Praise for *Valiant Dust*

Kirkus Reviews' Best Science Fiction and Fantasy Reads (November 2017)

"Fans of C. S. Forester's Horatio Hornblower will delight in discovering Baker's Sikander North."
—*RT Book Reviews* (starred review)

"Baker's military background only serves to raise this adventure above the rest."
—*Kirkus Reviews*

"This new series gets a grand start with fine attention to the details of starship engagements and operations, plus plenty of action as well as depth of character."
—*Booklist*

"*Valiant Dust* is an excellent example of military SF at its best."
—Michael A. Stackpole, bestselling author of *Rogue Squadron*

"In the finest tradition of Honor Harrington, Black Jack Geary, and Nicholas Seafort . . . an exciting new entry that fans of the genre won't want to miss."
—Dayton Ward, bestselling author of *24: Trial by Fire*

"Intelligent space opera with lots of vivid action . . . [A] sociological novel that examines the problems (on both sides) of a Third World aristocrat in a First World navy whose hierarchies are equally rigid."
—David Drake, author of the Hammer's Slammers series

"Intensely satisfying. Bravo! I look forward to more exploits of Sikander North!"
—Ed Greenwood, creator of Forgotten Realms™

"An excellent mix of military action and political intrigue."
—Eric Flint, author of the 1632 series

RICHARD BAKER

VALIANT DUST

A TOM DOHERTY ASSOCIATES BOOK
New York

VALIANT DUST

Copyright © 2017 by Richard Baker

All rights reserved.

A Tor Book
Published by Tom Doherty Associates
175 Fifth Avenue
New York, NY 10010

www.tor-forge.com

Tor® is a registered trademark of Macmillan Publishing Group, LLC.

ISBN 978-1-250-30385-1

Our books may be purchased in bulk for promotional, educational, or business use. Please contact your local bookseller or the Macmillan Corporate and Premium Sales Department at 1-800-221-7945, extension 5442, or by email at MacmillanSpecialMarkets@macmillan.com.

First Edition: November 2017
First Mass Market Edition: September 2018

Printed in the United States of America

0 9 8 7 6 5 4 3 2 1

FOR DAD.

I think you would've liked this one a lot.

ACKNOWLEDGMENTS

Thanks to my lovely wife, Kim, for keeping me going these last few years. The road's a little twisty but I think we'll like where we're going.

My first-draft readers helped me to make this a better book. So, my thanks to Cormac, Luke, Darrin, Chris, Chris, Ryan, and David. You guys rock.

A special thanks to my agent, Richard Curtis, and my excellent editor, Jen Gunnels, for their hard work in bringing this project to fruition.

And, finally, thanks to Alex and Hannah for sharing my appreciation for nerd culture. It's a lucky man whose daughters read Lovecraft.

For heathen heart that puts her trust
    In reeking tube and iron shard—
All valiant dust that builds on dust,
    And guarding calls not Thee to guard—
For frantic boast and foolish word,
Thy Mercy on Thy People, Lord!

—Rudyard Kipling, "Recessional"

VALIANT DUST

1

Lieutenant Sikander Singh North leaned forward in the shuttle's right-hand seat, eager to catch his first glimpse of the light cruiser *Hector*. The shuttle climbed slowly into low orbit, only four hundred kilometers above the feathered white cloud tops and gray-green dayside of New Perth. The white glare of Caledonia's sun illuminated dozens of freighters and tugs going about their business in the planet's busy approaches. Sikander quickly spotted the huge mass of New Perth Fleet Base—hard to miss, really, since the orbital structure was the size of a small city—and narrowed his eyes, peering in turn at each of the ships moored to the station's long arms. To his disappointment, the hulls of the Aquilan warships all looked the same at this distance; he felt he should have been able to spot his new ship as easily as he might pick out a pretty girl's face from a crowd. He'd certainly spent enough time memorizing every detail of CSS *Hector*'s lines and armament over the month and a half since he'd received his new assignment.

Beside him Petty Officer Second Class Robert Long, a pilot in *Hector*'s Flight Department, smiled. He'd guessed exactly what Sikander was doing, and he pointed out the docked cruiser for him. "Left-hand side of Fleet Base, sir, the second berth from the top. We'll be there in just a minute."

"Thank you," Sikander replied. He looked where the pilot pointed, and there was the Aquilan Commonwealth starship *Hector*, hull number CL 88. She was not the newest or largest of the ships moored at New Perth's orbital dock, but she was a handsome vessel nonetheless. He tapped the visual controls for the shuttle's viewports and zoomed in for a good look. Two hundred and sixty meters long, the Ilium-class cruiser (so called because all of her sisters were named for Trojan heroes from Homer's ancient epic, or so Sikander had read) had a graceful teardrop-shaped hull and powerful drive plates in sleek fairings aft. Her deadly kinetic cannons were housed in large, dome-like turrets that dotted her spine and keel, and the round ports ringing her bow concealed her potent torpedo battery. *Hector* might have been nothing remarkable by Aquilan standards, but she would have been the most powerful warship several times over in Sikander's native system of Kashmir, and it would be at least another generation before his homeworld could build a ship to match her.

"The Old Worthy's a fine-looking ship, isn't she?" Long observed. "Captain Markham is a stickler for appearances. She isn't happy unless the paint's still wet somewhere on the hull. But that's the way it ought to be."

Sikander agreed with the sentiment. If *Hector*'s captain took pride in her ship and wanted everyone to know it, he wouldn't argue. Of course, the Commonwealth Navy didn't actually use real paint on their warships, or at least not the sort that went on wet and dried into a coat; it was more of a nanoengineered polymer designed to stand up to the rigors of vacuum while displaying a handsome color scheme. Some star navies, such as the Dremish or the Nyeirans, favored all-black paint that made them a bit harder to spot with visual detectors, but stealth was generally pointless in normal space; simple physics dictated that ships couldn't hide their heat signatures. The Aquilans recognized that and chose colors designed to evoke a little institutional pride from their ships' crews. Accordingly, CSS *Hector* boasted a gleaming white hull, with buff-colored upperworks and beautiful red piping around the bow and the drive plates.

The shuttle continued its approach, while *Hector* seemed to swell up to fill the cockpit's viewports. Sikander dialed back the viewport magnification, and leaned over to call down to the shuttle's passenger area. "Come have a look, Darvesh," he called. "We have a few minutes yet before we dock."

"I am certain I shall see enough of *Hector* over the next two years, sir," Darvesh Reza replied in a carefully neutral tone. He generally disapproved of the fact that Sikander continued to serve in Aquila's star navy instead of returning to Kashmir to assume the proper duties of a North. Despite his reservations, the valet unbuckled his restraints and came forward to the cockpit, ducking through the low hatchway and steadying himself with a hand on the back of Sikander's seat. In deference to the requirement of being able to don a helmet in case of catastrophe, the tall Kashmiri wore a small round pakul instead of his customary turban. Darvesh functioned as Sikander's security detail, secretary, and general minder as well as his body servant. The impassive valet's eyes widened just a little as he took in the size and lethal beauty of the Aquilan cruiser.

"Impressive," Darvesh admitted. "And she is only a light cruiser?"

"Still three times the size of anything we can build back home," said Sikander. The Commonwealth of Aquila was a first-rate power, by some measures the foremost among the multisystem states that formed the core membership of the Coalition of Humanity. Decades or centuries ahead in technology and industrial capacity, the great powers far outclassed single-system backwaters, even populous and economically valuable ones such as Kashmir. Sikander's home system was merely a client state—or a colonial possession, more accurately—to Aquila. Building a fleet of large, modern warships remained out of reach for Sikander's people, but he hoped to change that someday. Until then, he wore an Aquilan uniform.

Darvesh merely nodded in reply. As a younger man he had served in a Kashmiri regiment of the Commonwealth Marine Corps; he was accustomed to displays of Aquilan power. He glanced at the shuttle pilot. "Did you call *Hector* 'Old Worthy,' Petty Officer Long? That seems a strange nickname."

"It is," Long agreed. "I understand that it's a reference to the ancient Earth hero Hector, the one who fought in the Trojan War. There have been a lot of ships—spacegoing and the old seagoing sort—named after him over the centuries. But I never have heard how that got turned into 'Old Worthy.'"

"It's a reference to medieval chivalry," said Sikander. "Hector was considered one of the Nine Worthies, heroes that young knights should strive to emulate. Except the part about getting slaughtered by Achilles, anyway." The Aquilans might have been a hundred years ahead of Kashmir in shipbuilding, but it seemed that he'd received a better education in the classics than his Commonwealth shipmates. Of course, very little about Sikander's upbringing had been normal. Even by Aquilan standards the Norths were extremely wealthy, an aristocratic clan who could afford to buy their sons and daughters opportunities most Kashmiris could only dream of—for example, appointment to Aquila's prestigious naval academy and an officer's commission upon graduation.

Long shook his head. "Huh. That's the best answer I've heard yet, and I've been on the ship for a year and a half. Can't wait to try it out on the fellows in the ready room. They—" He broke off as the comm unit came to life.

"Shuttle Hector-Alpha, New Perth Traffic Control," the

audio crackled. "You are cleared for final approach and recovery on parent deck, over."

The pilot nodded, even though this was only an audio link. "New Perth, this is Hector-Alpha. Clear for approach and recovery, roger, out."

"Better go take your seat, Darvesh," Sikander told his valet. A routine shuttle landing on a stationary dock was probably going to be about as rough as an elevator ride, but procedures were procedures, and passengers were supposed to strap down during departure and landing. For that matter, he was supposed to be ready to back up the pilot since he was riding in the copilot's seat. This was Long's boat and Sikander wouldn't touch the controls unless the petty officer invited him to, but like any Aquilan line officer he was rated for ordinary shuttle operations.

Darvesh nodded and returned to the passenger seating, buckling himself in. Sikander adjusted his own restraints and sat back in his seat, watching as Long expertly adjusted the shuttle's course and yawed the small vessel into a dead-center approach. *Hector*'s hangar was located in the middle of the ship's "belly," although that was mostly an illusion created by the customary Aquilian color scheme; there was very little real difference in what part of a warship was considered up or down. The large hangar door rolled open slowly with a puff of escaping atmosphere as the shuttle glided closer. No matter how many times a big compartment like a hangar deck cycled, traces of air remained to turn into a silver dusting of snow and drift out into the night.

Sikander watched carefully, but Long handled the shuttle with a masterly touch. He brought the boat into its cradle and set it down with a bump so gentle it wouldn't have spilled a glass of water. "There you go, Lieutenant North," he said. "Welcome aboard! Wait for the indicator to turn green before you crack the hatch, please."

"Thanks for the ride, Long," Sikander replied. He unstrapped himself and straightened up, tugging at his flight suit and stretching carefully in the cockpit. He was not particularly tall, standing five or six centimeters shorter than most Aquilans he met, but he was wide through the shoulders and solidly built. The gravity of Jaipur, his homeworld, was a little higher than one standard, and over centuries, natural selection had left most Jaipuri with stocky frames. Cramped spaces like a shuttle cockpit had a way of finding his elbows and shoulders if he wasn't careful.

He ducked back into the passenger compartment, seized one of his own duffel bags despite Darvesh's disapproving look, and waited for the atmosphere indicator by the shuttle's hatch to go from red to green. No doubt the Kashmiri servant thought it undignified for Sikander to carry his own luggage, but Sikander had learned it was necessary to show his Aquilan comrades that he didn't think he deserved any special treatment. No other officer on board besides the captain would have a personal attendant, after all, so the less he relied on Darvesh Reza, the better.

The light by the hatch turned green, indicating that the hangar bay was repressurized. Sikander cycled the hatch and stepped onto the hangar deck of the Commonwealth starship *Hector* for the first time. He turned and saluted the Aquilan flag displayed at the end of the hangar bay, then faced the watch officer in the hangar's control booth. "Lieutenant Sikander North reporting under orders," he said. "Request permission to come aboard."

The watch officer returned his salute behind the booth's wide viewport and answered through the intercom. "Come aboard, sir."

Sikander waited a moment for Darvesh to complete the time-honored ritual of boarding a warship—for purposes of Aquilan naval etiquette, he'd been assigned an acting rank of chief petty officer—while the watchstander, a first-class petty officer, stepped out of the hangar control station and logged in their datacards. If the rating was surprised by Sikander's identity, he didn't show it. He simply nodded and said, "You're expected, sir. The captain left word that you're to call on her as soon as you get settled."

"Very well," Sikander replied.

"If you'll follow Deckhand Parris, she can show you to your stateroom and give you a hand with your gear," the watch officer continued. "After that, you can signal the ship's info assistant to find anything you need—you're logged in to the system now. Chief Reza, I'll call for a messenger to give you a hand to the chiefs' quarters."

"No need," Darvesh replied. "I will accompany Mr. North to his quarters first."

The watch officer raised an eyebrow—he probably didn't see many chief petty officers toting officers' duffels—but made no comment. "Very good. Mr. North, Chief Reza, welcome aboard."

"Right this way, sir." Deckhand Parris was a short young woman who probably wasn't more than twenty standard years of age. She smiled broadly at Sikander and Darvesh, and seemed to grin even wider as she tried to maintain a suitably solemn demeanor. Sikander had seen the reaction more than once. Many Aquilans were simply unsure of how they were supposed to greet him, and couldn't help but get a little nervous or self-conscious. "Can I get your bag?"

The first of a hundred little decisions that might color how Hector's *crew receives me,* Sikander reflected. Kashmir was a little old-fashioned, and a gentleman would never allow a young lady to carry a bag he was perfectly able to carry. On the other hand, an Aquilan officer would not want to suggest that he thought that a female rating couldn't carry a duffel that a young enlisted person would be expected to tote for an officer . . . and a North would never carry a bag at all, but that was also an impression he would not wish to put forward. He decided that he'd rather look unconcerned about the whole business. "It's no trouble," he answered. "Lead the way."

Hector might have been more than two hundred meters

in length, but that didn't translate into a very spacious interior. Armor, power-plant shielding, drives, weapon capacitors, and space for fuel, water, oxygen, and other necessary stores took up a lot of the hull volume. Officers' country turned out to be just aft of the ship's bridge. The stateroom reserved for Sikander's use featured a decent-sized bunk, a desk and chair, a closet, a sink, and a small couch that faced the desk; as a department head, he rated his own quarters, including enough space to meet privately with a subordinate if needed. A screen on the outward-facing bulkhead showed the busy orbital approaches around New Perth Fleet Base, although it was a video feed from an exterior camera. Overall the room was not much bigger than three meters by six—spacious and comfortable for shipboard accommodations, and certainly a big step up from the tiny cabins he'd shared with other officers in his previous assignments.

Without a word, Darvesh went to work unpacking Sikander's clothes and hanging them in the closet. Deckhand Parris stared; in all likelihood she'd never seen a valet. Most Aquilan enlisted men and women came from the middle class, after all, and the Commonwealth Navy had a deep-rooted egalitarian tradition. "Thank you, Parris," Sikander told her. "I think we can manage from here."

"Yes, sir!" the young woman replied. Curious or not, she recognized a dismissal when she heard one. She saluted and hurried back down toward her watch station at the ship's hangar.

"Your whites, sir?" Darvesh asked, holding up Sikander's dress uniform.

"Yes, please." *Hector*'s crew wore shipboard jumpsuits for their in-port routine, but to report to a new commanding officer Sikander preferred to err on the side of formality. He quickly changed out of his flight suit, pulling on the clean white tunic and red-striped trousers of an Aquilan officer, and took a moment to splash a little water on his face and check his appearance in the mirror. He always liked the way he looked in his dress whites; the uniform complemented his copper complexion and dark, wavy hair. Those features were common enough in Kashmir, but he also had the North eyes—a striking jade-green hue rare anywhere Sikander traveled. It must have been a good combination, since he rarely had much trouble attracting the interest of the relatively tall and slender Aquilan women he encountered. "Right, I'm off to call on the captain. Why don't you go get settled in the chiefs' quarters?"

"As soon as I finish here," Darvesh replied. "Good luck, sir."

"Thanks." Sikander left the tall Kashmiri arranging his shoes in the closet, and set out to find his way to the captain's cabin. As the petty officer on watch in the hangar promised, he already had access to the ship's information network; a few quick taps on his dataslate produced a small map to show him the way. One deck up and halfway around the circular main passage, and he was at the captain's door.

Sikander paused for a moment to collect himself. In theory Captain Markham was fully briefed on his unusual situation, but there was no doubt that it would be awkward for any commanding officer. In his brief naval career he'd already seen resentment, distrust, cold formality, and—the most commonplace reaction—complete bafflement. It all struck him as more than a little unfair, but he'd learned to put up with it because his service in the Aquilan star navy was important to Kashmir. His home was in dire jeopardy of becoming as obsolete as the polearms carried by the guards who paraded in front of the Revered Kathakar's Palace. Like many of the second-wave colonies established in the early centuries of Terra's expansion to the stars, the worlds of the Kashmir system had fallen out of contact with the rest of humanity. By the time the Aquilan Commonwealth had reestablished contact, Sikander's people lagged generations behind less-isolated worlds in technology and industrial development. Kashmir desperately needed a thousand Sikanders—a *million* Sikanders—to help catch up by taking service with Aquilan corporations, universities, research facilities, and armed forces, learning everything they could. But that didn't mean Aquilans always welcomed the junior partners in their alliance or regarded them as equals, especially in conservative organizations such as the Commonwealth Navy.

"Easy things are not worth doing," Sikander murmured aloud—a favorite expression of his father's. Nawab Dayan North expected that any son of his would work tirelessly to make himself the master of his circumstances. Small obstacles such as growing up in a world decades behind the current technology of the Coalition powers or a wall of institutional discrimination did not matter. Much was expected of a North and a son of the nawab.

I am not doing this for him, Sikander reminded himself. But despite that, he found himself remembering the night he was sent away from home. It was ten years ago now, the night of the Bandi Chor Divas celebration. The Day of Release, ironically enough. He closed his eyes, remembering—

—*the terrace of the palace at Sangrur, sirens of emergency vehicles keening in the night. The doctors fight to save Mother and Gamand; he waits in the warm night just outside the palace's medical center, unable to watch. After an hour, Father emerges from the medical center, his face harder than stone.*

Sikander fears the worst until Nawab Dayan sighs and speaks: "Your mother will live, and Gamand as well. But I have just been informed that Devindar was attacked at the same time we were."

"Devindar, too?" Sikander grips the balcony rail to steady himself. His older brother is studying at the university in Ganderbal, not even on the same continent. The KLP means to eliminate all of us, *he realizes. "Is he—?"*

Nawab Dayan shakes his head, sparing him the rest of the question. "He is not seriously injured. But you must leave for High Albion as soon as possible, Sikander." It is always "Sikander" when his father addresses him, never "Sikay" or even "son." "I can arrange for you to join this year's midshipman class instead of next year's. We can never all be on the same planet again."

He stares at his father in horror. "People will call me a coward, Father!"

"This is not a matter for discussion," Nawab Dayan snaps—a rare failing in a man who habitually keeps his own fierce temper firmly in check. "I will not be defied on this."

Even though he is only eighteen standard years of age on this awful night, Sikander already knows that It's not fair! *has not the slightest chance to alter one of his father's decisions. He fights down the urge to say it anyway. "I know nobody at the Academy. And I will be the only Kashmiri there!"*

"Nothing has ever been difficult for you, Sikander. A little adversity might teach you something about yourself." Sikander's father turns then to set both hands on his shoulders. "This is an opportunity. Our enemies in the KLP are right about one thing: We will not always be tied to the Commonwealth of Aquila. Study hard, do what is right, and remember that you are a North of Jaipur. Make us all proud."

Standing at Captain Markham's door, Sikander opened his eyes and brushed away the past. In ten years he still hadn't found a good answer to his father's expectations. In his more honest moments, he could admit to himself that Nawab Dayan had been right about what the eighteen-year-old Sikander needed, no matter how much he'd hated it at the time. Now . . . now he could return to Kashmir any time he wanted to, but he'd come to define himself by his chosen profession, not his family name.

This is not about my father or his expectations, Sikander told himself. *This is for me, and whether I can be proud of myself. Father was right about one thing—it isn't supposed to be easy.*

He rapped his knuckle on the door.

"Come in," a woman replied in a firm voice.

Sikander entered. The captain's cabin doubled as her office and private conference room, much like his own stateroom, but her quarters were large enough to seat half a dozen people at once. There were a few personal touches in sight: a couple of digital images displayed in a frame on the bulkhead, a pair of small viewports that offered a peek at New Perth's darkening coastline far below, half a dozen small models of older starships (and one seagoing vessel), and, most uniquely, a large oil painting showing an equestrian in traditional riding dress jumping her horse over the water obstacle in a race of some kind. Physical artwork was quite uncommon, especially aboard starships; without meaning to, he allowed his gaze to linger on the painting for a long moment before he remembered himself.

He turned his attention to the officer seated at the desk and saluted. "Lieutenant Sikander North reporting for duty, ma'am," he said calmly.

"Captain Elise Markham, commanding the Aquilan Commonwealth starship *Hector,*" she replied, and acknowledged his salute. Captain Markham was a tall, thin woman with short red-brown hair and a deep, tawny complexion, perhaps forty-five years of age. She had stern, dark eyes—unusual for Aquilans, whose eyes usually ran toward a warm brown or hazel—and a serious set to her wide mouth. Most Aquilans and citizens of other cosmopolitan powers showed few characteristics of the old Terran races, which had blended together long ago; idiosyncratic phenotypes were usually found among people from more secluded systems. Her lips quirked upward as she took note of his distraction with the painting. "Welcome aboard, Mr. North. Please, have a seat on the couch."

"Thank you," Sikander replied. He took a seat in the cabin's small sitting area, while Captain Markham got up from behind her desk and came to join him, sitting on the opposite couch. He took the opportunity to study her more closely, and looked back to the painting again. "Wait a moment. Are you the rider in the painting, ma'am?"

"You have a sharp eye. Yes, that's me, although I was only nineteen then. My sister painted it."

"It's quite good," he said, and he meant it. Sikander had seen more real paintings than most people, and he could see that the artist had effortlessly captured the horse in mid-jump, with the young Elise Markham leaning forward and standing in the stirrups.

"Do you have horses in Kashmir, Mr. North?" Captain Markham asked. It was not a meaningless question; few colonists setting out from Old Terra during humanity's early migrations had brought horses along for the trip, and even fewer had managed to keep the creatures alive during the hard years most new colonies had faced in the distant past.

"We do, ma'am. I have done a fair amount of riding myself, but nothing like that sort of competitive jumping. Just trail riding." In fact, one of the North estates in Srinagar offered better than five thousand square kilometers of rugged and beautiful riding on the edge of the Kharan Desert. Sikander had spent a few summers there as a teenager.

"That's actually an ancient type of race called a steeplechase, not a jumping competition. I used to do some of those, too." Markham looked at the painting for a moment, and a small grimace passed over her face. "I broke my leg badly just two races later, and never raced competitively again. But I still like to ride every chance I get. Can I offer you some coffee or tea, Mr. North?"

"Coffee, thank you, ma'am." Sikander was not particularly

thirsty, but he very much wanted to make sure that Captain Markham felt comfortable pursuing the interview in her own good time. In Sikander's experience, some people in authority engaged in small talk simply because they enjoyed the sound of their own voices, while others seemed to sincerely try to put their subordinates at ease at the beginning of a conversation. Elise Markham seemed to be one of the latter, which he took as a good sign.

Markham retrieved a pitcher and a pair of cups and saucers from a small wall unit and set them on the low table between the couches. "How are you settling in?"

"Well, thank you," said Sikander. "This is not my first tour in New Perth. I have quite a few old classmates in-system, and I own a nice condominium in Brigadoon. For now I'm in one of the spare rooms, though. My cousin Amarleen moved in a few months ago while I was off-planet. She's studying at Carlyle." Most officers and senior enlisted personnel assigned to ships based in New Perth established homes down on the planet for their families; Brigadoon, the planetary capital, was a popular choice. For Sikander, raising a family was not yet a consideration, but establishing himself in the fleet's social circles ashore and entertaining friends were things he very much looked forward to. He could keep his boat in the marina and go fishing when he was off-duty, and it was only ten minutes by flyer from the city's orbital shuttle terminal.

"Carlyle, really?" Markham nodded in appreciation; it was one of the foremost medical colleges in the Commonwealth. "I'm impressed."

"We all are, although I can hardly tell her that to her face," Sikander admitted. "She'd be insufferable."

"Naturally," Markham agreed, and smiled. She set down her coffee and leaned forward. "Well, let's get down to business. As you might expect, I have reviewed your service jacket closely. And I've also had a conversation with a representative from the Admiralty, and another from the Foreign Ministry." She gave a small shrug. "I've been in the Commonwealth Navy a long time, Mr. North, but I confess that this is the first time I've had a diplomatic briefing about an officer serving in my command."

"I understand, Captain," Sikander said, setting down his own coffee. "It's an unusual situation. However, it is my sincere hope that you will treat me exactly like you would treat any of your other officers. I don't expect any sort of favoritism or prejudice. If I screw up—which hopefully will not be often—I expect to be corrected or reprimanded like any other Aquilan officer."

"So I was told by the Admiralty, and so I intend to proceed." Captain Markham studied him. "However, your service jacket suggests differently. You seem to have had a reputation at the Academy, your first shipboard tour on *Adept* was not terribly successful, and I can't help but notice that you are quite junior for assignment as a department head. You are taking over for an experienced and well-liked gunnery officer, and I have some . . . concerns."

Sikander tried not to wince. Fortunately he had been expecting to hear something along these lines, and did not allow himself to become angry or flustered by the sentiment. "I can't change what is in my service jacket, Captain Markham," he said. "Yes, I didn't always take things seriously at the Academy, and yes, I argued with my department head on *Adept*. I also suspect that the Admiralty is under some pressure to accelerate my career in order to foster good relations with my father—something I certainly never asked for, I should add." The Commonwealth had figured out long ago that it was easier to exercise influence through Kashmir's existing aristocrats than it was to build a local administration without their help. As a result, Aquila's Foreign Ministry placed a high value on the support and goodwill of potentates such as Nawab Dayan . . . which, incidentally, did nothing to endear the North clan to the Kashmiri Liberation Party or any of the other Kashmiri nationalist movements.

"Asked for or not, it's not the sort of help that is likely to make a favorable impression on your fellow officers," Markham observed.

"So I have learned, ma'am," said Sikander. "However, I think you will see that my tour on *Triton* was much more successful, and I received high marks in Department Head School at Laguna. I'd like to think I have matured a bit in the last couple of years, Captain. I ask only that you base your opinion—for good or for ill—on how I perform on *Hector.*"

Markham regarded him for a long moment before she answered. "Very well, Mr. North. You begin with a clean slate with me."

"Thank you, ma'am." Sikander decided that the captain meant what she said. Of course, what she didn't say was whether the rest of *Hector*'s officers would feel the same.

"As I just said, you're taking over a gunnery department that is running well at the moment. Do you know how you would like to proceed with assuming your duties?"

"I have already started reviewing the service jackets of my personnel—my thanks to the chief yeoman for forwarding them to me at Laguna. As soon as I can, I intend to meet with the division officers and chief gunner's mates. But what I would really like to do is get in some live-fire exercises and see how the team works together."

Markham offered a small smile. "A gunnery officer who isn't interested in shooting is a gunnery officer I have no use for. As it so happens, we have some range time already scheduled for next week. I'll see if we can add some torpedo practice, too."

"Thank you, ma'am."

"Don't thank me yet, Mr. North. I am a stickler for high range scores." Markham stood, and offered her hand. Sikander stood and shook it. "If you have any questions or trouble, my door is always open. Make sure you introduce yourself to Pete Chatburn—the XO—soon. He's running errands planetside right now, but he should be back in a few hours."

"I will, Captain," Sikander promised. He saluted again, and turned to go.

"One more thing, Mr. North." Captain Markham stopped him. "Out of curiosity, just what is the significance of the title Nawabzada of Ishar?"

"Ah. Ishar is the largest continent of Jaipur, the fourth planet in the Kashmir system. It's the next one out from Srinagar—Kashmir Prime. My father is the nawab, or prince, of Ishar. Nawabzada simply means 'son of the prince.'"

Markham's calm reserve cracked just a little at that. She blinked. "You are the prince of a *continent*?" she asked.

"It is mostly a ceremonial title, Captain. I am the fourth-born in my family, and since I am unlikely to succeed my father, I'm expected to find another way to make myself useful. Military service is a traditional alternative, but of course Kashmir's navy is almost nonexistent, so my father had me sent to Aquila's naval academy instead." Sikander offered a small shrug; as much as he might have resented being sent away at first, idleness wasn't really in his nature. Pursuing a competitive and engaging career helped to make up for ten years of virtual exile. "There are also diplomatic benefits. The Aquilan alliance is vital to Kashmir's development and will certainly remain so for many years to come. Serving alongside Aquilan officers helps me to appreciate Aquilan interests and traditions, and perhaps meet those who will play an important role in Kashmiri affairs in the future."

It might also demonstrate to the Aquilan Commonwealth that, while Kashmir was a backward system, it would not always be so, and Kashmiris were every bit as capable as native-born Aquilans if given the education and opportunity . . . but Sikander didn't feel that he needed to point that out. Many Aquilans held little respect for the peoples who were native to the colonial possessions of the Commonwealth, and harbored a sort of unthinking bigotry toward them. It was not founded on race, since Aquilans themselves represented a mix of many different Terran phenotypes, but there was no doubt that most Aquilans were quite convinced of the superiority of their *culture*. He hoped that Elise Markham wouldn't turn out to be that way, or it would be a trying tour of duty for him.

The captain quickly recovered her Aquilan aplomb. "I see," she said. "For what it's worth, Mr. North, I look forward to learning a thing or two from your assignment on *Hector,* too. Carry on."

"Yes, ma'am," Sikander replied, and left to get settled in his new home.

2

Aberdeen Fleet Gunnery Range, Caledonia System

"Main battery, engage target Alpha," Lieutenant Commander Hiram Randall said in a calm and unhurried manner from his station at *Hector*'s tactical console. "Helm, take us to the port side of Alpha at eleven thousand klicks." The tall, laconic Aquilan lounged in his battle couch as if he didn't have a care in the world, one hand tugging absently at the small dark goatee he wore. As head of *Hector*'s Operations Department, Randall served as the tactical officer when *Hector* was at battle stations.

"Engage target Alpha, aye," Sikander repeated. He was stationed at the cruiser's master weapons console, the customary battle station for the ship's gunnery officer, just a few paces behind the tactical station. It was Randall's job to decide which targets to engage and in what order, and it was Sikander's job to make sure that whatever Tactical wanted hit got hit *hard*. Captain Markham observed the exercise from her own station in the middle of the bridge. By long-standing tradition she left the details of the engagement to the tactical officer and focused on maintaining her overall situational awareness. If Randall started to do something she didn't want done, she'd step in—but so far

Randall handled *Hector*'s pass through the Navy's Aberdeen firing range perfectly.

Sikander checked his displays to confirm that *Hector*'s sensors held a good lock on the target drone, and keyed the engage icon, selecting the ship's forward kinetic-cannon mounts for the job. His battle couch overlooked the stations for the main-battery fire control, secondary-battery fire control, and the torpedo battery, each manned by a junior officer of the Gunnery Department. In fact, Sikander could easily see the main-battery console, manned by Ensign Michael Girard, from his station. Girard would actually do the shooting.

"Target Alpha, Mr. Girard," Sikander said. "Blue shot only!" The engage order on the console sufficed, of course, but Sikander felt it couldn't hurt to be a little specific the first few times he worked with his new team.

"Commencing fire!" Girard replied, unable to keep the excitement out of his voice. One of the youngest officers on board, only five months out of the Academy, he still looked like a schoolboy with his slight build and unruly hair. What Girard lacked in experience, he made up for with quick reflexes and a natural aptitude for his battery console: Even as he acknowledged the order, his fingers flew over the controls. From somewhere forward of the bridge and a few decks above, Sikander heard the electric whine of *Hector*'s turrets slewing their weapons onto target, followed by the deep, thrumming pulses as the electromagnetic coils launched their heavy slugs at the target drone. At the same time, *Hector*'s acceleration changed, the bow dropping and rolling left as the chief pilot at the helm maneuvered to keep the drone at optimal range. The motion pushed Sikander deeper into his battle couch for a moment until the ship's internal compensators caught up.

Sikander ignored the ship's movement and kept his eyes on the integrated sensor display. Kinetic rounds, even the general-purpose ones, moved *fast*: the big Mark V kinetic cannons in *Hector*'s main battery accelerated a ten-kilogram rod of tungsten alloy to a velocity of more than three thousand kilometers per second. Each rod hurtling downrange was moving at one percent of the speed of light when it left the driver coils. Even so, flight time between *Hector*'s cannon snouts and the armored drone stretched out for three full seconds. The target drone twisted and rolled, maneuvering like an enemy destroyer trying to throw off the cruiser's aim . . . and Girard's first volley missed, blasting through empty space just behind the drone.

The young officer raced through a set of corrections and fired again, this time overcorrecting and leading the target too much. Sikander's display plotted the path of the missed shots into the blue-and-brown mass of the gas giant Aberdeen, which served as a convenient backstop to the firing range. K-rounds that could have leveled a small city vanished into the huge planet without a splash.

"Let's tighten it up, Guns," Randall drawled. "Otherwise we're going to have a long day on the range."

"Sorry, sir," Ensign Girard stammered. "I'm on it!" He fired again. A little more than ten thousand kilometers away from *Hector,* the kinetic cannon's ten-kilo solid shot slammed into the drone's armored side. Fortunately for the drone, the practice round—or "blue shot," in Commonwealth Navy parlance—was built to shatter and dissipate most of its energy on impact. A real war shot from *Hector*'s main battery would have delivered energy comparable to a small nuclear explosion, and not even the toughest synthetic alloys and nanoengineered armor could stand up to that kind of abuse. The practice round still hit with enough force to crack one of the drone's replaceable armor plates and knock the robotic vessel into an end-over-end tumble; the drone began to flash its *I'm dead* beacon.

"Target Alpha destroyed," Sikander reported with a note of satisfaction. He couldn't help it; the little boy in him liked playing with the biggest firecrackers he could get his hands on, and the Mark V kinetic cannon was a very big fire-cracker indeed.

Hiram Randall promptly deflated whatever momentary satisfaction he might have felt. "About time," the operations officer drawled. "Three salvos is two too many."

Sikander suppressed a sharp retort. The firing range was supposed to be challenging, and the drone operators tried hard to make shots miss. Besides, Girard was a gunnery officer, not an ops officer, and that meant it was Sikander's place to come down on the young ensign, not Randall's. He'd intended to keep quiet and do a lot of watching on his first live-fire shoot with his team, but he certainly didn't like another officer chastising one of his new subordinates. *Or does Randall think he needs to do my job for me?*

Sometimes the best thing to say was as little as you could. "Aye," he answered, mostly to let Captain Markham—and Ensign Girard—know that he'd heard the criticism but wasn't about to add to it. Markham said nothing, but Sikander was sure she was paying close attention. As for Girard, Sikander couldn't see his face from his battle couch, but he thought he could make out a flush coloring the younger officer's neck as he waited for his orders.

"New target, target Bravo, bearing three-three-five, range twenty thousand k," Sublieutenant Keane, the sensor officer, reported. He was stationed on the right-hand side of the bridge, forward of the tactical officer's position. "New target, target Charlie, bearing one-zero-zero high, range fifteen k."

"Commence tracking targets Bravo and Charlie," Randall ordered.

"Let's get ready to split our fire," Sikander told Girard quietly, making a point of keeping his voice unexcited. He tagged the new icons on his board, marking Bravo for the forward mounts and Charlie for the aft mounts. "Take your time, and let the targeting system steady up just a bit more on the firing solution. At this distance we're not getting good returns on a small target like a drone."

"You've done some shooting with the Mark V board, sir?" Girard asked.

"I just finished the refresher course at Skye," Sikander replied, referring to the Navy's gunnery school. He had to work twice as hard on his technical proficiency as a native-born Aquilan; if he was anything less than very good, his fellow officers might wonder whether he was displacing a more qualified officer for political purposes. Fortunately, he'd always had a good feel for shooting, whether it was a hunting rifle or a target pistol. Targeting computers shot far faster and more accurately than humans, but enemy helmsmen had a way of never being quite exactly where a computer predicted. Human intuition and anticipation in just the right amount made a noticeable difference in the accuracy of most combat shooting. "Relax, Mr. Girard. This is the fun part of the job."

Girard glanced over his shoulder, startled, and managed a weak smile. "Yes, sir."

"Main battery, engage target Charlie," Lieutenant Commander Randall ordered.

"Engage target Charlie, aye," Sikander responded, and keyed the engage icon on his board. He glanced back to Girard. "Hit him just when he finishes a jink. Fire when you're ready."

"Commencing fire," Girard reported. He pressed the fire button, and once again *Hector*'s hull quivered and thrummed, this time from somewhere a little aft of Sikander's station, as the kinetic cannons opened up. Girard's first volley missed again—not entirely surprising, since it was a significantly longer shot than Alpha, and *Hector* continued to maneuver. But the ensign's second volley scored a direct hit and hammered the small drone.

"Target Charlie destroyed," Sikander reported.

"Very well. Engage target Bravo," Randall ordered.

"New targets Delta, Echo, and Foxtrot up on the board!" Sublieutenant Keane announced.

"Engage target Bravo, aye," Sikander acknowledged. He keyed the engage icon and started figuring out how to assign the ship's cannons to the next batch of targets. Ensign Girard hunched closer over his console, concentrating intently on the task at hand; the atmosphere in the combat center grew tense as more targets began to appear, and the pace of the exercise rapidly increased.

For the next twenty minutes, the cruiser drove aggressively through the firing range, hammering first one drone and then another as the range operators presented a dizzying array of targets for *Hector*'s main battery of K-cannons. They were relatively simple weapons; the principles had been worked out more than a thousand years ago. A kinetic cannon was simply a very powerful coil gun or mass driver, a tube ringed by electromagnets that accelerated a hunk of metal to the highest speed possible. But, as with so many things, the devil was in the details, and design trade-offs forced difficult choices on weapon designers. Unlike a gunpowder cannon of ancient Earth, a kinetic cannon wasn't measured by the heft of its projectile—its power was really a function of the velocity the cannon could impart. High velocities meant more impact energy and a reduced flight time for the kinetic round. The longer it took a round to reach its target, the more time the target had to detect the incoming round and dodge the attack. In general, flight times of more than seven or eight seconds were very unlikely to result in hits, unless the target was completely surprised or unable to maneuver. A battleship-caliber kinetic cannon threw rounds close to five thousand kilometers per second, so its effective range was perhaps thirty-five or forty thousand kilometers. A destroyer's smaller K-cannon might only achieve 2,000 kps, which meant that its effective range was more like fifteen thousand kilometers. As a light cruiser, *Hector* carried K-cannons that fell in between the two, and threw metal at a velocity of a little more than three thousand kilometers per second; she fought most effectively at ranges of twenty-five thousand kilometers or less.

However, velocity wasn't the only consideration for kinetic-weapon design. There was actually such a thing as *too much* velocity. A K-round traveling too fast might punch completely through its target, a less damaging interaction than transferring all of its staggering energy into whatever it hit. After all, any of the projectile's energy that it retained after passing *through* the target was energy that did not get used to break things *inside* the target. A Mark V round fired at full power against an unarmored freighter would leave two neat, round five-centimeter holes in the freighter's sides unless it happened to hit something big and heavy, such as an engine casing or a structural frame, in the target. But slowing down the shot of course increased flight time and decreased effective range. To counter this, kinetic projectiles came in "hard" armor-piercing rounds and "soft" general-purpose rounds, which were intended to squash and fragment in the moment of impact and therefore dump as much energy as possible into whatever they hit. Soft K-rounds were soft only in the most relative sense of the word, of course—if you fired taffy at 3,000 kps into a steel hull, you'd still punch a hole in it.

Most things CSS *Hector* would be expected to shoot at would be armored. Nothing could really stand up to ten kilos of tungsten moving at one percent of the speed of light, but layered armor plates and voids, thorough compartmentalization, and sturdy construction went a long way toward containing damage and protecting vital systems; Aquilan material technology could produce some very tough armor indeed. All these different considerations led the various navies of the great powers to make their own subtly different design trade-offs. The Dremish made a cult of achieving the highest launch velocities possible, trying to get the best range they could manage. The Aquilan navy preferred to give up some range and velocity in order to get a slightly better rate of fire and maximize energy transfer for K-cannon rounds. The Nyeirans, on the other hand, favored buckshot-like projectiles that delivered dozens of half-kilo darts to the general vicinity of the target instead of a single penetrator. Any of the schemes was lethal, but Sikander supposed that the ongoing debate about the advantages of one system over another gave naval experts across the galaxy a way to pass the time.

He observed carefully as Ensign Girard fell into the rhythm of locking on to targets, selecting rounds, and choosing firing profiles. *Girard's quite good when he stops thinking about what he's doing,* Sikander decided. The console skill Sikander had had to work so hard to attain came naturally to Girard; native Aquilans were immersed in modern information technology from early childhood, after all, and naval systems designers took advantage of a hundred everyday interface conventions and shortcuts Aquilans took for granted. Maybe all Girard needed was a little more confidence in his abilities.

Other than Girard's jitters, the rest of the weapons team seemed to function smoothly. Sublieutenant Karsen Reno, seated beside Girard, handled *Hector*'s secondary battery of UV lasers adroitly. At their posts in the ship's mounts, the gunner's mates responded well to simulated battle damage and casualties. That was Darvesh Reza's battle station. In his role as an acting chief petty officer he'd been assigned to the gun crew in the number-one main-battery turret, since marines usually doubled as gunner's mates during their shipboard service. Darvesh was not an Aquilan marine, of course, but he had similar training, and he'd served in gun crews during Sikander's previous shipboard assignments. Sikander noted that *Hector*'s gun crews shot quite well when the cruiser reached the part of the course where she was required to fire in local control—practice in case the cruiser's centralized fire control was ever taken out by a bridge hit.

I'll have to ask Darvesh for his impressions of the turret team after the exercise, but it certainly seems like they're pretty sharp. Captain Markham was right—the Gunnery Department is in good shape. My predecessor must have known what he was doing. That would make Sikander's job easier. Getting the best performance out of a good team was its own kind of challenge, but he'd much rather concentrate on helping people to excel than on correcting basic deficiencies. It meant that he would be hard-pressed to show a lot of improvement with the department, but Captain Markham seemed to have a good grasp on the state of the gunnery team; Sikander doubted that she would expect him to keep bettering range scores that were already pretty good.

"Mr. Randall, let's use the torps on this last target," Captain Markham said as they approached the final portion of the range. "I seem to recall that we've got practice weapons in tubes one and two."

"Yes, ma'am," Randall replied. He glanced back at Sikander and the weapons team. "Stand by for torpedo engagement. Target Sierra, two torps, range ten thousand kilometers."

"Solving for target Sierra, aye," Sikander replied. He punched the proper icons into his console and sent the orders to Sublieutenant Angela Larkin, *Hector*'s torpedo officer. She sat in the battle station beside Karsen Reno, and so far today she hadn't been very busy. Most firing-range work revolved around the main battery of K-cannons, because warp torpedoes were too bulky and expensive to use up in practice shots. They packed enough punch to threaten a battleship, but *Hector* carried only a dozen of the weapons. In a real engagement, the Aquilan cruiser would save the torpedoes for a high-value target she could hit at optimum range. Warp torpedoes left normal space during their run to the target, and required tricky timing to return to reality at their detonation point. Too soon, and the torpedo would be exposed to enemy defensive fire. Too late, and the dense matter of the target structure would incinerate the torpedo, preventing detonation. It would still be a damaging hit, but not the spectacular explosion expected.

"Good solution on target Sierra," Angela Larkin reported. She was a native of New Perth, slender with light brown corkscrew curls in a short mop, and her Standard Anglic had the soft burring accent common in the system. "Ready on tubes one and two."

"As torpedoes bear, fire," Randall said. "Helm, bring us to zero-three-five, full acceleration. Let's make these count." The cruiser came around toward the right, and the drive plates applied a steady but noticeable push to the center of Sikander's back. Any ship making a torpedo run naturally wanted to close the distance fast, and give the enemy less opportunity to rake her at close range. He watched as the range to the last target drone ticked down rapidly. Larkin hovered over her torpedo console, making small adjustments to the weapons' programming in the last few moments before firing. The better the sensor picture when the torpedoes launched, the better their chance to land hits.

The range indicator turned green. *Hector* shuddered as the magnetic tubes hurled the torpedoes, each one massing close to two thousand kilos, downrange. Within a kilometer of the launch tubes, each weapon vanished into its own warp bubble, driving invisibly toward the target. "Two torpedoes away!" Larkin reported. "Run time ten seconds."

"Very well," Captain Markham replied. She leaned back in her chair. "Now we wait."

Sikander took a moment to stretch, deliberately keeping his hands away from the console. Maintaining any kind of telemetry link with a torpedo in flight was impossible. Objects in warp could be detected with difficulty from normal space, but it was maddeningly imprecise, since they weren't really in the universe. That was the point of the warp torpedo—a physical missile maneuvering in real space between two modern warships was just too slow and fragile to make it through most targets' point defenses, but torpedoes didn't offer the enemy anything to shoot down, because they weren't even *there* until they struck. It was the same principle that allowed starships to travel faster than light, but torpedoes didn't compress space for speed, they merely bent it a little to hide as they approached their target. They didn't need to be fast to be lethal.

"Five seconds," Angela Larkin announced. "Four . . . three . . . two . . . one . . . impact!"

Right on cue, a bright burst of light announced the arrival of *Hector*'s torpedo spread. Unlike the drones they'd fired on with the kinetic cannons, drone Sierra simulated complete annihilation—a real torpedo's nuclear warhead would vaporize a small target vessel, after all. "Hit!" Larkin called out. She barely stifled a whoop, and settled for waving a fist in the air.

"My compliments to the torpedo battery," Randall drawled. "You certainly showed that drone what's what."

Sikander nodded in appreciation; sure, it was a practice-range shot, but it was good to see that the torpedo crew knew their business. "Nice shot, Ms. Larkin," he said quietly.

"*Hector,* this is Aberdeen Range Control," the comm unit crackled. "Firing run complete. Your weighted score is eighty-six point nine. You passed *Paris,* but *Pandarus* shot an eighty-nine nine, over."

Captain Markham grimaced. "Damn. I owe Captain Yarrow a bottle of scotch." She keyed the comm unit in her battle couch. "Aberdeen, this is *Hector* actual. Thank you for the range time, pleasure working with you today. *Hector* out."

"Second place to *Pandarus.* I suppose it sets the bar for next time," Randall observed.

"So it seems," Markham replied. "All right, let's recover our practice torps and be on our way."

Sikander frowned at his display. They'd launched two torpedoes, but he had only one torpedo beacon on his screen. The practice torpedoes were designed to be recovered and reused, since they were quite expensive. Each one was a miniature ship, after all—the sort of hardware the Navy wanted to keep track of. He leaned forward and spoke quietly to Larkin. "Ms. Larkin, do you have contact with torpedo two?"

"Number two?" Larkin tapped her display, then began rapping out more commands. She muttered under her breath.

"Ms. Larkin?" Sikander repeated.

The young woman shook her head in disgust. "No contact with the second torpedo. It hasn't emerged from its bubble."

Well, that's not supposed to happen, Sikander told himself. Torpedoes could return to normal space a few seconds early or late, but they very definitely *returned*—the warp generator cut off when the weapon decided it had been in its warp bubble long enough to reach its target. The torp had launched with good telemetry, so what had gone wrong? "Check the program," he told Larkin.

"I am!" Larkin snapped—not a very respectful reply, but Sikander let it go without correction for the moment. The torpedo officer was obviously busy.

"What seems to be the trouble, Mr. North?" Captain Markham asked.

"The second torpedo is still bubbled, ma'am," Sikander answered. "We're forty seconds over program. I think we lost it."

Heads turned throughout the bridge. "Lost it?" Randall snapped. "What kind of program did you punch in? It was a straight shot on a practice range."

Sikander glared at the operations officer. He was a department head, too, and he didn't answer to Hiram Randall once they secured from exercises. "We're checking the program now."

Elise Markham gave him a sharp look. "Please do, Mr. North," she said. "That's five million credits of torpedo now roaming around loose. We need to know where and when it intends to pop out again."

"Yes, ma'am." Sikander called up the ship's info assistant on his console and duplicated the torpedo-control console's log for the last half hour, scrolling down to check over every command Larkin had entered during the range run. Building the attack profile for a warp torpedo required far more programming than any human could do in the space of a few moments, but the engineers who'd designed the weapons-system controls had realized that; the attack program really consisted of only a dozen or so selections and variables that the user could assemble and set with a few quick gestures on the console. As far as he could tell from a quick inspection, Larkin's settings seemed fine, but she did have several personalized macros saved on her console. Many people liked to set up their own preferences and shortcuts for such things, but he'd have to pore over those to see exactly what she'd entered.

"The program is fine," Larkin announced. Naturally she'd finished going over it much faster than Sikander would have; native Aquilans raced through computer tasks that he had to work through with a good deal of care. "Both torpedoes had the identical attack program. Number one worked, so it must be a hardware fault on number two."

"Which, unfortunately, is not available for inspection," Captain Markham said. She shook her head. "Damn. All right, then. Mr. Randall, advise the range of our lost torpedo and make sure you give them all the firing parameters. It's probably never coming back, but they need to know. And tell the XO we'll need to get out the Admiralty report for lost ordnance as soon as practicable."

"Yes, ma'am," Lieutenant Commander Randall replied. He didn't bother to glare at Sikander or Larkin, but he didn't really need to.

"Mr. North, better pull the maintenance records for our wayward torpedo and see if there's anything in the previous diagnostics that might explain where it went."

"Yes, ma'am," Sikander answered. "We'll look over the launch-tube mechanisms, too." He'd also take a good long look at Larkin's programming, just in case. He didn't think she would deliberately attempt to conceal an error—that was an excellent way to turn an unfortunate accident into a career-ending blunder—but she'd reviewed her own work in quite a hurry, and she might have overlooked something.

"Good," the captain replied. She unstrapped from her battle couch and stood. "You have the deck, Mr. Randall. Secure from gunnery exercises and lay a minimum-time course for Fleet Base. Maybe we can beat the paperwork home."

3

The parade grounds of El-Badi Palace broiled slowly under fierce morning sunlight. Groves of moon palms at the far end of the field floated in the heat shimmer, while dazzling flashes of light danced on the waters of the Silver Sea to the south. The legendary summer heat in Tanjeer, the planetary capital of Gadira II and the seat of the sultanate, routinely reached 40 degrees Celsius before noon, but Ranya Meriem el-Nasir paid little attention. She was the descendant of thirty generations of Gadirans, and the colonists who had first settled the planet had been carefully selected from desert-dwelling peoples of Old Terra; sweltering heat rarely bothered her. Besides, the lethal mass of the Léopard grav tank resting on the field before had her full attention.

She studied the grav tank, carefully noting its various features and armament. The vehicle rested on its landing skids, hidden behind the tough dura-weave skirts of its plenum chamber. Not strictly a hovercraft, it was designed to take advantage of ground effect to maximize its speed and maneuverability under the weight of its thick armor and heavy weapons. A dual-barrel kinetic cannon—one barrel for high-velocity armor-piercing rounds, the other for lobbing low-velocity explosive shells—made up the Léopard's main armament. Two small cupola-mounted autocannons furnished more than enough firepower to deal with soft targets such as enemy infantry or unarmored vehicles, and its turret boasted a variety of sensors and accessories. Ranya slowly walked around the tank, admiring it from all sides. She noted that the vendors had finished the armored vehicle in a striking black-and-scarlet paint scheme that matched the house colors of the el-Nasirs, and smiled to herself at the impracticality.

Major Cheney of the Republic Marines took her amusement for approval. "The finest Montréalais military technology, Amira," he said proudly. Ranya might not have noticed the heat, but perspiration darkened the craggy offworlder's dashing uniform. "Just like the legendary Terran predator for which it is named, the Léopard is fast and lethal. Nothing short of heavy antitank weaponry or naval fire support can scratch it. Your uncle's Royal Guard would make a splendid sight mounted in armored vehicles such as this, no?"

"Yes, they would. And they would be seen from twenty kilometers away in such a ridiculous paint scheme," Ranya replied. "A broken rock-and-sand camouflage would make a lot more sense for desert operations. Or do you think I know so little about military equipment that a forty-year-old tank painted like a grav racer is sufficient to impress me?"

Cheney couldn't help exchanging a quick glance with Ambassador Nguyen and the other Montréalais from the embassy's military mission who stood nearby. Ranya waited patiently for the handsome officer to collect himself; it wasn't the first time she had caught someone off-guard with her knowledge of military affairs. Gadira's armed forces limited women in uniform to a handful of specialties that theoretically kept them out of direct combat roles, and few women of high station looked on military service as socially acceptable. It didn't help that Ranya happened to be wearing a light, flowing rose-colored caftan with delicate embroidered flowers, and left her blue-black hair in a long cascade of gentle curls. *It almost doesn't seem fair.* However, she wondered why Paul Nguyen hadn't warned the new military attaché that she was more interested in such matters than her uncle, Sultan Rashid.

She looked over at Ambassador Nguyen, and noticed a distinct twinkle in his eye. That explained it, then—Major Cheney, fresh off the ship from Montréal, was receiving a little lesson from the ambassador. No doubt the enthusiastic and dashing young major had arrived in-system with a boundless store of energy and dozens of grand ideas for showing the poor, backward Gadirans just how lucky they were to have Montréal for their friend. Paul Nguyen would have offered a few words about patience and circumspection, which Cheney would have ignored, so the canny old ambassador stepped out of the way to let the young major learn some things for himself.

"You are terrible," Ranya told Ambassador Nguyen.

"I am afraid I don't know what you are speaking of, Amira," the ambassador innocently replied.

Major Cheney finally rallied. "It is true that the Léopard is an older design, Amira Ranya. But it is highly reliable, cost-effective, and more than adequate for the threat environment your uncle's forces may encounter."

Ranya decided to take pity on Major Cheney, since it wasn't entirely his fault. Montréalais were overly sensitive to the fact that Gadira could be very traditional, since most of their troubles in the sultan's realm came from the highly conservative elements of society, but their predeployment briefings seemed to make little distinction between the urban classes and the more narrow-minded desert tribes. While it was true that Gadiran women did not *ordinarily* engage in male-dominated trades or studies, her people usually made room when extraordinary women defied those expectations. More important, wealthy Gadirans of both sexes enjoyed more personal freedoms—exercised with discretion, of course—than offworlders sometimes realized. As the daughter of one sultan and the niece of another, Ranya had benefited from a first-class education and the freedom to pursue any field of study she took an interest in. Seven years ago, she'd discovered that she needed to know more about military affairs and politics than any proper Gadiran princess ought to, and she'd thrown herself into acquiring that knowledge as efficiently and thoroughly as possible. Ranya couldn't command troops in the field—Gadira simply wasn't ready for that—but she'd instead made herself an expert on the Royal Guard, the military aid provided to the sultanate by the Republic of Montréal, and the forces and tactics of Gadira's urban radicals and restless tribal chieftains.

"You make a good point, Major," she told Cheney. "The Caidists have no armored vehicles at all, and few antitank weapons. Your Léopard is certainly sufficient to control any battle space we establish. The difficulty is that rebellious tribesmen won't oblige us by engaging our tanks." She turned back to the grav tank, found the handholds and footsteps built into its armored flanks, and scrambled up on top of the vehicle. She knew that she looked ridiculous standing on top of a tank in her gauzy pink-white robes, but she wanted a closer look. The driver's hatch stood open, so she set her hands on the deck—hot enough in the sunlight to singe her palms—and dropped into the seat below, disappearing from sight.

She examined the controls, rubbing her hands absentmindedly as she noted the field of view from the armored ports and the access to the rest of the vehicle. Outside, she heard someone quickly scramble up the side of the grav tank. A moment later, Major Cheney appeared above her open hatch. "Be careful in there, Amira!" he said. "Please don't start the vehicle, it can be difficult to control if you are not trained in its operation."

"Have no fear, Major. I'm not going to drive off with your tank." Ranya settled herself into the seat, and identified the principal controls without touching anything. "These seem straightforward enough. I assume you'll provide trainers for our crewmen and maintenance personnel?"

"But of course, Amira. The basic instruction course takes about six weeks. Advanced tactics and maintenance qualifications require additional training regimes."

"What is its operational endurance?"

"The onboard reactor only needs to be fueled about once per six months in operational use. It takes a few liters of a deuterium fuel mixture." Cheney seemed to be a little more comfortable on ground he knew well. "The real limitations are onboard ammunition storage, and the crew's endurance."

"Do we have the ability to produce the deuterium fuel mix in-system? Or the ammunition, for that matter?"

"Not yet, Amira. We will provide ample stores of both for any foreseeable operations. However, you will probably want to contract with SGS Industries—the manufacturer of the tank—to build a fuel plant under license, if you feel that local production of fuel is important."

Only if we want tanks that we can use when we need to without begging for fuel. Well, the ability to produce advanced fuels was something Gadira needed anyway. If her uncle's generals wanted tanks, she would have to convince them that maintenance and logistical support were just as much a part of buying a tank as picking out something with heavy armor and a big gun. Unfortunately, the Montréalais had figured out soon after Sultan Rashid's succession that the easiest way to secure friends close to the throne was to shower them with toys—the bigger, the better.

"Amira!" From outside she heard the voice of Captain Tarek Zakur, the commander of her personal guard. "Bey Salem approaches!"

Ranya glanced out the viewport that faced the palace.

Two figures were indeed making their way toward the parade ground. Well, she had seen most of what she needed to see of the Léopard, and she had probably done enough damage to her daily calendar by taking the time to educate herself on the newest addition to the sultan's arsenal. She scrambled out of the driver's seat, using her loose sleeves to protect her hands from the broiling black-painted hatch rim.

Major Cheney offered his hand, and she allowed him to help her up out of the hatch. "Thank you, Major," she said.

"My pleasure, Amira," the Montréalais officer replied. "Would you like to see the gunner's position?"

"Not right now." Ranya brushed her hands on her robes, and turned her attention to the two men walking up the palm-shaded arcade leading from the palace. Salem el-Fasi she'd known all her life; he was a rotund little man of middle years dressed in a modern Montréalais-style white silk suit, with a blue fez as a nod to Gadiran tradition. The other man she did not recognize, but he appeared to be an offworlder. "Captain Zakur may want a look, though."

"Indeed I do," Tarek replied. He was a huge man, easily two meters tall and at least 120 kilos, with a fierce-looking black beard and a plumed turban that added another fifteen centimeters to his height. For all his size, he was a superior athlete, quick and nimble, and if his dress uniform was just as impractical as the Léopard's parade paint scheme, the mag pistol holstered at his hip was not just for show. He helped Ranya down from the grav tank, and climbed up to take her place. At once he and Major Cheney fell into an animated discussion.

Salem el-Fasi approached Ranya and salaamed when he reached her. "Good afternoon, Amira Ranya," he said. "Did my eyes deceive me, or were you climbing on top of that tank just a moment ago? That hardly seems like the sort of thing that would interest a princess of the royal house."

"I wished to educate myself on my uncle's next major

purchase, Bey Salem." She returned his salaam. The bey pretended to disapprove of her involvement in military procurement, but he'd long ago given up any serious hope of shooing her into the sorts of pursuits he thought more fitting for a princess of the royal house. "What brings you to the palace today?"

"Business, my dear," Bey Salem replied with a wide smile. Ever since her parents had been assassinated by extremists, seven years ago, Bey Salem had insisted that she could look on him as her special protector. He had been one of Sultan Kamal's political allies and a key figure in the old regime, although Sultan Rashid had installed his own favorites after assuming the throne. Ranya had gradually developed the sense in the years after her father's death that he hadn't particularly trusted el-Fasi; as a class, the beys had always been quite wealthy, and contact with foreign powers had benefited Gadira's nobles more than anyone else on the planet. The beys practically bathed in offworld money these days, and Ranya was sure that some had foreign patrons who might someday want to put a different puppet on the throne. Of course, the fortunes of Salem el-Fasi were closely tied to those of the el-Nasir sultanate.

Bey Salem motioned toward his companion. "This is Mr. Otto Bleindel. He represents Dielkirk Industries, a major manufacturer based in Dremark. We are discussing importing and licensing arrangements for establishing a plant to build Dielkirk power cells here in Gadira. Mr. Bleindel, may I present Amira Ranya Meriem el-Nasir, niece to Sultan Rashid and Crown Princess of Gadira?"

Bleindel refrained from offering his hand, and bowed from the waist instead. Evidently he had been briefed on Gadiran etiquette about introductions to women of high rank. "Amira," he said in accented Jadeed-Arabi. "I am honored to meet you."

"Welcome to Gadira, Mr. Bleindel." She studied the offworlder with interest. Bleindel was a young man, probably not more than thirty standard years or so, with a slim build and refined features. He had the brownish-amber skin tone common among the offworlders from the great powers of human space, with dark blond hair and a pair of spectacles shaded against the bright sun. Seemingly without effort, he projected an aura of confident competence. "Why don't we walk under the palms as we speak? Our sun can be harsh for those who are not used to it."

"I am grateful for your consideration, Amira," Bleindel replied.

"Just one moment more," Ranya told him. She turned to Ambassador Nguyen. "Thank you for arranging the inspection, Ambassador. Have your military attaché forward the proposed terms for the purchase to my secretary. I will review them and speak with my uncle about how many Léopards we need."

"Our pleasure," Nguyen replied. "We will send you all the information by the end of the day."

"And thank the major for me when Captain Zakur finishes with him." Ranya glanced up to the grav tank's turret, where Major Cheney and her guard captain were still discussing armament. "Perhaps we can arrange for a firing demonstration soon. I don't think Tarek will be satisfied until he sees the cannon blow up something."

"I'll have the major set it up. Until next time, Amira." Nguyen bowed.

Ranya nodded to him, and turned back to Bey Salem and his Dremish friend. She noticed Bleindel studying the grav tank with a thoughtful expression while waiting for her to finish. *A soldier?* Something in Bleindel's pose suggested that he had a more than casual interest in the armored vehicle, but she could not see his eyes beneath his dark spectacles.

"Are you a military man, Mr. Bleindel?" she asked as the three of them strolled beneath the palms, trailed discreetly by two of her guards. The shade felt quite pleasant after the baking heat of the dusty parade ground; the noise and bustle of the surrounding city subsided as people settled down for the midday *qaylulah,* the time for rest or quiet work indoors to escape the heat of the afternoon.

"Ah, no," Bleindel said. "My education and experience are all in business matters. But as the bey remarked, it struck me as unusual that a Gadiran princess would be knowledgeable in modern military technology."

"Have you met many Gadiran princesses?" Ranya asked him. Bleindel hesitated, perhaps trying to determine whether he'd offended her. *That's two offworlders skewered in the space of ten minutes, Ranya,* she told herself. *If you keep that up, no one is going to come to you about anything.* She gave the businessman a small smile in an attempt to soften the sting of her words, waving away the question. "Forgive me. I understand that visitors from the Coalition worlds aren't sure what to expect when they learn that Gadira is a sultanate with a planetwide religious tradition. However, our Quranism is derived from the reformation movements of the twenty-second century, not the *hadith* teachings that gave rise to the Terran Caliphate. We are a good deal more liberal than you might think."

"I see," said Bleindel. "You are correct, of course. I have some familiarity with Caliphate worlds and I assumed Gadira would be similar."

"You might be surprised by how things work beneath the surface even in the more restrictive Caliphate worlds, Mr. Bleindel." Ranya had never visited them herself, but her family had ties to aristocratic houses in the Terran Caliphate. Over the years, she'd had some very interesting conversations with visiting relatives. "But, to answer your original question, it's true that few women of my station are familiar with military affairs. Unfortunately the house of el-Nasir has a distinct shortage of princes, which means that the events of the last few years have compelled me to take an interest in such things."

"The rise of the caids?" Bleindel stumbled a bit over the Gadiran word.

Ranya nodded. "It's 'cah-eeds,' not 'ky-yeeds.' But yes."

"My apologies, I am still learning, Amira," Bleindel said with a small smile. "My company's security consultants provided me with only a basic overview. The desert chieftains do not like your uncle's dealings with the Montréalais, correct?"

"The Republic of Montréal isn't really the problem," said Ranya. "It's the explosion of interstellar commerce. In the past, Gadira sometimes went decades without a starship visit. But since Montréal reestablished regular contact a couple of generations ago, our people have seen their native industries wiped out by the flood of cheaper, better goods from other worlds. They've seen their financial system swallowed up by interstellar banks. They've seen the popular culture of the great powers overwhelm their entertainment, drowning their children in what they regard as borderline pornography. Montréal is simply the face of the modern world to Gadira's more traditional people, and they don't like what they see."

Bey Salem snorted. "They want to turn back the clock, and they are frustrated because it can't be done."

"Can you blame them?" Ranya said. "Interstellar commerce has enriched some Gadirans—the beys, for example. But the rural people and the less-educated urban workers have seen few of the benefits. They've lost lands and livelihoods to foreigners who appear to show contempt for their values."

"That may be true, at least in part," Bey Salem said. "But it is not the whole story, Ranya. Standards of living are improving around the planet. Some people have lost jobs, true, but others have found better jobs, and more are coming. The working classes have no rational reason for their anger, and they certainly have no excuse for acts of terrorism."

"You need not remind *me* of that, Bey Salem," said Ranya. She glanced at the palace, gleaming in the white sunshine. It had been her father's until the day a Caidist suicide bomber had slipped past the Royal Guard. "For the record, I suspect the people of the working classes do not share your rosy view of their economic prospects. But whether their anger is justified or not, it is *real*. If the Caidists get their way, Gadira will close its spaceports to all contact with non-Islamic powers and ban most modern technology. I can think of no better way to guarantee centuries of poverty and backwardness."

"I can see why the Montréalais are so interested in supporting the sultanate," Bleindel said. "If the radicals have their way, they'll lose fifty years of investments and development here."

"Exactly," said Ranya. She did not add that the more the sultan leaned on the Montréalais for support, the more caids became radicalized. Helping an offworld investor to understand why the Caidists were upset was one thing, but laying bare the harsh paradox of the sultan's weakness was another thing entirely.

"How much of a threat do the Caidists pose?" Bleindel asked.

"They have already made several attempts to seize control of outlying cities and destroy offworlder facilities. They are not well organized or well armed, but they enjoy a good deal of popular support in some quarters, and they are quite determined." Ranya nodded back in the direction of the grav tank. "There is a reason we are modernizing the Royal Guard."

"An excess of caution, Mr. Bleindel," Bey Salem quickly pointed out. "The attempts the amira refers to were unsuccessful. I assure you that protecting foreign investments in Gadira is of utmost importance to Sultan Rashid. You need have no concerns about doing business here."

"Indeed. I am sure that your caids"—this time Bleindel

got the pronunciation correct—"will come to terms with the futility of their position soon enough. But it occurs to me that an army strong enough to deter the Caidists is probably strong enough to simply put an end to the unrest altogether. How long before your new tanks are in service, Amira?"

Ranya paused in their stroll and turned to study the Dremish businessman carefully. A small fountain played nearby. "Is Dielkirk's investment contingent upon the suppression of Caidist unrest, Mr. Bleindel?" she asked.

Bleindel hesitated. "I am only here to gather information for my company's executive leadership, Amira," he said. "That would be up to my superiors. I simply wish to provide the most complete report possible so that they can make good decisions."

"Many beys support Sultan Rashid in dealing sternly with the unrest, Mr. Bleindel," Bey Salem said. "Our taxes pay for his army, after all, and we too would like to see a good return on our investment. I have been urging the sultan to consider more stringent measures for some time now, and to settle the question once and for all."

"Why does the sultan hesitate, then?" Bleindel asked.

Because he leaves everything to his ministers? Ranya wanted to say. *Or because he does not trust the army and worries they might turn on us?* But once again those were not the sorts of concerns to share with an offworlder she had just met. Instead, she shrugged. "The sultan is not eager to turn heavy armor loose on our fellow Gadirans, even the most defiant ones," she said. "Ultimately, we can buy all the grav tanks we want from Montréal, but tanks won't change minds. Good jobs and a little more sympathy for Quranist sensibilities are the weapons that will defeat the Caidists. Companies such as Dielkirk can bring the jobs to Gadira. If their representatives are careful to pay attention to cultural concerns, so much the better."

Bleindel bowed. "The sultan's restraint is commendable. Forgive me if I have been impolite in my questions, Amira."

"There is nothing to forgive," Ranya replied. She glanced toward the palace's west veranda, which was only a short distance away. "Shall we go inside and perhaps have some lemonade? I would like to hear more about your company's plans—and why Bey Salem is so enthusiastic about them."

Salem el-Fasi laughed softly. "A healthy percentage, of course," he replied. "But I am sincere in my belief that Mr. Bleindel's company represents an opportunity all Gadirans should welcome."

"At least you are honest about your venality, Bey Salem," Ranya said, but she gave the businessman a small smile to make light of the remark. She had to be careful about whom she trusted, and if she couldn't count on Salem el-Fasi to always do the *right* thing, at least she could predict how he might act in his own self-interest. So long as he saw that his fortunes would flourish alongside those of House Nasir, he could be counted on.

She motioned toward the veranda. "This way, Mr. Bleindel. And, while we walk, I hope you'll allow me to tell you a little about the palace and its gardens."

"I would be delighted, Amira," Bleindel replied, and followed her inside.

4

Brigadoon, New Perth

Sikander North climbed out of the luxurious flyer on the landing pad of the governor's mansion, and unconsciously adjusted his finest dress uniform. The magnificent residence was lit with hundreds of golden hover-lights, a lazy swarm of fireflies drifting over the pools and gardens, and the soft sound of a live string quartet came from a bandstand not far away. Hundreds of men and women dressed in formal wear—short jackets and wide cummer-bunds for the men, glittering gowns in countless spectacular hues for the women, and of course dress whites for military personnel—were already present, strolling about the grounds or gathering in small groups to talk over cocktails. Sikander was impressed; Aquilans could pull off elite elegance better than almost anyone.

It's like the Bandi Chor Divas festival back home—the celebrations at the palace after the public processions, anyway. He smiled at the old memories: At dusk, throngs of people and thousands of golden lights would fill the streets of Sangrur as the raucous processions made their way through the city, passing by the nawab's box in the review-ing stand for the traditional blessing. Afterward, Nawab Dayan always hosted the notables of his domain at a grand banquet, the highlight of Jaipur's social calendar. Sikander remembered standing in his princely finery beside his father and older brothers, all too conscious of the beautiful young women in the crowd trying to catch his eye. As the fourth-born of his father's children, Sikander was always much better positioned than his dutiful older brothers to take advantage of his aristocratic name. While Devindar and Gamand squirmed under the constant scrutiny of the planet's elites and the crowds of journalists who followed them, he was free to engage in the much more enjoyable task of choosing his company for the evening. . . .

I am forgetting my date, Sikander realized. He took a deep breath, returning his attention to the governor's mansion on a cool Brigadoon evening. He gave his tunic a tug and shrugged his shoulders to adjust his uniform, then turned to assist Lara Dunstan as she emerged from the luxury flyer. She was his companion for the Governor's Ball, the daughter of an important Aquilan senator and a close friend of his cousin Amarleen. A deep sapphire gown perfectly complemented her eyes, and her hair was swept up into a jeweled coiffure that sparkled in the soft light.

Lara beamed with delight as she took in the scene. "It looks like everyone who is anyone is here," she murmured to Sikander.

"Well, now that we have arrived, I suppose so," he said, and smiled.

"Oh, this will be so much fun!" Impulsively she leaned over and kissed his cheek. Lara was petite by Aquilan standards; she had to stand on her tiptoes to reach him comfortably. "Thank you for inviting me!"

"The pleasure is all mine," he said. Already he thought he saw heads turning to take in Lara's striking dress, and he grinned even more. There was nothing like walking into a party with a gorgeous woman on one's arm and knowing that she was the most stunning beauty present. He almost forgot about his cousin Amarleen, and it was only the gentle throat-clearing of Dr. Ondrew Tigh—a wealthy young physician from another upstanding senatorial family, and Meena's date for the evening—that reminded Sikander that he was standing in the way. He quickly took Lara's arm and led her a few steps from the flyer so that Ondrew could enact the time-honored ritual of offering his date assistance she didn't need to get out of the vehicle and make her arrival.

The evening promised to be a welcome change of pace. Sikander had spent much of the last two weeks looking over Sublieutenant Larkin's shoulder in the effort to figure out what had happened with their stray torpedo, to no avail. Fortunately, the Governor's Ball offered a suitable excuse for setting aside the day-to-day work of a gunnery officer, and the fact that Amarleen happened to have a beautiful friend in need of a date had worked out well for him. Things were comfortably casual between Sikander and Lara, but that was how he preferred it, especially when they both came from such prominent families. Of course, the Governor's Ball was a very prominent event. Every socialite in Brigadoon—and every well-connected fleet officer whose personal fortune or family pedigree rated mention in the social register—was there, and for the foreseeable future the gossip of the capital would revolve around who had been seen with whom.

"Shall we make our way to the bar?" Sikander asked the others. The buffet had not yet been served and the dancing would come later; most of these events started with cocktails in the garden.

"Only one for me," Amarleen declared. She wore a brilliant green gown that complemented the famous North eyes, and would have been the most striking woman present if Sikander didn't have her friend Lara on his arm. "If I don't pace myself, I'll be as giggly as a little girl in no time at all."

"Yes, let's avoid that at all costs," Ondrew Tigh agreed

gravely. He had an excellent deadpan; Sikander liked the fellow already. "That doesn't sound fun at all."

"Well, I remember a wedding in Jaipur a couple of years ago . . ." Sikander began.

Amarleen wheeled around and threatened him with a raised finger. "Oh, no you don't! That story does not need to be told tonight, or ever. Am I clear?"

"As you wish." Sikander waited until Amarleen had turned back to her date, and leaned close to whisper to Lara. "Just remind me to tell you about Meena and the cake later."

Lara laughed. "I will!"

They strolled slowly down the path leading from the landing pad to the extensive gardens behind the manor. It was a cool, breezy evening, not unusual for springtime in Brigadoon, but the hoverlights provided heat as well as illumination, and the mansion's staff had carefully arranged hidden screens in the shadows of the surrounding forest to mitigate the breeze. The night was clear and starry above the golden glow of the drifting lights, and the Fleet Base was clearly visible as a bright, crooked crescent directly overhead, surrounded by scores of tiny moving stars crisscrossing the sky—ships joining or leaving New Perth's busy orbital traffic.

As Sikander expected, most of the guests gathered in the gardens for cocktails. Lara and Ondrew pointed out various celebrities among the civilian guests for Amarleen, while Sikander did the same for high-ranking members of the Admiralty or noteworthy captains. Amarleen and her date soon fell in with a large group of university types; Sikander caught a few glimpses of her laughing and chatting with Ondrew Tigh's colleagues and a number of her fellow students. For his own part, Lara introduced him to many of her friends, who proved to be a good sampling of New Perth's aristocratic families. If any of them thought it unusual to see a Dunstan escorted by a prince of Kashmir, they were too well-mannered to comment.

Around a bend in the garden path Sikander spied a knot of officers from *Hector* surrounding Captain Markham. He looked to Lara. "Would you like to meet my shipmates? Most of them are decent people, and I'd love the opportunity to show you off for them."

"You're incorrigible," Lara said. "But yes, I'd like to meet your colleagues."

They strolled down to the patio where *Hector*'s officers had gathered. "Good evening, Captain," said Sikander. He nodded to the rest: Hiram Randall, Karsen Reno, Michael Girard, as well as Peter Chatburn—a tall, somber man who was actually the sitting Senator Malgray as well as *Hector*'s second-in-command—and Magdalena Juarez, *Hector*'s chief engineer. "May I present Ms. Lara Dunstan? Lara, this is Captain Elise Markham, commanding officer of CSS *Hector*."

"A pleasure to meet you, Ms. Dunstan," Captain Markham said. "You're Senator Dunstan's daughter, aren't you?"

"Yes, I am," Lara replied. "Do you know my father?"

"I met him during my last staff tour." Markham took Lara's hand firmly. "He was in charge of the Naval Appropriations Committee when I was serving with the Office of Construction and Repair. Senator Dunstan was always very well informed on budget issues."

"By which you mean he badgered you mercilessly, I think," Lara said with a small smile. "I know he can be difficult at times, but he really does have the service's best interests at heart."

"I would much rather defend our designs from an informed critic than someone whose only interest is scoring points in the press," Markham replied. She released Lara's hand.

"Allow me to make some more introductions," Sikander said. One by one he introduced his shipmates to Lara. In turn, his colleagues introduced their own dates to Lara and him. Captain Markham was in attendance with her husband Nicholas, a tall, silver-haired civilian with a bluff good cheer to him. Sikander gathered that he worked as an attorney for the government. Neither Peter Chatburn nor Michael Girard had dates for the evening, but a commander from squadron operations stood close by Magdalena Juarez. Karsen Reno was accompanied by a handsome young man, his longtime partner, while Hiram Randall had on his arm a pretty, dark-haired woman in a ruby-red dress. Sikander always found it strange to meet the spouses or romantic interests of his shipmates; he often fell into the habit of thinking that the officers he saw every day had no existence of their own outside the ship. For example, he hadn't realized that Karsen Reno was committed to another young man—something common enough in Aquilan worlds, although not usually acknowledged openly in Kashmiri society. He'd known that Juarez was dating Commander Nilsson, but he'd heard only the vaguest rumors about Elise Markham's husband. As captain of *Hector,* she'd struck him as complete in and of herself, and it was somehow unexpected to see her as half of a couple.

"How do you know Mr. North?" Juarez asked Lara when the introductions were concluded.

"Actually, his cousin Amarleen is a dear friend of mine from our college days," Lara replied. "She introduced us. In fact, she is here tonight, although I don't see her at the moment."

"Another North is loose in the capital?" Hiram Randall remarked. "Good heavens, I believe they've discovered space travel!" He adopted an expression of mock terror that was ridiculous enough to earn a round of mild laughter from the group.

Sikander acknowledged the barb with a good-natured smile, although he never liked being the target of someone else's gibe. "As it turns out, we have discovered medicine, too," he said. "Amarleen is studying at Carlyle. I for one am very proud of her; they only accept eighty students a year, or so I'm told."

"They must—" Randall started to say, but the soft tone of a chime sounding from the mansion above interrupted him. That was probably for the best, since Sikander did not intend to let another wisecrack directed at him or his family pass by.

"It seems dinner is served," Captain Markham observed. "Might I suggest that we make our way inside?"

Hector's officers and their dates joined the throng heading inside. Dinner was a vast buffet, but Sikander took care to partake lightly. Lara had made it clear that she expected to *dance* at the Governor's Ball, and he'd learned early on that stuffing himself to the gills was not the best way to prepare himself for a long night of dancing. He collected the makings for a steak salad while Lara helped herself to a mix of lighter pastas, and they rejoined *Hector*'s officers at a round table in the corner of the banquet room.

Hiram Randall watched Sikander eat with a bemused expression. "I thought New Sikhs were vegetarians," he observed. "You do know you're eating steak, I hope?"

"Indeed I do, and it's delicious," Sikander replied between forkfuls. "I am not a vegetarian. Only *deri-amritdhari* refrain from eating meat."

"So you are a *sahajdhari,* then?" Lara asked. She, like her friend Amarleen, was pursuing a doctorate, but hers was in international relations. Sikander had been quite pleased to discover that Lara had studied Kashmiri culture and social norms as part of her postgraduate work; most other Aquilans were not as well versed in the traditions of his homeworld.

He nodded for the benefit of the others. "Indeed I am. That means I have accepted the tenets of my faith, but have not yet committed myself to being fully observant."

"That seems like a convenient place to be," Peter Chatburn said. In Sikander's first four weeks aboard *Hector,*

Chatburn had struck Sikander as a rather unforgiving and results-oriented executive officer. That was part of the job, of course, but Sikander found him difficult to like, despite the shared bond of aristocratic rank. "All of the benefits of salvation, and none of the silly restrictions."

"There is a little more to it than that," Sikander said. "Even as *sahajdhari,* we practice meditation, engage in charitable work, and study the gurus' teachings. And eventually I'll be expected to undergo *amrit deri-sanskar*—baptism—and begin living in a strictly observant manner."

"It all seems like a tremendous waste of energy," said Randall. "If there's a divine spirit out there in the universe, I doubt whether it cares if you eat meat or not, as long as you get the other parts straight."

"I take it you are not religious, Mr. Randall?" Lara asked.

"Good God, I hope not," Randall said with a laugh. That did not particularly surprise Sikander; something like seventy-five percent or more of Aquilans did not claim any religious affiliation, and were proud agnostics or atheists. "I have no use for magical men in the sky telling me how to live, thank you."

"And yet you swore by His name just then," Sikander pointed out. Soft laughter followed around the table. "Perhaps you are more religious than you think, Mr. Randall."

Randall shot Sikander a hard look, but joined the laughter after a moment. "The one thing I suppose He's good for, then," he said. "Humankind has outgrown the need for such fables."

"Fairy tales to your thinking, perhaps," Sikander said. "The search for truth and meaning to countless other people, including millions of Aquilans. What is so contemptible about that?"

Randall gathered himself for another retort, but a glance from Captain Markham stilled his words. An awkward silence fell over the table for a moment; the captain cleared her throat. "I believe the palace staff would like us to finish up so they can clear the dance floor," she said. "I think I'm ready for another drink, myself."

By ones and twos, the table broke up. Lara excused herself to head for the restroom; Sikander waited by the hallway, and did his best not to glare in the general direction of Randall or Chatburn as they wandered off. The infuriating thing was that New Sikhism was actually very open to scientific inquiry and was hardly the blanket of oppressive ignorance that people like Randall railed against. Kashmir lagged behind the great powers of human space because of poverty and long isolation, not its dominant faith. And even if that weren't true, Sikander had never understood how any decent human being could take *pride* in holding the sincere beliefs of others in contempt.

"Thank you, Mr. North." Sikander looked up, and found Magdalena Juarez nearby. She was apparently waiting for her date as well.

"You're welcome, but for what?" Sikander replied.

"Standing your ground against Hiram. I've heard that tirade more times than I care to relate. For someone who claims to be the embodiment of reason and scientific inquiry, he can be a close-minded bigot toward people of faith."

"Mr. Randall is not the first person who has shared those views with me." Sikander offered a small shrug. "You need not concern yourself with my sensibilities."

"Oh, I am not annoyed on your account," the chief engineer answered. "I'm a Nicosian Catholic. My whole family is. I'm afraid I don't know much about New Sikhism, but I suspect it deserves more respect than Hiram Randall cares to show it."

Sikander nodded. The Papacy had left Old Terra centuries ago, driven into exile by the rise of the Caliphate. Rome was no more, but her children roamed the stars, and the Nicosians were the most numerous and unified of the Christian denominations. "In that case, I am happy to have been of service, Ms. Juarez," he told her.

"Magdalena, please, or Magda for short." The engineer raised a finger for emphasis. "Never, under any circumstances, Mags or Maddie or Maggie."

"So noted. Sikander, then, although my friends call me Sikay—just like the letters C-K."

"Sikay, then," Magda said. She shook his hand, and a wicked gleam came to her eye. "Now, more importantly: Did I hear correctly that you keep a *boat* on Brigadoon Bay? And that you go fishing most weekends?"

"My reputation precedes me, apparently," Sikander said. "I take it you are an angler, too?"

"New Seville is nine-tenths water. I learned how to troll for glow-tuna before I could ride a bicycle."

Sikander grinned. "I have no idea what a glow-tuna is, but I'd be delighted to take you fishing on Brigadoon Bay, Magda. When we get back to the ship, let's look over our duty schedules and pick a day."

At nine o'clock precisely, an orchestra took its place in the mansion's ballroom and struck up the music. The banquet room, as well as the surrounding veranda, soon filled with elegant couples gliding gracefully across the floor. Sikander thoroughly enjoyed the next couple of hours; Lara Dunstan was a delight in his arms, as delicate as a wisp of cloud, her eyes filled with a mischievous light that promised a very fine conclusion to the evening when they finally decided to quit the party. From time to time they parted briefly to entertain other partners, since Lara simply couldn't decline all the requests she received for a single dance, but she quickly returned to him after each instance. When they grew tired, they strolled outside to admire the evening or refresh themselves with drink.

A little before midnight, Captain Markham issued her apologies. She and her husband made one more round to say their good-nights, and left the party. The orchestra began their last set; Sikander and Lara decided they were ready for a nightcap or two, and retreated to one of the mansion's quieter verandas. This one faced south, commanding a striking view of Brigadoon's skyline. Amarleen was determined to finish out the very last bit of the dancing and had not yet released Ondrew Tigh, but several of *Hector*'s officers gathered on the veranda with Sikander and Lara, enjoying the end of the entertainment.

Sikander leaned against a balustrade, one arm around Lara's waist, the other gently swirling a flute of Andalusian champagne. The evening seemed suffused in a pleasant glow fueled by dancing, dining, drink, and the company of a beautiful woman all in their proper proportions. He raised his glass in the direction of the mansion's residential quarters. "My compliments to the governor," he announced. "She throws an excellent party."

"I don't think I actually saw her this evening," Lara said. "Was she even here?"

"I saw the governor at dinner," Ensign Girard answered. "I think there's a rule that says she has to come to her own party."

Hiram Randall and his date wandered out onto the veranda. It seemed that Randall's date had perhaps had a little more champagne than was good for her. Her face was flushed and she wasn't entirely steady on her feet; she clung to Randall's arm as she laughed loudly at something he'd said. Randall grinned at his own wit and steered her out into the cooler air. He caught sight of the group standing by the balustrade and headed over.

"I should have known that Mr. North would see the party through to its close," Randall said as he joined them. "His talents in that regard are legendary."

"I see my misspent youth follows me still," Sikander replied. He'd intended to linger just a little bit longer, but he found that he was not terribly interested in trading jabs with his fellow department head. "However, in this case, you are mistaken. I fear that things are winding down here. We were just saying our good-nights; I must see Ms. Dunstan home soon."

"Indeed?" Randall turned to Lara, and gave her an appraising look. "I must say, Ms. Dunstan, it's very kind of you to take an interest in Mr. North's introduction to Aquilan society. I can only hope the Foreign Ministry is compensating you handsomely for your work among the less advantaged cultures of the galaxy." He enjoyed a merry laugh at his own humor, but his eyes remained cold and hard.

Lara gave Randall a sharp look, but a moment later she smiled coolly and intertwined her arm with Sikander's. "I am sorry if it was not clear before, Mr. Randall, but Sikander is my date for the evening. And I certainly wouldn't refer to a culture as rich and artistically mature as Kashmir's as disadvantaged in any way."

"If you say so," Randall replied. "I suppose primitive belief systems are quite fascinating. The fact that they have survived up to the modern day says quite a lot about human nature—although not much that is complimentary, I am afraid."

"Oh, here it comes again," Magdalena Juarez said. "Hiram, no one cares what you think about their beliefs. Leave it alone."

"I don't mean to offend," Randall said. "I am sincerely trying to satisfy my own curiosity. What exactly is the nature of Ms. Dunstan's interest in this arrangement? Political? Charitable? Anthropological, perhaps?"

"Ms. Dunstan's interests are none of your business, Mr. Randall," said Sikander in an icy tone.

"I don't see that they ought to be yours, either." Randall gave a small shrug, and took a level sip from the highball glass in his hand. Sikander realized then that Randall was drunk—in fact, he'd had a drink in his hand every time he'd seen him throughout the evening—but he was one of those people who carried his liquor in his words. Instead of getting loud or red in the face or boisterous, Hiram Randall grew colder and viciously deliberate as he drank. The idea of baiting Sikander and teasing Lara Dunstan about him was something that a sober Randall might have entertained, but would never have acted upon. The drunk Randall couldn't resist the temptation to stir up trouble, and the alcohol he'd imbibed fueled a cruel streak in him that was never very far beneath the surface.

Even understanding that, Sikander was furious. Hiram Randall had said all that he was prepared to put up with. "You're drunk, Randall," he said. "Go home before you say something you'll regret."

"Perhaps, but tomorrow when I sober up, I'll still be an Aquilan and you won't, no matter how much you pretend otherwise," said Randall. He glanced at Lara, and his gaze lingered until she flushed and looked away. "Or who you . . . date."

Sikander flexed his fists and took a step toward Randall. At that moment, he frankly did not care that he was about to end his career in the Commonwealth Navy in the most spectacular fashion imaginable. Striking another officer was a court-martial offense, regardless of the provocation that had been offered, and the witnesses standing nearby would be bound by duty and honor to testify about what happened next. He'd be sent back home in disgrace, but wiping the arrogant sneer off Hiram Randall's face might just be worth all that trouble.

Magda Juarez took two quick steps and set a hand on Sikander's shoulder. "For God's sake, Sikay—*don't do it*," she said in a low whisper. "If you throw the first punch, you're giving him exactly what he wants."

"At a loss for words?" Randall met Sikander's eyes. The Aquilan officer deliberately dropped his glass; it shattered on the flagstones of the veranda. The other guests nearby stood shocked into silence. "Don't let Ms. Juarez keep you from speaking your mind!"

Sikander angrily shrugged off Magda's hand, but just as he was about to step forward and knock Hiram Randall's teeth down his throat, his personal comm beeped urgently. Randall's went off at the same moment, along with Magda's, Reno's, and Girard's. Despite his anger, he hesitated a moment and glanced at the device clipped to his belt. The other officers likewise looked down, surprised.

"What in hell?" Randall growled. He backed away from Sikander and brought his communicator to his hand. Sikander glared at the Aquilan, but held his place while his own unit continued to warble.

"Ship's recall," Michael Girard reported, listening carefully to his communicator. "All the officers and crew of CSS *Hector* are to report aboard immediately. It sounds like they'll need us to get under way as soon as possible, sir."

Recall? Sikander wondered. He turned his attention to his own communicator and accepted the call. In a moment he heard the cool, automated tone of the ship's info assistant announcing the general recall. In six years of duty aboard three different ships, he had never seen a ship's company called back from liberty. It simply wasn't done . . . except in case of emergency.

"Damn," Magda muttered. "They called us back from the Governor's Ball? Did somebody start a war somewhere?"

"It's only *Hector,* ma'am," Girard pointed out. He nodded at the rest of the ball guests. Scores of uniformed personnel from other ships and stations were in sight, but none were looking at their own communicators or making their way toward the landing pad.

Something urgent, then, but urgent only for CSS *Hector.* The cruiser was needed somewhere else in a hurry. Some sort of disaster relief? An urgent delivery too big for a fleet courier? Sikander couldn't even begin to guess. He returned his comm unit to his belt and faced Randall. "We will continue this another time, Randall," he said. "I am available at your convenience."

"I won't forget," Randall said. He put away his own communicator, caught his date by the hand, and headed for the landing pad.

Lara turned to Sikander. "What is it, Sikander?"

"I am afraid I must cut our evening short. We've all been recalled to the *Hector*." He took her hand and grimaced. "There is a good chance we'll sail at once. I don't know where we're going, or when I will be back."

"The hazards of dating a naval officer, I suppose," Lara answered. She sighed. "Well, it was a fun evening. I suppose I can see myself home."

"I'm sorry," he apologized. "And, Lara—I am sorry about the way Randall treated you. He shouldn't have said those things. I promise I will teach him better manners."

"Don't let him get to you, Sikay. He's an ignorant bigot." Lara pressed herself close and kissed him with a warmth that made Sikander very sorry indeed that he had to go. When they broke apart, she whispered in his ear. "Send word when you can, and be careful out there."

"I will," he said. "And I am truly sorry to spoil the evening." He embraced her again, and then hurried away toward the mansion's landing pad and the waiting flyers.

5

CSS *Hector* got under way six hours after the general recall. As the mottled green-blue crescent of New Perth faded behind them, Captain Markham summoned the ship's officers to a briefing. A few minutes before 0800 ship's time, Sikander made his way to the wardroom. He had just enough time to pour himself a mug of coffee before Captain Markham entered the room.

"Attention on deck!" Peter Chatburn called. Everyone present rose and faced the door.

"Please, be seated," Markham replied. She took her place at the head of the table as *Hector*'s officers sat down and waited for her to continue. "I suppose you're all wondering what exactly is going on. I'll get to that in a moment. First, a navigation report?" She looked to Chatburn.

On most Aquilan warships smaller than a battleship, the executive officer also served as the ship's navigator. "We're aligned for warp transit and accelerating to our ring-activation velocity, Captain," Chatburn replied. "We expect to bubble—" He glanced down at his dataslate. "—at ten percent *c*, which we'll reach at 1555 hours. That should give us a thirteen-day transit. We could boost harder and bubble at a higher velocity to cut the transit time a bit, but that will use a lot of fuel."

"Thirteen days is sufficient," Markham answered. "We're supposed to be on station by the end of the month, and I don't want to arrive with our fuel bottles empty. Transit at 1555 approved. Ms. Juarez, engineering will be ready?"

Magda nodded. "Yes, ma'am. But I confess I'm curious about where we're going."

"Gadira, Ms. Juarez. We are headed for the Gadira system."

Sikander considered himself reasonably well educated on galactic geography, but he hadn't ever heard of the place. It wasn't within the Aquilan sphere of influence, anyway. He noticed that most of the other officers in the briefing seemed just as puzzled as he felt.

Captain Markham took in the confused looks of her officers with a small smile. "I only learned of the system last night. Yesterday the Foreign Ministry informed the Admiralty they needed a warship on station there as soon as it could be arranged. The Admiralty in their wisdom decided that the Old Worthy was just the ship for the job and called me as I got home from the Governor's Ball." She glanced around the table, and Sikander thought that her eyes lingered on Hiram Randall a little longer than the others. Had she heard something about his behavior at the end of the ball? "I understand many of you were still there when the recall was sent—my apologies for cutting your evening short."

"You wouldn't have called if it wasn't important, Captain," Chatburn said. "The needs of the service come first, and all that."

"Indeed." Markham looked back to Randall. "Mr. Randall, why don't you fill everyone in on what we know about Gadira?"

"Yes, ma'am." As the ship's operations officer, Randall was the most closely involved with mission planning and intelligence summaries. While the rest of the crew had been loading stores or quickly finishing routine maintenance tasks to make ready for departure, the Operations Department had been examining every detail of *Hector*'s orders to find out where they were supposed to go and what they were supposed to do. Randall picked up a remote in front of him, and pointed it at a screen on the bulkhead. A moment later the image of a gold-and-blue planet with a single, prominent moon appeared.

"This is Gadira—the name of both planet and planetary system," Randall began. "Technically this is Gadira II; there's a mercurian planet close to the star, and three uranian-type gas giants further out. Gadira itself is a temperate semi-terran world, originally colonized by the Caliphate in the Second Expansion. As you can see, its seas are small and landlocked, and tend to lie in the tropical zone. That's where most of Gadira's population lives. The higher latitudes are quite arid, with minimal ice caps."

"The planet seems ordinary enough," Markham observed. "What about the people?"

"The planetary population is a little under a billion. The system developed more or less independently, especially after the Terran Caliphate fell into decline. Contact with the rest of human space was sporadic at best for several hundred years. The Montréalais reestablished contact forty years ago; Gadira's still catching up to Coalition standards today."

Sikander nodded to himself—Kashmir's story was similar. In humanity's first waves of emigration from Old Terra, the early starfaring powers launched colony ships to many promising worlds, but the drive technology of that time meant that establishing any kind of interstellar commerce or regular communications would be impossible. The people who felt the need to settle their own world were often trying to preserve vanishing cultures; as a result, long-isolated colonies often retained stronger racial phenotypes and cultural patterns than the more cosmopolitan star nations in the Coalition of Humanity. By the time the Gadiras and Kashmirs of the galaxy had been rediscovered, they'd fallen centuries behind the leading powers of human space.

Randall continued. "Politically, Gadira is a system monarchy ruled by a sultan by the name of Rashid el-Nasir. The sultanate is allied to the Republic of Montréal with a treaty of mutual defense and support, although it should be noted that the other Coalition powers don't entirely accept the arrangement. When contact was first reestablished, several great powers—the Kingdom of Cygnus, the Dremark Empire, and of course our own Commonwealth—believed they had interests in Gadira. As I understand it, our Foreign Ministry favored more of an open-door policy, but over the years Montréal has become the de facto colonial administration of the system. We haven't pushed the question."

"I can't say I like the idea of Montréal shutting an open door in our faces," Chatburn said. "Have they noticed our fleet is twice the size of theirs?"

"I suspect we haven't protested too much because we wouldn't want Montréal to push us on some of our own colonial interests," said Captain Markham. "Or maybe it's a quid pro quo for some other arrangement. Interstellar politics is a tangled web indeed. Go on, Mr. Randall."

"Of course, ma'am," Randall said. "Economically, a class of titled aristocrats controls most of the planet's commercial interests. A good number of people in the outlying districts are actually seminomadic herders who eke out a subsistence-level existence on the verge of the high-latitude deserts. Finally, Gadira is dominated by a post-Terran tradition of Islam, Tharsisi Quranism. Religious participation is almost universal. The history of the planet is punctuated by various violent movements toward stricter interpretations of the role of religion in public life."

"It almost sounds medieval," Angela Larkin said.

"Mr. North should feel right at home," Chatburn observed. That earned a couple of quiet chuckles from around the table.

Sikander kept his face impassive. He'd already had enough of Hiram Randall's barbs, and he was in no mood to let more wisecracks go unanswered. But Chatburn was his superior, and he had to be careful about how he responded. If he reacted with anger, the situation would be escalated right in front of the entire wardroom. If he laughed at himself to show that he fit in with his Aquilan colleagues, he would only be inviting more gibes in the future—and he would hate himself afterward. *Don't let them see an emotional response. But don't let it pass without comment, either.*

"If you mean that I feel like I understand the Gadirans, sir, then yes—I do," Sikander answered. "They find themselves at the mercy of foreign cultures that have little respect for their most cherished traditions. You should not underestimate the injury of wounded pride, especially in systems that are controlled by less . . . *enlightened* powers than the Commonwealth." He measured his sarcasm very carefully, allowing just a hint to color his tone and make his point; most of the officers at the table frowned or looked away. Then he continued on. "I believe I am not just speaking for myself when I say that I don't yet see why our presence is required. What's on fire in Gadira, and what are we supposed to do about it?"

"That's the question, isn't it?" said Captain Markham. "Why don't you skip ahead a little, Mr. Randall?"

"Yes, ma'am." Randall looked down the table at Sikander. "The short version is this: Sultan Rashid's government faces serious unrest driven by economic distress and native xenophobia. The tribal groups openly defy the sultan's authority, and the poor urban classes resent the fact that the beys are the only ones profiting from interstellar trade. Montréal is propping up the sultan, which of course makes the sultan even more unpopular with the xenophobic elements in Gadira. Our diplomatic agents in Tanjeer—that's the planetary capital—believe the sultanate may fall, which means the Montréalais may lose control of the system."

"That seems unfortunate for the Republic, but perhaps Montréal shouldn't have grabbed the whole system or backed an unpopular ruler," Magda said. "Picking winners in local politics is certain to inflame resentment from the losing side."

"And I don't understand why an Aquilan presence is important," Chatburn added. "Isn't this a problem for Montréal?"

"It is," Captain Markham answered. "But Montréal is not the military power they were forty or fifty years ago, and there are strong sentiments in their domestic politics for getting out of their colonial responsibilities. When or if the sultanate falls, there will be a significant power vacuum in Gadira. The Montréalais will be out, but there will be other great powers anxious to bring Gadira within their sphere of influence."

"Specifically, the Dremish," said Randall.

"Exactly." Markham leaned back in her chair. "The Foreign Ministry's learned that the Empire of Dremark informed Montréal that it is very concerned about the ongoing unrest in Gadira and worries that its interests in the system are under threat. They will take steps to protect their own citizens and property. It seems clear that if the Montréalais are thrown out, the Dremish intend to move in."

Sikander nodded again. Even if he hadn't heard of Gadira before, anyone serving in the Aquilan navy knew the strategic situation of the Empire of Dremark quite well. Dremark was a powerful state but had been slow to organize when the era of great power expansion began. As a result, other powers established control over territory that now hemmed in Dremark's natural avenues for growth. Dremish strategists and statesmen constantly called for access to sectors with better prospects, but the question no one had yet answered was who exactly would surrender territory to satisfy Dremark's ambitions.

"How long do we expect to remain on station, ma'am?" Magda asked.

"Until relieved or recalled. Unofficially, I've heard that we can expect to be spelled by *Paris* or *Memnon* two to three months after we arrive." Captain Markham looked around the table. "Any other questions? Ms. Larkin, what's on your mind?"

"Yes, ma'am," Larkin said. She sat up straighter and collected her thoughts. "You said that we wouldn't want to see a power vacuum develop in Gadira, and I can see that. But a squadron of Montréalais warships above Gadira ought to guarantee that the sultanate stands, or at least make sure the Dremish don't try to seize the system. I don't see what we can do that they can't. If anything, I'd imagine they would prefer us to mind our own business."

A good question, Sikander thought. He'd come to think of Larkin as the sort of officer who didn't volunteer anything she didn't have to. It didn't help that most of their interactions in Sikander's first month aboard *Hector* had revolved around the issue of the lost torpedo and the lack of progress in determining the cause. It surprised him now to see that she was following the discussion and speaking her mind.

Captain Markham gave Larkin an approving nod. "Two or three years ago, I think that would have been exactly how Montréal would have handled the situation," she said. "At this particular moment, the Republic needs to tread lightly. Fleet Intelligence thinks there may be a deeper strategy in play here. I've seen some analysis that suggests Dremark may be looking for an opportunity to confront Montréal and wring concessions out of them."

"I think I understand, ma'am," Larkin told the captain. "If the Dremish force Montréal to surrender a strategic system like Gadira, they gain a valuable new possession. If Montréal chooses to fight for Gadira, the Dremish gain the opportunity to start a war they know they'll win."

"That's the idea. Montréal can't afford a direct confrontation with Dremark—and we have no interest in allowing Dremark to push the Republic into one." Markham looked around the table. "I think that covers the bases. Transition to warp at 1555; department heads, I'll expect your readiness reports by 1300. Dismissed."

The assembled department heads and junior officers rose as Captain Markham stood, and waited for her to exit. Then they began to gather up their dataslates, finish their coffees, and head for the hatch. Sikander quickly organized his own materials, thinking about what he needed to do next. Then his eye fell on Hiram Randall, who was topping off his own coffee. *That business is unfinished.*

"Mr. Randall, a word," Sikander called.

Randall stopped and turned as the others filed out of the wardroom. "Mr. North?"

Sikander waited for the rest of the officers to leave, then shut the door behind them. He and Randall were alone in the wardroom. He studied Randall in silence for a moment; Randall regarded him coldly. "I have a lot to do," he finally said. "What is it?"

"We did not finish our conversation at the Governor's Ball," said Sikander. "I am available to resume the discussion at your convenience."

"I don't think I have anything else to say to you, North." Randall started to push past him.

Sikander threw out an arm and stopped the Aquilan. "Then perhaps we could meet in the gym tomorrow. We'll pick a quiet time so that we can have the place to ourselves, and finish that conversation."

Randall narrowed his eyes. "Is that a threat?"

"No, Mr. Randall. It's an opportunity for you to shut your mouth and *show* me who's the better man." Sikander let his arm drop. "You were full of opinions last night. I'd like to hear what you might say to me in the gym when no one else is around."

The operations officer glared at Sikander, but he did not back down. "All right, North, but you ought to be careful what you wish for. I won the Academy's silver belt for kickboxing three years running."

Sikander simply held Randall's gaze a moment longer, then yanked the hatch open and left the room. He set up the gym reservation on his dataslate before he reached the Gunnery Department office and returned to the transit preparations.

Hector activated her warp rings precisely on time, and the ship settled into its FTL routine. A bubbled ship was a strange little island universe, cut off from outside communications and events. The gym was naturally popular during warp transits, so the first free time Sikander could schedule was late in the evening. That suited him just fine. He skipped dinner, and used the opportunity to retrieve vids of Randall's Academy kickboxing bouts from the ship's extensive files. If Randall was proud of his record, then Sikander was more than happy to study his technique ahead of time.

Sikander found Hiram Randall waiting for him when he arrived in the ship's gym a few minutes before 2200. The Aquilan officer wore long athletic trunks and light striking pads on his fists, elbows, and feet; he bounced on the balls of his feet and threw quick punches in the air as he warmed up, until his torso was gleaming with sweat. Chief Petty Officer Trent, the ship's master-at-arms and the supervisor of all hand-to-hand combat training on board *Hector,* stood nearby, watching with her arms folded. She was a tall, broad-shouldered woman with a studied lack of curiosity in her posture, and any kind of sparring or other use of the gym was under her purview. There was simply no way that Randall and Sikander were going to be able to fight without Chief Trent standing ready to intervene if things got out of hand.

Randall gave Sikander a single contemptuous glance and went back to his warm-ups, but when Darvesh followed Sikander into the gym, he scowled and lowered his hands. "What the hell is this?" he demanded of Sikander. "Is your butler going to step in and take your beating for you?"

"Mr. North has instructed me not to interfere, Mr. Randall," Darvesh told him. "I must caution you that I will be forced to do so if I see you make use of a lethal technique or continue to strike Mr. North after he has been rendered defenseless."

"I'm not going to kill him," Randall snarled. He looked at Chief Trent and jerked his thumb at the valet. "Make sure he stays out of this."

Trent shrugged her heavy shoulders. "I kind of agree with Chief Reza, sir. I'll step in if I see either of you make this any stupider than it has to be. For that matter, I'll step in if either of you cries uncle, because the XO will have my head if I don't. But we'll both stay out of it as long as you two *gentlemen* keep it clean. Right, Chief Reza?"

Darvesh nodded to her. "As you say, Chief Trent."

"Fine," said Randall. He turned his back on Sikander and went back to his warm-ups.

Sikander peeled off his workout gear, stripping down to sparring trunks. He ignored Randall and began his own warm-up routine, a set of standing yoga exercises mixed in with plenty of stretching and some shadow-boxing. For his own part, Sikander preferred Kashmiri *bhuja-yuddha*. It was a mixed style that emphasized locks, throws, and close-in strikes. Every North received a decent amount of training in both armed and unarmed combat as soon as they were old enough, and it had been one of the few interests he'd developed as a young man that his parents approved of.

When his muscles felt loose and warm, he allowed Darvesh to strap on his striking pads. He would have been happy to dispense with them, but this was ostensibly a friendly sparring session—the equipment was required. He tested the snugness and fit of the pads, then looked over to Chief Trent and nodded. Randall was already waiting.

The master-at-arms motioned for Randall and Sikander to step onto the mat. "Okay, gentlemen. You know the rules—no lethal techniques, otherwise unlimited. We'll observe three-minute rounds. If you step out of the ring, I'll issue a warning the first time, and stop the bout if it happens again. No contact after the bell or outside the ring. If I call a stop for any reason, you will immediately break contact and return to your corners. Understood?"

Sikander nodded. "I understand," he said. Randall just nodded.

Trent looked at each one in turn. "Three rounds enough?"

"Two more than I'll need," Randall said.

"Three rounds are fine," Sikander said. He didn't think it would last that long, either.

"To your corners. Mouth guards in, and wait for the bell." Trent retreated out of the way as Sikander and Randall waited. She studied the two fighters for a moment, then pressed the signal device at her belt. The ring's bell chimed sharply.

Sikander settled into his fighting crouch and advanced. Randall came out to meet him, light on the balls of his feet. They circled warily for a moment, as Sikander studied his opponent's stance and compared it to what he'd seen in the vid records. *Close, but not quite the same,* he decided. Randall was still quick and light on his feet, but his footwork was quieter, a little less energetic; he seemed a little more cautious than he had in the records Sikander had watched. More discipline and experience? A little rusty and conscious of being out of practice? Or had he studied vids of Sikander's own wrestling bouts from the Academy and worked out a different set of tactics?

The distance between them steadily narrowed—and then Randall launched his first attack, throwing a hard front kick at Sikander's midsection. Sikander got his knee up to block, and Randall threw a quick round kick from the other side. Sikander took a hit to his thigh and tried to get outside Randall's legs, but the Aquilan circled away. In a long bout, Sikander might have stayed at a distance and waited for a chance to catch a kick and turn it into a takedown, but this wasn't about outlasting his rival; he wanted to *hit* Randall, and just make sure he didn't let a fight-ending punch or kick get through before he could.

He pushed forward, and in the space of an instant the two were engaged in a furious exchange of knees, elbows, and short jabs. Neither gave much thought to defense, punching hard and taking hard hits in return. Sikander took a stiff jab to the jaw and a knee to the side that just about lifted him off the mat; he landed a hard right hook in Randall's ribs, a knee to the thigh, and then he ducked under the next punch and got his hands on the Aquilan's back leg. Randall punished him with a couple of off-balance hits to his head and shoulders, but Sikander got him up off his feet and drove him into the mat. On the ground Randall balled up and raised his hands to defend himself while Sikander attacked furiously, scoring brutally through Randall's guard. Then Randall got one foot up into position to push Sikander away from him, and scrambled to his feet before Sikander could get back on top of him.

"Round! Round!" Chief Trent called. Sikander backed off, and realized that the three-minute bell was ringing. He'd almost forgotten there would be a break; slowly he retreated to the side of the ring, and took stock of his injuries. His thigh ached, his ribs were sore, he had the taste of blood in his mouth—but looking across the ring at his rival, he could see that Randall's eye was already swelling and he was wincing as he walked around. *When did I punch him in the eye?*

"Do you want to continue?" Darvesh asked quietly.

Sikander was breathing hard, but so was Randall. "I'm fine."

"Do not spend so much time boxing with him," Darvesh said. "You're a good enough boxer, but that is Mr. Randall's strength. Get him on the ground and lock him down."

Sikander nodded. He was fighting with anger, not with strategy. He wanted to pummel Randall, so that was what he was trying to do in the ring. *Use your head, Sikay. Randall does not want to wrestle me, he wants to be free to strike. Fight your fight, not his!*

"Second round," Chief Trent warned. "On your guard, gentlemen!" The bell chimed again.

Sikander came out looking for a chance to grapple. Randall danced away, keeping him back with long-range kicks. Sikander pushed aggressively to close in, and took a side kick in the gut that half knocked the wind out of him and put him on one knee. Randall followed up at once with a spinning round kick as Sikander was still getting to his feet; he barely ducked under it, and was clipped hard enough by Randall's heel that he saw stars. But Sikander surged up as Randall completed the kick, caught him by thigh and waist, and put him on the mat again.

Randall replied with a vicious barrage of elbow and knee strikes—pure savage improvisation, with no technique to speak of. But Sikander got the hold he wanted, twisting his adversary into a half-sitting position and pinning an arm behind his back. "Give!" he snarled through his mouthpiece.

"Go to hell!" Randall snarled back. He snapped his head back, catching Sikander in the ear hard enough to make his eyes water.

Blind fury overwhelmed Sikander. He gave Randall's arm a half twist and shoved hard, dislocating the Aquilan's shoulder. Randall let out a strangled cry and sagged to the ground.

"Stop! Stop! Stop!" Chief Trent shouted. She rushed into the ring; Sikander released Randall at once and backed away. "That's it, sir. We're done here. Mr. Randall, you hear me? We're done."

Sikander stripped off his striking pads as Trent helped Randall to his feet. His ear still rang from Randall's head butt, and he gingerly reached up to rub it. Darvesh came up to him and silently handed him a towel.

Randall spat out his mouthpiece and turned to glare at Sikander. "Goddamn it, you did that on purpose!"

"I had you in the lock and I told you to yield," Sikander replied. "If you do not want your shoulder put out of joint, don't let me get you on the mat, don't let me get you in that hold, and don't head-butt me!"

"Next time—" Randall growled.

"There will be no next time," Chief Trent interrupted. "Not under my watch, sirs. You can go try to kill each other someplace other than my gym." She looked at Randall's shoulder, and shook her head. "I guess we'd better get you to sick bay, Mr. Randall. What do you want me to tell Dr. Simms and the XO?"

Randall reached up with his good hand, pressing it to his injured shoulder. It must have pained him greatly; his face was white and his jaw was clenched tight. He glared at Sikander for a long moment, then gave a small snort and looked to the master-at-arms. "It was an accident, Chief. Mr. North and I got carried away during a practice bout. Nobody's fault but mine."

"Does that suit you, Mr. North?" Trent asked.

Sikander inclined his head to Randall. "As Mr. Randall says—it was an accident."

"All right, then. That's what I'll say." Chief Trent studied Sikander, then looked over to Darvesh. "Chief Reza, make sure Mr. North gets some ice and medical spray on those bruises." Then she took Randall by his good arm and steered him to the door.

"That was very foolish, Nawabzada," Darvesh said quietly. "He nearly had you early in the second round. And if he presses charges, there will be serious repercussions for you."

"Foolish?" Sikander buried his face in his towel, wiping the sweat from his eyes. "No, Darvesh, it was necessary. Some words are worth fighting over." He tossed the towel into the hamper by the door, and headed for the shower.

6

Tanjeer, Gadira II

Otto Bleindel sat in the shadows of the coffee shop, sipping at a strong Gadiran roast and idly watching the crowd. The only bars on Gadira were tucked away in off-worlder districts, but coffeehouses served as a cultural replacement. There were hundreds upon hundreds of cafés in Tanjeer, each serving up its own particular décor and conversation. Just like the nightlife of less modest societies, café culture acted as the social outlet for students, young professionals, and both rich and poor alike. Bleindel had little use for the cultural traditions that shackled Gadira to archaic social norms, but he found that he greatly approved of Tanjeer's coffee shops. He appreciated the rich and complex flavors of Gadiran-style coffee, but he also enjoyed the free-ranging discussion and polite debate of public issues that characterized the café crowd. Even the tension between cultural liberalization and Quranist modesty was a permissible subject in coffeehouse conversations, although Bleindel noted that Gadirans universally supported—or at least claimed to support—the place of religion in civic life.

This is an intelligence agent's bonanza, he decided as he studied the crowd. Talk that would be considered seditious or shocking in other settings was openly aired in Gadira's cafés. All a sultanate spy needed to do in order to identify malcontents and potential revolutionaries was to wander into a café, order a cup of coffee, and listen attentively. Of course, as one of the top special agents in the Security Bureau of the Empire of Dremark, Otto Bleindel noticed things that others might miss. For example, while coffeehouse philosophers never argued that their world would be better off if people abandoned their antiquated faith, Bleindel could see that better-educated individuals guarded their feelings about the outsized influence wielded by Gadiran allamehs and imams and their so-called schools. It would be an interesting question for a future colonial administration; economic development and the adoption of Coalition cultural norms would be greatly accelerated by making mosques into museums, but of course few things provoked people like efforts to suppress their religious beliefs.

A man in dark trousers and a sky-blue shirt entered the café, surreptitiously sweeping the room with his eyes. He had a young man's beard, thin and scraggly, with surprisingly light-colored eyes set in a broad, open face, and hair that was a shaggy mass of dark ringlets. His gaze rested briefly on Bleindel; then he turned to another table and struck up a conversation with a group of professionals. Bleindel picked up his dataslate and resumed his study of the local news features, waiting patiently. After a few minutes, the young man came and joined him at his table.

"*Salamu aleikum,* Mr. Hardesty," he said as he sat down. "I am Alonzo Khouri. Did you have any trouble finding the place?"

"None at all," Bleindel replied. Khouri did not look like a Gadiran rebel; he'd half expected to meet a stern desert tribesman in a robe and keffiyeh. "Extend your hand, please."

Khouri took a sip of his own coffee and set it down, holding it between thumb and forefinger as he rested his hand on the table within easy reach. *Good tradecraft,*

Bleindel noted. He made a show of reaching for his own coffee, and quickly brushed a small skin sampler against Khouri's hand. A quick glance at the indicator confirmed that he was indeed speaking with the man he was here to meet. "Very good, thank you. Do you wish to see my bona fides?"

"No need, Mr. Hardesty." Khouri nodded at the café around them. "You have been under observation for some time now."

Bleindel affected a look of mild surprise. He'd known as soon as he entered, but he didn't want to look *too* confident. "Well, I suppose that explains why you'd feel comfortable discussing our business in such an open setting."

"We can account for everybody here. Offworlders often patronize this particular shop, and discuss business here with Gadirans who deal with their companies." Khouri smiled. "Hiding in plain sight attracts much less attention than trying to not be seen."

"I am sure that your knowledge of the local conditions exceeds mine, Mr. Khouri. If you say we're safe to talk here, then I believe you."

"Safe enough," Khouri replied. He leaned back in his chair, adopting a casual pose, but his eyes remained cold and intense. "I understand that you have come to Gadira to offer us help with our present situation. Excellent—we can use all the assistance we can get, especially since the *khanza* Montréalais are selling tanks to the sultan's army now. But I need to know who you are and why you want to help us, Mr. Hardesty. If I am not satisfied with the answers, this café may not be all that safe after all."

"A reasonable precaution," Bleindel said. "Hardesty is not my name, of course."

"That we knew already. Salem el-Fasi seems to be under the impression that you are a Dremish businessman named Bleindel."

"A cover identity. Bey Salem deals with offworld interests, and I needed a plausible reason to come to Gadira, travel more or less freely, and meet lots of people."

"Does el-Fasi know the true nature of your business on Gadira?"

"Not exactly. He does, however, know quite a lot about moving cargo to or from this planet, so he is useful as a conduit." Bleindel sipped at his coffee. This was potentially tricky; he didn't want Khouri and the caids he represented to become too curious about el-Fasi's role in this whole business. "If I were you, I would not assume that Bey Salem's assistance implies any particular zeal for your cause. He's interested in getting paid, and we plan to pay him handsomely to ignore some shipments that will soon be arriving at his port facilities in Meknez."

"Trust a bey to close his eyes and fill his pockets," Khouri said with a sour look. "That is exactly the sort of corruption that must be rooted out."

"In this case, Salem el-Fasi's greed will prove very useful to both of us. There will be plenty of time to convince men like el-Fasi to mend their ways after your revolution succeeds."

Khouri thought for a moment, then nodded. "Perhaps. So why are you interested in helping us, Mr. Hardesty?"

"I'm a mercenary, Mr. Khouri. My employers are devout and wealthy emirs in the Terran Caliphate who look for opportunities to support various Islamic movements throughout Coalition space. Important people in the Caliphate remember that Gadira was settled by the Faithful. They are offended by the influence secular powers such as Montréal hold over this world, and they want to see similarly devout men come to power here." That, of course, was not remotely true, but Bleindel's superiors in the Imperial Security Bureau had carefully arranged the necessary background elements if Gadira's rebels were inclined to investigate more closely.

"Are you a Believer?" Khouri asked him.

"No, I am not. Your cause isn't my cause, Mr. Khouri. But I am a professional, and my services have been retained to provide you with the very best assistance I can render." Bleindel sipped his coffee again, allowing Khouri to digest that for a moment. He had considered the idea of posing as a fellow Quranist—after all, many Muslims throughout Coalition space came from non-Arabic phenotypes and cultures—but ultimately he'd settled on the mercenary approach as the simplest. In the first place, he'd been afraid that even with weeks and weeks of study, he might find himself unable to successfully pass himself off as a devoted follower of the Prophet. More importantly, he hadn't *wanted* to. Quranism struck him as fundamentally irrational, obsolete, even in the rather moderate consensus that had emerged from the Martian schools a few centuries ago. "Is that a problem?"

"I am a revolutionary and a socialist." Khouri smiled without humor. "Yes, I am also a Believer, but we are not interested in imposing some form of medieval law, Mr. Hardesty. We only want to protect our culture, and put an end to the offworld plundering of our economy."

"What about the desert caids? Do they feel the same way?"

"They're more concerned with the cultural questions, and less conscious of their economic interests. The fact that you are a mercenary and an infidel will trouble them."

"The caids are, of course, free to decline my services. But I hope you'll hear me out, and let me prove my reliability. I am being paid *very* well to help you, and I'm anxious to deliver on the contract."

Khouri snorted. "I suppose a man working toward a large paycheck has a certain dedication to the task," he admitted. "Very well, then. What sort of help can you provide us?"

No one nearby seemed to be listening closely, but Bleindel lowered his voice anyway. "I have a shipment of Cygnan mag rifles, antitank weapons, and antiair missiles. I can also offer my own personal expertise in how they should be employed."

"The Kingdom of Cygnus is involved in this, too?" Khouri asked, frowning.

"No, it's not—my apologies for the confusion. It just happens that my contacts can get their hands on Cygnan surplus weaponry, and that's the best match for your needs."

"How big of a shipment are you talking about?"

"Four full standard cargo containers." Bleindel leaned close. "Two thousand rifles, two hundred disposable antitank missiles, and one hundred surface-to-air missile launchers. The arms lag a generation or so behind current leading-edge military tech, but they're as good as anything Montréal shares with the sultanate, and far ahead of anything your people have employed so far. And they're in-system *now*. I need to coordinate with your people to ensure they get into the right hands."

The young revolutionary could not keep the surprise from his face. He simply stared at Bleindel for a long moment. "We can arrange continued support for the foreseeable future," Bleindel added. "Shipments that size every three to six weeks, plus medical supplies, communications gear, some transport assets, maybe even a handful of combat flyers, although those will require special arrangements . . ." Bleindel noticed that Khouri was still staring at him. "Is there a problem, Mr. Khouri?"

It took a moment for Khouri to gather his thoughts. "Our mythology is full of tales of foolish men who accept gifts from *jinn* without asking the price," he finally said. "Mag rifles and antitank weapons would be a great help to us, there is no point in denying it. But I must know who is aiding us, because this seems too good to be true."

"Well, on a personal note, I hope to establish a profitable relationship with the revolutionary government that assumes power after defeating the sultanate and evicting the Montréalais. That is my price." Bleindel leaned back again, and adopted a thoughtful expression. "Regarding the patrons who provide the Cygnan arms, I've been instructed to maintain their confidentiality. But I will be glad to convey to them any message you care to send. If you ask for more information about their identities they may choose to tell you more, but due to travel times, it will be five or six weeks before you get an answer."

"You say that the arms are already in-system?"

"Mr. Khouri, they are currently about ten kilometers from where we are sitting. The sooner we can arrange delivery, the better. You may have a need for the antitank weaponry soon."

Khouri's eyebrows rose. "The containers are in Tanjeer? Very well, Mr. Hardesty. I will consult with my superiors and pass along your offer."

"Excellent." Bleindel handed Khouri a slim card. "This is my private contact information. It's a secure channel. I will await contact from your people to coordinate the delivery."

"I understand."

"Also, tell your people to find a place well away from prying eyes where we can conduct live-fire training. I'll need to instruct some of your fighters in the operation of the weapons."

"Our fighters are quite skilled with rifles, I assure you."

"Then they'll love their new Cygnan mag rifles. And they'll still need instruction on the heavier weaponry."

"I will see to it," Khouri promised.

"I'll speak with you soon." Bleindel drained his coffee, reached into his pocket and pulled out a few credits for the drink before leaving. When he reached the street, he took a ground taxi to a nearby shopping district, circling the stores several times to ensure he was not under observation before he walked over to his hotel. Attention to everyday precautions might someday spell the difference between life and death after all. It always took time to do things right, but Otto Bleindel was nothing if not meticulous about his own survival.

The call came in the morning. Bleindel worked out the arrangements for the meeting, exercising all due care. Naturally, the insurgents had no reason to trust him, but they needed arms badly, and they recognized that they needed to take a chance that his offer might be genuine.

He spent the day making a show of attending to Dielkirk business in the capital, but three hours after sunset, he made his way over to the city's port facility in a battered old ground van and drove up to a darkened warehouse. The huge bulk of a star freighter rested in the water alongside the pier. On more developed worlds, spaceships rarely landed on the surface and did all their cargo handling in orbit. Gadira simply didn't have the orbital infrastructure for that, but as it turned out, basins suitable for large ocean-going transports worked well for spacegoing freighters, too. The existing cargo cranes and maglev rails meant that cargo containers could be quickly distributed through the planet's ground transport systems instead of waiting for lighterage service in low orbit.

Bleindel got out. A modern lock secured the warehouse door. Keying the combination, he let himself in. The cargo containers and a pair of heavy ground transports waited inside the otherwise empty interior; no one normally used the place, which was why he'd appropriated it. Bey Salem's mercantile empire included port facilities, ground- and water-transport lines, rail networks, and warehouses in half the cities on the planet. As it turned out, the best place to hide a container full of contraband arms was in the middle of a facility handling thousands of containers, especially one where the inspectors and police could easily be directed away from sensitive areas by el-Fasi's managers.

A single dim light illuminated the cavernous interior of the building. Ahead of him, five men stood by one of the containers, apparently engaged in a vigorous debate.

Bleindel quickened his pace. He recognized Alonzo Khouri and two men from the coffeehouse, but the others wore the plain uniforms of el-Fasi security guards. Khouri and his men seemed agitated, but the echo of their voices died away as they noted his approach.

"What seems to be the trouble?" Bleindel asked as he walked up to the group.

"Customs inspection," Khouri said, nodding at the two security guards. "They wish to examine the cargo and assess the appropriate duties. I have explained that these arrangements are not needed in our case, but they insist."

"We understand you wish to arrange private inspections instead of making use of the normal clearance procedures," the older of the two security guards said to Bleindel. "We are of course happy to comply, but there is a special customs fee. Your drivers refused to pay the fee, so we're going to have to open the containers and confirm the manifest."

Bleindel studied the scene. The guards stood a short distance from Khouri and his fellows, pistols holstered at their hips in plain sight. Most likely they were simply freelancing, hoping to collect a decent bribe from an offworlder and his local hirelings clearly trying to dodge an inspection. After all, scores of watchmen worked in the cargo facility, and it was unlikely that they were all in on contraband operations. For whatever reason these two had not gotten the word to stay away from this particular warehouse—or they had received that message, and decided to exercise a little initiative and see if they could shake down some smugglers.

"Open the containers for the inspectors," he told Khouri. The tall rebel stared at him in surprise for a moment, but Bleindel gave him a reassuring nod. "Go ahead. I don't mind a reasonable fee."

"As you wish," Khouri replied. He turned and unlocked the heavy door at the end of the cargo unit.

The instant the two guards glanced at the container, Bleindel drew a mag pistol from his coat pocket, aimed deliberately, and fired. The weapon coughed once with a harsh, buzzing chirp as its internal coils hurled the dart out of its barrel. The younger guard's head snapped sideways with a gruesome spray of blood and brain matter; he crumpled to the concrete floor.

The older guard gaped for half a second in astonishment before he went for his own firearm. He never got it out of the holster; Bleindel smoothly swung his weapon over and fired again, taking the second man in the throat. The guard spun half around, reaching for the gaping wound in his neck with clumsy fingers, and then he collapsed to the ground. The echoes of Bleindel's two shots slowly died away.

The three insurgents stared at Bleindel, shocked. In the sudden silence, he calmly walked over to the second guard and made sure of him with one more shot to the head.

"God is merciful," one of the other rebels murmured, his voice shaking. "This is bad, very bad. Those men will be missed, Sidi."

"Not for another hour or two, and by then you'll be well on your way," Bleindel told him. He thought it over carefully for a moment, studying the bodies in their spreading pools of blood. "I think it's very likely that no one knows that they are here. After all, would you tell your supervisor or your colleagues that you're going to collect a bribe from someone?"

"Wouldn't it have been better to simply pay them?" Khouri asked.

"The money is nothing. I do not want *witnesses.*" Bleindel looked around for security cams, and spotted one pointed at the vehicular door at the other end of the building. All the recorders in this warehouse were supposed to be turned off, but it might be for the best to make sure of that before they left. "Go ahead and put the bodies in the container. You can take the bodies with you and find a good spot to dump them outside the city."

Khouri and his friends looked a little sick at the idea.

Strange that they think nothing of taking up arms against their government, but they shrink from handling dead bodies, Bleindel reflected. It must be a cultural predilection. Well, it was a little more work he'd have to do before he left Tanjeer. Salem el-Fasi's people might be helpful in making sure that no one became too curious about the missing guards and collecting any awkward security footage.

He noticed that the three Gadirans were still staring at the bodies on the floor. "Go on," he urged Khouri. "It has to be done."

Khouri nodded at the other two men, who picked up the bodies with distaste. "What next?" the tall rebel asked.

"I'd like to take a few minutes to talk about how you're going to use these weapons to make this revolution of yours successful. I have some specific operations I think you should consider, now that you've got the firepower to execute them." Bleindel glanced down on the floor, and frowned at the amount of blood pooled on the concrete. "But first, let's see if we can find a mop."

7

When Sikander got up the next day, he felt every one of the kicks Randall had landed on his legs and ribs, and he discovered that he had a very noticeable black eye. He had Darvesh dress it up as best he could with a medical spray. However, he noted with great satisfaction that Randall failed to appear for the morning officer's call. In fact, it was all he could do to stop himself from grinning like an idiot when Commander Chatburn gave him a long and thoughtful look after Dr. Simms, the ship's medical officer, announced that Mr. Randall was in the sick bay and unable to muster this morning.

After the muster, he went up to the bridge to assume his watch and found Sublieutenant Karsen Reno occupying the command station. As one of the older junior officers on board *Hector*, Reno took a turn in the officer-of-the-deck watch rotation. "Good morning, Mr. Reno," Sikander said. "Anything I should know?"

"Good morning, sir," Reno replied. He stood and stretched for a moment. "No significant dust out here. The bow shield hasn't sparked once, engineering reports all equipment on-line, and we're still eleven days from arrival. Should be a quiet watch."

Sikander nodded. There usually wasn't much to do during a warp transit; ships in warp did not maneuver, they coasted. All the velocity ships achieved for faster-than-light travel had to come from acceleration in normal space before they activated their warp rings, since physical thrust from inside a warp bubble had no measurable effect on the ship's course or speed. The only decision to be made was when to deactivate the warp rings and return to normal space—a simple matter of very precise timing based on the ship's course and velocity at the moment the ship entered warp. Sikander certainly wouldn't cut the warp generator early during his watch. Recharging warp rings with exotic matter—in the case of an Aquilan warship, a molten lithium alloy made from pentaquark matter—was terribly expensive, so a ship stayed bubbled unless something disastrous occurred. Every now and then a ship in warp transit struck a speck of interstellar dust large and dense enough to generate a nasty burst of radiation as the leading edge of the warp bubble ripped it apart, but the heavy armor shielding the cruiser's bow could handle a routine impact—or "spark," as Aquilan watchstanders described it.

He checked the display screens for status reports on the ship's systems; everything was well within normal parameters. "I am ready to relieve you, Mr. Reno."

"I stand relieved," Reno replied. "Thank you, Mr. North. Have a good watch."

"Thank you," Sikander replied. He took the command couch as Reno headed down for a late breakfast, and studied the ship's estimated position for a moment. The bridge viewscreens showed nearby stars drifting slowly sternward against the luminous glory of bright nebulas and dazzling globular clusters in the distance. The navigation system generated the image, of course. A ship encased in a warp bubble could perceive nothing of the universe outside, and even if it could, the apparent velocity of the ship would have stretched the stars into tiny streaks ahead or behind. The viewscreens simply showed what the galaxy would have looked like to a ship moving past the stars, ignoring the distortions of faster-than-light travel. While wildly inaccurate as to the real conditions of warp transit, it did do a good job of showing where the ship was in relation to the rest of human space. More to the point, it never failed to mesmerize Sikander.

The bridge watch passed quietly, with only one spark to speak of. To distract himself from his general stiffness and soreness, Sikander drilled the bridge crew on basic battle maneuvering problems for most of the watch, using the ship's tactical computer to conjure up squadrons of phantom allies and adversaries. Only a handful of the crew members currently standing watch were actually assigned to the bridge for battle stations, but one never knew when someone might have to stand in at an important station. Additional aches and pains announced themselves as the day wore on; Sikander was forced to admit that he hadn't gotten away completely unscathed from his encounter with Hiram Randall.

When Sublieutenant Keane relieved him at the end of his watch, Sikander headed for his quarters, hoping that a hot shower might help to soothe his sore body. Instead, the ship's info assistant pinged him as soon as he left the bridge. "Lieutenant North, your presence is requested in the captain's quarters," the computer announced.

"I will be there in a moment," he replied. The hot shower would have to wait a little longer, it seemed. He took the passage leading toward Captain Markham's cabin instead of his own; it was quite close to the bridge, the customary arrangement on any warship Sikander had served on. He paused at the door, collecting himself; then he knocked and went in. "You wished to see me, ma'am?" he said.

Captain Markham looked up from her work. "Mr. North. Please, have a seat." She nodded at the chair in front of her desk, and regarded him in silence. She had a stern set to her mouth, and a line creased her brow; Sikander realized that he was about to be called on the carpet, and braced himself for it. The captain studied him for a long moment, and then asked, "Can you explain to me why my ops officer is on the limited-duty list today?"

I should have guessed this would come up. Whether or not Hiram Randall had said anything, a mysteriously injured officer would naturally attract the captain's curiosity within a matter of hours. "Mr. Randall and I engaged in some full-contact sparring last night in the gym, ma'am," he said. "I am afraid we got a little carried away. I dislocated his shoulder."

"Dislocated his shoulder," she repeated. "Why in the world did you do that?"

"I caught him in a hold he didn't know how to get out of, ma'am. Mr. Randall tried an escape he wasn't in position to pull off, and I reacted without thinking." Sikander squirmed—he did not like being dishonest with his commanding officer, and that skated close to the line.

"Is unarmed combat one of your duties aboard *Hector*?" Markham asked. "Or Mr. Randall's?"

"No, ma'am. It was sport—exercise."

"So, your *hobby* leaves me with a key officer unable to perform his duties for several days. Did you think about that before you and Mr. Randall decided to work out your differences by brawling after hours in the gymnasium?"

"We agreed to a freestyle sparring match, ma'am, not a brawl. And Chief Trent was present to make sure the rules were enforced."

"Don't insult my intelligence, Mr. North. I had Chief Trent retrieve the gym's security vid; Mr. Chatburn and I have already watched it." Captain Markham kept her eyes fixed on Sikander. "The XO thinks I should bring you up on malicious assault charges and have you arraigned for court-martial. The only reason I'm not doing so is that Hiram Randall refuses to press charges for the shoulder injury, and if I charge you on any lesser assault, I'd have to charge him, too."

"I see." It seemed like the safest thing Sikander could say. He was surprised that Randall would pass up the opportunity to press a charge against him. The operations officer certainly hadn't been shy about his opinion of Sikander before their bout in the gym. Either Randall had a better-developed personal character than Sikander had realized, or he'd decided that neither of them would look good if the whole business came out in a formal inquiry.

"While there won't be any charges filed, Mr. North, you may rest assured that I will make a note of the incident in your service jacket. And I'll tell you this, too: Whatever ill feeling exists between you and Mr. Randall, you will put an end to it *now*. I don't care if you like the other officers on *Hector* or they like you, but I expect you to work together as professionals. When you put another officer in sick bay, you're making your personal disagreements *my* problem, and I won't stand for it. Do I make myself clear?"

"I didn't pick the quarrel with Randall, ma'am," Sikander replied, unable to keep the anger from his voice. "He has goaded me since the moment I set foot on board. And any officer would have been justified in seeking satisfaction for the way he treated my date at the Governor's Ball."

"I don't care, Mr. North. Am I *clear*?"

Sikander scowled, but nodded. "Yes, ma'am."

"Good," Captain Markham said. "The next time you feel the need to make a fellow officer eat their words, remember that it's your good fortune that Hiram Randall doesn't feel like pressing charges against you. Perhaps you don't understand him as well as you think. And if you ever injure one of my officers again—'accident' or not—you will be off this ship so quickly your head will spin. Dismissed."

"Thank you, ma'am." Sikander stood and saluted, then marched out of the room.

As far as reprimands went, it was not as bad as it could

have been. He probably deserved worse. But even so, it left him fuming. He couldn't afford to draw the captain's ire, and if Lieutenant Commander Chatburn had it in for him, too, then Sikander's life could become complicated and unpleasant. A hostile executive officer could make any junior officer's life a living hell even without looking for a reason to bring him up on charges. *The XO has one friend on this ship, and that's Hiram Randall,* Sikander told himself. *Nice going, Sikay.*

It didn't take long for Peter Chatburn to make his displeasure known. The next morning, after the officers' muster, Sikander detoured through the wardroom to brace himself for the day with some strong coffee. He had just poured himself a mug when Chatburn stepped through the hatch, and joined him by the wardroom's coffee service.

"Mr. Chatburn," Sikander said. "Good morning."

"Mr. North," the XO replied with a nod. He loomed over Sikander without even meaning to as he poured his coffee. Chatburn stood a good twenty centimeters over Sikander's own 175, and unlike many Aquilans he was broad-shouldered and strongly built. Sikander remembered hearing that he'd been a standout rugby player during his Academy days. Chatburn was also *Hector*'s only other title-bearing officer, heir to a large estate on High Albion, the capital world of the Commonwealth. Not all Commonwealth worlds possessed a peerage system, but enough did that family connections often mattered a great deal in the Navy's higher ranks; *Hector*'s executive officer would likely go far in the service.

Sikander waited for Chatburn to bring up the fight, but the XO surprised him. "Any new insight about our missing torpedo yet?" he asked as he stirred his coffee.

Sikander quickly changed gear, bringing the details of the investigation to mind. He'd had the Torpedo Division working on little else for weeks now. "Nothing much, sir. I watched the torpedo mates take Tube Two apart and put it back together again for hours last week. We are confident it is not the launcher, but other than that . . ."

"A problem with the tube was a long shot at best. Those things have been in service for twenty years—there's nothing the torpedo mates don't know about them." Chatburn took a long sip from his mug. "Did you confirm the maintenance records and update installations?"

"Yes, sir. As far as we can tell, the scheduled maintenance and software updates were all performed. If the fault wasn't in the launcher and the torpedo was properly maintained, the only other possibility I can see is that Ms. Larkin's customization of the torpedo console settings caused some sort of software fault. Maybe she used a bad macro without knowing it."

"I doubt Larkin's user preferences would have caused a major fault. She's too sharp for that."

"So I hear, but we might as well eliminate what possibilities we can, sir." Sikander shook his head. "Unfortunately, without the torpedo we may never know what exactly failed."

"That's not going to be good enough," Chatburn said. "Captain Markham expects something better than 'We don't know.' For that matter, so do I. It's not the way we do things on *Hector,* Mr. North."

"Yes, sir," Sikander replied with a grimace. He didn't appreciate being talked to as if he were a brand-new ensign, but he couldn't really say anything else.

"If I was missing a torpedo, I'm not sure I would spend my evenings socializing ashore. Perhaps a few hours reviewing Ms. Larkin's code would have been a better use of your leisure time than picking fights with other officers. Especially if you think that might be the reason we lost a multimillion-credit torpedo on the range."

"Yes, sir." Sikander just barely managed to answer without snarling, and swallowed the next few words that came to his lips. By tradition, a ship's executive officer served as the whip cracker and disciplinarian in the command structure. It was Chatburn's job to get results, not to win friends. Still, he couldn't help but wonder whether Chatburn would have criticized an Aquilan about the level of effort devoted to the problem. He set down his mug, and nodded to the XO. "With your permission, I will return to my investigations. There is one more thing I can try."

"Carry on, Mr. North," Chatburn replied. He returned his attention to his own coffee.

Sikander left the wardroom, careful not to slam the door behind him. If the problem really did turn out to be an error in routine maintenance or a failed installation of new software, it almost certainly had occurred before he had even reported to *Hector*. It was hardly fair to hold it against him, but sometimes things weren't fair. He didn't know what more he could do about the damned torpedo than was already being done . . . but as he stormed toward the Gunnery Department's compartments, several decks below the wardroom, an idea began to take shape.

In the department office he found Sublieutenant Larkin studying a screen full of code—one of the recent software updates, or so he guessed. A junior deckhand named O'Neal, who served as the Gunnery Department yeoman, worked alongside her, pulling maintenance records from the ship's info assistant. O'Neal started to rise, but Sikander waved a hand. "As you were," he told the enlisted man.

Larkin was fixed on the information in front of her. "Software update?" he asked her.

She nodded without looking up. "From three months back. The control code for the torpedo's drive received a minor upgrade. I'm looking to see what changed."

"Have you found any significant differences?"

"Not really, and I suspect this is a dead end anyway. Both our practice torpedoes received the same update. If the code was bad enough to make one fail, they both should've failed."

Sikander nodded; that was probably true enough. In fact, it suggested that perhaps they should focus their efforts on things that had happened to one torpedo but not the other. "I think we need to look at the technicians who performed the regular maintenance on the torpedoes," he told her. "The records show that the torpedoes received the same maintenance on the same dates, but we don't know that the torpedo mate actually performed each procedure exactly the same way."

Larkin gave him a sharp look. "You think the torpedo maintenance was gundecked?"

That was precisely what Sikander suspected, but he didn't want to throw around a serious accusation lightly. As long as sailors had served in ships, they'd been tempted to skip out on jobs no one was likely to check, and fill out the paperwork saying the work had been done. Why they called it gundecking, Sikander had no idea, but it was a very serious matter and could get a torpedo mate in a great deal of trouble.

He chose to downplay his suspicion for the moment. "I suppose that is a possibility, but I think it's more likely a simple oversight or seemingly minor accident—a dropped screwdriver that damaged a relay, absentmindedly reinstalling an old part instead of the new one, or overlooking a step that seemed unimportant. O'Neal, you have the records there. Which of the torpedo mates signed off on the regular maintenance?"

The young crewman checked his dataslate. "Torpedo Mate Second Class Harris, sir."

Sikander looked back to Larkin. "Let's have Petty Officer Harris crack open the practice torpedo we did recover, and demonstrate the maintenance procedures for everything he's done in the last few months. Chief Maroth should watch, too. We can make sure the maintenance was done properly."

"That would be a waste of time," Larkin said. Sikander

shot her a stern look—after the unpleasant conversation he'd just had with the XO, he was in no mood to have one of his own subordinates speak sharply to him—but Larkin did not notice. She continued. "The maintenance procedures haven't changed in two years, and no one in the fleet has had a problem like this. It's got to be a hardware defect in the missing weapon. They sent us a bad torpedo."

"Humor me, Ms. Larkin. Harris may have made a mistake, or perhaps he'll be reminded of something that did not go right. I want to verify the maintenance procedures."

Larkin looked dubious. "All right. I'll have Harris and Chief Maroth go over the procedures as soon as they can find the time."

"Immediately," Sikander told her. "I will be in the torpedo room in half an hour, and I expect them both there. In fact, I would like you to join us. If someone is on watch, pull them off and send a substitute. It's time to solve this riddle if we can."

The torpedo officer stared at Sikander for a moment before remembering her basic military courtesy. "Yes, sir," she said. "Immediately."

Sikander spent most of the next two days in the torpedo room at *Hector*'s bow. As it turned out, Petty Officer Harris knew his duties well. The two officers and Chief Torpedo Mate Maroth had Harris walk them through the normal maintenance procedures on the Phantom Type 12-P torpedo, and nothing struck them as particularly out of place. Harris had a couple of shortcuts that weren't strictly by the book, but Chief Maroth pointed out that every torpedo mate in the fleet had been using those same shortcuts for years, and they had nothing to do with the drive anyway. Larkin had the good sense not to tell Sikander "I told you so" to his face, but after two long days in the confines of the torpedo room, she didn't have to say it to let him know what she was thinking. Sikander grudgingly admitted defeat, and withdrew to wrestle with the problem privately.

For a few miserable days, no new possibilities came to him. But during casualty simulations on a bridge watch an idea occurred to him, and after the watch section finished up their drills, he gave it quite a bit of thought. By the time he was relieved, Sikander determined to put it into action. After a quick review of the personnel files, he summoned Ensign Girard and Sublieutenant Larkin to the Gunnery Department office. When both officers arrived, Sikander invited them to sit at the small conference table.

"What's up, sir?" Girard asked as he sat down.

"I took a look at your service jacket, Mr. Girard," Sikander said. "You graduated from the Academy with degrees in data architecture and information science?"

"Yes, sir," Girard replied. "I haven't used them much on board *Hector,* but I have a few pet projects I like to tinker with to keep my hand in things."

"Such as?"

"Well—games, sir." Girard offered an embarrassed shrug. "I like taking apart entertainment software and fixing the parts that annoy me."

"Excellent," Sikander said. "In that case, I have a special assignment for you. As you know, Ms. Larkin and her torpedo mates have been tearing down every line of code and reviewing every step of maintenance procedures for our missing torpedo. I think we need some fresh eyes on the problem."

"Sir, I don't know anything about torpedoes, really."

"In this case, I don't think that will be a hindrance," Sikander told him. "I have a new line of inquiry I want to try out, and I need a topflight software tech for the job. I think that might be you."

Larkin frowned. "Sir, we've done everything we can without the actual torpedo to examine. You saw us take the other torpedo apart and put it back together again a dozen times, and you watched us crawl through the code. There is nothing more we can do."

"I want to try something new," Sikander told her. He looked back to Girard. "Mr. Girard, I want you to make a copy of the torpedo-control software and set up an emulation program that verifies each command input or output during weapon flight. Then I want you to run combinations of events that cause the torpedo to launch normally but fail to return to normal space. Since we're getting nowhere by retracing the steps we thought we took, let's figure out what would have to happen to make the torpedo fail in exactly the right way. Find ways to break torpedoes, Mr. Girard. Can you do that?"

Girard nodded slowly, his eyes distant as he thought it over. "I think so, sir. Cloning the software and setting up an emulation system shouldn't be too hard."

"What's the point?" Larkin said. "The software was identical for both torpedoes. The only cause that makes sense is a hardware failure on the missing torpedo, and we'll never know what that might be, because it's missing!"

Sikander bit back his own response, and studied the angry young woman for a long moment before he trusted himself enough to speak. "Ms. Larkin, tell me this: If, God forbid, we have to launch a torpedo in anger when we get to Gadira, will it hit or will it disappear?"

"We've had no problems with the war shots," Larkin countered.

"We've never *launched* one of the war shots. I checked the ship's records. It's been three years since *any* ship in the entire fleet fired off a Phantom Type 12 that wasn't a practice torp. So at this moment, I have no confidence that the problem we encountered is limited to our inventory of 12-Ps, and I can't honestly tell Captain Markham that if she orders me to fire a torpedo, I know beyond the shadow of a doubt that it will actually reach the target. Or am I missing something about the significance of this problem?"

Larkin stared at him. "That's insane. Our battle sims

haven't shown any hint of a problem like that with the 12-Js on board." Those torpedoes carried real warheads.

Sikander counted silently to ten, then looked at Girard. "Mr. Girard, would you excuse us? I think you have enough to get started on."

"Uh, yes, sir," the young officer said. He stood up, gathered up his dataslate and notes, and hurried out of the department office.

Sikander stood up as well and saw him to the hatch. He waited for the hatch to seal shut behind Girard before rounding on Larkin. "On your feet, Sublieutenant!" he barked.

Larkin stared at him for a moment, and slowly got to her feet. "What are you—" she began to say, but he cut her off immediately.

"Enough is enough, Sublieutenant Larkin. I have been on this ship for six weeks now, and it has not escaped my notice that you have yet to show me the respect expected from a subordinate officer. You are free to think of me whatever you like, but in front of others you will maintain a professional bearing. Do I make myself clear?"

Larkin's eyes blazed. "Yes, *sir*."

"Do you know why I dismissed Girard? It wasn't to spare your feelings. I sent him off because junior officers don't need to see higher-ranking superiors arguing. This discussion is between you and me, and no one else needs to hear what I have to say to you, or you have to say to me. I don't reprimand you in public, so you refrain from showing me disrespect in front of others. Is that understood?"

Larkin looked straight ahead at the bulkhead, but she nodded. "I understand."

Sikander folded his arms deliberately and leaned against the corner of the desk. "I do not want to have this conversation again, and I suspect you do not either," he said. "So, Ms. Larkin, let's go ahead and get to the bottom of this: What exactly is the nature of your problem with me?"

He waited for a response. Finally, Larkin steeled herself

and spoke. "I doubt that you are qualified for the rank and position you hold, sir," she said.

Sikander stopped himself before he said something he would regret, and forced himself to answer evenly. "Well, that's straightforward enough," he said. He'd encountered that sort of distrust before, although few people had the nerve to express it in so many words to a superior officer. Then again, Angela Larkin had made it plain that if she had something on her mind, she wasn't inclined to hide what she thought. "Ms. Larkin, have I given you reason to form that opinion in the time that I have been on *Hector*? Other than the torpedo business, on which we obviously disagree?" he asked.

She hesitated before answering. "No, sir."

"Then reconsider your position, or request a transfer. Or, if I prove as unqualified as you fear, simply wait me out. You'll soon have the opportunity to see if my replacement is any better. But whichever option you choose, do not dismiss my concerns or challenge my orders in front of other officers or crewmen again."

Larkin gave a grudging nod. "Yes, sir."

"Very well. I consider the matter closed. Provide Mr. Girard with whatever assistance he requires, and continue with your duties. Dismissed."

"Yes, sir." Larkin saluted, performed a crisp about-face, and marched out of the office.

Sikander watched her leave, wondering if he had handled the matter properly. Perhaps Larkin would give him a chance and perhaps she wouldn't, but at the very least he thought that she would be more careful about maintaining a semblance of professional courtesy in front of others. He sighed and ran a hand through his hair. For now, that was all the victory he needed.

On the last day of the warp transit, Sikander took his station on the bridge an hour before *Hector*'s scheduled arrival in Gadira. The main bridge display featured a prominent countdown to warp termination. During the last few minutes of a warp transit, ships traditionally adopted a posture of maximum damage readiness. The odds that a vessel might end its warp and find itself in danger of collision were literally astronomical, but ships returned to normal space with the same velocity they had when they initiated their warp transit. CSS *Hector* had accelerated up to ten percent of light speed in the outskirts of the Caledonia system, so that would be her speed when she arrived. A ship that made even a tiny navigational error could return to normal space and discover that it was headed into a dangerous situation at thirty thousand kilometers per second; simple prudence dictated that the ship should be ready for trouble.

As the counter approached 0:00:00, Captain Markham keyed the ship's announcing system. "All hands, this is the captain. Arrival imminent; take your stations."

Sikander watched the last few seconds tick down—and then *Hector* dropped her warp bubble, right on time. If his eyes had been closed, he never would have noticed. Bubbling and unbubbling offered no physiological cues to humans on board, since after all a vessel remained in perfectly normal space within the confines of its warp field, and warp generators in operation were not any louder than the ship's normal machinery noises. All that happened was that the displays on the bridge gave a sudden lurch and recalibrated as the computers switched from providing estimated positions to accepting actual sensor input. The main vid display that curved around the front of the bridge compartment switched to an enhanced local view, marking the location and distance to the central star and each of the system's planets, and quickly populating the screen with the tracks and identifications of dozens of commercial and industrial vessels under way in the area.

"Clear arrival," Sublieutenant Keane reported from the sensor console. "Nothing within ten million kilometers, ma'am." Given the potential dangers of arrival in the relatively cluttered inner reaches of a planetary system, captains preferred to cut their warp generators in the outlying regions of a system, even if that meant a long trudge in normal space to finish their journey.

"Very well," Captain Markham answered. "Depower and retract the ring. Navigation, what's our position?" Back around the cruiser's slim waist, the large motors controlling the fairings that deployed the warp ring hummed, producing a slight tremor in the deck under Sikander's feet. A moment later, the ring sections retracted into their sockets with a series of audible thumps.

"Gadira II is eleven light-minutes distant, bearing three-one-zero down thirty, ma'am," Commander Chatburn said. "We're about ten million kilometers off our estimated position; looks like a minor deviation in our transit alignment."

Captain Markham nodded. "Not bad for a long transit. Helm, set course for the planet, standard acceleration. Communications, please transmit our arrival notification to the local traffic-control authority."

Sikander tapped at his console. That meant . . . a six-hour passage from their emergence point to the system's inhabited planet. It was in fact quite good navigation; once during his tour on *Adept,* they'd arrived almost fifty light-minutes from their destination after a particularly long transit.

The bridge display slowly swung to the left and down as Chief Quartermaster Holtz at the helm adjusted the ship's attitude to bring her nose to the proper intercept course. Then he activated the main drive plates; a soft shudder shook the hull. *Hector* now traveled almost backward at thirty thousand kilometers per second, her bow pointed about three-quarters of the way around from her actual course, but it would take hours of steady thrust to kill off the speed they'd built up back in Caledonia.

Captain Markham studied the ship's course for a moment, and nodded in satisfaction. "Very good. Secure from transit-arrival stations; Mr. Randall, I believe you have the watch."

"I have the watch, Captain," Randall confirmed. His left arm was still in a light sling, but he'd made a point of reporting to his station for the ship's arrival in Gadira.

Sikander powered down his weapons console, getting ready to leave the bridge. But before he finished, Sublieutenant Keane spoke up from his post. "Sir, there's an unidentified warship in high orbit around Gadira II," he reported. "Mass fifty-five thousand tons . . . looks like a cruiser."

"Montréalais?" Randall guessed.

"No, sir. One moment, we've got its transponder. It's Dremish, sir, hull number seventy-three, SMS *Panther*."

"What in the world is a Dremish warship doing here?" Markham said aloud. She had paused by the hatch when the sensor officer announced the contact. She glanced at Randall. "I saw nothing about a Dremish deployment in the threat assessments."

"Nor did I, ma'am," Randall answered. "This is a new development. They must have shown up while we were in transit."

"So are they just passing through, or are they here to lean on the locals?" Chatburn asked.

"I have no idea, XO," Markham replied. "Communications, send this on over to our Dremish friends: To commanding officer SMS *Panther*, my compliments. This is Captain Elise Markham, commanding officer of the Commonwealth starship *Hector*. We are approaching Gadira II and intend to assume an orbit at three thousand kilometers, over."

"Transmitted, ma'am," the comm tech reported. "It's an eleven-minute delay one-way."

"Very well." Markham returned to her seat to wait as the

bridge crew rotated from the fully manned transit-arrival stations to the ordinary watchstanding team. Sikander was not on duty, but out of curiosity he decided to wait and see what the Dremish ship had to say. While he waited, he activated his console again and called up the ship-recognition function to study the few details available on the Dremish warship. *Panther* seemed quite comparable to *Hector*—a little bigger, but the two ships possessed similar armament and they were closely matched in speed and maneuverability. The info assistant had little else to offer, since it was a new class and the database had to rely on public-domain sources from Dremark. At least sharing an orbit would give *Hector* plenty of opportunities to record close-up vid of *Panther* and add to the Commonwealth Navy's database on the Dremish cruiser.

Twenty-two minutes after *Hector*'s arrival in the system, the communications tech announced, "Incoming message from SMS *Panther,* ma'am."

"That was pretty quick," Captain Markham observed. *Panther* could not have observed *Hector*'s arrival until eleven minutes after the Old Worthy actually terminated its warp, and any message she sent would of course have the same delay to reach *Hector*. "Put it on-screen, please."

A window opened on the main vid display, showing the face of a middle-aged man in the uniform of a Dremish naval officer. Lean and dark, he had a hatchet-like nose and a close-cropped beard, but his smile was surprisingly warm. "Welcome to Gadira, *Hector*," he began. "I am Fregattenkapitan Georg Harper of His Imperial Majesty's warship *Panther*. My compliments to the commanding officer; we are maintaining a high orbit above Gadira II and do not expect to maneuver for some time. SMS *Panther,* out."

"They must have transmitted as soon as they saw us arrive," Sikander observed.

"The Dremish are nothing if not punctual." The captain shrugged and stood up. "Well, we've observed the formalities. I suppose we'll be sharing orbits for a while. Call me if anything interesting happens, Mr. Randall."

8

Tanjeer, Gadira II

Three days after *Hector*'s arrival in Gadira, Sikander jolted and bounced his way down to the planet's surface in one of the ship's shuttles as the dazzling waters of the Silver Sea raced by underneath its stubby wings. The inertial compensators could not quite mask out all the sharp maneuvers; Sikander, seated in the passenger cabin, felt his seat restraints tightening automatically in response. He glanced around. Dr. Isaako Simms, the cruiser's medical officer, looked faintly green, but Magdalena Juarez only raised an eyebrow in response, and Captain Markham seemed perfectly at ease, reading her dataslate without even looking up. She'd chosen three officers to accompany her down to the planet's capital, leaving Peter Chatburn in command of *Hector,* which now circled Gadira II a few thousand kilometers overhead.

The shuttle leaned into a steep, banking curve. The captain didn't seem to take notice, but she finally spoke. "Petty Officer Long, are you in some special hurry to land the shuttle?"

"Sorry, Captain!" Long called down from the cockpit. "Tanjeer Traffic Control sent us a minimum-time approach vector and included some steep evasive maneuvers. Apparently they have some concerns about potential ground fire."

"The controllers think someone might *shoot* at us?" Dr. Simms asked. He was a short, dark-haired young man with a wide face and very dark eyes. Other than a certain professional coolness toward Sikander over Hiram Randall's dislocated shoulder, he struck Sikander as a decent fellow. Like many medical officers, Simms was a doctor first and a naval officer second.

"I'm afraid so, sir," Long answered him. "Don't worry too much. We'll be on the deck in just a minute." Sikander could see the pilot through the small companionway between the cockpit and the cabin; Long's tone revealed no concern, but his head swiveled left and right as he brought the shuttle down, and his copilot kept busy with a constant stream of tower instructions.

"Just a precaution, or have they had some trouble with shuttles making descent?" Magda wondered aloud.

"They would have routed us to another landing zone if they were really worried," Sikander pointed out. He tried to shrug in his seat restraints. "Good practice for our pilots, at any rate."

He glanced out his viewport, and saw the glittering waters of the coast give way to dun-colored tarmac. The shuttle streaked past a row of old hangars, then suddenly slewed into one velocity-killing turn and deployed its landing struts with a mechanical whine. Long expertly cut the power, bringing the shuttle to a sharp landing in front of a concrete revetment. "You can unbuckle, ma'am," the pilot called. "But let me crack the hatch for you. The skin'll be blistering hot after that descent, so make sure you keep your hands off the doorframe."

"Very good," Captain Markham replied. She, Sikander, and the other two busied themselves with removing their restraints and gathering their things as the pilot came back to the shuttle's passenger hatch and cycled it. Bright sunlight flooded into the cabin, along with a wall of humid heat that instantly reminded Sikander of home. There were plenty of warm Aquilan worlds—even New Perth had its tropics, of course—but most big cities and naval installations were located in middle latitudes. It was refreshing to feel air that was as warm as it was supposed to be.

One by one, they filed carefully down the shuttle's steps and moved away from the sizzling hull to stand blinking in the sun. In deference to the Gadiran climate, *Hector*'s officers wore their summer dress whites, almost painfully bright in the brilliant daylight. A small group of people stood in the shade of the revetment, alongside a long, sleek ground transport. In addition to a pair of fit-looking Aquilans who wore light jackets despite the heat—security specialists, or so Sikander guessed—a short, balding, middle-aged civilian waited for *Hector*'s officers to debark.

The older man strode briskly out to greet them. "Captain Markham?" he asked. "I'm Franklin Garcia, Commonwealth system consul. Welcome to Gadira."

Markham shook his hand. "A pleasure to meet you, Mr. Garcia." She motioned to the others in turn. "Lieutenant Commander Magdalena Juarez, our chief engineer; gunnery officer Lieutenant Sikander North; and Lieutenant Isaako Simms, *Hector*'s medical officer."

"It's good to see some faces from home," Garcia remarked. A quick round of handshakes followed; Sikander noted that the security agents deliberately averted their attention from the introductions, keeping an eye on the surroundings. "I took the liberty of arranging ground transportation for the ride over to the palace. The Royal Guard is very touchy about anything flying near the sultan's location, which is why they had you land out here in the commercial spaceport."

Garcia motioned to the ground limo, and they climbed inside one by one; the security agents took their places in a chase car. The car hummed into motion, and accelerated away from the revetment. Sikander gazed out the window at the striking palmlike trees and brass-colored sky. The Aquilan consul must have had some sort of special clearance for his vehicle; as they left the spaceport and ventured into the city's boulevards, traffic halted to let them pass. He had an impression of streets crowded with old ground cars and pedestrians, and cluttered storefronts marked with foreign lettering.

"Given the political instability of the system, I would imagine that the sultan's personal security must be extremely sensitive," Magda said to Garcia. "After all, he inherited the throne after his brother was killed, didn't he?"

"It's worsened in the last few weeks," Garcia said. "The local insurgents have gotten their hands on modern offworld arms. It has significantly upped the ante, so to speak."

Sikander glanced from the window to the consul. "Modern arms? The reports we saw didn't mention that."

"The Royal Guard is keeping those details out of the press for now. They don't want it publicly known that the Caidists are well-funded enough to bring in offworld arms."

"Who would want to support the extremists?" Magda asked. "Islamic hardliners from the Caliphate? Foreign operatives inclined to make a little trouble for Montréal?"

"There's a Dremish cruiser just over our heads," Sikander observed.

Garcia shook his head. "The *Panther* showed up a few days after the weapons were first employed. Wherever the new arms came from, they weren't on board the warship," he said. Then he leaned forward a bit and pointed out the window behind Sikander's seat. "Not to change the subject, but if you'll look to your right, you can get a good view of El-Badi Palace. It's really quite impressive."

Sikander turned in his seat and peered out the window as the others looked past him. The palace compound sprawled over a low, flat-topped hill between Tanjeer's downtown quarter and the Silver Sea. Domes sheathed in gold leaf glittered with blinding brightness in the sunlight; elegant marble colonnades and arcades ringed the main structure, decorated with patterns of blue tile. The ground car sped along a tree-lined boulevard at the foot of the hill, heading toward the palace gate.

"Are there any special considerations of etiquette we should be aware of?" Markham asked the consul.

"Address the sultan as 'Your Highness.' Under no circumstances should you initiate contact, so don't offer your hand. If he offers you his, it's acceptable to shake." Garcia thought for a moment. "The sultan's niece Ranya may be in attendance. Her title is amira. The same rules apply for her. Oh, and one last thing—are any of you title holders? I should include that in any introductions."

"My executive officer is the senator Malgray, but he remained on the ship today," said Captain Markham. Senatorial families were well represented in the Commonwealth Navy, making up a good ten or fifteen percent of the officer corps. Naturally, the percentage only increased once one reached the flag ranks. "And Mr. North here is Nawabzada of Ishar."

"Ah, a Kashmiri title." Garcia looked back to Sikander. "May I ask where that falls in precedence?"

"It's equivalent to senator-viceroy," said Sikander.

The consul raised an eyebrow. That was about as close to royalty as one could get in Aquila's patrician ranks. "That may be helpful," he observed. "Sultan Rashid understands that our senatorial families are title holders, but the lack of letters-patent colors his perception of Aquilans just a bit. You are certainly the highest-ranking individual in Commonwealth service to visit in quite a while, Mr. North. I wouldn't be surprised if he warms up to you because of that."

"Captain Markham is my commanding officer, Mr. Garcia. The sultan shouldn't overlook her because I happen to have a title," said Sikander. The ground limo turned in to the palace gate, and climbed slowly up a winding road under the shade of stately rows of palms that led to the top of El-Badi's hill.

Captain Markham gave Sikander a wry smile. "Don't be concerned on my account, Mr. North. I asked you to join the landing party specifically because I guessed that the local aristocrats might be impressed by your pedigree. From what I understand, the sultan leaves most important matters to the officials in his court. Mr. Garcia will be introducing me to the decision makers while you keep the royals occupied."

Sikander inclined his head. "My duty becomes clear, ma'am. I will strive to be as interesting as possible."

The ground limo turned in to a circular driveway by the palace's grand main entrance. Delicate fountains and pools stood on either side of the drive. Servants in traditional Gadiran garb hurried up to open the doors and offer the Aquilans assistance in climbing out of the car. For a moment, Sikander wondered if they would be escorted through the gilded front doors with blasts of trumpets, but Franklin Garcia motioned for them to follow him to a winding path that led around the building. From somewhere ahead of the Aquilans came the soft sound of music playing and the buzz of voices in conversation. Then they rounded a wing of the palace, and found an elegant party in progress among the gardens and pavilions behind the palace. Colorful canopies draped between marble columns provided shade; at a glance, it seemed that about half the attendees were offworlders, and half were well-off Gadirans.

Garcia spoke briefly with a palace attendant, who announced their arrival. Sikander thought that a few heads turned at his own rather colorful title, but most of the attendees took little notice; if one moved in these circles, the formalities quickly ceased to draw one's attention. Then the consul ushered them toward a buffet. "Refresh yourselves if you like, but stay close by," he told them. "An attendant will come find us when the sultan is ready to meet you. It shouldn't be long."

Sikander hadn't thought he was very hungry, but the lavish spread in front of him changed his mind. He helped himself to a small selection of fruits and cheeses, and discovered that no alcohol was being served. Instead, he found a wide selection of teas and fruit juices, so he settled for some lemonade, taking great care not to spill anything on his spotless uniform. The other officers followed suit and stood together taking in the crowd as they ate and drank. Most of the men wore military uniforms or modern Montréalais-style suits, although the native Gadirans added a fez or close-fitting caps not unlike the pakuls many Kashmiri men wore. The women dressed in colorful, flowing dresses with delicate embroidery; most were bareheaded.

"I rather expected burkas and veiled faces," Magda Juarez observed, echoing Sikander's own thoughts. "This seems a good deal more open than some of the Caliphate worlds."

"The guests may not be very representative of Gadira as a whole," said Markham. "We are standing in the sultan's garden, after all."

They had just finished their first small plates when a stoop-shouldered, silver-haired man with a broad face and flat features approached. He wore a light summer suit of modern cut, and smiled warmly. "Good afternoon, Franklin," he said to Garcia. "Unless I am badly mistaken, these must be some of the officers from the Commonwealth cruiser that arrived recently."

"Nothing gets past you, Paul." Garcia shook the other man's hand, then turned to make introductions to *Hector*'s officers. "May I present Mr. Paul Nguyen, the Montréal Republic's ambassador to Gadira?"

"A pleasure to meet you, sir," Captain Markham said, shaking Nguyen's hand. The others did so in turn. "How long have you been posted here?"

"Six years as ambassador, Captain. But I served two tours

in Gadira as a more junior representative of the Republic at the beginning of my career." Nguyen gestured at the palace grounds and the low, sprawling city beyond. "This is something of a homecoming for me. How was your voyage?"

"Uneventful, which is the preferred state of affairs," Markham replied. "However, we were a little surprised to find upon arrival that we weren't alone here."

"Our Dremish friends," the Montréalais replied with a nod. "It seems that Gadira's troubles are attracting a good deal of attention."

"Our foreign ministry was concerned that Aquilan citizens and investments might be in danger from the Caidists."

"Funny, Captain Harper said the same thing."

A small frown creased the captain's brow; Sikander doubted that anyone who didn't know Markham well would have noted her displeasure at the comparison. "I assure you, Mr. Nguyen, my government is opposed to *any* attempt to alter the status quo in Gadira. *Hector* is here only to make sure our people are safe."

"My apologies, Captain; I did not mean to imply otherwise. The remark was supposed to be ironic." Nguyen glanced up toward the sky to indicate the warship overhead, and gave a small shrug. "Several Aquilan corporations have been doing business in Gadira for decades, but the last time I looked, there weren't more than half a dozen Dremish citizens in-system. Your concerns seem a little more . . . proportionate."

Magdalena Juarez glanced around the party. "Are the Dremish here?" she asked.

"No, Dremark has no diplomatic representation in the sultan's court," Garcia answered. "There's a local consul in the city of Meknez, but he's a newly arrived business representative. This is not the sort of event that he would be invited to. In fact, I haven't even met him yet."

"Nor I," said Nguyen. "I am sure he will turn up sooner

or later. In the meantime, Captain, I suggest you exercise some care in granting shore leave to your crew. It would be best to stick to the offworlder-friendly districts in Tanjeer to avoid any incidents with Caidist sympathizers. The poorer neighborhoods may not be safe. I can recommend some good—" The Montréalais broke off. "Ah, perhaps later. It seems the sultan is ready to see you."

Sikander glanced around. A palace guard in a crisply pressed uniform approached from behind him. The fellow bowed to Captain Markham, and said, "Captain Markham, will you and your officers follow me? The sultan will receive you now."

"Please, lead the way," Markham replied. The palace guard escorted them to a large pavilion that stood a short distance from the assemblage of guests, partially screened by an elegant hedge. Several more guards stood silently nearby, motionless and vigilant. Inside the pavilion, a richly attired Gadiran man reclined on a couch, surrounded by several more men dressed in similar fashion, and one young woman who wore an embroidered caftan in rose and burgundy. The Gadirans spoke softly among themselves in their own language, but the man on the couch looked up with interest as *Hector*'s officers were shown into his presence.

"Your Highness, Captain Elise Markham of the Aquilan Commonwealth Navy, commanding officer of CSS *Hector,* and her officers," the guard announced. "Lieutenant Commander Juarez, Lieutenant Simms, and His Highness Lieutenant Sikander Singh North, Nawabzada of Ishar. His Royal Highness, Sultan Rashid el-Nasir, Monarch of Gadira and Defender of the Faithful. Her Royal Highness, Amira Ranya el-Nasir."

"Your Highness," Captain Markham said, bowing. The others followed suit. Sikander quietly studied the ruler of Gadira. The sultan was a short, round-bellied man of middle years, but his fleshy face lit up with an almost childlike delight as the introductions continued. On the other hand, the sultan's niece was not much older than twenty-three or twenty-four, with raven-black hair and a tall, graceful figure. Her chin was perhaps a little strong and her expression a bit too severe for her to be a classic beauty, but she studied *Hector*'s officers with an expression of keen interest.

"Captain, welcome, welcome," Sultan Rashid said. "We are honored by the visit of a Commonwealth warship. Aquila is one of our oldest and most valued friends among the great powers."

"The pleasure is ours, Your Highness. The opportunity to visit new worlds and meet new friends is one of the things I enjoy the most about the naval service."

"Tell me, how do you find Gadira?"

"Warm, Your Highness. My homeworld is quite a bit cooler and rainier than Tanjeer." Markham smiled easily. "Your gardens are very beautiful—already today I have discovered dozens of flowers I have never seen before. Are they native species?"

"Many of them are," the sultan replied. "It is one of the little ironies of our planet; so much of Gadira is desert, but we are blessed with many exquisite native blossoms. Come, let me show you some of them."

"I would be honored," Markham replied. Sultan Rashid got to his feet and led the way over to one of the nearby flower beds, launching immediately into a description of the various blooms. The captain allowed herself one brief moment of polite surprise, then followed along and paid attention to Rashid's enthusiastic discussion.

Sikander exchanged bemused glances with Magda Juarez and Dr. Simms. Somehow he doubted that Captain Markham had intended to dive into a botanical discussion with the ruler of Gadira, but she'd found herself there anyway. It was a credit to her natural composure that she adapted to the unexpected diversion without a hint of confusion, as if her whole purpose in calling on the sultan had been to discuss his gardens. With small shrugs, Magda and Simms hurried over to join the captain and take an interest in the discourse as Sultan Rashid chattered on about the flowers. Sikander was about to follow them, but as he glanced around for a cue of what was expected, he noticed the amira giving him a thoughtful look.

"Are you interested in gardens, Lieutenant North?" she asked him.

"I appreciate them, Amira," he told her. "I am afraid I don't know much about Gadiran botany, though."

"Neither do I," she said. "However, gardening is one of my uncle's dearest pastimes. Your captain may learn a lot more about flowers today than she anticipated. Let's escape while we can."

"As you wish, Amira," Sikander replied automatically. He covered his surprise with a warm smile while he collected his thoughts. Was this unexpected meeting nothing more than the pleasantries of a dutiful hostess? A diplomatic ploy to exchange views the sultan would not want to bring up in person? Or did the sultan's niece have something else on her mind?

The amira took his arm and steered him toward the other side of the pavilion. For an instant Sikander wondered if he'd committed a faux pas, but he realized that the men and women at the sultan's party mixed and chatted just as they did in similar settings on any other world. It seemed Gadiran society was not quite as puritanical or sex-segregated as he'd expected. The two of them strolled slowly out along a garden path, trailed unobtrusively by one of the guards. *The sultan's niece really is quite pretty,* he decided.

"Did I understand correctly that you are from Kashmir, not Aquila?" she asked him.

"Yes, Amira. Kashmir is an independent system, but we have been under Aquila's protection for more than a century."

"Just as Gadira is . . . allied . . . to the Republic of Montréal."

"More or less," Sikander said. "I grew up on the planet Jaipur, but I was sent off when I was eighteen to study at the Commonwealth's naval academy. I am unusual in that my father is a man of some standing in Kashmir, and he arranged for my appointment."

"The nawab, of course." The amira gave him a playful smile. "Are you royalty, Nawabzada?"

"Not really. My father's rank probably falls somewhere between the Gadiran titles of sultan and bey. I'm certain yours is the superior title, Amira."

"Ranya, please," she said. "Everybody calls me by my title. If you have half an excuse not to, I would sincerely appreciate it."

Sikander laughed. "I have much the same experience on the rare occasions when I return home. Very well, Ranya. I would be delighted if you called me Sikander, or just Sikay."

"Sikander, then." The Gadiran princess turned along one of the shaded paths leading toward the garden fountains. Sikander fell in easily beside her. "I have met many off-worlders, as you might imagine. Most are Montréalais, of course, although I have met Aquilans, Cygnans, and a few distant relatives from the Terran Caliphate. But I have rarely had the chance to speak with someone who comes from another colonial system. How do the people of Kashmir perceive their relationship with Aquila?"

"Well, the phrase 'colonial system' is not generally favored," Sikander admitted. "Most Aquilans are too polite to describe the arrangement in those terms, and most Kashmiris are too proud to allow themselves to look at things like that. Our bureaucrats and officials choose to speak of 'the Aquilan alliance,' or 'our development agreement,' or 'our chief trading partner,' not our colonial patron. The people who describe the relationship as colonialism tend to be the nationalists and the radicals."

"Things are not very different on Gadira. Of course, our radicals aren't concerned with words like 'colonialism.' The terminology is not terribly important; the dynamics of the relationship are the same." Ranya paused to gaze at a bed of blooming flowers that Sikander did not recognize. "Kashmir and Gadira share a situation that many less-developed peoples have been caught in down through the centuries. They rarely end well."

"I suppose I am a little more optimistic," Sikander said. "Economically and technologically, Kashmir had fallen a hundred years behind the Coalition powers when Aquila brought us into their sphere of influence. Now Kashmir is only twenty or thirty years behind the times. Within my lifetime I think I'll see my homeworld catch up to the worlds of my Aquilan peers. The same forces that are shaking Gadira today shook Kashmir a generation or two ago, and we survived them. I see no reason why your world should be any different."

She glanced up at him. "You truly believe that?"

"I think you'll find that I rarely manage to stop myself from saying what I think about things, Ranya."

"That is something of a handicap for a diplomat."

"Which is why my father thought military service better for me," Sikander replied.

Ranya laughed. "That was probably for the best, then."

The guard following ten feet behind them quietly cleared his throat. He stood almost two full meters in height, and wore an impressive turban that made him seem even taller; Sikander would not have cared to give the fellow a reason to remove him from Ranya's presence. "Amira, Bey Hurat and his party are arriving," he said to Ranya. "The sultan is about to greet them."

"I will be right there, Captain Zakur." The amira gave

Sikander a small shrug. "Duty calls, I fear. It was a pleasure to meet you, Sikander."

He took her hand. "Likewise, Ranya. I look forward to our next meeting."

"I do, too, although I am afraid that must wait." She held his hand for a long moment, measuring him with her dark eyes. "My uncle is flying to Nador tomorrow to preside over the opening of a new power plant, and I will be accompanying him. We won't return until early next week . . . but I hope you'll visit again when we get back."

"I will," Sikander promised. "Have a safe journey."

Ranya smiled warmly, then turned and glided back toward the sultan's pavilion. Sikander stood watching her for a moment, then took a deep breath, glanced around the palace garden, and headed off to find his shipmates again.

9

Tanjeer, Gadira II

Five days after the garden party, Ranya el-Nasir gazed out the window of the luxury flyer, daydreaming as the golden cliffs and dazzling waters of the coastline east of Tanjeer passed by below. Nador was eight hundred kilometers behind her, a little less than an hour of flying time; she leaned back in her seat half-asleep, her mind drowsily sorting through the discussions and events of the whirlwind state visit to Gadira's second-largest city. But just as she began to actually doze off, Sultan Rashid brought her pleasant languor to a very sudden end. "I think it is high time that we found you a husband, my niece," he said.

Ranya couldn't have awakened any faster if her uncle had pushed her into a pool of icy water. "Uncle, I am not sure—" she began.

"Allow me to finish, Ranya." Sultan Rashid smiled benignly and cut her off with a broad gesture of his hand. He reclined in the comfortable seat across the narrow aisle from her. "I have been giving this a good deal of thought lately. You are twenty-four years old now, and Gadira expects princesses of the royal house to do their duty to the dynasty. And more to the point, my brother would have wanted a grandchild."

The route of the sultan's luxurious transport happened to pass just a kilometer or two above some of the most magnificent desert landscape on Gadira, but it seemed that Sultan Rashid had more on his mind than the view. Ranya paused to gather her argument. She had no time or interest for husband hunting at the moment, but she didn't want to hurt her uncle's feelings—or, worse yet, spur him into some grandiose plan to helpfully interfere in her romantic life. She settled on the most honest answer she could give him. "I simply don't feel that I am ready for marriage yet," she finally said. "I've been so caught up in my duties that I haven't even met anyone that might be a suitable match."

"And that is in part my fault, my dear." Sultan Rashid shook his head. He was less than twenty years older than Ranya, but he'd developed the manners and studied indolence of a much older man. He was already fat enough that his doctors constantly urged him to moderate his diet, but Rashid had a sweet tooth that could have shamed a ten-year-old. "You are a beautiful young woman, but you have the mind and temperament of your father. I have relied on you as I might have relied on a son, instead of allowing you to blossom as a daughter. It is not fair to you."

"It's what I wanted, Uncle." This topic came up every few months, and it seemed that every time it did, her uncle sounded as if just a little more of Gadira's chauvinistic ideas had seeped into his way of looking at the world. Years ago she had found it endearing; now it was becoming tiresome, although Ranya did her best not to show her annoyance. If nothing else, she was fond of her uncle. "As you say, I have my father's temperament. I wasn't meant to spend my days as a palace ornament."

"That you have made clear to me more than once. Nevertheless, Yasmin and I have been talking, and we have come up with a plan of sorts."

Ranya frowned. This was something new. Her uncle had never gone beyond making simple observations about her eligibility for marriage, and he rarely consulted with his wife on anything. Extremely shy, Sultana Yasmin disliked the capital and the public routine of the palace. She and her two daughters spent most of their time in the Khalifa Palace, a highly secluded fortresslike retreat high in the mountains above the picturesque town of Toutay, a couple of hundred kilometers from Tanjeer. It wouldn't be quite accurate to say that Rashid and Yasmin were estranged from each other, since as far as Ranya knew there was no real disagreement between them. But Rashid seemed content to allow his wife to enjoy her seclusion, and it didn't seem likely that the sultan and sultana would ever produce a male heir for House Nasir. For now, Gadira's elites maintained the polite fiction that a crown prince would be born in due course, but in all likelihood the throne of Ranya's father would eventually pass to any of a half-dozen distant cousins who had had the foresight to be born with a penis . . . unless Ranya happened to find the right marriage.

So that is what this is about, she decided. Her uncle was worried about establishing a clear line of succession. "A plan?" she asked cautiously.

"It seems to your aunt Yasmin and me that there are not many suitors of your station on Gadira," Sultan Rashid said. "As the daughter of a planetary sovereign, you should most properly be married to the son of a royal house of similar rank. So we have settled upon the idea of sending you on an extended visit to the core systems of the Caliphate. You can begin by making your *hadj* to Terra. Then you can undertake studies at any of the proper schools, and attend various royal courts. We have relatives in the Caliphate worlds willing to sponsor you, and introduce you to men of suitable rank. I think three years should be sufficient."

"Three years?" Ranya felt a flutter of panic at the idea. While it was true that she was not likely to find a husband on Gadira, she didn't particularly *want* a husband at the moment. She had friends and interests at home that she did not wish to leave . . . and she was also very concerned that no one else in House Nasir could replace her in the administration of the sultanate's affairs. The Montréalais would see to it that Sultan Rashid did not fall, but what kind of world would she come home to? "Uncle, I am not sure I can afford to leave Gadira for three months, let alone three years. The Caidist troubles grow worse every day. They demand the full attention of our house, and I can be of great help to you."

Sultan Rashid reached over to pat her arm. "My dear, there will always be troubles. I cannot ask you to delay your own happiness forever simply because we can't look past the challenges of the day. And no one is indispensable—it will be good for the rest of us to take on some of your burden."

Ranya did not answer immediately. She glanced out the window again, gathering her thoughts; the coastal mountains faded into the dusty haze behind the aerial motorcade, while the multicolored sprawl of Tanjeer's fields, orchards, and outlying districts passed by two thousand meters below. She felt that she was a good deal more indispensable than her uncle realized, but Rashid could be surprisingly stubborn if openly defied. Besides, a part of her was not entirely opposed to the idea. She hadn't ever left Gadira, and the opportunity to see dozens of new worlds tempted her. She could think of a friend or two who would come with her if she asked; it might be something of an adventure. *But not right now,* she decided.

She glanced back to Sultan Rashid. "When do you want me to go?" Her uncle had a habit of coming up with grand ideas, but then forgetting about them when something else caught his attention. In the time between this conversation and the day she was supposed to leave Gadira, the whole idea might slip his mind.

"It may take some time to finalize the arrangements," Rashid answered. "I have taken the liberty of sending messages ahead to some of our offworld relations—the Birkols of Tau Ceti, the al-Firats, Shah Norouzi of Khorasan III. We won't see any replies for a month or two yet. But I see no reason why it shouldn't be later this year."

He means well, Ranya reminded herself. It grated on her to learn that her uncle was laying plans to float her around the Caliphate worlds like a fly fisherman trying to hook a prize catch. And the fact that he'd already sent letters ahead meant that for once Sultan Rashid was putting one of his grand ideas into action. She might not be able to evade this offworld tour after all, and of course, she would be expected to return with a husband, or at least some good prospects for one. She wasn't completely inexperienced with men— the more permissive quarters of Gadiran society turned a blind eye to affairs carried on with discretion, and even a princess was entitled to some privacy. But opportunities for serious relationships, as Rashid observed, were more than a little limited for Ranya. She knew next to nothing about the process of catching a husband.

"Later this year?" she said, still trying to grapple with the thought. "I will give some thought to passing my responsibilities along to a replacement. And finding some companionship for the trip."

"That's the spirit." Sultan Rashid beamed. "I had the good fortune to make a similar journey as a young man, when your grandfather was still sultan. Oh, I wasn't looking for a wife at that point, but I had the opportunity to visit dozens of worlds and see wonders that I could not have imagined before I left Gadira. We live on one small planet, Ranya, but there is a much greater universe out there. You can't truly understand that until you see it for yourself."

Ranya glanced out the window again, wondering how much she would miss her home. She dealt with offworlders every day, and she knew that many of them privately considered Gadira to be a miserable and backward system indeed. The contrast between the sprawl of Tanjeer's squalid suburbs, now passing beneath the sultan's skycade, and the white walls of El-Badi Palace, with its surrounding gardens and parks, certainly offered little to be proud of. There were cities in the core worlds of the Coalition that were a hundred kilometers across, skyscrapers like artificial mountains, orbital palaces, markets where the goods of a hundred worlds were bought and sold . . . *What was that?*

Five thin smoke trails suddenly leaped into existence from the tree-covered expanse of a large cemetery just off the flight path of the sultan's flyer. Ranya happened to be looking out the window at the very moment they launched, so she saw them before anybody else. Pure surprise froze her for a half second as the weapons streaked up from the ground; the exhaust plumes looked like gray daggers reaching up for her. Then she found her voice. *"Missiles right!"* she screamed.

Lieutenant Colonel Raoul Yusir, a highly experienced veteran, had the honor of serving as the sultan's personal pilot. The position was perhaps the most prestigious assignment in the entire Royal Guard, and he'd fought his way through months of competitions and training to win the post. Today that rigorous selection process proved its value—the instant Ranya shouted her warning, Colonel Yusir slammed the throttle to the stops and dove down and away from the threat.

The luxury transport's inertial compensators did their best to accommodate the violent maneuver, but even so Ranya was thrown against her window. Her uncle grunted in surprise as he flailed sideways against the restraints in his seat. When Ranya got her bearings again, the missiles were almost on top of them.

Smoke trails—rockets, not induction motors, she noted with an oddly clinical interest. Years of familiarizing herself with the sultanate's military aid from Montréal had its benefits. Cutting-edge ground-to-air weapons were hypersonic missiles with gravity induction drives. They wouldn't have left any smoke for her to spot, and would have hit the sultan's skycade in the blink of an eye. Metallic hydrogen rockets or more primitive chemical propellants powered older weapons. She watched the first of the rockets swerve suddenly to one side to follow one of the escort flyers. *And they're guided, too!* That almost certainly meant they were offworld arms. Plenty of industrial facilities on Gadira could manufacture an unguided rocket, but building a seeker head was another matter altogether.

The question abruptly ceased to be of merely clinical interest when the first rocket reached the Royal Guard flyer escorting the sultan's transport. The weapon detonated in a powerful blast that ripped one engine off the escort and peppered its fuselage with lethal shrapnel. The stricken flyer—four Royal Guards, men who'd been around Ranya all of her life—tumbled end over end toward the crowded city streets below.

"Hang on!" Colonel Yusir shouted as he wrestled with the controls. The oversized personal flyer that served as Sultan Rashid's transport was armored and equipped with defensive systems for just such a situation, but it couldn't outclimb surface-to-air missiles. The pilot instinctively dove to get the transport on the deck as fast as he could and use ground clutter to break the missile lock. Of course, that meant throwing the transport toward the streets below in a reckless power dive. Ranya looked forward, saw the ground rushing up, and screamed again despite herself.

Behind the sultan's transport, a second missile clipped another one of the escort flyers. This one survived the hit, just barely; it veered wildly out of control and wound up making a hard landing in a vacant parking lot two kilometers distant. The third missile never locked on to anything; in his excitement, the young insurgent who'd fired it had neglected to activate the seeker head before launching the weapon, although no one in the sultan's skycade saw where it went or learned why it missed. The two remaining missiles established a good lock on the sultan's transport, and they streaked after the diving and twisting vehicle despite Colonel Yusir's desperate effort to escape.

Only fifty meters behind the sultan's transport, the third flyer in the escort squadron dove headlong into the path of the oncoming missiles. The brave Royal Guardsman piloting the craft could not intercept both weapons, but he traded his life and the lives of the other guardsmen with him to stop one missile streaking toward the royal transport.

It was almost enough.

The last missile exploded just above the sultan's transport, shredding the vertical stabilizer and blasting shrapnel through the engines and the cabin. Shrieking wind and the sound of tearing metal filled the cabin as a dozen fist-sized holes suddenly appeared in the ceiling, with bright blue sky showing through. Ranya felt a hot searing sting crease the nape of her neck, and missed decapitation by a matter of centimeters. Sultan Rashid was hit in the left arm and shoulder; an aide sitting just behind him was killed instantly by a piece of shrapnel that struck between his eyes. The engines failed with a burst of sparks and flame, and the transport dropped sickeningly as alarms wailed in the cockpit. Ranya screamed again. And this time Sultan Rashid and the two Royal Guards who were still alive in the damaged transport cried out as well.

The sultan's transport glanced off the side of a water tower, digging a ten-meter gash across the tank. The impact threw the heavy flyer into a violent horizontal spin, wrenching Ranya from one side to the other as blinding bursts of daylight and black shadow strobed madly through the cabin. Then the sultan's flyer smacked into the street below, crushing a pair of parked ground transports and hurling debris in all directions. She heard screeching metal, shrieking alarms—and then nothing, as merciful darkness rose up and claimed her.

Some time later—seconds, minutes, she could not tell—she came to back to her senses when she felt someone fumbling at her restraints. Her neck stung, her back ached, and her mouth was full of the metallic taste of blood. Numbly, Ranya reached up to push the hands away. "No," she mumbled.

"Let me help you, Amira. We must get you out of here, there is a serious risk of additional attacks."

Ranya opened her eyes, and found herself looking up at Captain Tarek Zakur. Blood splattered his singed tunic, and his face was grim with anger. "What happened?" she said. Blood trickled from her mouth. "Where are we?"

"The transport was shot down. We're in Tougana, about three kilometers from the palace." Captain Zakur gently moved her hands aside and unfastened the seat restraints. "Are you hurt, Amira?"

"I don't know," she said. "I don't know."

"Come with me, please," Zakur said. Without waiting for her answer, he pulled her upright and somehow maneuvered her through the twisted wreckage of the cabin to the door. Then Ranya found herself outside, standing in the street beside the broken transport.

She saw that the sultan's flyer had landed hard on its belly and skidded two hundred meters or more along a residential street before a large tree had stopped it. Several medical techs clustered around the nose of the vehicle, where Colonel Yusir and his copilot appeared to be trapped in wreckage. The two surviving flyers of the escort had landed in the middle of the street, bracketing the crash site; two more now orbited overhead with gunners manning heavy autorifles perched in their doors. Several ambulances and firefighting vehicles were already on the scene, their bright red and blue lights flashing, and the wailing sirens of more on the way echoed through the city. Everywhere Ranya looked, soldiers of the Royal Guard swarmed over the scene, their faces full of fear and anger. Scores of bystanders stood outside the cordon or watched from their front doors or windows.

What a nice neighborhood, she noticed. *Why did we decide to land here?* Then she realized that she was not making sense, even in the privacy of her own thoughts. Clearly she was not at her best. It was hard, but somehow Ranya forced herself to focus on what was going on.

She steadied herself on Captain Zakur, ignoring everything else except for his face. "The sultan?" she demanded.

"He is injured but alive, Amira," the guard captain replied. He glanced at a medical transport that rested alongside the wreckage of the royal transport; Ranya saw a number of medical techs clustered around a stretcher there. She pushed herself away from Zakur and hurried over to the side of the stretcher.

Sultan Rashid groaned and shifted, his arm encased in a pressure sleeve and bloodstained wound dressings taped to his bare shoulder. Small cuts and abrasions marked his face, but his eyes were alert. He looked up at her as she reached the side of his stretcher. "Ah, good," he murmured in a weak voice. "I was worried for you, my dear."

"I am fine, Uncle," she said. "Don't concern yourself about me, save your strength!"

"I do not mind that they tried to kill me," he murmured. "After all, they killed Kamal, and Grandfather, too. But I could not stand it if something happened to you, Ranya. Enough is enough. If it's a war the Caidists want, we will give them one."

Ranya had difficulty in following Rashid's words, but she managed to organize her thoughts with sheer effort of will. "The insurgents are trying to provoke you, Uncle. Don't give them that power over your actions."

Rashid spat a mouthful of blood onto the stretcher. "I am provoked," he snarled—perhaps the first time in her life that

Ranya had ever seen him truly angry. "Trust me, my dear, I am very much provoked. And our enemies will be sorry indeed for it."

Captain Zakur appeared by her side, and set a hand on Ranya's arm. "Please, Amira, we must get the sultan onto the med transport," he said. She allowed him to draw her away from the stretcher; the medical technicians immediately lifted Rashid up and into the flyer. "One will be here for you in a matter of moments."

"But I'm not hurt," Ranya told him.

Zakur shook his head. "That is for the doctors to say, Amira. You have a cut on the back of your neck, and another one on your leg. And you probably have a concussion, too. Please, this way."

Ranya put her hand to the back of her neck and felt that it was warm and wet. When she looked at it, her palm was covered in her own blood. "Oh," she managed to say. Captain Zakur just managed to catch her when her legs gave out.

10

CSS *Hector*, Gadira II Orbit

The brown, gold, and blue surface of Gadira seemed to drift slowly past the wall-sized vid display in the wardroom. From the altitude of three thousand kilometers, almost half of the hemisphere was visible. Sikander gazed absently at the view from his seat at the large table in the middle of the room, enjoying a coffee break as he mentally organized the rest of his day. Judging by the position of the terminator dividing the planet into day and night below him, it was midday in Tanjeer, but there was little point in adopting local timekeeping for ships in low or middle orbit; *Hector* currently circled the planet in a little less than three hours. The crew instead observed Naval Standard Time, and accepted the fact that visits or communications to the planet below might sometimes come up in the middle of the ship's "night." *It's close to noon for Ranya,* Sikander noted. *I wonder what she does for lunch?*

Magdalena Juarez helped herself to some coffee from the service on the nearby credenza, and gave Sikander a wicked smile when she noted his absentminded gaze. "Thinking about the amira?" she asked—a lucky guess indeed.

Sikander pulled his attention away from the image of the

planet below. "I suppose I was," he admitted. "Ranya el-Nasir is not what I expected to find here."

"You seem to have made quite an impression on her."

"She made an impression on me, as well. She's a very intelligent woman—insightful, curious, and quite fluent in Standard Anglic, which I imagine is at least her third language. Mr. Garcia says that she just about runs the place for her uncle."

"The dashing offworld prince descends from the stars and meets the bookish princess," Magda teased. "To his surprise he finds a woman of fiery passions stifled by the expectations of those around her! The romance novel almost writes itself."

"Did you just call me dashing?" Sikander grinned. "I like the sound of that, but I have to admit that our conversation was not in the least romantic. The amira asked about Kashmir and Aquila."

The chief engineer gave him a measuring look as she sat down in the opposite seat. "Really? What did you discuss?"

"She was curious about how I came to be in the Commonwealth Navy. From there the conversation turned to colonial relationships and interstellar politics, and the similarities between Gadira's situation and that of Kashmir a generation or two ago. Nothing about her fiery passions, thank you very much!"

"Too bad," said Magda. "It was a lot more interesting in my head, I suppose."

Sikander shrugged, and sipped at the dregs of his coffee. "What did the sultan talk about while I was off strolling with the amira?"

"Nothing at all to do with politics, insurgencies, or colonial affairs. However, I'm now certain that the sultan's gardens will be well prepared for any eventuality." Magda smiled. "I think Captain Markham had hoped that indulging his botanical interests would establish a bit of a connection, which in turn might shed insight on the strategic situation. Unfortunately, all we gained from the conversation was a vastly increased understanding of Gadiran sunrose varietals."

"You never know when that might be useful," Sikander replied. "For example, you might—"

He was interrupted by the ship's info assistant. "Ms. Juarez, Mr. North, your presence is requested in the captain's cabin," the computer announced. "The matter is urgent."

Sikander exchanged looks with Magda, and read the same sudden disquiet in her expression that he felt. It was not all that unusual to be summoned for an impromptu discussion, but the "urgent" wasn't included unless something was in need of immediate correction. "We're on our way," he said to the computer, and pocketed his dataslate as he stood.

"What's going on?" Magda wondered aloud. She allowed herself one long sip from her just-poured coffee, then set down her mug and stood as well.

"I've no idea," Sikander answered, even though he knew she hadn't really been asking him. The two officers hurried out of the wardroom and headed forward, climbing up one deck to the captain's cabin. Sikander did not quite run, since that would have been undignified. But he did reach the captain's door less than two minutes after the announcement.

He knocked once and entered, Magda a step behind him. Captain Markham waited by the small conference table in her cabin. "You wished to see us, ma'am?" he asked. Then he noticed that Peter Chatburn and Isaako Simms were already seated in their customary places. Apparently the captain had summoned all the senior officers, not just Sikander and Magda.

Captain Markham merely nodded at the empty seats by the table. "Ms. Juarez, Mr. North, have a seat. Events are taking an unpleasant turn down on Gadira."

Sikander took his customary seat, halfway down the

table. The vidscreen on the cabin wall showed a scene on the ground, the highly magnified ship's-eye view of a tree-shaded boulevard filled with the flashing lights of emergency vehicles and what appeared to be a crash site of some kind. He studied the view for a moment. The lights flashing, the hastily erected barricades, the firefighting vehicles and medical transports . . . he knew the scene well. *It's like Sangrur,* he realized. *Something has happened to the sultan.*

There was a knock at the cabin door, and Hiram Randall entered, a dataslate open in one hand. He had finally shed the arm sling he'd been wearing for the last two weeks. "My apologies, Captain," he said as he came in and took his seat at the table. "I thought it best to pull together the newest intel before joining you." As operations officer, it was Randall's job to keep a close eye on all planetside developments and determine which of those merited the direct attention of *Hector*'s leadership team.

"Good thinking," Captain Markham replied. "Go ahead and bring everyone up to date, Mr. Randall."

"Yes, ma'am." Randall shifted in his seat to address the rest of the officers at the table. "Insurgents shot down Sultan Rashid's flyer with surface-to-air missiles thirty-five minutes ago. We picked up a major military alert about twenty minutes ago, and the news is just now breaking on Gadiran vid channels."

Sikander nodded; his intuition had been all too accurate. Around the table, his colleagues likewise winced, straightened in their seats, or took in sharp breaths as they absorbed the news. "Is the sultan dead?" Chatburn asked.

"We don't believe so, sir." Randall reached for the display controls. "Let me bring up the live newscast feed—that's our best source at the moment."

He clicked the wall display over to a Gadiran broadcast channel. The screen shifted from the overhead view of *Hector*'s vidcams to a live street-level view from a local news team. Ground transports were parked unevenly on both sides of the tree-lined street, and ugly black smoke climbed up to stain the colorless sky over the nearby buildings. In the middle of the image, charred debris soaked in firefighting foam was scattered down the boulevard, leading to the wreckage of a large luxury flyer. Text in Jadeed-Arabi crawled slowly across the bottom of the screen while a woman—the news anchor, or so Sikander guessed—spoke rapidly in a voice-over.

"Dear God," Magda murmured. "Where is this, Mr. Randall?"

"It's in Tanjeer, a few kilometers from the palace," Randall replied. "The sultan was on his way home from an official visit to Nador, where he's been for the last few days."

"Is anybody claiming responsibility for the attack?" Dr. Simms asked.

"Not yet, but our best guess is that we're looking at the work of a large and well-funded group of urban insurgents," said Randall. "Surface-to-air missiles would almost certainly be offworld arms, and the attackers fired off a whole volley at the sultan's skycade—three of the escort flyers were hit at the same time as Rashid's transport. It appears to have been a coordinated ambush."

"The Royal Guard has a major security leak," Chatburn observed. "The insurgents had to know the sultan's schedule and the flight plan in order to set up this kind of attack. Someone on the inside is feeding them intelligence."

"Not necessarily," Captain Markham said. "I'd bet that someone watching the sultan's comings and goings from the palace over a few months could make a very good guess about the Royal Guard's typical flight paths, and an observer on the ground at Nador could call ahead to provide a couple of hours' advance notice. For that matter, orbital observation could provide the same information."

Sikander studied the imagery, wondering how many of the sultan's bodyguards had lost their lives. That thought led to another, more personal concern: Ranya el-Nasir had told him that she'd be accompanying her uncle to Nador. "What about Amira Ranya?" he asked. "Was she with the sultan? Was she hurt?"

"The amira?" Randall checked his dataslate. "One moment. . . . The reports indicate that she received minor injuries and is currently being treated."

"Thank God for that much." Sikander allowed himself a sigh of relief, surprised at the depth of his sudden worry. He'd met Ranya only once, after all, but he had enjoyed his conversation with her; the amira was intriguing and, as Magda had pointed out, the centerpiece of a situation that seemed almost designed to inspire visions of romantic folly. He tried to ignore the speculative look that Magda gave him.

"Agreed," Captain Markham said. "If the sultan is out of commission for a time, she might be able to hold things together."

"How are the Gadiran people reacting to the news?" Chatburn asked.

"Not well," Randall replied. He adjusted the vidscreen, showing several different feeds from other locations around the planet—an unruly crowd gathering in front of a large government building, another march or protest of some kind proceeding down a wide street in a city Sikander didn't recognize, a column of police vehicles taking up position on a bridge. "It's just breaking, but we already have indications of demonstrations and riots shaping up in different areas, including Tanjeer's offworlder district."

The captain looked back to the operations officer. "Is our consulate threatened? I can't imagine why locals would react to the attempt on the sultan's life by attacking offworlders, but we'd better be ready to do something about it if they do."

"I don't know, ma'am. Let me see if I can find a better view." Randall opened his dataslate and rapidly entered several commands, taking control of one of *Hector*'s high-resolution vidcams. The vidscreen abruptly jumped to a new image, a view of an elegant older neighborhood in the downtown area. The image was distinctly off-vertical, since *Hector*'s orbit now carried her away from the capital, but it still clearly showed a walled courtyard-style house with an iron gate. Several dozen Gadiran men gathered in the street just outside, shaking their fists and waving signs. Randall adjusted the view, zooming out a bit to show the area for several blocks around. A much larger crowd seemed to be taking shape about five blocks away.

Sikander watched the silent scene, looking for signs of weapons or rioting. He didn't see any, but he did spot a small group of Tanjeer police a block away from the large crowd. They milled around, evidently conferring with each other as they watched the crowd. Then they got into their vehicles and withdrew from the scene. "I think the police were just called away," he pointed out. "Or they decided that the crowd was too big for them to handle."

"Or they were instructed not to interfere," said Randall. "I have to say it strikes me as a bad sign that the Gadiran police are getting out of the way."

"It doesn't look good," Captain Markham agreed. She leaned back in her chair, and studied the vidscreen for a long moment. Then she arrived at her decision. "Let's ready a landing force and have it standing by in case we need to pull out the consulate personnel. Mr. Randall, touch base with Consul Garcia and find out what he needs from us. Mr. North, tell Sublieutenant Larkin to pull her people out of the watch rotation and muster in the hangar bay."

"Yes, ma'am." Sikander nodded. During the transit to Gadira, they'd done some preliminary planning for evacuating civilians from just this sort of situation. That involved organizing a thirty-hand landing force from the ship's crew and having them brush up on their small-arms handling, since *Hector* did not carry a contingent of marines. Angela Larkin had the most recent security training among the junior officers, so she'd been assigned as the officer in charge. It was a perfectly sensible way to make the decision . . . but as he watched the crowds gathering in the streets of the capital, Sikander found himself growing uneasy.

Captain Markham noticed his hesitation. "What is it, Mr. North?" she asked.

"Captain, with your permission, I think I'd better accompany the landing force."

"You lack confidence in Ms. Larkin?" Chatburn asked sharply.

Sikander did, but he was not willing to denigrate one of his subordinates to the XO and the captain. "I think she is more than qualified for tactical command of the landing force," he told Chatburn, which was mostly true. "What I worry about is that this might not be a tactical situation—a certain amount of judgment or restraint may be called for. I would feel better if a department head were on the ground." *And no other officer on this ship has actually commanded troops during civil disorders,* he added silently. In the tense months leading up to the attack that had resulted in his departure from Kashmir, Sikander and his older brothers had each deployed with the Jaipur Dragoons on several occasions. Even as a teenager, Sikander had been expected to meet the duties of a North; he'd gained a hard education in political violence as a result.

Captain Markham hesitated, perhaps reviewing her instructions about appropriate duties for a prince of Kashmir. But whatever those might have been, Sikander was correct: Hiram Randall and Magda Juarez were needed on board, and no other officer on board was more qualified for command of a landing force unless she decided to send down Peter Chatburn. "You make a good point, Mr. North," she said. "Take charge of the landing force, and stand by for orders. Dismissed."

Sikander stood, saluted, and made his way out of the cabin, followed by the rest of *Hector*'s leadership team. He'd been looking forward to the opportunity to visit Tanjeer again and explore a little more of the city, or perhaps find an excuse to call again on the amira. This, however, was not the sort of sightseeing or café hopping he'd had in mind. *I doubt that the marketplaces are going to be open today,* he reflected. Instead he was likely heading into a riot, but perhaps he'd find a way to check on Ranya and make sure she was all right while he was on the ground.

"Message for Sublieutenant Larkin," he told the ship's info assistant as he hurried down the passageway. "The landing force is to muster immediately in the hangar bay. Arrange watch substitutions as needed. I will join you there shortly."

Sikander headed first to his stateroom to change. He pulled out his Navy battle dress—a mottled blue-gray urban-camouflage uniform reinforced with panels of light, flexible armor—and tossed it on the bunk. For routine duty a matching fatigue cap completed the uniform, but Sikander took a moment to add the inserts that turned the cap into a light helmet. People tended to throw things during riots, and he had a feeling he might need it when he got down to the ground.

Three soft knocks came at his stateroom door, and then Darvesh Reza entered. The valet studied Sikander's change of clothes. "Are we going ashore, sir?"

"I'm afraid so," Sikander answered. It never failed—throughout his Navy career, Darvesh's ability to sense when his services might be needed was simply uncanny. If his duties took Sikander anywhere near personal danger, then by order of Nawab Dayan, Darvesh had to be close by. "How did you know?"

"Chief Trent informed me the landing force was needed. She also mentioned your intention to join the shore party—which, I must note, you are not assigned to."

Word travels fast in the chief petty officers' quarters, it seems. Sikander supposed he shouldn't have been surprised by that; things had been much the same since the days of oared galleys. "The situation calls for more experience and judgment than we might expect from a sublieutenant," he told Darvesh. "I'm afraid Captain Markham doesn't have many other choices."

Darvesh regarded him with a stern look. "You know very well that you should not go out of your way to find dangerous situations to leap into, Nawabzada. This is exactly the sort of duty your father would disapprove of. For that matter, I disapprove of it, too. There is a difference between accepting the ordinary risks associated with the naval service, and putting yourself in the middle of thousands of angry people when you are not required to do so."

"The fighting around Sangrur or Manigam was worse than what's going on here."

"Yes, but your father deployed whole battalions of soldiers on those occasions. Thirty armed sailors is the very definition of a token force."

"It's more than enough to defend a building or deter a crowd armed with cudgels and stones." Sikander stripped off his jumpsuit and began to don his battle dress. Darvesh was correct, up to a point; he was obligated to avoid unnecessary risks. But he was also obligated to do his duty without shirking. He pursued his career in the Aquilan navy not only to learn, but also to teach. If an Aquilan officer would be expected to do something, then Sikander had to show the men and women around him that a Kashmiri officer would do no less. "Besides, I can hardly reverse course now."

Darvesh stood in silence for a moment, then collected the jumpsuit from Sikander and folded it neatly. "No, sir. I suppose you cannot. But in the future I must insist that you take your father's wishes into account before volunteering for such duty."

"I have my reasons." Sikander shrugged on his camo uniform, then gave Darvesh a confident smile in an effort to downplay the bodyguard's concerns. "I can finish here.

You'd better get dressed—we may be called away at any moment."

Darvesh gave Sikander a stiffly formal bow to express his disapproval one more time. "Very good, sir. I will meet you on the hangar deck." Then he left to gather his own gear.

Sikander glanced around the stateroom, looking for anything he might have missed. The vidscreen on the bulkhead showed the same Gadiran news feed he'd been watching from the wardroom; the news crews focused on live reports from the crash site of the sultan's transport, although smaller windows showed images of unrest in various places.

Ranya's lucky to have survived, he realized as the news vid zoomed in on the wrecked flyer. He found himself unable to look away, wondering what those last few moments in the flyer must have been like, whether she'd realized what was happening or even had time to be terrified. He remembered how he'd felt on the night of that last Bandi Chor Divas celebration, and the streets of Sangrur—

—echoing with the pounding of a hundred drums and the singing of ten thousand voices. Fantastic floats and troupes of dancers pass before the nawab's box in the review stand as the warm dusk settles over the city like a blanket.

Sikander entertains himself by picking out pretty girls from the crowds. He can't take his eyes off the young woman dancing on the grand float just now entering the city square. It's designed to resemble a fantastic castle, and the lead dancer holds the place of honor on the loftiest of the colorful battlements. He wonders who she is, and whether he'll be able to find her later when it's time for the revels to begin.

Nawab Dayan gives a small nod, and the whole family rises together, holding the light globes before them. By old custom the nawab will make a few short remarks, and then his children—all young men and women now, none of them small any longer—will release their hoverlights to drift away over the crowd, joining hundreds of other lights overhead. Sikander and his siblings turn expectantly to Nawab Dayan to hear his words.

Then the bomb goes off.

Later on, the Khanate investigators would determine that it was hidden in the chassis of the ground transport beneath the castle float, and that no one in or near the gaudily decorated vehicle had any idea what was about to happen. It's a small device, only a few kilos of molecular explosive, which is why the death toll is limited to scores instead of hundreds or thousands. The bomb is still powerful enough to knock down everyone within sixty meters, and performers dancing on top of the float are flung six or seven stories in the air. The blast hurls Sikander and everyone else in the nawab's stand back over their seats. The flimsy grandstand buckles; he lands in a tangle of chairs and scaffolding.

Ears ringing from the blast, he struggles to his feet, clambering over the wreckage. There is no sign of the pretty girl he'd been watching in the center of the float. At first he hears nothing but the echoes of the explosion rolling back from distant buildings, but as his ears clear, he hears the first of the screams. . . .

Sikander shook himself and turned off the vid input.

"Enough of that, Sikay!" he muttered aloud. The bombing at Sangrur was ten years ago and three hundred light-years away; it had no more power to hurt him, not unless he allowed it to. *Ranya is not seriously hurt,* he reminded himself. Then again, he hadn't been seriously hurt at the Sangrur bombing, had he? But he carried scars of a different sort.

He hesitated, then turned the vid unit back on and activated the messaging system. "Hello, Ranya," he said as he looked into the recorder. "I just heard the news about the attack. I am terribly sorry that your uncle and others in your escort group were injured; it was a cruel and callous act. My family has been targeted by such attacks, too, and I know how you must be feeling now. I . . . I am very relieved to hear that you survived, and I wish you a quick recovery. If there is anything I can do for you, I hope you'll let me know. And I promise that if I can help in some way to bring the perpetrators to justice, I will. In the meantime, may God be with you and your family today. Sikander, out."

He thought over what he'd said, and decided that it captured his sincerity and concern well enough. A few taps on his dataslate cued it for delivery. Strictly speaking, it might not be appropriate for a serving officer to address a personal note to a high-ranking royal of another government. There was a real risk of creating a diplomatic faux pas or offending local sensibilities, and no captain would care for a subordinate causing that kind of trouble. But Sikander could defend his actions as an expression of sympathy on behalf of the Kashmiri government if he needed to—and, more to the point, he thought Ranya was his friend, and as far as he could tell she was probably having a very bad day.

He pocketed his dataslate and donned his fatigue cap, heading down to the hangar bay. But before he got ten steps from his stateroom, Michael Girard overtook him. "Excuse me, Mr. North?" he asked. "I think I have a question about that assignment you gave me."

Sikander stopped and waited for him, suppressing his impatience. Girard carried an oversized programmer's dataslate under his arm, and his brow was furrowed with intense concentration. "Make it quick, Mr. Girard. I need to get down to the hangar bay."

"Which torpedo model am I supposed to be emulating, sir?" Girard asked.

Any hope that Sikander might have felt about his most junior officer somehow noticing something that everyone else had missed evaporated. CSS *Hector* carried only one model of torpedo—well, two, counting the practice shots. In fact, pretty much all the cruisers and a good number of the destroyers in the Aquilan navy carried the exact same weapon. He'd known that Girard could be unusually focused on his own specific duties as fire control officer, but Sikander would have thought that *all* of the ship's officers knew what kind of torpedoes the ship carried. *Don't cut him down,* he admonished himself. *The whole idea was to give him an opportunity to excel at something without expectations.*

"The practice models, Mr. Girard," he said patiently. "Phantoms Type 12-P. God help us if our war shots have the same fault, but that's a problem we can tackle after we figure out what happened on the Aberdeen range."

To his surprise, Girard actually waved off the answer. "Oh, I know that, sir," he said. "What I mean is, which series of manufacture? Type 12-P-2, 12-P-5, or 12-P-6?"

"There's a difference?" Sikander asked. Now it was his turn to be confused. He'd learned a lot about warp torpedoes in the last few weeks, and he hadn't seen anything that suggested that there was any variance at all between manufacture series. "The maintenance procedures for any 12-P are the same, aren't they? And the control software, too, as far as I know."

"Well, no, there isn't any difference in software or maintenance procedures," Girard said, "but the torpedoes are actually just a little bit different. The 12-P-2s were fleet depot yard upgrades of the old 11-P Phantoms. The two torpedo models have the same drive and the same casing, so when the fleet switched to the Type 12, they just replaced the old warheads, control boards, and software with an upgrade kit. The 12-P-5s and later series were manufactured new. So which one did you want me to set up the emulator for, sir?"

Sikander stared at him for a long moment. Then he quickly referred to his own dataslate. A few quick keystrokes in the ship's magazine records confirmed what Girard was saying . . . and maybe, just maybe, solved the never-to-be-sufficiently-damned Torpedo Mystery once and for all. He grinned in triumph. "The 12-P-2, Mr. Girard," he answered. "Our missing torpedo is a Phantom Type 12-P-2. And the one that we recovered was a Type 12-P-5. In theory they're identical, but now we know that somehow they are *not*."

Girard frowned. "Sir, I know I asked the question, but after the depot upgrade, they're really the same torp. I was just trying to make sure I had the precise versions for the emulation program."

"Don't sell yourself short," Sikander told him. "I think you may have cracked the case, whether you know it or not. Hold off on running that set of emulations I requested. What I want you to do now is set up a component-by-component comparison of the series-2 and the series-5. Find out *exactly* what is different between them."

Girard began nodding. "And that will tell us which specific software updates and maintenance procedures to focus on as the cause of the torpedo failure."

"Exactly." Sikander adjusted his cap on his head. As curious as he was about what Girard would find, that was clearly a secondary priority at the moment. "Advise me as soon as you have any progress—"

He was interrupted by the ship's info assistant. "Lieutenant North, the landing force has been ordered to deploy. Your presence is requested in the hangar bay."

"Understood. I am on my way," Sikander answered the computer. He turned back to Girard. "Thank you, Mr. Girard. Good work. I look forward to your report."

"I'll get on it immediately," Girard promised. "Good luck, sir."

"Thanks," said Sikander. "It sounds like we might need it." He clapped the young ensign on the shoulder, then hurried on down to the hangar bay.

11

Tanjeer, Gadira II

Chaos reigned in the streets of the capital as two of *Hector*'s orbital shuttles streaked low over dun-colored buildings and dusty palms. Sikander checked his seat harness and tried to ignore the lurching sensation in his stomach as the shuttle pilots jinked and slalomed between the taller buildings and the occasional minaret or comm tower. They had to avoid the controlled airspace around the palace, which meant spending more time over Tanjeer's crowded outlying districts than Sikander would have liked, especially since the local insurgents had so recently demonstrated that they had the capability of knocking flyers out of the sky. Petty Officer Long and the other shuttle pilot certainly proceeded as if they expected to be fired on at any moment.

"I do not like the looks of this," Darvesh Reza murmured, watching the rooftops and crowded streets passing by beneath the small viewports in the shuttle's passenger area. Like the rest of the landing force, he wore battle dress and carried a mag rifle, although he wore a small turban instead of a fatigue cap. He gave Sikander a long look, but did not voice any more objections. They were commited at this point, after all.

"Nor do I," Sikander admitted. "At least we're not Royal Guards or Montréalais. The locals have no particular reason to be upset with us."

"I suspect one offworlder looks like another to most of these people, Nawabzada. I would not count on a different uniform to deflect their anger."

"So noted," Sikander replied. Then he gripped his seat as the pilot threw the shuttle into one more sharp turn and dove down to the ground, landing heavily inside the walls of the consulate compound. The hatch by Sikander cycled open, and a barrage of impressions—the bright late-afternoon sunlight, the humid air, the smell of smoke, and more ominously the distant pop-pop or chirp-chirp of distant gunfire—assaulted his senses all at once.

Darvesh gave him one more look, but Sikander ignored him and scrambled out of the hatch. The valet and fifteen more of *Hector*'s sailors armed for ground combat followed him. Forty meters away, on the other side of the courtyard, the second shuttle likewise landed and opened its hatches; Sublieutenant Larkin, Chief Trent, and the rest of the landing force quickly exited and fanned out. Sikander moved aside and studied the scene, allowing Larkin to direct the sailors to take positions around the consulate grounds. He had no reason to believe he would do it better than she would, and he wanted to keep focused on overall situational awareness.

The consulate itself was a small palace in the heart of Tanjeer's Sidi Marouf neighborhood. Over the last forty years, the Sidi Marouf had grown into the heart of offworlder activity on Gadira; the picturesque manors that had formerly sheltered Gadira's wealthy old families had been quickly bought up by Montréalais or Aquilan businessmen, who were fantastically rich by Gadiran standards and could afford to live in the planet's most affluent neighborhood. Handsome low-rise buildings nearby harbored banks, corporate headquarters, luxury apartments, theaters, and restaurants catering to offworlders with money to spend. Sikander observed that some of the nearby rooftops commanded the area inside the consulate walls; snipers overhead might be a real concern if a siege situation developed. Bricks and broken bottles littered the courtyard, and most of the consulate's windows were broken.

He turned his attention to the front entrance, an ornamental iron gate that was currently closed. Two plainclothes Aquilan security agents stood guard nearby, while scores of Gadiran men—some dressed in Montréalais-style working clothes, others in more traditional Gadiran robes—protested just outside, shouting angrily or waving signs with Jadeed-Arabi slogans Sikander couldn't read. He found the experience unsettling, since he'd never been to a planet where he couldn't understand what the people were saying; Standard Anglic was universal among Commonwealth worlds, and of course he understood the High Panjabi and Tari Urdu spoken in Kashmir. In any event, the sudden arrival of two large shuttles and deployment of well-armed soldiers momentarily quieted the crowd.

Larkin trotted up to Sikander, with Chief Trent a step behind her. "We've secured the compound walls, sir," she reported. "I've got two squads on the perimeter, and one reserve here in the courtyard with our shuttles. The back gate and the alleyway behind the consulate seem clear, but we think they're being watched. We'd better assume that trouble might come from that direction at any time."

"Do we have any drones in the air?" Sikander asked.

"Four Dragonflies, sir," Chief Trent answered. The thumb-sized remotes combined excellent vidcams with stealthy profiles, good endurance, simple operation, and the ability to perch, creep, or hover as needed. Combined with *Hector*'s orbital cameras, they'd go a long way toward keeping anything from surprising the landing force.

"Very well," Sikander replied. "Your dispositions seem

good to me, Ms. Larkin. Make sure we keep an eye on those rooftops, and instruct your troops to set their rifles for non-lethal fire. I'm going to find Mr. Garcia and see what else we can do to help."

"Yes, sir," Larkin answered. She remembered not to salute; one never knew who might be watching, after all.

Sikander headed into the consulate building; Darvesh followed him. Inside, the place was in almost as much chaos as the streets outside were. Half a dozen consular employees in the outer office busily collected dataslates and sterilized information-storage devices, or locked up valuables against a possible attack. Sikander continued on in to the interior office, and knocked on the doorframe. "Consul Garcia?" he called.

Franklin Garcia sat on the edge of his desk, watching several vid feeds at the same time. An administrative assistant worked around him, stashing small valuables and important documents in sturdy boxes. Garcia looked over at Sikander, and allowed himself a sigh of relief. "Mr. North," he said. "Words cannot express how happy I am to see the Navy this afternoon. Most of our local security guards have chosen to call in sick today. We've been afraid that the mob outside would decide to scale the walls while we were short-handed."

"Hopefully we'll deter them from anything like that," Sikander replied. "We've got the compound secured for now. What else can we be doing?"

Garcia pointed at one of the vidscreens. "First Bank of High Albion," he replied. "They've called me five times in the last half hour. We've got a dozen Aquilan citizens and local employees pinned in by another large crowd, and they tell me they're taking small-arms fire."

Sikander studied the screen that the diplomat indicated. The consulate sat on a relatively quiet residential street, but it looked like the bank occupied the corner of a major intersection, and the crowd gathered outside it was substantially larger. A vehicle burned just outside the bank's front door. "Where is this?" he asked.

"Five blocks west of here. Can you send some troops over to disperse the crowd or escort the people back to the consulate?"

"That's a much larger crowd than the one outside your door," Sikander said slowly. "Darvesh, what do you think?" Darvesh had twenty years' more experience with civil disorders and urban combat scenarios than he did, after all.

"We don't have the numbers to disperse a crowd of that size without employing heavy weapons," Darvesh told him. "The repercussions of such a decision I leave to your imagination, sir."

Sikander suppressed a shudder. Most of the demonstrators on-screen were unarmed. They might be hostile toward offworlders at the moment, but he was certain that slaughtering scores or hundreds of Gadirans would in no way advance Aquila's interests in this system. "We'd better look for a way to get the bank employees out of there, then," he said. "Did you say this was just five blocks away, Mr. Garcia?"

"I did," the consul confirmed. "I can't tell you much about the condition of the streets between here and there, though."

"We've got reconnaissance assets in place, so we'll know more soon," said Sikander. "But I think that it would be very dangerous to put troops on the street right now. No, the way to go is to fly the civilians out of there. If they can get to the roof, we can have one of the shuttles pick them up."

"Ground fire may be a risk, sir," Darvesh pointed out.

"It's the best option I see," Sikander replied. "Mr. Garcia, contact the bank and tell them to get to the roof, or even a higher-floor window. We'll make arrangements to move them to safety."

"I'm on it," the consul replied. He picked up his desk comm, and started to dial.

Sikander hurried back outside to the courtyard, and motioned to Larkin and Trent to meet him by the first shuttle. The angry roar of the crowd seemed to fill the air, echoing between the low-rise apartments and businesses of the Sidi Marouf. A rock thrown over the consulate's outer wall clattered off the shuttle's stubby wing; he jumped in spite of himself, and turned to keep half an eye on the front gate while waiting. *Maybe bringing civilians to the consulate isn't the right move,* he thought. *Maybe we should be evacuating everyone we can to some safe place out in the countryside.* The problem was, he didn't know what might qualify as a safe place.

Petty Officer Long cracked the hatch by the shuttle's cockpit, opening it just enough to speak to Sikander while taking advantage of the cover it provided. "What's going on, Mr. North?" he asked.

"One moment." Sikander waited for Larkin and Trent to join him, then addressed all three together. "We need to rescue some civilians trapped in a bank building a few blocks over. Getting them out on the ground seems problematic, but we might be able to take them off the roof. Here, let me show you." He opened his dataslate and picked up the feed from the nearest Dragonfly, steering the tiny drone to show the First Bank of High Albion and the ugly mob surrounding it.

The three Aquilans watched for a long moment. "The flight space is a little cramped, but I think I can get the shuttle in there," Long said. "I don't like the look of the crowd, though."

"I'll take a half squad of riflemen along for security," Sikander said. "Ms. Larkin, find me half a dozen steady hands. Long, figure out the best way to get in and out of there."

"Yes, sir," Long replied. He ducked back into the cockpit and pulled up his own recon feed.

"Chief, let's send half our reserve squad," Larkin told Trent. "I don't want to pull anyone off the perimeter."

"Yes, ma'am." Chief Trent nodded, and hurried off to gather a crew.

The instant the chief was out of easy earshot, Larkin turned on Sikander. "Sir, you shouldn't go. You're in command here—I should go instead."

"I need you here to maintain tactical control of the consulate," Sikander told her. "I'm the extra officer. I'll go."

Larkin fell silent, fixing her eyes on the shuttle hull behind Sikander. He could almost feel the barriers slamming into place behind her expressionless face. For a woman who wasn't more than twenty-five years in age, Angela Larkin had some of the densest armor he had ever seen; her finely shaped features might as well have been carved out of surgical steel. "Do you lack confidence in my ability to get this job done, sir?" she asked.

Now what do I do? Sikander wondered. That was exactly his concern, although he could hardly be honest about it. He decided to make the decision about him, not her. "No, Ms. Larkin," he answered. "I know you are trained for landing operations. But I have some personal experience with riots and civil unrest. I am sorry to say that this sort of situation comes up from time to time on my homeworld."

"I know." A shadow of old pain flickered across the younger officer's face. "My father was very nearly killed serving in Kashmir. As I understand the story, it was a situation a lot like this one."

Her father was wounded in Kashmir? Sikander remembered seeing a note in Larkin's service jacket that her father was a retired officer in the Commonwealth Army, but he hadn't paid attention to the exact date or the circumstances; normally, they wouldn't have been any of his business. A suspicion took shape in Sikander's mind. "When was your father injured?"

"It was 3077, the Palarist Uprising. He was shot and blinded while under orders not to fire back." Larkin took a deep breath. "The doctors did the best they could, but he's never seen me with his own eyes."

Sikander nodded to himself. All of the sudden, many things about his difficult start with the younger officer made a good deal more sense. Twenty-five years ago, the Palarist movement had racked large parts of Jaipur and Srinagar. Nationalists and extremists had rioted for weeks, protesting Aquilan rule over Kashmir and demanding more autonomy. Thousands of Aquilan troops had been involved in the fighting. In fact, the terrorists who had struck at Nawab Dayan and the North clan during the Bandi Chor Divas had been Palarists, fighting on fifteen years after their defeat. *No wonder she finds it difficult to serve alongside me. Every time she sees me, she is reminded of her father's injury.*

He met Larkin's eyes. "My family, too, fought against the Palarists. You must understand that many Kashmiris died at their hands. Their reckless violence hurt both my people and yours."

"I didn't know that, Mr. North," Larkin admitted.

"This is not Kashmir. Most of the demonstrators outside the walls are not our enemies—they are angry and misguided, and they don't know what else to do. Yes, we can't let them hurt people we're here to protect. But we have to be careful not to make things worse."

Larkin nodded. "Yes, sir."

"Very well, Ms. Larkin." Sikander took a step back and signaled to Chief Trent, waiting a short distance away with the armed sailors she'd gathered. "It's your shuttle. Inform your team that they are not to fire unless you release them to return fire, and do so only as a last resort. We don't want to take any chance of hitting noncombatants."

"Understood, sir." Larkin motioned to the sailors of her detachment. They quickly boarded the shuttle as Sikander backed away to give Long plenty of room to lift off. With a shrill whine of the engines, the stubby vehicle kicked up off the ground. It hovered just above the consulate grounds for a moment, and then slewed around and disappeared over the surrounding rooftops.

Darvesh watched the armed shuttle fly off. "You allowed the sublieutenant to go?"

"She was right to insist—it's her job. And I seem to recall that you had some words for me about choosing my risks more carefully."

"I am surprised that for once you heeded my advice, Nawabzada."

"I promise I won't make a habit of it," Sikander told him, watching the feed from the Dragonfly drone as the shuttle moved into position and alighted on the bank's rooftop. Then he made himself put away his dataslate and pay attention to the neighborhood immediately around the consulate. Plenty of people would be watching the shuttle's rescue attempt, and he didn't need the temptation of micromanaging Larkin's efforts via vid feed. He settled for quickly circling the compound, checking the positions of the landing force. Four sailors protected the front gate, staying back around the wall to minimize their exposure. The low roof of a garage that stood up against the compound's eastern wall provided a good vantage for another fire team to protect that whole side of the grounds, while the windows and roof of the consulate building itself offered good positions for another fire team to guard the back of the compound. He left Chief Trent in charge there. But the western wall offered no good places for a rifleman to stand and look over its four-meter parapet—anything could be going on just on the other side of the wall, and the Aquilans would have no idea. Sikander settled for repositioning one of the Dragonflies to provide a constant view of the street on that side of the compound, and instructed the fire team there to keep a close eye on its video feed.

"Is there anything we're overlooking?" he asked Darvesh as he studied the compound defenses again.

"The consulate cannot be held against a determined

attack, sir," said the Kashmiri soldier. "It simply comes down to whether or not the people in the streets outside have the motivation to make such an attack. Your guess about that is as good as mine."

"I do not find that reassuring," Sikander muttered. He glanced at the video from the Dragonfly watching over the bank evacuation. The shuttle remained parked on the rooftop. Several of Larkin's squad knelt with mag rifles raised as they covered different quadrants around the rear hatch, while the rest of the team hurried to move a handful of civilians from a roof access panel to the shuttle. It seemed to be going slowly.

He keyed his comm device and spoke. "Status report, Ms. Larkin?"

"Taking fire, sir. Several of the civilians are wounded. We're moving as fast as we can."

"Very well," he replied. Larkin had enough on her mind for the moment; he didn't need to distract her with extra orders or suggestions. Instead, he keyed the two medics in the landing force. "Thierry, Niles, it sounds like Ms. Larkin will have wounded civilians on board when she returns. Be ready to treat casualties."

"Yes, sir," the two medics answered. A few moments later, they appeared by the consulate building entrance and hurried over to wait beside Sikander. He glanced again at his vid feed just in time to see *Hector*'s shuttle lift off from the rooftop. Silent puffs of paint and dust showed the impact of bullets on the hull. Small-arms fire posed little threat to the orbital shuttles; they were rugged craft. But if the Caidists in the crowd had any more of their antiair missiles, it might be a different story.

The shuttle darted out of the Dragonfly's view, accelerating hard as soon as it was clear of the rooftop obstructions. Sikander heard the low hum of the returning shuttle's induction engines echoing through the streets, growing louder as it quickly spanned the short distance between the bank and the consulate. Then the shuttle suddenly appeared overhead, circled around just above the rooftops, and set down again in the consulate courtyard. The crowd outside the front gate shouted in consternation and anger, and a new shower of bricks and bottles came over the wall. Sikander hurried over to the main hatch, with the two medics just a few steps behind him.

The hatch slid open, and Angela Larkin hopped out. Without a word to Sikander she turned and immediately helped down a crewman bleeding from a bad leg wound. More than a dozen civilians—three Aquilans judging by their clothing, the rest Gadirans dressed in business attire now torn or rumpled in some cases—tumbled out of the shuttle as soon as the wounded sailor was clear. "Head for the consulate!" Sikander shouted to them, and pointed the way. "Right over there!"

An old-style rifle barked from somewhere high and behind Sikander. One of the civilians running for the consulate door, an older Gadiran man in a good suit, grunted and stumbled, falling on his face. A neat round hole between his shoulder blades oozed red.

"Sniper!" several voices called over the tactical comm network at the same time. Civilians and sailors alike scattered in terror, seeking cover anywhere they could find it or throwing themselves flat on the ground. Sikander ducked back under the shuttle's stubby wing, and managed to knock his helmet against the fuselage hard enough to bite his tongue.

I have been here before, he realized. *The panic, the screams, the taste of blood—*

—in his mouth. Then he becomes aware of the sounds: shouts of dismay, thin wails of pain, the ringing echoes of the blast all strangely dull and distant to his ears.

Sikander slowly levers himself upright from the wreckage of the reviewing stand. It's difficult to make out what he is looking at. Ceremonial costumes are nothing but colorful tatters; smoke roils across Sangrur's central square while Jaipur Dragoons scramble to reach the nawab's family. He can see his own fear and confusion mirrored in their expressions.

To his left, Nawab Dayan seems to be sitting up, but his mother, Vadiya North, rolls from side to side, her hands clapped to her face. Sikander's brothers Devindar and Manvir, his sister Usha, his cousins, likewise begin to pick themselves up. Thank God, Sikander thinks. They're all alive. But Mother—!

He picks his way through the wreckage to go to her side. Then, not two meters from Sikander, his brother Gamand suddenly spins in a half circle and falls back into his seat with a grunt, blood pouring from his shoulder. An instant later the chirping report of a high-velocity mag rifle echoes through the air.

"Shots fired! Shots fired!" his cousin Amarleen shouts. She is only fourteen, but she dashes to Gamand and tears the sash off her ceremonial dress. Blood splatters the rich gold cloth as she does her best to apply pressure to the wound.

Sikander whirls around, looking for the shooter. From the time he was old enough to absorb the lessons, he was taught to evaluate security threats and survive worst-case scenarios. That training kicks in now, overriding his shock and horror. He grasps the plot in a sudden flash: The Palarists set off the bomb to wreck the grandstand and blow down the bulletproof glass panels, while a rifleman waits to take advantage of any shots presented.

"Across the street!" Sikander yells to the nawab's dragoons. One of the stand's dislodged glass panels lies almost at Sikander's feet. He stoops down, gets his hands under the glass, and lifts. The panel weighs almost ninety kilos, but Sikander doesn't need to pick it up—he only needs to stand it up on its edge. He rips his fine tunic raising the *armored glass, but he wrestles the panel upright and holds it there, interposing it between his wounded brother and the sniper. A heartbeat later, something punches the center of the panel right in front of him with a heavy* thunk! *and a white spiderweb cracks the armored glass. The impact almost carries the panel out of his hands.*

"I have it, Nawabzada Sikander." A tall, black-bearded soldier—Darvesh Reza, a senior sergeant in the Jaipur Dragoons—moves to stand beside him, taking the panel from his hands. "Please, go with the others. We must get the nawab to safety."

Sikander relinquishes his burden. Dragoons in gaudy parade uniforms swarm around him, sweeping him out of the ruined stands toward the waiting flyers, shielding him and the rest of his family with their own bodies. . . .

Someone grabbed Sikander's arm and jerked him back as another rifle shot rang out. The bullet kicked a puff of dust from the ground not far from where the Gadiran bank manager fell. Harsh daylight and the smell of smoke in the air brought him back to Tanjeer's streets. Darvesh—leaner, grayer, and less splendidly attired than he'd been in Sangrur that night ten years ago—gave him a sharp look, and returned to scanning the rooftops surrounding the Aquilan consulate.

This is not Jaipur, Sikander told himself. *And these are not Palarists.* He pulled his eyes away from the dead or dying man in front of him, and made himself lock away the terrible memories of the Bandi Chor Divas bombing. "Thank you," he said. "That was careless of me."

"Think nothing of it, sir," Darvesh replied.

From his safer vantage, Sikander studied the rooftops overlooking the compound. He thought he glimpsed a shadow of movement at the edge of a rooftop, a long block away. "West side, rooftop at one hundred and fifty meters," he reported to his team. "If anyone's got a clean shot at the sniper, you're authorized to fire."

"Lieutenant, this is Chief Trent." The master-at-arms keyed Sikander's private channel. She was posted on the consulate building roof behind him. "I think the crowd by the bank is following the shuttle. There are a lot of people moving in this direction."

"Understood," he replied. The situation was getting complicated in a hurry. He turned to Sublieutenant Larkin, who sheltered behind the shuttle right beside him. "Good work at the bank, Ms. Larkin. It looks like you had your hands full there."

Larkin nodded, but kept scanning for more snipers on the rooftops. "I'm afraid we didn't get everybody, sir. Two of the bank employees were picked off as we were boarding the shuttle."

"I think this is turning into one of those days where we just do the best that we can," he told her. He risked another quick glimpse over the shuttle's nose. There was definitely more movement on the rooftops in that direction, and the shower of stones, bottles, and debris increased by the moment. Then a sudden commotion by the front gate caught his attention: Two men in traditional robes brought up a large loop of chain and started threading it through the bars. Sikander couldn't see if they had a vehicle ready to yank the gates out of the wall or if they hoped to do it with nothing more than human muscle power, but he couldn't let them carry out their plan. He pointed it out to Larkin. "We'd better put a stop to that," he told her.

"Yes, sir," she replied. "First fire team, single volley through the gate, nonlethal velocity! Torso or lower, we're trying not to kill anybody here. On my command . . . take aim . . . fire!"

At the gate, the half squad of sailors guarding the consulate's front entrance quickly popped out of their cover and leveled their mag rifles. The Gadirans pressed up against the gate by the crowd behind them shrieked in sudden panic and turned to move away, but none succeeded in clearing the line of fire before the mag rifles chirped. Unlike older weapons with cartridges full of chemical propellant, mag weapons could easily be adjusted for high-velocity or low-velocity shots. A low-velocity mag-rifle dart could still cause a great deal of injury, but the sabots encasing the dart-like rounds remained in place for a low-velocity shot, turning a lethal arrowhead into a thumb-sized blunt cylinder that wouldn't break the skin. It would, however, knock a strong man off his feet and leave quite a bruise. Half a dozen Gadirans yelped, tumbled, or sagged back from the volley, and suddenly the people pressing against the gate were no longer interested in standing right in front of the bars. The crowd immediately in front scattered; two of *Hector*'s sailors hurried up and disentangled the chain from the bars.

"That's better," Sikander said. Then the distant rifle cracked again, and a bullet bounced off the shuttle hull not half a meter over his head. He ducked and swore. "Does *anybody* have a shot at that damned sniper?" he demanded. No one answered.

He looked down at his vid feed from the Dragonflies, studying the crowds beginning to thicken around the consulate. One image captured several Gadiran riflemen lying prone on the rooftop, in plain sight to the tiny drone flying by overhead. If only Dragonflies were armed . . . but they were simply too small to carry anything remotely lethal, and too valuable to kamikaze into someone's ear in order to send a message. Sikander looked over to Darvesh, and met his eyes. *Motivation,* he reminded himself. He was beginning to form his own best guess about the insurgents' determination, and he didn't like the answer he was coming up with.

"*Hector,* this is Lieutenant North," he said into his comm.

"I recommend that we evacuate all consulate personnel and abandon the facility. This situation is becoming untenable."

There was a long pause; then the comm beeped in reply. "Mr. North, this is Lieutenant Commander Randall. We've been watching developments closely. I concur with your assessment, and I'm forwarding your recommendation to the captain. Stand by."

Larkin grimaced. "I hate the idea of letting our consulate get overrun. It's a bad message to send, sir."

"If you can see a way to stop it without killing a lot of people, you're smarter than I am," Sikander said. "We'll stand our ground if the captain orders us to stay. Otherwise, I intend to get our troops out of the way and let this mob burn itself out."

"Mr. North, this is Randall. You are ordered to withdraw. We're sending your pilots a flight path to a safe location fifteen kilometers northeast of the city. Get the civilians and your people out of there, over."

"Acknowledged," Sikander replied. The consulate staff and bank employees would be a tough fit in the two shuttles alongside *Hector*'s landing party, but for a short flight they'd make do. He met Larkin's eyes. "Time to go, Ms. Larkin. Pass the word, please."

"Yes, sir," she said. She took a deep breath, then broke cover and ran back toward the consulate in a low crouch, already shouting orders as she went along.

Sikander watched her move off, thinking about the implications of what Larkin had told him earlier, and replaying any of a half-dozen interactions with her over the last couple of months. She should have told someone about her family history with Kashmir before he'd ever set foot on board . . . but of course she wouldn't have wanted to seem like she was prejudiced against Kashmiris, even if she had reason to associate him with difficult emotions. But perhaps by bringing her story out into the open she could begin to move past it.

Another rifle shot interrupted his thoughts, and he ducked again. His eye fell on the Gadiran bank manager, lying motionless a few meters from the shuttle. In just a minute or two, they'd need to bring all the consulate personnel through the courtyard again. *We've got to do something about the snipers,* he realized. Suppressing fire might keep their heads down—and might play directly into the narrative the initiators of the riot hoped to create. But if there were some way to screen the civilians from potshots as they moved to the shuttles . . .

"Landing force, this is Lieutenant North," he said over the tactical net. "I want everybody to pop your smoke markers inside the courtyard. First squad, smoke the east wall. Second squad, smoke the west wall. Third squad, cover the front gate." The consulate building itself would cover the fourth side. "We need a smoke screen to cover the evacuation."

"Yes, sir," the various squad leaders replied. Sikander pulled out his own smoke grenade, pulled the pin, and rolled it a few meters away, producing a thick white cloud by the shuttle. He heard the sharp hiss of other grenades going off all around him, and saw dozens of smoke clouds billowing up from the ground along the walls before he was completely engulfed. Outside, the roar of the crowd swelled and echoed; the Caidist demonstrators could see that something was happening, but they didn't know whether it was dangerous or not.

"Good thinking, sir," Darvesh told him.

"We'll see," Sikander replied. He keyed his comm button. "Ms. Larkin, get the civilians to the shuttles. Lead them by hand if you have to." He waited in the shifting smoke. Shots still echoed through the air. Some of the snipers were shooting blindly into the smoke, he guessed. Well, there was nothing he could do about that. A moment later, a line of gray shapes appeared in the smoke, shuffling forward in single file with joined hands—the consulate civilians, coughing and cringing as they hurried to the shuttle hatch.

"Everyone aboard," Sikander told the first of them. He turned his attention back to the perimeter, trying to gauge how long the billowing clouds would last. People in business dress clambered into the shuttle one after another, murmuring words of thanks or stifling sobs of terror as they passed by. Then Chief Trent jogged up, with the squad of sailors from the consulate building and Consul Garcia at her side.

"The consulate's clear, sir," she reported to him.

"Good." Sikander raised his voice and called into the smoke. "Ms. Larkin? Embark your troops."

Garcia paused by the hatch, checking to see that his people were on board. Then he turned to Sikander. "My thanks, Mr. North. I hate to leave like this, though."

"I do, too," Sikander replied. "You'd better—" That was as far as he got, because at that moment Garcia suddenly grimaced and clapped a hand to his neck. A distant rifle report echoed above the noise of the crowd; whether the persistent sniper had found a clear patch of air to shoot through or had simply gotten ridiculously lucky, Sikander never knew. But a terrible spurt of blood burst out of Franklin Garcia's mouth, and he sagged to his knees with a wet, strangled gasp.

"Mr. Garcia!" Sikander cried. The consul clutched at Sikander's trouser leg, fighting for breath. Sikander reached down, grabbed him by the shoulders, and half carried, half threw the wounded man through the hatch into the shuttle's passenger compartment. A woman, one of the consulate secretaries, screamed at the sight, but Sikander didn't see what else he could do; the smoke was thinning, and his sailors pelted in from all sides, throwing themselves on board the shuttles.

"The compound's clear, Mr. North," Larkin reported over

the tactical comms. "All the landing force is accounted for. We're buttoning up Shuttle Two."

Sikander stared for a moment at the bloody handprints Garcia had left on his trousers and arm. "Buttoning up Shuttle One," he replied, and climbed through the hatch. "Petty Officer Long, get us out of here."

He had one last glimpse of the smoke-filled consulate and the surging crowds filling the streets outside before the shuttle streaked away. Franklin Garcia died five minutes later.

12

Harthawi Basin, Gadira II

Otto Bleindel counted forty-one operational grav tanks camped around the water station—the better part of an armored battalion. A third or so were the new Léopards. The rest were older Tatous, slower and less heavily armored than the recent additions, although still quite immune to anything short of a small K-cannon or antitank rocket. Mounted infantry in heavy-duty scout cars accompanied the Royal Guard armor, although in the heat of the afternoon none of them moved about the laager. City-dwelling Gadirans cultivated the midday *qaylulah* as a matter of comfort and ease; here, in the depths of the planet's unforgiving desert, resting during the hottest part of the day was a matter of life and death.

Good enough, Bleindel decided. He'd been following the reports from Tanjeer on his news feed all morning long. The capital was almost halfway around the planet; it was a few hours before dawn there now. Alonzo Khouri and his revolutionaries had kept the Royal Guard busy all night with riots and attacks in their backyard, but now it was up to the desert tribes to strike the next blow. Toppling a government was like chopping down a tree; no one was strong enough to bring it down with one clean stroke, but the cumulative effect of many small ax bites would serve just as well . . . and if you knew what you were doing, the weight of the tree itself would finish the job for you.

The Dremish agent swept his binoculars over the force below him one more time, looking for anything he might have missed. Not many trees here, that was for certain. More important, he didn't see any combat flyers, either. The desert Caidists had made a point of targeting the sultan's airpower at every opportunity, expending surface-to-air missiles at a prodigious rate to whittle down the Royal Guard's most important advantage.

Bleindel finished his observation and scooted back carefully behind the brush, moving slowly to avoid raising a telltale puff of dust on the long, low hillside. He turned to Caid Harsaf el-Tayib, who likewise was lying on his belly studying the sultan's tanks. "It looks like they've settled exactly where we thought they would, Caid Harsaf," he said. "I can't see any reason to wait."

Caid Harsaf snorted. "By which you mean you are ready for me to poke this nest of scorpions whenever it suits me." He was a wiry, gray-bearded tribal chieftain, his skin burned to dark brown leather by a hard life in the Harthawi Basin, a vast region of scrub plains and broken hills between two dry mountain ranges. The water station currently occupied by the sultan's soldiers belonged to Harsaf el-Tayib's tribe, providing a rare source of clean, pure water in the middle of what was otherwise one of the more inhospitable places Bleindel had ever visited. "The el-Manjouri had better be ready."

Bleindel checked his dataslate. "They're in place," he told the desert chieftain. Convincing the hardheaded desert fighters to let him track their tactical movements hadn't been easy, but results were what counted. The green icons representing the el-Tayib tribe and their neighbors (and occasional rivals), the el-Manjour tribe, were arranged more or less as he intended. They wouldn't stay there for long, of course—sooner or later one of the fighters would get bored or anxious, and begin firing without regard for what should be a clear and simple tactical plan. However, that suggested just the right way to handle the proud Harsaf. "Best to get started, before Caid Ahmed and his men find a way to ruin the surprise."

Caid Harsaf spat and nodded. "Maybe you're right." He rolled over and looked back down the slope to where his fighters were gathered. He gave one shrill whistle and waved his hand; below them, five teams of el-Tayib fighters quickly dropped their mortar bombs down the short barrels of their weapons and fired off a volley in the direction of the encampment two kilometers distant.

The mortars were simple and ancient weapons indeed; even Gadira's backward industrial complex could have produced the tubes without trouble. Importing any kind of heavy artillery from offworld was not very practical, but modern mortar bombs weighed only a few kilos each and made locally produced tubes into very effective weapons for their size and portability. These rounds included a mix of guided armor-penetrating antivehicle rounds that could identify grav tanks and transports, steering themselves toward likely targets as they came down, and air-burst fragmentation weapons that showered troops in the open with lethal shrapnel. Even before the first rounds hit, the crews dropped more bombs into the tubes; the steady *whump! whump!* of the mortars firing battered Bleindel like big, soft punches.

"Hah!" Caid Harsaf shouted as the first volley hit. Airbursts exploded above the encamped battalion; one mortar bomb found a scout transport and blew it up in spectacular fashion, creating an orange fireball and a cloud of black smoke that rose slowly into the hot desert air. Bleindel felt the explosions through the ground beneath his belly, and grinned. One of the old Tatou grav tanks brewed up a moment later, killed by the shaped charge of an armor-penetrating bomb, but he saw a small black burst of smoke on the turret of a Léopard where another such weapon failed to destroy the newer tank.

"Damn it!" the caid snarled, pointing at the grav tank Otto was watching. It now began to move, its turret slewing from side to side. "Your bombs are too light for the newer tanks!"

"I thought that might be the case." Bleindel shrugged. "It doesn't change the plan. Keep firing, you're doing plenty of damage to the other vehicles." *And any Royal Guards unfortunate enough to be outside of armor plating, as well as the station's pump mechanisms,* he thought. Well, the el-Tayibs could always fix their pump later.

He took a moment to scan the horizon in a full 360 degrees, looking for any other threats. It was all too easy to get caught up in the spectacle of a barrage and forget that sometimes your enemies weren't where they were supposed to be. The Harthawi Basin was not as flat as its name implied. Long, rolling slopes covered in clumps of thorny desert vegetation two or three meters high provided surprisingly good cover to those who knew the terrain—and whatever one might think of the desert tribes' lack of discipline or antiquated beliefs, they certainly did. Caid Harsaf had easily brought two hundred fighters within mortar range of an alert enemy equipped with modern fighting vehicles. In fact, if Bleindel had asked, Harsaf might have been able to get his men within rifle range without being spotted. Fortunately, that was not required today.

"They are moving out," Caid Harsaf growled.

Bleindel looked back toward the encampment. Sure enough, dozens of the grav tanks pushed out of their laager, heading in his direction. They left at least six or seven armored vehicles burning behind them in the wreckage of the water station. *That's what will really hurt them,* he decided. It was fifty kilometers to the next source of water.

"Time to let them see us run," he told Harsaf. "Leave the tubes, but take the mortar bombs."

The caid nodded and shouted orders at his tribesmen in Jadeed-Arabi. Bleindel had been studying diligently for weeks now, but he still found the language hard to make out. Fortunately most of Harsaf's exhortations consisted of swearing at his followers. The Dremish agent got up and hurried down the reverse slope of the low hill to where half a dozen light transports waited. Getting them into position without raising suspicious clouds of dust had required hours of driving along at a walking pace and choosing a circuitous route that kept the rise and fall of the land between the tribe's vehicles and the water station, but now that painstaking effort would pay off—or so he hoped.

"This would be a good time to pray, infidel," Caid Harsaf told him as they climbed into one of the flatbed vehicles. He grinned, a flash of bright teeth. "The allameh Hadji Tumar says that God in his mercy heeds the prayers of unbelievers and believers alike, although I have my doubts."

"Then I will hope for both our sakes that your allameh"—some sort of teacher or scholar, if Bleindel remembered correctly—"is correct in this regard." He held on as Caid Harsaf gunned the transport's motor and surged up out of the shallow valley behind the hill, with half a dozen more fighters clinging to the jolting transport's back and sides. There was no hiding their movements now; speed was their only hope, although the thick dust kicked up by the bouncing transports certainly helped to obscure them from the pursuing soldiers.

Bleindel anchored himself in place by bracing one arm against the dashboard. They raced off across the desert, flattening small clumps of brush and dodging around the thicker ones. To either side, the rest of the el-Tayib transports bounced and sped alongside them, forming a great uneven semicircle as they fled toward the north. Behind them came the Royal Guard grav tanks and scout cars, relentless in their pursuit. The military vehicles were a little slower than the tribesmen's own civilian transports, but they were built to handle tougher terrain—and they were armed with K-cannons that could reach out and kill from a very long way on open ground. The flatbed racing alongside Bleindel's own vehicle suddenly erupted in a burst of mangled metal and flying bodies, wrecked by a hypersonic round whose report came two heartbeats after it hit. Then another one of the el-Tayib transports slewed aside and buried its nose in the sandy ground, knocked out by a second shot.

"Damn good shooting!" Caid Harsaf shouted. He was right—there was so much dust behind the fleeing tribesmen that the grav tanks behind them couldn't have been shooting by sight. Belatedly Bleindel recalled that the Léopards had both advanced radar and thermal targeting capabilities. He wondered how long it would take for one of the sultan's grav tanks to get around to blowing his own light transport to bits, and did his best to ignore the crawling, itching sensation between his shoulder blades as he heard the earsplitting whine of additional K-rounds streaking past the fleeing tribesmen. He was not ashamed to heave a sigh of relief when the shrinking convoy finally reached the cover of a broad wadi a couple of kilometers behind their original position, and momentarily broke line of sight.

"That was entirely too close," he admitted. "To your left, Caid Harsaf."

"I have not forgotten," the desert chieftain replied. He slewed the transport into a broad curve and streaked off down the dry riverbed, the remainder of his tribe's vehicles following him. They rounded a large outcropping of worn boulders, and the caid quickly turned their light transport behind the rocks while the rest of his men continued on.

Bleindel hopped out of the cab and scrambled up to peer

over a boulder at the pursuing force. They came speeding over the desert, firing wildly as they followed the fleeing tribesmen. *Nest of scorpions is not quite the right metaphor,* he decided. *More like a herd of blood-maddened bulls goaded into a killing rage.* The leading vehicles broke out from the thorny brush and into the relatively open wadi, turning to chase the el-Tayibs.

At that moment, Caid Ahmed and his el-Manjouri struck. From the heavy brush on the opposite bank of the wadi, a score of antiarmor rockets streaked out to hammer the Royal Guard grav tanks, while insurgents armed with new mag rifles opened up on the lighter scout cars. Explosion after explosion rocked the desert, as Tatous brewed up and Léopards staggered under the warheads. Maybe half the rockets missed—after all, the Caidist fighters hadn't had much practice with antiarmor weaponry before—but the ones that hit did plenty of damage, and even the misses contributed to the chaos of the moment by rocking the ground with stray blasts that showered vehicles nearby with fountains of dirt.

"Ha!" shouted Caid Harsaf, joining Bleindel behind the boulder. "Kill those city-dwelling dogs, you Manjouri bastards!" He waved a fist in the air as shrapnel hissed and pelted off the boulders around them. A piece of barrel from a grav tank's main armament actually sailed completely over the boulder jumble sheltering the two men, and thudded into the sand twenty meters behind them. It must have weighed at least five hundred kilos.

"My men stand and fight, while yours run for their lives!" Another gray-bearded tribesmen, this one a short, round-bodied fellow in a dusty keffiyeh, scrambled into the sheltered vantage where Bleindel and Caid Harsaf watched the battle.

"That is unfair, Ahmed," Caid Harsaf said, glaring at the other chieftain. "We diced for which tribe would stand and which would pretend to run. This is as God willed it, and my men played their part well."

Caid Ahmed of the el-Manjour answered Harsaf's angry look with a wide grin. "As you say, Harsaf. Your men run very well indeed."

Bleindel ignored the two chieftains, keeping his eyes on the battle. He'd spent only a few hours with them—after all, he was doing his best to be in a hundred places at once as he coordinated arms deliveries, stirred up riots and protests in the major cities, and urged the pugnacious desert tribes into useful action—but he'd already come to the conclusion that despite all their protestations, Harsaf and Ahmed were firm friends. Better yet, they seemed eager to find out what they could do with the modern weapons he was able to deliver through el-Fasi's shipping network. This deadly skirmish seemed to be a matter of sport to them.

More rockets fired off, now shooting in ragged volleys as different teams struggled to reload their weapons and fire at their best speed. The Royal Guards opened up on the brush and boulders of the wadi's dry bank, autorifles whining and chirping as they scythed back and forth. The grav tanks still had plenty of teeth, and the concentrated firepower was terrible to behold. They simply sterilized whole patches of desert with storms of mag darts, but most were firing blindly; the ambushers were well hidden. The furious barrage silenced some of the el-Manjour tribesmen, but others kept up their fire. Three of the rocket teams happened to target the same Léopard at once, and this time the Montréalais tank's armor didn't hold—it blew apart, its main turret spinning through the air. Abruptly the remaining Royal Guard combat vehicles spurred into motion again, wheeling about to flee back the way they had come and escape the killing ground. The autorifle fire slackened as the targets disappeared into the ever-present dust.

Bleindel scrambled up on top of a low boulder for a better vantage. Yes, there was no doubt of it. The badly mauled battalion was in full retreat, heading back toward the water station, most likely inoperable now. Nine more Royal Guard combat vehicles burned in the wadi, adding their thick black smoke to the billowing dust. He smiled in satisfaction. "Well done, Caid Harsaf. And you, too, Caid Ahmed. The sultan is going to miss those grav tanks sorely, I think."

"We should hit them again tonight," Caid Ahmed said. "One or two more shocks like this and we will chase them completely out of the Harthawi."

"I think you might be correct, but that's not what we need from your fighters. The best place for the Royal Guard is right here in the middle of your desert. Let's see if we can keep them here for a few more weeks." Bleindel lowered himself back to the ground again. "Draw them in deeper after you. Encourage them to chase you, and when they give up, sting them again to goad them on, or feign weakness and lure them in."

Caid Ahmed and Caid Harsaf exchanged glances. "It is the height of folly to allow an enemy to learn your strength," Harsaf said. "If blows are to be struck, strike hard and finish your foe."

"True," Bleindel admitted. "But the goal is not just to defeat the sultan's army. You also need to break Montréal's grip on your planet, and right now, the best way to do that is to help the Royal Guard waste the better part of its strength here in your desert. Speaking of which, it is time for me to move on. I think I can count on a pair of sly old desert foxes to look after things here for now."

"Where are you going?" Ahmed demanded.

"To and fro in the earth, and walking up and down in it," Bleindel said with a cryptic smile.

Caid Harsaf gave him a sharp look. "That is from the story of Job," he said. "I thought you were not a Believer."

"I have been reading up." Of course, that was what

Satan had told God when God asked what he'd been up to lately. He salaamed to both men. "I should have another shipment of weapons for you in a week or so. Contact me if anything unexpected comes up." Then Otto Bleindel jogged off into the desert, headed for the spot where his flyer was hidden. He had a lot to do, and not enough time.

13

CSS *Hector*, Gadira II Orbit

The riots in the capital lasted for three days. When the Royal Guard finally succeeded in restoring order in Tanjeer, a huge strike by disaffected workers in Nador paralyzed the sprawling offworlder industrial plants there. *Hector*'s landing force was obliged to execute two more evacuations of local consular offices, as well as protect a new Aquilan-owned tidal power station from an unruly demonstration, disperse a crowd immobilizing a lev train carrying Aquilan goods, and rescue a news team from High Albion that managed to wander into the wrong neighborhood at the wrong time. And those were just the disturbances that directly touched on Aquilan interests; there were two or three times as many Montréalais investments on Gadira, and the sultanate's forces were hard-pressed to protect them all. Sikander himself made three landings within a week of the Sidi Marouf riot, and Angela Larkin at least five or six more without him.

He was just finishing a report on the news-team incident at the desk in his stateroom when his comm beeped at him again. Sikander sighed and keyed it, wondering where he'd be headed next. "Lieutenant North," he answered.

"Mr. North, this is Sublieutenant Larkin. I'm in the

gunnery office with Ensign Girard. We think we've made some progress on the torpedo failure."

"You did?" Sikander had almost forgotten about the missing torpedo over the last few days. "When in the world did you find the time to work on it?"

"I'm not on the watch rotation now, so I've been working with Mr. Girard whenever I'm back on the ship," Larkin replied. "I suppose it gave me something else to think about instead of riots and snipers."

Sikander could certainly understand the desire to put the troubles down on the surface out of mind for an hour or two. "I'll be right there," he said. Stretching his legs and thinking about something different for a while sounded like a good idea to him, too.

He grabbed his cap and headed down to the Gunnery Department office. Larkin and Girard were waiting for him, along with Chief Torpedo Mate Maroth, the senior enlisted man in Larkin's division. Sikander could see Larkin's fatigue in the set of her shoulders and rumpled uniform, but her eyes remained bright and alert, and she greeted him with a confident smile. "Mr. North. Thank you for coming down."

"I'm in need of some good news today, Ms. Larkin." He joined the others at the table. "What have you found out?"

Larkin picked up the remote controlling the office's vid display, and brought up an image of the schematics of a Phantom Type 12 torpedo. "You'll recall that the older Phantom Type 12s were upgrades from the Type 11 with new warheads. The top image is the Type 12-P-2, which was the torpedo that went missing. Later Type 12s were manufactured new. The second image is the Type 12-P-5, which is the torpedo we recovered."

"They look identical," Sikander remarked.

"They are—almost," Larkin said. "A Type 12 is simply a Type 11 fuselage and propulsion system with a new warhead bolted on. It was an easy conversion for fleet-level repair depots, and hundreds of old Phantoms were upgraded to match the new model when it came out. But Mr. Girard discovered a crucial difference here, sir." Larkin moved a pointer to a specific point in the schematic. "This is a power supply to the flight-control unit. That's the hardware that converts maneuvering signals from the guidance system into operations such as cutting off the warp generator at the termination of an attack run. The power supply on the old Type 11 was replaced with a newer unit with a bigger capacity for new Type 12 torpedoes, but the older upgrades kept the same power supply."

"The old power supply wasn't a problem for the Type 11," Chief Maroth said. A twenty-year veteran with thinning hair, he spoke with the nasal twang of Hibernia, his home system. "Those were in service before I joined up, and no one had much trouble with them."

Girard cleared his throat and answered. "That's true, Chief. The problem is in the interaction between the Type 11 power supply and the Type 12 control unit. Under the right—well, wrong—settings, the new unit draws more power than the old power supply can handle. When that happens, the whole thing resets, and the fault recurs before the reset is complete. Our missing torpedo is probably resetting over and over again while we speak. In a few months the onboard generator will be exhausted, and it will pop out somewhere in interstellar space."

"So what are the wrong settings?" asked Sikander.

"The ones I used at Aberdeen," said Larkin. She changed the vid image to show a control console's display; Sikander recognized the icons and menus for the torpedo officer's station on the bridge. "When the standard attack program is selected and the seeker head is set in continuous homing, it generates a power demand that triggers the reset."

Sikander glanced over to Chief Maroth. "What do you make of it, Chief?"

"That's a pretty normal attack program, Mr. North. At

torpedo school, they tell you to choose those settings for practice shots because they might give you a slightly better score on the range. I'd bet that half the torpedoes in the fleet are probably set to run the same way."

"And God knows that every ship in the Navy is fanatical about range scores." Sikander nodded slowly. "So what does this mean for our war shots?"

"They use that same power supply and flight-control unit, and some of those were conversions from the old Type 11, too," said Girard. "This problem isn't just limited to our practice torpedoes."

"I was afraid of that," Sikander said. "Very well, then. We'd better check our torpedo inventory and make sure we know which of our war shots are upgrades and which are new weapons. I'll recommend to the captain that we put the new ones in the launch tubes on the off chance we might need to use one."

"We already checked, sir," said Larkin. "We have only two of the 12-J series 5 on board. The rest of our torpedoes are the older series 2, so they might fault out. I'm sending you the list of weapons we ought to replace in the torpedo tubes."

"We have only two good torpedoes on board?" Sikander winced. He didn't look forward to explaining that to the captain and the XO.

"If we had to, we could probably use the questionable torps with a different attack program, sir. But we'd need to run a lot of simulations to make sure the power-supply fault wouldn't crop up."

"Better that we know that now, I suppose." Sikander took one last look at the vid display, then turned back to his junior officers. He'd known that Michael Girard was sharp as a tack in technical issues, and the landing operations over the last few days had showed him a different side of Angela Larkin. "Excellent work, both of you," he said. "Clear your afternoons—I want you to present your findings to the captain as soon as possible."

Girard grimaced. "The captain, sir?" Like many ensigns fresh out of the Academy, he was more than a little intimidated by the idea of speaking with his commanding officer, even someone as reasonable and even-tempered as Elise Markham.

"The captain," Sikander affirmed. "Far be it from me to take credit for your work, Mr. Girard."

Larkin's response was more guarded, but she gave him a small nod, and allowed herself another smile. "Thank you, sir," she said.

Later that afternoon, after the two junior officers had made their report to Markham and Chatburn, Sikander spent an hour watching the Torpedo Division carry out the painstaking work of unloading two of the cruiser's torpedo tubes and replacing the potentially defective weapons with Phantoms of newer manufacture. Each weighed over two thousand kilos, and the torpedo room was a crowded workspace; changing weapons required no small amount of care. But the exchange went well, and by dinnertime Sikander was able to report to Markham that at least two of the ship's torpedoes were fully ready again.

He returned to his stateroom, intending to turn in early and catch a few hours' sleep before he was inevitably awakened by another deployment of the ship's shore party or further deterioration of the situation on the ground. He found Darvesh there, folding freshly laundered shirts and arranging the shoes in his closet. "Good evening, sir," said Darvesh.

"Good evening," Sikander replied. Personally, he saw little reason to waste time on the tiny details of military grooming during ordinary shipboard routine, but Darvesh refused to allow him to be seen with anything less than crisply pressed clothing and shoes shined to a mirror polish.

He'd learned long ago to simply allow Darvesh to have his way. He sat down on the edge of his bed, but before he could even kick off his boots, his personal comm beeped.

Wondering who would call him directly, he keyed it and answered. "Lieutenant North."

"Hello, Sikander. This is Ranya el-Nasir. I just found your message, and I wanted to thank you for your concern."

He glanced down at his comm unit in surprise. Sure enough, Ranya's blue-black curls and dark eyes filled the small screen. "Ranya? This is a pleasant surprise. I wasn't expecting to hear from you."

"Is this a good time to call?"

"Yes, absolutely. It's just after dinner for me, and I'm not due to go on watch for hours."

Darvesh looked up from the task of stowing Sikander's shirts in the cabin's dresser unit. "The amira?" he asked, one eyebrow raised.

Sikander nodded, and muted his pickup for a moment. "The amira," he confirmed.

"Begum Vadiya will find this a most interesting development," Darvesh remarked. "She has long despaired of you taking a serious interest in a woman of noble background."

"Leave my mother out of this," Sikander told Darvesh, and shooed him away. The valet gave a small shrug and withdrew; Sikander returned his attention to his comm unit and activated the vid to be polite. *No need to let Ranya speak to a blank screen, after all.*

Ranya smiled when she caught sight of his face. "There you are. I was worried I might be calling in the middle of the night for you."

"I wouldn't have minded much. We're accustomed to odd hours around here," he said. He studied her image in the small device, and noted what seemed to be a small cut on her brow with a bandage. "I'm glad to see you again, Ranya—well, your image anyway. I feared the worst when

I heard what happened to your uncle's flyer. Are you okay?"

She gave a small shrug. "I have some stitches, and there was some minor surgery for a shrapnel injury in my ankle. I am back at home now and recuperating well, or so they tell me."

"How is your uncle?"

"He is recovering from a more serious surgery on his shoulder, but it isn't life-threatening. He should be fine with a few weeks of rest, or at least as much rest as the present circumstances allow." She frowned. "Speaking of which, I understand you had a close call of your own recently. I saw the newscasts about the consulate and the Sidi Marouf riots. I heard that *Hector*'s landing party suffered some casualties, and I was worried that you might have been hurt."

He shook his head. "A couple of our sailors were wounded, but I came through without a scratch. Unfortunately I was standing right by Franklin Garcia when he was shot. There was nothing I could do for him."

"I am terribly sorry about Mr. Garcia. He was a good man, and I liked him quite a lot."

"I think you probably knew him better than I did. I only met him a couple of times." Sikander gazed at her image in the small vidscreen. "I wish I understood why people are so upset," he continued. "I've seen civil unrest a time or two in my own home system, but there was so much anger in the crowd at the consulate . . . How do they think Aquila has wronged them?"

"They are not necessarily angry at you," Ranya replied. "Many Gadirans are quite poor, and they have been held down by the beys for a long time. When Gadira was brought back into contact with other star nations, the beys were naturally positioned to benefit first and most from offworld trade. So, to many of our people, you represent a force that has enriched and propped up an already oppressive class for forty years now. Combine that with offworld mores that conflict with the more traditional teachings of Quranism, and you have an explosive mixture." She sighed. "I'm afraid you picked a poor time to visit Gadira, Sikander. Matters have worsened significantly in the last few months."

Sikander smiled ruefully. "I wish we'd met under better circumstances, Ranya. All we seem to talk about are interstellar politics and planetary troubles."

"I'm afraid they are in the forefront of my mind these days." She looked away, then met his eyes again. "I suggest we change the topic, then. Tell me about your homeworld."

"There are two of them, really," Sikander replied. "Kashmir has two near-terran planets, Srinagar and Jaipur, and my family spent a good deal of time on each one. But I suppose Jaïpur is what I think of as home." He fell into a description of his family home near Sangrur, and before he knew it, he was chatting with Ranya, trading small stories about their childhoods and schooling. She was easy to talk to, and her Montréalais-accented Anglic was delightfully exotic in his ears.

Half an hour passed by as they talked, but then Ranya glanced aside and made a small face. "I am sorry, Sikander, but I must go. I have an appointment in just a few minutes."

Sikander nodded. "I understand. I hope we'll speak again soon."

"Good night, Sikander."

"Good night, Ranya," he said.

She held his gaze a moment longer, smiled, and then ended the connection. Sikander stared at the blank screen, somewhat bemused. He hadn't intended to spend half an hour chatting about idle nothings with the sultan's niece, but somehow it had happened anyway. *She must have received thousands of messages in the last few days, but she took the time to reply to mine,* he reflected. Was it simply the novelty of a note from an Aquilan officer? He replayed the conversation in his head, and decided that there was definitely more to it than that.

"Careful, Sikay," he told himself. Reaching out to express sympathy and see how she was doing after the missile attack was within the bounds of friendship. Late-night calls and stories about their homeworlds seemed a good deal more . . . complicated. Ranya wasn't an Aquilan socialite he could date casually, after all. In fact, it wasn't really clear how he could date her at all, even if he was so inclined. But that didn't stop him from dwelling on her when he closed his eyes and tried to go to sleep later that evening.

The next day, Sikander rose early to take the morning bridge watch. Ships didn't normally maneuver much in orbit, but monitoring the traffic even in a backwater system such as Gadira was a never-ending chore, and of course events on the ground required constant attention. When he assumed the watch, Sublieutenant Larkin and the landing force were already on the ground seeing to the evacuation of a mining survey team cut off in the small desert outpost of Ksar Lake—something of a misnomer, since the "lake" was actually a vast salt pan. Caidist raids had closed the access road, stranding a dozen Aquilan engineers and geologists working for Clayne Industries. Larkin's team extracted the Clayne group without much trouble, but then a new demonstration broke out in the large city of Oujad, threatening a storage facility where hundreds of new Aquilan heavy ground transports waited to be distributed to local dealers. Sikander didn't think that *Hector*'s sailors ought to risk their lives to protect someone else's new trucks, but the Operations Department recommended a demonstration of resolve, so they dispatched an orbital shuttle and a squad of armed sailors as soon as the mining survey team was transported to safety.

The chime of the bridge's contact alert interrupted Sikander as he watched the orbital imagery of the landing at the transport facility. "Mr. North, two new contacts arriving in-system, thirteen light-minutes out," announced the sensor officer of the watch, a senior chief petty officer in the Operations Department. "They're Dremish transponder codes, military."

"Two more Dremish warships?" Sikander rose from his station and walked over to the consoles of the sensor operators, looking over the chief's shoulder. He frowned at the sensor picture. Sharing an orbit with *Panther* was one thing; if Aquila was interested enough in Gadira to send a cruiser, then Sikander could grudgingly accept the possibility that the Empire of Dremark had the right to express its own concerns by dispatching a warship, too. But a whole Dremish flotilla was another matter entirely. "What classes are we looking at?"

"One moment, sir," the sensor chief replied. She quickly correlated the transponder codes and visuals with a library of Dremish ships. "It looks like a Waffe-class destroyer, escorting a General-class assault transport. They're identifying as *Streitaxt* and *General von Grolmann*."

Sikander studied the readouts on the Dremish ships. The destroyer did not worry him overmuch—after all, the Imperial fleet was already represented in Gadira. But the assault transport was a different story. It had a capacity of well over a thousand Dremish marines, plus heavy combat vehicles for ground operations. *Hector*'s thirty-hand landing force of armed sailors suddenly seemed extremely inadequate in comparison. *Nothing on this planet could stand up to a large landing force of Dremish infantry,* he realized. *This completely changes the strategic picture.*

"Damn," he muttered. "Communications, send the standard greeting to the new arrivals, and inform them that we're conducting landing operations and do not anticipate maneuvering for some time yet." Then he returned to his station. Standing orders did not require Captain Markham to be notified of routine traffic, but this was the sort of development she expected her deck officers to alert her to.

He keyed the captain's direct link. "Captain, this is Lieutenant North."

Markham replied a moment later from her cabin. "A busy watch this morning, Mr. North. Where are the locals rioting now?"

"Nothing new on that front, Captain—this is a system traffic update. Two additional Dremish warships have just arrived in-system, range thirteen light-minutes. It's a destroyer escorting an assault transport. I sent the customary greeting."

"Any change in *Panther*'s status?"

Sikander checked his displays. "No, ma'am. She is maintaining orbit."

"What in the world are they doing here?" The captain paused for a long moment, absorbing the new information before speaking again. "Very good, Mr. North. Let me know when the new ships take station."

"Yes, ma'am," Sikander replied. He waited and watched as the two new arrivals began their maneuvers; a few minutes later, the customary messages and captains' compliments arrived. *General von Grolmann* turned her blunt bow toward Gadira and began moving in to assume an orbit near *Panther,* but *Streitaxt* reported that she was not remaining in Gadira long and maneuvered to establish a new warp transit. Sikander relayed the news to Captain Markham; thirty minutes later, *Streitaxt* bubbled up again on a new course, heading for parts unknown. He made a note to have the intelligence team analyze the destroyer's departure course and figure out where she was bound; there was no harm in being a little nosy, after all.

General von Grolmann was still en route to Gadira when Sikander's watch ended. He headed down to the wardroom to find some lunch, but managed to eat only half his sandwich before the info assistant signaled him. "Lieutenant North, your presence is requested in the captain's conference room."

"On my way," he replied. He took one more bite and washed it down with a gulp of iced tea, then headed up to the captain's cabin. When he arrived, he found Peter Chatburn, Hiram Randall, Magdalena Juarez, and Isaako Simms already there. The vidscreen on the bulkhead showed the orbital view of Gadira's night side, with thin threads and clusters of yellow light marking out the planet's inhabited areas.

"My apologies for being late," he said. "I just finished my watch."

"Have a seat, Mr. North," Captain Markham replied. "We're discussing the implications of the Dremish assault force and what we could do to step up our presence if the Dremish become more heavily involved in the security situation on the ground."

"We can't compete with a full brigade of heavy assault troops," Randall remarked. "Dremark now has far more combat power to influence events on the surface than we do. They will presumably employ that power to look after their own interests."

"What interests?" Magda Juarez asked. "We've been keeping tabs on a hundred different Aquilan companies and citizens for the last few days, but as far as I know there isn't a single Dremish shipping crate on the ground—only stories about Dremark's plans to invest in Gadira. If they're so involved here, where are the Dremish businesses?"

"That's the question, isn't it?" Markham said. "Let's take it for granted that we are outgunned on the ground. How else can we influence events?"

"We can provide the benefit of our orbital observation to the Royal Guard and help them monitor the movement of insurgent forces," Sikander suggested. "And we can provide orbital gunfire support to help the sultan's forces repel insurgent attacks or neutralize Caidist strongholds. We might not have as much ground power as Dremark here, but our help might make the difference between Sultan Rashid's survival or defeat."

"Preserving the el-Nasir sultanate is not our primary objective in Gadira," Captain Markham said. "That is Montréal's problem, not ours. Our principal concerns are to make sure that the extremists down on the planet don't hurt or kill Aquilan citizens, and that our Dremish friends don't use any local disorders as a cover for an unwarranted intervention. Other than that, we need to stay out of the way and allow the sultan and his Montréalais allies to deal with the Caidist problem—or not."

Sikander hesitated. While it was strictly true that Aquila was more or less ambivalent about the survival of Sultan Rashid's government, he could not help but think of Ranya el-Nasir and wondering what would become of her if the Caidists succeeded in overthrowing her uncle. *The right thing to do is to keep the peace as best we can. But it would be more pragmatic to determine who's going to hold the throne at the end of the day, and make sure they're indebted to the Commonwealth. If I think the right course of action is to assist the el-Nasirs, I need to tie that argument to something that Captain Markham sees as the simple demand of duty.*

"There is a good argument to be made that a new sultanate might be more amenable to the open-door policies we favor than the el-Nasirs," Chatburn said, explicitly stating the concern that Sikander was privately wrestling with. "If the Caidists win, they'll see Montréal as the ally of the enemy they just fought for twenty years to defeat. They'll need a new friend among the great powers. It might as well be us."

"I suspect the Caidists won't be inclined to be friendly with *any* offworlders for quite some time," Randall countered.

"They don't seem like they're very interested in making Gadira into a place where foreigners might want to do business."

For once, Sikander found himself in agreement with the operations officer. "Mr. Randall is right," he said. Randall glanced at him in surprise, but Sikander kept his attention focused on Markham. "And that is exactly why we should be prepared to intervene on behalf of the el-Nasirs, Captain. If the Caidists gain power, no offworlder will be safe on Gadira. The surest way to protect our citizens—and, incidentally, deflect any Dremish ambitions in this system—is to help the sultanate defeat or pacify its enemies. By helping them restore order swiftly, we are helping ourselves."

Captain Markham leaned back in her chair, considering his point. "There may be something to that, Mr. North," she admitted. "But I must be clear about this: We are not authorized to attack local insurgents unless Aquilan citizens are in immediate danger from them. My orders do not permit me to begin an open-ended military commitment for the Commonwealth."

"Sharing our intelligence with the sultan's Royal Guard and making plans to coordinate fire support would appear to be within your discretion, ma'am," said Sikander.

Captain Markham fell silent for a long moment, gazing at the vidscreen with its view of the planet below. Sikander held his breath; he thought Markham was a reasonable person and that he'd made good points, but he also felt that he'd pushed her about as far as it was safe to go in arguing his case. Finally, she nodded. "Very well. Mr. Randall, make arrangements to share our orbital observation with the sultan's forces. Mr. North, go ahead and prepare your fire plan. Give me a range of options from nonlethal crowd suppression to targeted interdiction of military movements. I seriously doubt that we will need them, but it doesn't hurt to be prepared."

"Yes, ma'am," Randall replied. "I'll get on it immediately."

"Yes, Captain," Sikander said. He made a mental note to speak to Michael Girard; this was a job for the fire-control officer. "We will examine a range of responses."

Markham glanced over to Commander Chatburn. "While we're at it, XO, let's touch base with the senior surviving consulate personnel and verify the Aquilan citizens known to be in-system." Chatburn nodded his assent, and made notes on his own dataslate. "Anything else? Then let's meet again tomorrow to—one moment." Her dataslate beeped softly with a new communication. The officers gathered at the table waited politely as Markham quickly checked her message. Her comm preferences would not interrupt a senior leadership meeting for routine business, so anything that triggered a notification had to be at least a little unusual.

"What is it, Captain?" Chatburn asked after a long moment, unable to restrain his curiosity.

"Some of our preparations will have to wait until tomorrow," Markham replied. "We've been invited to dinner."

"The Gadiran government? Or the Montréalais?" Sikander asked.

"Neither." Markham allowed herself a wry smile, savoring the opportunity to surprise her officers. "We'll be dining with Captain Harper and the officers of SMS *Panther* tonight."

14

CSS *Hector*, arriving!" The shrill, piping call of the bosun's whistle echoed through the large hangar deck of the cruiser *Panther* as Captain Markham descended the steps from the shuttle. By old tradition, commanding officers were identified by the command they held when boarding or leaving another warship; the Dremish navy observed the same rituals that the Aquilan navy did. As Elise Markham reached the deck, an honor guard of eight sideboys in resplendent black uniforms with blue trousers snapped to attention.

Captain Markham returned the honor guard's salute and strode ahead between the two lines of sailors. Captain Georg Harper and several other Dremish officers waited at the end of the sideboy line; Sikander debarked from the shuttle just in time to see the two commanding officers exchange salutes, then shake hands. "Captain Markham, welcome aboard," Harper said. His voice had a strong, slow drawl; Sikander wondered where he'd learned his Standard Anglic. "We're glad you and your officers could join us."

"Captain Harper," Markham replied. "It was courteous of you to invite us. I hope you'll allow *Hector* to return the compliment in the near future."

Harper smiled broadly. He was shorter than Sikander had expected, not much more than 1.7 meters or so, although of course he'd seen Harper only from the shoulders up in their message exchanges. "Of course, we'd be delighted."

The two commanding officers exchanged more pleasantries; Sikander took a few moments to study *Panther*'s hangar deck. It was definitely a little larger than *Hector*'s, with several dangerous-looking armed shuttles stowed efficiently in davits suspended from the overhead. On the forward bulkhead, a large flag in blue, black, and gold hung from brackets—the Imperial ensign. On the opposite bulkhead, the Dremish placed a similarly sized ensign in white and red, the insignia of the Commonwealth of Aquila. "It seems they are rolling out the red carpet for us," he murmured to Hiram Randall, who happened to be standing nearby.

Randall snorted. "Foresighted of them," he replied. "I'm pretty sure we don't have a Dremish banner in our flag locker."

Captain Markham finished with her initial greetings, and gestured at the rest of *Hector*'s officers. "Allow me to introduce the rest of my party," she said to Harper. In addition to Sikander and Randall, the group included Dr. Simms; Angela Larkin; Sublieutenant Keane; Ensign Perry, the auxiliaries officer; and Ensign Kang, the ship's disbursing officer. It was only half of the wardroom, but given the necessities of watchstanding—and a little elementary military caution in a potentially volatile situation—Markham had made sure to leave Commander Chatburn behind with enough officers to handle *Hector* in combat if the unthinkable happened. Sikander was still getting to know the younger officers in the dinner party, but they seemed comfortable and competent as they exchanged greetings with the Dremish captain.

"A pleasure to meet all of you," Harper said. "May I present my executive officer, Kapitan-Leutnant Anton Braun? Our gunnery officer, Oberleutnant Helena Aldrich? And here is Major Owen Kalb, executive officer of the Third Silesian Rifles. They are the regiment embarked on *General von Grolmann*." He continued with several more junior officers, but Sikander quickly lost track of their names and positions; the most important impression he came away with was that *Panther*'s crew was about the same size as *Hector*'s, and the officers had similar duties. The only differences he noted were that ranks had slightly different names. Then Harper turned to a thin, sandy-haired man in civilian clothing who stood beside *Panther*'s officers. "Oh, and I almost overlooked Mr. Otto Bleindel, our leading trade representative in Gadira. He works for Dielkirk Industries, but he is also accredited by the Imperial government."

The two groups of officers mixed together, exchanging handshakes and quick greetings. Sikander found himself shaking hands with Oberleutnant Aldrich, the woman that Harper had introduced as his gunnery officer. She was a tall, strong-featured woman with short rust-brown hair and a stern, rudder-like nose, but she had a surprisingly warm smile. "It would seem that you are my counterpart," she said, her voice marked by a noticeably throaty accent. "I am Helena Aldrich, gunnery officer."

"Sikander North. A pleasure to meet you." Sikander returned her smile. "May I say that *Panther* is a very impressive-looking warship? I was admiring the main battery from the shuttle as we flew over. Those are the new Type 9 K-cannons, aren't they?"

"Indeed they are," Aldrich said. Her smile broadened; it was a rare gunnery officer who didn't like to talk about his or her work, after all. "I see that you know your armament."

"I read a feature piece about the *Löwe*-class cruisers in *Naval Review* a few months back. They garnered quite a bit of praise from the naval-affairs establishment in Aquila." Sikander was curious about some of the specifications on the Dremish cruiser's guns, but it would seem a little impolite to ask. After all, the exact performance of *Hector*'s own Mark V kinetic cannons was considered confidential; he would have declined to offer any details if Aldrich asked him. The Empire of Dremark was not an enemy, but it was a rival with a fast-growing, modern, powerful navy. Quite a few strategists in Aquila worried that Dremark's rise would lead to conflict, although Sikander sincerely hoped they were wrong. There hadn't been any kind of great power war in almost fifty years, and the size and power of the battle fleets maintained by most of the stellar polities meant that a serious conflict would certainly result in destruction on an unimaginable scale.

"If I am not mistaken, your Ilium-class cruisers influenced the design of our own class," the Drémish officer said. "Our navy was almost nonexistent two generations ago, so our shipbuilders made a habit of basing their work on the most successful foreign designs. Imitation is the sincerest form of flattery, they say."

Sikander inclined his head, and decided to change the subject. "Which of the Empire's systems do you call home, Ms. Aldrich?"

"I am from Gotland. Are you familiar with it?"

"Not much more than the name, I fear. It's an older system, isn't it?"

"The second-oldest in the Empire," Aldrich said. "It's renowned for its excellent university, and its rings. Gotland is one of the few terrestrial planets with visible rings, although one really can't see them in the middle of the day. Where are you from, Mr. North?"

"Kashmir. I grew up on the planet of Jaipur."

"Kashmir, really? I was not aware that Kashmiris served in the Commonwealth officer corps."

"There aren't many of us." Sikander indicated the emerald-green sash on his dress uniform. "That's why my insignia is a little different from everyone else's. I hold a Kashmiri rank as well as an Aquilan one."

"Do you—" Oberleutnant Aldrich started to ask, but she was interrupted by Captain Harper, who raised his voice for attention.

"Rather than standing about in the hangar bay, might I suggest that we repair to the wardroom?" *Panther*'s captain said to the officers mingling on the deck. "Our mess stewards have quite a dinner planned, and we shouldn't keep them waiting. This way, if you please." With Captain Markham beside him, he led the way to a passageway heading forward from the hangar bay.

"We'll continue the conversation later," Aldrich promised Sikander. They fell in with the rest of the group, following the two captains.

The internal passageways of SMS *Panther* did not look very different from those of *Hector*, Sikander decided. The paint was a different color—a bright eggshell white, as opposed to the slightly darker taupe that filled the passages and compartments of Aquilan warships. Markings on hatches and fittings were in Nebeldeutsch, just similar enough to the Anglic spoken in Aquila that many words were the same, only spelled a little differently. Enlisted men in parade-dress uniforms stood at intersecting corridors, helping to mark the path to the wardroom and perhaps discourage any of *Hector*'s officers from wandering off to examine sensitive areas of the ship.

The Aquilans found the Dremish wardroom appointed with white linen tablecloths and formal place settings. Sikander noted that small placards showed each officer's place at the table; Captain Markham must have provided a list of guests ahead of time. When he took his seat, he found himself between Owen Kalb and Otto Bleindel; Helena Aldrich sat across from him. Harper, Markham, Braun, and Randall were seated around the head of the table; as the third-ranking Aquilan present, Sikander was closer to the head than the foot. *No doubt the Dremish checked everyone's date of rank to make sure they arranged the table cor-*

rectly, he reflected. The Dremish navy had a reputation for punctiliousness, although Sikander hadn't spent enough time around Imperial officers to see if it was deserved or not.

"Drink, sir?" a mess steward asked him as he settled in his place.

Sikander glanced over at the two captains. Two more stewards poured wine from elegant-looking decanters for both of them; in case of doubt, it was always good practice to follow your captain's lead. "What is the white?" he asked.

"Gray Mountain Viognier '96, sir."

He'd never heard of the vintage, but if it was six years old and Captain Harper was serving it to impress, it was probably good. "Excellent," he told the steward.

"Mr. North, correct?" the Dremish civilian said as Sikander sampled his viognier—a dry and crisp vintage, quite good. "I hear that you've met the sultan. Tell me, what do you think of him?"

Sikander glanced over, remembering the introductions. *Otto Bleindel,* he recalled. "We only exchanged a few words, Mr. Bleindel. He seemed like a man with a gentle disposition, although I think Captain Markham could tell you a thing or two about his zeal for gardening."

"I've heard a few stories to that effect, too." Bleindel sipped at a glass of ice water. "In ordinary times I would think the Gadirans lucky to be in the hands of a ruler whose chief concern was his own palace grounds. Regrettably, there are times when rulers cannot afford to be gardeners. In Gadira, this might be one of those times."

Major Kalb gave a sour laugh from Sikander's other side. "The only reason the sultan holds on to his throne is because Montréal lavishes arms, military advisors, and economic aid on his regime. Without the Republic's support, Rashid would be deposed within a day."

"Perhaps, but his policies have succeeded in bringing quite a bit of offworld investment to Gadira," Sikander pointed out. "I wonder if Sultan Rashid is cleverer than we all think he is. I am fairly certain that his niece is, anyway."

"Ah, you have met the amira, then?"

"Yes, I have. I received the distinct impression that she pays attention to a lot of things her uncle doesn't have time for."

"I thought so, too," Bleindel said. "In fact, the first time I met her, she was climbing on a grav tank and interrogating a Montréalais major about the proper maintenance and training procedures."

"As they say, amateurs study tactics, and rank amateurs study strategy," Oberleutnant Aldrich observed. "Professionals study logistics."

Sikander laughed, and sipped his wine. "That saying has been around forever."

The talk turned to the peculiarities of Gadiran society, but was soon interrupted by a dizzying array of courses from the wardroom galley—soup, salad, a cheese-plate appetizer, and the main course, small roasted fowl stuffed with rice pilaf and lamb kebobs made with local vegetables. "Our chief mess steward suggested that featuring the local cuisine might be a novel experience," Captain Harper explained as the meal was served. "And, of course, the ingredients and seasonings are fresh, since we were able to purchase them in the market of Meknez just yesterday."

"We appreciate the efforts of your mess stewards, Captain," Markham replied. "I can see that we'll have to think up something special when it's our turn to host you."

No warship could truly replicate the fine dining experience of a five-star restaurant or a formal diplomatic dinner, of course, but Sikander had to admit that Captain Harper's mess stewards had made a very credible effort indeed. *Hector*'s own cooks would be hard-pressed to equal the effort when the time came to reciprocate. The kebobs were especially good; lamb was something that Sikander enjoyed at home but that rarely turned up on Aquilan menus.

Over dessert and after-dinner drinks, the conversation turned back to Gadira. "I must say, it is a relief to know that there is another warship representing a responsible power here in-system with us," Captain Harper observed. "Should conditions continue to deteriorate on the ground, the fire-power of a second cruiser might make a great difference in efforts to restore order."

"I sincerely hope that it will not come to that," Captain Markham said. "The best outcome would be for the Gadirans to work out their own troubles without overt interference from any outside power. I suspect we could only make things worse in the long run."

"*Someone* needs to take matters in hand," Harper said. "The Caidists are about to overthrow Montréal's puppet sultan, and the Republic doesn't have the will—or the right—to subdue the planet for the el-Nasirs. I for one don't believe that Dremark or Aquila must stand aside and do nothing when the Montréalais have allowed this disaster to develop. It's time to secure our own interests."

"For better or worse, the Republic of Montréal has invested a good deal of effort in the economic and political development of this system," Markham replied. "We're inclined to avoid the disruptions involved with any effort to change the status quo by force. Choosing this faction or that to support seems like a recipe for turning a rebellion into a full-fledged civil war. Surely that is in no one's interest."

"The Tanjeer Agreement of 3062 specifically called for an 'open door' policy whereby all the signatory powers would have equal access to development opportunities in Gadira," said Kapitan-Leutnant Braun, *Panther*'s executive officer. A thickly built man with a gleaming bald scalp, he sat beside Captain Markham. He spoke with a loud voice and forceful motions of his hands. "But somehow forty years later, Gadira is a Montréalais colony. One wonders if the Montréalais negotiated the previous agreement in good faith."

"How would you amend the agreement, Mr. Braun?" Hiram Randall asked. He maintained an even tone and a polite smile, but Sikander detected a hint of condescension in his tone. He'd been on the receiving end of Randall's sarcasm enough times to know it well, although he didn't think that new acquaintances such as the *Panther*'s officers would pick up on his skepticism. Captain Markham, on the other hand, made a show of taking a deliberate sip of her own wine.

"At the very least, I would consider dividing the planet into zones of development for each of the great powers with interests here," Braun said. "And each power could determine for itself the appropriate level of its presence and support."

"That would only be fair," Oberleutnant Aldrich pointed out.

"Indeed," said Harper. "I am afraid we must insist on establishing and maintaining public order in the regions where our interests are threatened. Clearly, we cannot count on the Montréalais to do that, since Caidist rebels are running amok on the planet. Fine—we won't try to tell the Republic how to manage its affairs. All we need is for them to step aside and let us look after our own concerns."

Braun nodded. "Exactly! Although if you asked me, I would say that the whole system would be better off under the administration of an enlightened power such as Dremark—or Aquila, of course—than they are now."

"The Gadirans might not see it that way," Sikander observed.

"Yes, but the question isn't for them to decide, is it?" Braun waved his hand around airily. "If the best they could arrange on their own was a feckless monarchy, it's time for more advanced states to step in and help them along."

"Dremark is a monarchy, isn't it? You have an emperor instead of a sultan, but what is the practical difference?" Sikander asked.

Smiles vanished from the Dremish officers at the table. Braun's face actually turned red, but he bit back whatever retort he intended. The awkward silence hung in the air for a long moment, but then Captain Harper set down his glass and cleared his throat. "That seems like an unfortunate comparison, Mr. North," he said in a light tone. "Emperor Klaus Lenard has little in common with that helpless idiot sultan."

"My own home system is ruled by a khan, Captain Harper," Sikander replied. "I merely meant to point out that the Gadirans believe their form of government is just as legitimate as you believe yours to be."

"The legitimacy of our government is not a matter of *belief*," Kapitan-Leutnant Braun said icily. "The House of Ritterblau has ruled in Dremark for over four hundred years with the full support of the democratically elected parliament. Considering the fact that the upper chamber of your own Commonwealth Assembly and many of your planetary governorships are comprised of hereditary plutocrats, I think you have little room for criticism. When was the last time any of your senators stood for election?"

Now it was the Aquilans' turn to fall silent. Sikander repressed a small smile at his colleagues' discomfiture. Kashmir was in no way, shape, or form a democratic system, but at least his own people didn't pretend that the leading families were anything other than a titled aristocracy. It was one of the aspects of Kashmiri culture that his Aquilan friends looked down on, without recognizing that their own system had no particular moral superiority. On the other hand, it seemed that everyone at the table had now been insulted by one comparison or another, and the tension was now thick enough to cut with a knife.

Fortunately, Captain Harper was determined to salvage the evening. He stood slowly, and gave Captain Markham a slight bow from the waist. "Captain, I apologize to you and your officers for allowing the conversation to take an unfortunate turn. Perhaps we should leave these matters to the politicians and the diplomats. We are all sailors here, travelers of the stars, warriors who accept the burden of long watches and constant vigilance in the service of the worlds we love. Let us speak of the things that we share, not the issues our governments fence over."

"Well said, Captain Harper," Markham replied. "Please, there is nothing to apologize for. What would you like to talk about?"

The Dremish captain took his seat again, and surveyed the table thoughtfully. "I don't suppose any of you are anglers?" he said with a small smile.

"I am not, but you're in luck. Mr. North here is an avid fisherman."

Harper's face positively lit up. "Is that a fact? None of my own officers are so enlightened. Tell me, Mr. North: saltwater or freshwater?"

"It depends on the planet, Captain Harper," Sikander said. "But in general, saltwater sport fishing is my favorite."

"Ah, too bad. I thought you might be a fellow devotee of the fly rod." Harper moved on to a colorful description of his last vacation in the mountains of Thuringia; slowly, the down-table conversations resumed, this time steering clear of the political situation. The mood around the table noticeably lightened, and after-dinner drinks flowed freely. After Sikander and Harper had traded fishing stories, Captain Markham and Helena Aldrich discovered that they were both equestrians, while Hiram Randall and Major Kalb both entertained a great (and previously unsuspected to Sikander) love of old Terran-style beer crafting. When Captain Markham and *Hector*'s officers finally took their leave an hour later, the awkward moments earlier in the meal seemed long forgotten.

The whole dinner party proceeded back to the hangar deck, and the Dremish officers saw the Aquilans to their shuttle hatch. The farewells were cordial enough, but Captain

Markham breathed a sigh of relief as the shuttle hands secured the hatch and the Aquilan half of the party found seats. Through the passenger-cabin viewports, Sikander could see the Dremish clearing the hangar before they cycled the bay door.

"Well, that wasn't so bad," Markham said, adjusting her seat restraints. "For a moment there I thought they were about to ask us to leave."

"They're a little touchy about their emperor, aren't they?" Randall observed.

"Indeed," said Captain Markham. She gave Sikander a stern glance. "Did you do that on purpose, Mr. North?"

"My apologies, Captain. That loudmouth Braun was beginning to annoy me."

"Me too, but next time please leave the diplomatic sallies to me." Markham shook her head. "I would have thought a man raised in a palace might have a better instinct for not offending people over a formal dinner."

"There's a reason my family sent me off to join the Navy, ma'am," Sikander said.

"Ha!" Randall gave a sharp bark of laughter. The other officers nearby joined in. "Well, I will say this much, North—you found a way to make things a good deal more exciting than they needed to be."

"You don't have much room to talk, Mr. Randall," Captain Markham said, turning her attention to the operations officer. "Don't think I didn't notice that you egged on Braun with that innocent little question about fixing the Tanjeer accords."

Randall grimaced. "Guilty as charged, ma'am. I was curious about what sort of rationale the Dremish might employ, so I took the liberty of performing a little experiment."

The shuttle's induction drive hummed, and *Panther*'s hangar deck gently rotated out of Sikander's view. The pilot smoothly accelerated through the open bay door, climbing up and away from the Dremish cruiser to rendezvous with

Hector in its higher orbit. "Remind me to put you both on watch when the Dremish come over," said Captain Markham. "Clearly neither of you is fit for company."

"When will we have them over, ma'am?" Sublieutenant Larkin asked.

"Let's give it a week or so," Markham decided. "In the meantime, I think it would be good to offer a show of support to the Montréalais. I suspect we're going to wind up backing their position, not the Dremish demands. I'd like to show Captain Harper and his XO that we're on friendly terms with the Republic, regardless of what they might think of it."

"Shall I arrange a social occasion with Ambassador Nguyen?" Randall asked, now serious again.

"Please do," the captain replied.

15

For the first time since the shootdown of her uncle's luxury flyer, Ranya el-Nasir's leg did not ache. She'd been on her feet all day, and in odd moments she noticed that it wasn't sore at all—a testament to the effectiveness of Montréalais medicine and the care lavished upon her since her injury. On the other hand, her temper was rapidly fraying. For all the study and effort she'd put in over the seven years since her father's assassination, too many of the sultan's officers treated her as a child playing with things beyond her years, and it positively infuriated her.

At this moment, the object of her anger was Major Louis Cheney of the Republic Marines. She'd called over to the Montréalais embassy first thing in the morning to speak with him, only to discover that he was already in the palace, meeting with the sultan's military advisors. Naturally, none of them had thought to advise her that any important discussions might be taking place. Ranya could almost understand that from her own countrymen; they simply didn't think of including her in anything resembling strategy discussions or operational planning. But she'd hoped that the Montréalais—especially Major Cheney, after the lesson she'd imparted a few weeks ago while examining the grav tank on the parade ground—would have figured out by now that she needed to be included in any conversations about the ways and means of supporting the sultan's military establishment. She'd had to wait until the private meeting broke up, then send Tarek Zakur to fetch Cheney before he left the palace grounds.

She waited in the Sultana's Conservatory, a room that she often used for meetings and discussions with visitors to the palace. Since Sultana Yasmin avoided long stays at El-Badi, the room was pretty much hers to use when she liked. Its outer wall consisted of sliding glass doors in a decorative iron framework, leading out to the well-shaded eastern gardens. The morning sun helped to warm the room swiftly, but the shade trees kept it from getting unpleasantly hot before the sun moved to the other side of the palace. Ranya could keep the whole outer wall opened up for most of the day, listening to the birdsong and the sounds of the fountains outside as she worked.

Footsteps echoing on the marble floors caught her attention. She closed the documents and reports in front of her, and turned to face the parlor's door. After two soft knocks, Captain Zakur entered with the Montréalais major Cheney in tow. "Major Cheney, Amira," he said.

The major crossed the room and bowed. "Good afternoon, Amira," he said. "I was just leaving the palace when Captain Zakur summoned me. What can I do for you?"

"Major, I was hoping you could help me solve a little mystery," Ranya began. She glanced at her dataslate to check the numbers. "As best I can tell, our Royal Guard took delivery of one hundred and twenty-two Léopard grav tanks three weeks ago. But when Tarek checked on the depot where our new Léopards are supposed to be refitting for desert service and our troops are supposed to be training with their new machines, they weren't there. It turns out that they were deployed out to our field commanders already, and they're now scattered over half the planet, chasing Caidists. Is that correct?"

Cheney stood easily with his hands clasped behind his back. "Yes, Amira. The grav tanks have already been deployed."

"I thought we had agreed that Montréal would furnish training programs and desert-ops modifications for these grav tanks."

"Yes, Amira," Major Cheney said. "We did. We sent a training cadre to the depot at Nador, along with sufficient mod kits to ready all the Léopards for Gadiran operations."

"The training course is supposed to be six weeks long, isn't it? And our planning anticipated that it would take about the same time to complete the mods, didn't it?"

"That is correct, Amira."

"So, why in the world were these grav tanks put into immediate operation without the proper training or equipment?" Ranya glanced again at her dataslate. "I see that we've already had eighteen of our new Léopards immobilized due to mechanical failures. More are failing every day. Did you even bother to apply some desert camouflage, or are they still painted in the parade-ground colors I saw a couple of months ago?"

Major Cheney looked uncomfortable. "Amira, the decision was made to provide the crews with an abbreviated training course so that the new grav tanks could be employed in the sultan's current offensive against the Caidist strongholds. Only essential refits—mostly additional dust filters for the fuel and ventilation systems—were carried out."

"Who made that decision?"

"I think it was General Mirza, although the sultan's military council concurred." Cheney frowned. "I advised against rushing the Léopards into service, Amira Ranya. Your uncle's officers thought that operational demands required their immediate availability."

Ranya glanced over to Tarek Zakur, standing by the door. The Royal Guard officer gave her the tiniest of shrugs, reminding her that it was not Major Cheney's idea to dispense with training and maintenance in order to rush grav tanks to battlefields where they weren't needed. Over the last few years she had managed to establish some basic oversight of purchasing and logistics, the elements of military readiness that Gadiran generals found boring. But gaining any kind of access to operational decisions remained out of her reach, thanks to her gender. As a result, she had to find out that the sultan's new tanks had been rushed into the field by quizzing the Montréalais who had provided them to the Royal Guard.

It is not Major Cheney's fault, she told herself. And she could hardly blame him for acceding to the demands of Gadiran generals, even when they were being foolish. The Montréalais were certainly aware of the fact that Dremish and Aquilan warships were orbiting a few thousand kilometers above the sultan's domain, and that if they didn't give the sultan's generals what they asked for, somebody else might. She consciously set aside her anger, and took a deep breath. She would take it up with a more appropriate target later on.

"Very well, so the grav tanks have been deployed," she said in a calm voice. "What can we expect as a result of inadequate training and desert readiness?"

"It shouldn't be too bad, Amira. In all honesty, the Léopard is a pretty reliable machine, and simple enough to operate. I would worry about damage to the plenum skirt and lift plates from ground impacts—the most important rough-terrain refit is a heavy-duty shield for the undercarriage, such as it is. Boulder fields and rocky, uneven ground are pretty punishing on grav tanks." Cheney considered the question for a long moment. "At a guess, I think you'll lose about ten percent of your effective force per week of hard operations to minor failures. Those vehicles can be recovered and put back into service fairly easily."

"If we had any tank recovery vehicles," Zakur observed from his place by the door.

Cheney winced. "Well, yes. But any heavy-lift grav transport could do the job of moving a Léopard back to the depot."

I'd wager we don't have a lot of those either, Ranya thought. The districts where the Caidists operated, and where the Royal Guard attempted to go, noticeably lacked modern heavy construction equipment and transport assets. And the Caidist rebels loved nothing better than ambushing sultanate forces when they tried to clear crash sites or recover damaged equipment.

"I will make sure to pass that along to our field commanders," Ranya told the Montréalais. "Thank you, Major Cheney. Please let me know the next time you receive a request to put Republic equipment in service without adequate preparation first. I may be able to do something about that."

"I will, Amira," Cheney promised. He bowed and left, striding quickly across the marble-floored hallway outside the salon.

"Idiots," Ranya muttered.

"In the major's defense, he is new here," Zakur reminded her.

"I wasn't speaking about the major," Ranya replied. She thought of a roomful of overdecorated Gadiran colonels and brigadiers, and wondered which one had convinced General Mirza to throw an expensive new weapons system into conditions that virtually guaranteed a force crippled by preventable faults within five or six weeks. "What do I have to do to make an impression on the generals? If they're not comfortable listening to me, you would think they'd at least listen to common sense! Or do they think that a pair of breasts invalidates whatever advice might follow?"

"I would not presume to comment on . . . that," Zakur said, which earned him a sharp look from Ranya. As it happened, the guard captain was happily married and very, very careful to avoid anything close to impropriety, except when he thought that a dry remark might do her some good. "I'm afraid it's the message, not the messenger. You happen to have a good deal of expertise in a field that General Mirza is inclined to overlook. Even if you were the crown prince instead of the sultan's niece, he would not pay much attention to issues of logistics and infrastructure."

"Yes, but if I were a prince rather than a princess, I could at least put on the uniform and *make* him pay attention," Ranya said. "The Montréalais and Aquilans seem to run perfectly competent militaries with females in the ranks."

"Just because it is right for them does not mean it is right for us, Amira—not yet, at any rate. Do you really wish you had been born a man?"

"Not particularly," Ranya admitted. If she'd been the son rather than the daughter of Kamal el-Nasir, her father's death would have forced her onto the throne as a teenager. As a member of the royal household and a woman in Gadira's chauvinistic society, she chafed under some annoying limitations, but she enjoyed her little freedoms. The sultan, on the other hand, could do *nothing* without careful calculation of the outcomes. Yes, she had to put up with patronizing behavior or annoying expectations such as finding a husband, but she'd been encouraged to gain a first-class education and she was more or less free to speak her mind; Gadira was not nearly as hidebound as some of the old Caliphate worlds. "But that does not mean I don't find it frustrating at times, Tarek."

The guard captain shrugged. "I was not born in the right family to hope for a brigadier's star. The general staff is full of men who gained their positions through the merits of their titles, not their experience. That does not diminish the value of my service."

Ranya allowed herself a sigh. Zakur came from a solidly middle-class background, but the most prestigious posts in the Royal Guard were traditionally given to bey families to curry favor or ensure loyalty. He'd probably never rise above major, through no fault of his own. The irony was not entirely lost on her.

She met the guard captain's eyes, acknowledging his point, then returned her attention to the reports stacked on the fine desk. "The worst part of it is that using up the Léopards isn't doing much good, by all the reports I can get my hands on," she said. She picked up a handful of documents, and let them drop to the tabletop. Sultanate forces were bogged down in half a dozen districts, unable to press forward without heavy fire support, but every time armored forces deployed, civil protests and riots broke out like wildfire. "I'm beginning to wonder whether any amount of escalation would actually make a difference."

"What other options are the Caidists and the urban radicals giving you, Amira?"

"Not many," she admitted. *And that begs the question of whether fighting is the right answer.* She looked up at Zakur again. "I think I need to have a word with my uncle. Is he free?"

Zakur murmured into his comm unit, comparing notes with the rest of the palace's security detail. "He's just finishing a private discussion, Amira. You can find him taking coffee on the south terrace."

"Thank you," said Ranya. She gathered up her dataslate and a folder full of reports, and headed for the other side of the palace. As a member of the royal family, she could interrupt her uncle at almost any time, but as a matter of simple courtesy she tried to avoid derailing whatever schedule his handlers had worked out for the day. The sultan, of course, was never considered late for any meeting or audience, but the palace just ran better if disruptions were kept to a minimum.

The sunny south terrace, with its expansive swimming pools and vine-covered arbors, faced the bluffs overlooking the Silver Sea. Most non-Gadirans would have found it unpleasantly hot, but a light breeze blew in from the sea this afternoon. Sultan Rashid sat in the shade of a table-sized umbrella at his favorite reading spot, his wounded arm in a sling. Ranya could tell it pained him by the way he favored it. Beside him sat an older, white-bearded man in the long, plain robes of a scholar. As she approached, the old man rose and took the sultan's hand.

Sultan Rashid exchanged some words with the scholar, then noticed Ranya's approach. "Ah, good afternoon, my dear! Have you met Hadji Tumar ibn Sakak?"

"I don't believe so, but I certainly know of him," Ranya answered. Hadji Tumar was one of the most respected imams on Gadira, an allameh—or Quranic scholar—widely regarded as a moderate voice among the planet's clerics. Finding him meeting with the sultan surprised her, since most imams took a dim view of House Nasir's friendship with nonreligious offworlders and lack of zeal for policing moral infractions among the population; Tumar ibn Sakak visited El-Badi at his peril. Not even the most fanatical Caidist would think about physically threatening a well-known allameh, but the risk to his moral authority was very real.

Hadji Tumar salaamed, and then took her hand. "It is a pleasure to see you again, Amira," he said. "We met when you were very small—I used to visit your father and speak with him from time to time. Sultan Kamal was a generous patron to my school."

"I am afraid I don't remember."

"I would not expect you to. You were very young." The old cleric turned to Sultan Rashid. "I will think on what you have said, Your Highness. I will do what I can, but so many men are ruled by their passions in these days. Changing minds is hard enough, but changing hearts? Only God has that power, I think." He bowed and withdrew.

Ranya watched the old scholar go, thinking back to her childhood and searching her memory for any recollection of him meeting with her father. It would have been at least ten or fifteen years; Hadji Tumar's hair would have been gray, not white, and perhaps his beard would not have been quite so long. *Why is he here today?* she wondered. Had her uncle invited him to the palace to seek his counsel on some question of policy? Or did he hope that Hadji Tumar could use his influence to calm some of the current unrest? Would any of the insurgents listen to him?

Sultan Rashid interrupted her speculation by patting the chair beside him. "Come, sit, my dear. What is on your mind?"

Ranya set aside her curiosity, and sat down. "Have you been briefed by the general staff on our equipment losses in the last few weeks?" she asked.

Rashid sighed. "And here I was hoping that perhaps you merely desired the pleasure of my company. It is not seemly for a young woman to take an interest in military matters, Ranya. You know how I feel about this."

"I am afraid I had no opportunity to choose my gender, Uncle."

"While that is certainly true, I think you probably had a little more choice about your interests. Most other women your age occupy themselves thinking about young men in general, not just soldiers." Rashid raised a hand to forestall her protest. "No, never mind that now. I can see that you have something important on your mind. Tell me what it is you think I need to know."

"We are using up equipment and supplies too quickly to sustain the offensive we launched after the missile attack, Uncle." Ranya pulled her dataslate out of a hidden pocket in her caftan, and brought up the figures she had been looking at. "We might succeed in reducing a couple of the Caidist strongholds in built-up provinces like Nador or Meknez, but our sweep is stalling out in the remote regions. I think we need to consider a change of strategy."

"Really?" Rashid frowned. "General Mirza told me just yesterday that he was pleased with our progress, and especially pleased that our casualties have not been too bad. We're wearing down the caids, Ranya. It seems like we should maintain the pressure."

"I agree that we haven't suffered too many personnel losses—well, I agree that no serious casualties have been reported so far. But the problem is the same one we've been experiencing for years in dealing with the Caidists. They're avoiding contact with our heavy forces and allowing us to wear ourselves out chasing them all over the desert. There is not much fighting, but it's brutal on our equipment. Almost fifteen percent of our brand-new Léopards are out of action already, just from operational tempo. And when the Caidists choose to stand and fight, the casualties will be a much different story."

"If all this is accurate, why does the general staff remain optimistic? They can certainly count up tanks and vehicles as well as you can, Ranya."

"Because they're looking at maps, not logistics reports," Ranya told him. "General Mirza sees that he has a heavy brigade operating out in the Harthawi Basin where the Royal Guard hasn't dared to patrol in three years, and he thinks that he is winning a war. I see that next month he'll be lucky to have half that force still ready for operations, and I worry about what happens when the Caidists launch their counterattack."

"What do you suggest, then?" Rashid asked.

"Suspend the offensive, or at least the parts of it that we know are going nowhere. Bring those forces in to rest, reequip, and train before we launch another effort." Ranya took back her dataslate. "Or see if we can open direct talks with key caids, and buy their loyalty with the right concessions. Settle this uprising at the negotiating table before we lose in the field."

"Lose?" The sultan sat up sharply, and winced as his wounded shoulder repaid him with a jolt of pain. "The caids don't have a single modern war machine, Ranya! Even if we can't run them to ground in the desert, they have no ability to take the battle to us in the cities. General Mirza has pointed out to me a dozen times that, down through history, irregular skirmishers have never managed to defeat a well-organized, well-armed professional army fighting on open ground."

"General Mirza might do well to acquaint himself with the Peninsular War or the Narnian Uprising," said Ranya. "And it's not clear to me that our army is terribly professional."

"I doubt that General Mirza would be pleased to hear you say that."

"Probably not. Still, the fact remains that continuing the campaign risks overextending ourselves, Uncle. If General Mirza does not recognize that, you might need to find a commander who does."

Sultan Rashid shook his head. "Replacing General Mirza is simply not possible, Ranya. He is the choice of the beys, and if the beys withdraw their support for us . . . well, whatever follows will not be our concern, because the house of el-Nasir will be finished. Allowing our current offensives to end without achieving their goals might be just as dangerous. Not only would the Caidists be emboldened by their victory, the more ambitious beys would be emboldened as well. And what would happen if Montréal decided to write off our house as a lost cause? No, for political appearances, we cannot admit to weakness at this moment."

Ranya was silent. It greatly surprised her to hear her uncle voice such a clear summary of his concerns; she'd fallen into the habit of assuming that he was disengaged on matters of state. *His generals don't know how to win this war,* she decided. *And he doesn't know how to replace them.* "Then we must have more help from offworld," she finally said. "We need a commitment from Montréal to suppress the caids and make sure that none of the beys decide to move on the throne."

"That would be helpful," Sultan Rashid agreed. "But of course, Montréal refuses to commit ground forces. They don't want to be drawn any further into our war—which, by the way, would expand tenfold if Republic troops were called upon to suppress the desert tribes—and their own rivals among the Coalition powers won't stand for a Montréalais occupation of our world. For that matter, I should not like to live out the rest of my life as nothing but a Montréalais puppet."

"I am sorry, Uncle. I—I think I have not appreciated the difficulties of your situation until now."

"You mean that you thought I was not paying attention," said Rashid. He smiled wryly. "I look up from my gardens every now and then, my dear."

She smiled, but she could not completely dismiss her concern. "We still have to figure out a way to conserve our strength, Uncle Rashid. I can promise you that unless something changes soon, the Royal Guard is going to exhaust itself in our current offensives. It seems to me it would be better to negotiate from a position of relative strength, so if we have a way to bring any of the caids to the table, now is the time to do it."

"Keep this to yourself, my dear, but I am working on that already," the sultan replied. "Why do you think Hadji Tumar ibn Sakak was here?"

Ranya regarded her uncle for a moment, surprised. "I didn't know that any of the moderate clerics had any influence over the caids. What does he want for his support?"

"Some hope that he is backing the winning side, for a start. And guarantees that our traditions will be respected by offworlders, so that we won't all be godless Montréalais within a generation or two." Rashid set down his cup. "I am afraid I must excuse myself, my dear. I believe that Bey Salem wants me to help that Dremish trade representative increase his already vast fortune with some agreement or another."

"Of course," she said. "Thank you, Uncle. Don't let Bey Salem talk you into doing anything foolish. And don't say too much in front of that Dremish fellow, either. I have a feeling he is interested in things other than business deals."

Rashid got to his feet and gave her an elaborate salaam. "Have you not yet learned that I can talk all day long and not say one thing of importance, my dear?" Then he headed back inside the palace, his attendants moving in to brief him on his next discussion before he even left the terrace.

Ranya watched him go. Sultan Rashid was not the ruler her father had been, but the self-awareness to know that seemed like a rare quality in a sultan. The fact that he continued to entertain visits from Salem el-Fasi and his Dremish friend while SMS *Panther* lurked overhead troubled her; it seemed like negotiating with someone pointing a pistol in your general direction. *A move intended to elicit some more assistance from Montréal, perhaps?* she thought. Giving the Montréalais reason to believe they had competition for the sultan's loyalties and might need to up their offer seemed like a shrewd tactic.

She glanced at the clear sky overhead. *There is another warship in orbit,* she reminded herself. If Montréal's hands were tied by the considerations of its internal politics, maybe another power would be inclined to show support for the sultanate. She would have to be careful in exploring those options; the last thing in the world House Nasir needed was a rift with its Montréalais sponsors, after all. Something quiet, a back-channel approach, that would be the way to go. And she thought she knew where to begin. Lieutenant Sikander North of the Commonwealth starship *Hector* might understand the el-Nasir position better than anyone else in the system, and he could serve as a conduit to his own superior officers and the Aquilan diplomats in the system. Besides, she'd enjoyed their conversations, and she thought he had, too.

Is he thinking about me? she wondered, and instantly chastised herself for such a silly thought. Romantic daydreams had no place in her world at this moment. But the fact remained that she wanted to know what Sikander thought about their situation, and what he thought Aquila's position might be. If a social occasion offered the best way to speak with him again, well, she would just have to make that sacrifice, wouldn't she?

16

Silver Sea, Gadira II

Sikander reclined on the cushioned bench with his eyes closed, enjoying the feel of the warm sun on his face, the creaking of the rigging, and the endless whispering of the water against the boat's hull. He'd never actually *sailed* before, and he loved the experience. All of his previous boating had been aboard powered vessels of one sort or another—usually sport fishing—and generally involved racing to the best or most scenic spots at whatever speed he could manage. The idea that people might take pleasure in going somewhere slowly, or not really going anywhere at all, had never taken hold of him, but a few hours on the sultan's royal yacht *Shihab* had changed that. Sikander was a romantic at heart, and the sheer extravagance of sailing gracefully over a blue sea beneath a brilliant sky just as his ancestors had a thousand years ago on Earth was overwhelming.

"Are you well, sir?" Darvesh Reza asked him. The valet stood nearby, busying himself with arranging sliced fruit and iced drinks provided by the yacht's crew at a nearby table.

"Never better," Sikander answered. "Why do you ask?"

"You were lying with your eyes closed; I wondered if perhaps you were seasick."

"Merely enjoying the elements, Darvesh. And you should know that I have never had any trouble of that sort, or I wouldn't have taken up fishing." Sikander propped himself up on his elbow and glanced over the low wooden rail ringing the yacht's expansive stern. The brown jumble of Tanjeer's buildings and factories had long since vanished over the horizon behind *Shihab;* the line of barren mountains and sea cliffs outside the capital slowly receded to the north as the yacht glided out onto the Silver Sea, leaving land behind.

Idly he wondered for perhaps the tenth time in the last hour or so why Ranya had invited him to come for a sail. A simple desire for companionship outside her customary circles? A quiet effort to ascertain more about the Commonwealth's interests in Gadira, or perhaps a subtle message to Montréal or Dremark that the sultan's allegiance might be flexible? Or was it a romantic overture—in which case, how exactly should he respond to any intimacies that were offered? Sikander had been surprised to receive the invitation to spend a day or two on the sultan's yacht without the rest of *Hector*'s officers along, and a little uncertain of how to reply, but Captain Markham hadn't hesitated. "If the amira enjoys your company and wants to spend some time with you, consider yourself under orders to attend," she'd told Sikander. "It offers a unique opportunity to gain the ear of the sultan. But don't sleep with her, Mr. North. We don't need any more complications here."

Of course, not *sleeping with someone might also cause complications,* Sikander reflected. Which order took precedence—avoid physical intimacy, or avoid diplomatic complications? And if a romantic situation developed, how would it complicate matters with Lara Dunstan when he returned to New Perth? He was fond of her, too, and hoped to renew their acquaintance after his deployment. "Don't get ahead of yourself, Sikay," he muttered. So far the outing appeared to be perfectly chaste, and in fact it was hard to imagine how he could initiate anything else with two dozen Royal Guard sailors and stewards aboard.

"What was that, sir?" Darvesh asked. He, of course, had to come along as well. Sikander had been surrounded by Aquilan officers at the sultan's garden party and at dinner aboard the *Panther,* but traveling unaccompanied on a planet in such turmoil as Gadira was out of the question, especially after the recent attack on the sultan's skycade.

"Nothing," said Sikander. "Just reflecting on complications."

"The entire point of sailing is to simplify things for a time," said Ranya, stepping through the companionway that led to the main cabin below. She had changed into a light, gauzy sundress, and tied her hair back in a long dark ponytail. "That's why I love it so much. The palace is busy around the clock, and there is always more to do. Getting away on *Shihab* compels me to set aside my concerns for a time. It's good for the soul, I think."

"In that case, I am gratified by your concern for mine. Thank you for inviting me."

"I'm glad you were able to break away from your duties when I called." Ranya crossed the sitting area at the stern and sat near Sikander; Darvesh finished rearranging the tray of refreshments to his liking, and left the two of them alone. "I see you're sitting in the sun. Most offworlders find this part of Gadira to be too warm for their liking."

"I grew up in the tropics of Jaipur. This is a pleasant change from New Perth, *Hector*'s home port. It's a rare day that gets above twenty degrees C in Brigadoon." Sikander smiled at Ranya, and nodded up at the great sails and slanted masts that loomed overhead. "I'm not very knowledgeable about sailing ships. What kind of vessel is *Shihab*?"

"She is modeled on an old Terran type called a dhow. They were common in the Red Sea and Indian Ocean during the preindustrial centuries, or so I am told." Ranya gazed up at the clean white sails, bellied out in the afternoon breeze. "Of course, most dhows were working vessels—the trading ships of the ancient Mideast. *Shihab* is built for pleasure sailing, although she has power turbines belowdecks, satellite navigation, and a variety of hidden defensive systems. The Royal Guard wouldn't dream of allowing the family to set foot on her otherwise."

Sikander nodded. "My family's Srinagar estate is similar. It looks like a rustic Terran lodge on the outside, but it's fitted with the most modern comm and security systems my father can afford. I spent many summers there when I was a boy, riding and hunting in the hills near the Kharan Desert. It's a good place to get away from things, but the realities of our situation demand that my father is never out of touch for emergencies."

"Do you have any sailboats in Kashmir, Sikander?"

He shook his head. "No sailing yachts like *Shihab*, at least not on Jaipur. There just isn't a yachting culture on my homeworld. The coastal regions are subject to powerful storms during cyclone season, so most settlements grew up well inland. On the other hand, Srinagar—the larger and more densely populated of Kashmir's planets—is home to quite a few pleasure craft. But most of those are powered boats."

"A shame," Ranya said. "It's not the same experience at all."

"I am beginning to appreciate that."

They passed most of the afternoon comparing more stories of their upbringing and the customs of their homeworlds. It was a pleasant way to spend the day, watching the mountains of the coast recede behind them, surrounded by the creaking of the rigging and the cool spray of the small waves slapping against the hull. Ranya was an only child, and Sultan Rashid's two daughters were a good ten years younger than her, leaving Ranya without any relations close to her own age. She told him about the servants' children she had played with when she was small, the gentle and good-humored side her otherwise fierce father Kamal had shown his family, and how much she had missed him over the last seven years.

"My circumstances were a little different," said Sikander when they finished a late lunch. "The Norths are more of a horde than a household."

"You come from a large family?"

"Oh, yes. I have four siblings: my older brothers Gamand and Devindar, my older sister Usha, and my younger brother Manvir. Not to mention a dozen or so close cousins who are more or less about my age." Sikander smiled ruefully. "The only time I seemed to get my father's attention was when I did something bad."

"I find that hard to believe. Like what?"

Sikander glanced up at *Shihab*'s sails. "Well, there was the time Devindar and I stole the family yacht."

"I thought you said you didn't sail!"

"*Ketu* is a powerboat, and a very fast one at that. I was twelve, and Devindar was fourteen. Our parents were away visiting colleges with Gamand and Usha, and the two of us decided to take the boat out on Long Lake to impress Hamsi and Jaya Lawton." He smiled. "The Lawtons had a handsome estate fifty kilometers down the lakeshore, and we were both quite smitten with Hamsi. I think we had some idea of zipping down to their place and asking the girls to join us for a boat ride."

"And the household staff let you just take the boat?"

"Of course not. We weren't supposed to be on *Ketu* without an adult, but we told them Father had given us permission to take the boat out to fish nearby if we wanted to. We simply bluffed our way on board." Sikander shook his head. "Apparently our confidence was quite convincing."

Ranya laughed. "Your father must have been furious when he found out!"

"We were sentenced to landscaping work for the whole summer. My father had the head gardener rip out a perfectly good sprinkler system and install a new one just so the two of us would have ditches to dig. Although Devindar had it worse than I, since he was supposedly old enough to know better." Sikander grimaced. "I'm afraid Devindar and my father still don't get along."

That led to stories of other escapades and punishments, which occupied them for the next hour or more. In the middle of the afternoon, the green hills of an island crept into view ahead of the yacht. It steadily grew higher and clearer, until *Shihab* sailed into a magnificent half-moon bay surrounded by headlands covered in dense foliage. Sikander smelled the rich scents of exotic blooms, and listened to birdsong echoing in the forest. He glanced over to Ranya, who stood by the rail beside him. "I was led to believe that Gadira was a desert planet," he said to her. "What is this place?"

"This is the island of Socotra, named after a similar place on Old Terra," she told him. "It belongs to my family. The el-Nasir sultans have used it as a sort of getaway and refuge for a couple of hundred years. There is a small villa just past that headland over there, but I asked our crew to stop here for an hour or two before continuing on. There is something here every visitor to Gadira should see."

"It's beautiful," Sikander admitted.

"Oh, I am not talking about the island," Ranya laughed. "Go below to your cabin and put on a swimsuit, Sikay. We're going in the water."

He shrugged and did as he was told. In a few minutes, he returned to the deck in his swim trunks and a T-shirt. The afternoon was drawing on, and the harsh Gadiran sun was mellowing to a golden twilight. He admired the scenery until Ranya joined him by the rail. She wore a demure green one-piece that showed no cleavage or midriff—a pity, in Sikander's estimation, since Ranya looked quite good in a swimsuit otherwise. A formfitting suit with bare legs and arms fell within acceptable bounds for Gadiran swimwear, but local custom frowned on the notion of a bikini or, God forbid, the topless suits popular on some Coalition worlds.

If Ranya guessed anything about the direction of his thoughts, she gave him no sign other than a slight smile. She handed him a diving mask and a pair of fins. "It's easier to put these on in the water," she said, and then she stepped off the side, disappearing into the bay with a silver splash.

Sikander pulled off his shirt, then hopped over the side to follow her. The deck was about two meters above the surface; he sank into warm, startlingly clear water. He could see the entire length of *Shihab*'s dark hull, looking like a toy sitting in a bathtub. Ranya hovered in the water a few meters away, already dressed in her mask and fins. Her green suit shimmered like emerald, rippling with dappled light from the wavelets above. It complemented her olive skin and dark hair perfectly.

Sikander surfaced to clear his mask and fit it to his face, slipping the rebreather tube into his mouth. More modern masks used a nasal rebreather and fitted a subvocal pickup so that you could talk to your companions underwater, but it seemed those hadn't yet reached this corner of the Montréalais empire. Then, pulling on his fins, he dove again and swam down toward Ranya. She waited a moment to make sure he was following, then led the way over the sandy bottom to a large reef head. Hundreds of tiny, brightly colored fish cruised and darted around the rocky outcropping, which was covered with flowering plants like an aquatic meadow. The fish seemed much like those Sikander had seen on other worlds; convergent evolution selected for streamlined, gilled, finned body plans, although the Gadiran species were beautifully colored. The sea plants, on the other hand, were something Sikander had never seen on any other planet. He decided that it had to be a combination of the Gadiran sun's particular spectrum and the clarity of the water. Green plants in Gadira's waters managed just as well in the shallows as they would on land, and the water chemistry explained how the colors remained vibrant to great depth. But the flowerlike structures he could attribute only to the randomness of evolution.

Ranya waved an arm to gain his attention. He glanced over, and saw that scores of small fish were circling her body. The shimmer of her emerald swimsuit drew their attention, just like the flowering plants of the reef. The fish evidently had no fear of humans; in fact, Sikander noticed that quite a number of the tiny creatures followed him as well, swimming lazily around him. One variety featured a striking combination of scarlet and gold with a black chinstrap marking, reminding him of the uniforms the Khanate Guard wore back in Kashmir; they bumped softly at his fingers when he reached out to touch them.

They swam together for a long time, exploring more of the reef. Sikander found new things to look at every minute, and slowly came to realize that the reefs of Gadira might be one of the most interesting and beautiful environments he'd ever wandered into. Of course, his company might have colored his experience somewhat. In their last stop before heading back to the boat, Ranya removed her rebreather to grin at him, at which point he removed his to grin back and pull her close for a stolen kiss. The kiss itself was not particularly great—he tasted nothing but salt water, and their masks got in the way—but the feel of her slim body pressed close to his and the soft firmness of her breasts against his chest more than made up for the logistical problems. Her hand wandered down to give him a playful tug before she broke away to surface.

He glided up to surface beside her. "What was *that*?" he said, stripping off his mask.

"I have no idea what you're talking about," she primly replied, and swam over to the ladder to climb back onto the yacht. Sikander made a point of swimming vigorously back and forth across the stern of the ship for a few moments more, mostly so that he could climb out of the water without announcing a conspicuous erection to everyone on board. When he judged it safe, he scrambled up the ladder and gratefully accepted the towel offered by a steward waiting for him.

"That was amazing," he told Ranya, who was toweling off nearby. "I've never seen anything like it. It's like a field of wildflowers underwater."

Ranya nodded. "We call them *zahrabarh,* sea flowers. Every planet has its own unique treasures, of course. The reefs are one of ours." She finished with her towel, and slipped on a long white robe; Sikander realized that the air was growing chilly, and that the sun was already touching the horizon. "This might be my favorite place in the world."

"I can see why." Sikander toweled himself. "So what's next?"

"We'll be at the island villa in half an hour. We'll have dinner and spend the night there—you'll have one of the guest bungalows, of course—and perhaps swim or hike in the morning before sailing back." Ranya's smile faded a little. "Unfortunately, I really can't stay away for more than a day or so right now."

Shihab weighed anchor and got under way again, although this time she motored along slowly on her turbines— they were in the lee of the island, and there wasn't enough breeze for the sails. Sikander rinsed off the seawater in an abovedecks shower, then went below to change into casual evening wear. By the time he finished and returned to the deck, the sun had sunk below the horizon, and the yacht was approaching an estate spread out along the beach of yet another bay. Some of the wooden buildings stood on piers extending out over the bay, while the palm trees and forested hillside screened the others. Festive lanterns hung from the trees.

Ranya personally showed Sikander and Darvesh to his

bungalow when the yacht moored to the dock. They ate a leisurely dinner of Gadiran seasoned seafood kebobs and fine white wine on a veranda of the main house. "It's sort of frowned upon in the more observant quarters, but the Montréalais can't go anywhere without importing their wines, and many city-dwelling Gadirans have become enthusiasts," Ranya explained. "In public functions at the palace, the sultan usually does not serve alcohol. Privately, wine in moderation is considered acceptable, and Socotra is a place where we may enjoy our privacy."

After dinner, Sikander and Ranya strolled out to an open-sided bali hut perched at the end of a pier. Gadira's moon gleamed low in the eastern sky, striking yellow-white reflections off the water. Sikander noticed that the small staff of servants remained in the main house, allowing the two of them quite a bit of space. They sat together for a long moment, gazing out at the moonlit bay.

"Thank you for sharing Socotra with me," Sikander said. "The sailing trip, the swim at the reef, the dinner, and this beautiful place . . . I think my shipmates would be very jealous of me."

"You are welcome, Sikay." Ranya glanced back at the buildings and verandas of the sultan's retreat, and sighed. "I shall miss it when I leave."

"You are leaving?"

"In a few months. My uncle wants me to travel. He is sending me on an extended visit with distant relations in different parts of the Terran Caliphate." Ranya shrugged. "I will have a chance to visit Terra, which I am looking forward to. How many people get a chance to see the home-world of us all?"

"I haven't yet, but I hope to one day," said Sikander. "You sound as if you are not entirely satisfied with the arrangements, though."

"I may be gone for two or three years." Ranya gestured at the villa. "I worry about what I will find when I return."

Sikander studied her features in the dim light. "What do you fear?" he asked.

"I worry whether my uncle will be in power much longer, and who will replace him if House Nasir falls," she said in a quiet voice. "If it was just a matter of balancing the interests of the caids and the beys, I think we could manage it. But the offworld influences complicate everything. Someone is arming the Caidists with modern weapons. The Montréalais have supported our own forces for years, but now their own internal politics leave them unable or unwilling to help us meet this new threat. And I don't know what to make of the sudden interest other powers have developed in Gadira." She glanced back at him. "In fact, I have to admit that one of the reasons I asked you to join me on *Shihab* was to see whether I could learn something about Aquila's intentions from you."

Sikander smiled in the shadows. He had half an idea of what some of the other reasons might be, but he wasn't particularly offended if she chose to mix some business with pleasure. One of the things he admired about Ranya was her intelligence. She was nobody's fool; he suspected that things on Gadira might not be in such a state if her countrymen had been just a little more progressive about the notion of a female head of state.

"I don't know what new insights I can offer, Ranya," he answered. "Keeping in mind that I am not a diplomat . . . it's my understanding that Aquila prefers the status quo. We want to see Montréal and Gadira continue their relationship, and we want to see an end of the current unrest so that Gadira becomes a safe place to do business again. I think that the el-Nasirs represent the best instrument for preserving the current balance of power, and helping you would be the easiest way to achieve our goals. Others think we ought to wait and see which faction or combination of factions gains the upper hand, and make them our new friends. I don't agree with that point of view."

"I am just an instrument for your goals?" Ranya asked with a mischievous smile.

"Well, you're the one who lured me down to the ground so you could extract my secrets with your feminine wiles."

"Feminine wiles?" she laughed. "Who says that?"

Sikander grinned. "I confess, I've been waiting for years to find the occasion to use that turn of phrase."

She laughed again, and Sikander joined her. Then she sighed. "I'm sorry, Sikander. I suppose this wasn't what you anticipated when we wandered out here. I wish I could put these things from my mind."

"You are who you are, Ranya," he said to her. "And I wouldn't say I anticipated anything. Well, perhaps I hoped a little, but I wouldn't have wanted to presume."

"A few centuries ago, your head would have been struck off for entertaining those sorts of notions about the daughter of a sultan." Ranya got to her feet and glanced back at the veranda; no one was in sight. Then she leaned down close over Sikander to kiss him soundly. He drank in the taste of her lips, the lovely scent of her perfume—and her sudden soft gasp as he slid one hand up under the hem of her dress to boldly caress her, counting on the shadows to conceal his movements.

"Presume, indeed," she breathed, and leaned into him for one long, delicious moment. Then a clatter of motion from the main house interrupted them; two of the serving staff came out onto the veranda to cover the table and adjust the shutters for the night. The servants seemed absorbed in their duties and Sikander didn't think they had seen anything, but Ranya pulled away with a nod in their direction.

"Well, turnabout is fair play," said Sikander. He stood and moved closer.

"I know." Ranya set a hand on his chest, keeping her distance as she watched the house for a moment. "Still, perhaps we had better call it a night. The staff is very discreet, but . . ."

He started to reach for her, but stopped himself. "I understand," he made himself say. "I do not want to put you in a difficult spot."

Ranya gave him a smile, and kissed him once more—a much more chaste brush of her lips against his. "Thank you," she said. "Sleep well, Sikander. I'll wake you early for breakfast, and show you around the island before we set out for home."

"Good night, Ranya." Sikander watched her walk slowly back down the pier toward the main house, and allowed himself a sigh of regret. Ranya el-Nasir was rapidly becoming a lot more interesting to him than a sultan's niece ought to be, given the trouble that could come of any indiscretions here. After all, Captain Markham had given him clear instructions on that score.

"Keep your head clear, Sikay," he murmured aloud. Sleep well, indeed! He knew what he would be thinking about once he was in bed. Did she expect him to presume just a little more, and find his way to her room? Or did she intend to visit him? And what would he do if she did?

He returned to his bungalow, changed for bed, and slipped beneath the sheets. The bungalow's bedroom featured a louvered wooden sliding door leading out to a deck and a view of the sea; the moonlight glimmered on the water, painting the ceiling with a pale glow. It did not take him long to recall the feel of Ranya's body pressed close to him, the fleeting touch of her hand on him, the soft brush of her breasts against his chest as he stroked her between the legs for that one delicious moment . . . He sighed and got up, walking over to the door and stepping out onto the balcony. The air was cool and humid on his bare torso. He watched the waves break on the shore, but when he looked away, he noticed that the sliding door two bungalows down stood open.

That was Ranya's room.

Before he could think better of it, Sikander padded down

the steps of his own deck and made his way along the path behind the bungalows, half expecting to be confronted by scimitar-wielding harem guards. There was no way the Royal Guard would not be keeping an eye on their amira . . . but Ranya had told him that Socotra was a place where Gadira's royals could enjoy their privacy. His heartbeat quickened as he considered the implications of that remark, and before he knew it, he was climbing up the stairs leading to her door. *I hope this is what Ranya intended,* he thought. *Otherwise this is going to be very hard to explain to the captain.*

He paused in the open doorway, silhouetted by the moonlight but momentarily unable to see much in the deep shadows of the bedroom. "Ranya?" he called softly.

He heard a rustle of sheets. In the silver gloom he saw her sit up in her bed, the sheets pooled around her waist. She wore a thin sleeping shift that clung to her breasts, her nipples barely veiled. "I wondered if you would come," she answered.

Sikander advanced into the room, feeling the familiar excitement in his loins. His silken pajama pants wouldn't do much to hide what was on his mind. "Do you want me to go?" he asked.

She shook her head. "I am not entirely sure this is a good idea . . . but no."

"Good, because right now, I am." He clambered onto the bed beside her and covered her mouth with his, kissing her long and passionately. Ranya sighed and seemed to melt into his kiss with a soft sound, sinking back into her bed as he leaned over her on his hands and knees. With one hand he brushed aside the sheets; she gasped softly when he caressed her again, and lowered himself down beside her. Sikander devoted himself to the task of undressing her one gentle move at a time, and exploring her lovely body as he kissed her neck and nuzzled at her soft breasts. When he finally entered her, she quivered and cried out, clasping him close.

Afterward, they lay in a tangle of arms and legs, the moonlight shining in through the louvered door. Ranya idly stroked her hand across Sikander's well-muscled chest, while he caressed her back. "Did I say you were a little too bold for your own good?" she murmured.

"That might have come up, but I'm not always good at taking advice," he admitted. "The sultan's guards aren't going to behead me now, are they?"

"I do enjoy *some* privacy. What happens behind closed doors is nothing to concern them, especially in a secluded retreat like Socotra. But it might be best if you allowed your bungalow attendant to find you in your own bed in the morning."

"Which is still quite a few hours away, the last I looked."

Ranya smiled. "You may not be good at taking advice, but you seem to be able to take a hint," she replied. Her hand wandered downward, and of course, that was just the sort of hint that Sikander needed to stop talking again.

17

Socotra, Gadira II

An hour before dawn, Sikander slipped back to his own room, leaving a delectably nude Ranya sleeping in her luxurious sheets. He'd just drifted off to sleep again in his own bed when the chirp of his comm unit on the nightstand interrupted him.

A little groggy, he sat up and keyed the audio-only icon. "Lieutenant North," he answered.

"Mr. North, this is Ensign Girard. Sorry to disturb you, sir, but I think I've found something interesting."

Sikander rubbed his eyes, trying to bring his attention back to his ship and the mission. In the last few hours he hadn't thought about *Hector* once. *Good thing he didn't call a couple of hours ago,* he decided. "Go ahead, Mr. Girard."

"Sir, I've been doing some traffic analysis of Gadira's shipping, and trying to correlate it with Caidist attacks across the planet. I think I've identified a ship engaged in smuggling arms to the rebels. She's just made atmospheric entry, heading for the port facilities at Meknez."

"Traffic analysis? Isn't that something for Mr. Randall and the Operations Department?"

"Well, yes sir, it is." Sikander could hear the apologetic note in Girard's voice over the audio link and imagined the shy Aquilan turning red. "I got the idea after I started developing a target list of rebel strongholds and noting which ones seemed to be stockpiling advanced arms. Mr. Randall and his intelligence specialists are focused on direct observation, looking for where the weapons are and examining shipping as it enters the system. I started wondering when the weapons that were already here actually arrived, so I built and ran a set of traffic sims and compared them to rebel activity." Girard hesitated a moment. "I didn't even think I would find anything, but I guess I got interested in the puzzle of setting up the programs."

"You have a very useful hobby, Mr. Girard," said Sikander. "And your initiative is commendable, too. What have you found out?"

"Sir, there is a ninety-three percent chance that the vessel currently landing in Meknez delivered two shipments of offworld arms to Caidist rebels in the last two months. She's a Cygnan-registered independent freighter named *Oristani Caravan*. What should we do, sir?"

"Intercepting illegal arms shipments is one of the reasons we're here. Go find Mr. Randall or Mr. Chatburn immediately, and let them know what you've found out." Sikander thought it over for a moment; some officers might think that Michael Girard was trying to show them up by doing their job for them, although anyone who knew the ensign well would understand that he simply didn't have the sort of competitiveness to do something like that. It was, however, possible that Randall or Chatburn might not take him seriously. "I will call the captain, and advise her of your suspicions."

"Thank you, sir. I'll organize my information and take it to the XO."

"Good work, Mr. Girard," Sikander told him. "This might be the opportunity we've been looking for to change the trajectory of events in this system. North, out."

He glanced across the beach at Ranya's bungalow.

Lanterns glowed softly in the predawn gloom, and a chorus of birds and insects beginning to rouse themselves for the day filled the air. The last thing in the world he wanted to do was leave; a day of hiking or swimming in Ranya's company, perhaps followed by another nighttime visit to her bedchamber, struck him as an excellent plan. Unfortunately it seemed that Michael Girard's curiosity might have brought his sojourn with the amira to an early end. *I hope she understands,* he thought. If she believed that he was looking for a way to slip away from her after the night they'd shared . . .

He sighed, and keyed his comm unit again as he got out of bed to get dressed. "*Hector,* this is Lieutenant North. Put me through to the captain, please."

Two hours later, Sikander found himself at the controls of a Royal Guard combat flyer above the dark waters of Gadira's Bitter Sea, fifteen hundred kilometers west of Socotra. It was still dark here, although a pearly rose glow hovered on the eastern horizon. Sunrise was not far off in this part of the world. He checked the nav system of the flyer, and switched off the autopilot. The flyer bounced softly in the air as he settled his hands on the control yoke. The city of Meknez was thirty kilometers distant, only a couple of minutes away at his current speed. "Tell everyone to strap in, Darvesh," he said. "We're getting pretty close."

"Yes, sir." Darvesh Reza sat in the middle bench of the flyer's small passenger area, along with three Gadiran Royal Guards. The Kashmiri soldier wore Navy battle dress, with a light helmet snugged over his pakul. A heavy mag pistol hung in a shoulder holster beneath his left arm, and a combat knife was strapped to his right thigh; Sikander wore the same uniform and weapons. Montréalais mag carbines for each of them were racked behind the pilot's seat. They had borrowed the flyer and the carbines from the Royal Guard detachment at the small Socotra Island barracks, but the rest of the gear came from Darvesh's luggage. The bodyguard kept his combat dress close at hand, even when the day's plan called for a pleasure cruise and an overnight stay at a remote retreat.

The flyer's comm unit beeped. "Flyer Socotra-Two, this is Shuttle Hector-Alpha. Confirm your ETA, over." Sikander recognized the voice of Petty Officer Long, the shuttle pilot.

"Hector-Alpha, we can be skids-on-the-ground in two minutes, over," Sikander replied.

There was a pause as Long checked his own approach. "Socotra-Two, roger that. Make your touchdown on the south side of the landing zone. We're coming in from the northeast, and we'll be skids-down at the same time, over."

"Confirmed. See you on the ground. Socotra-Two out," Sikander replied. He turned his attention to his flying. He'd been descending steadily for fifteen minutes, and the borrowed Gadiran flyer raced along only a few hundred meters above the moonlit swells of the Bitter Sea. The streetlights and traffic signals of the city of Meknez covered a vast, curving crescent of coastline ahead of him. Instead of palm-lined avenues like those he'd seen in the capital, old maglev rails crisscrossed Meknez, carrying massive ore trains from the strip mines out in the desert. The harbor district was crowded with ore carriers and transshipment facilities where spacegoing freighters could disgorge their containerized cargo and load gigantic hoppers full of the rare earths that had brought miners to these southern wastelands three hundred years ago. Bright work lights harshly illuminated the port facilities; the city's industrial areas worked around the clock.

He glanced over at Captain Tarek Zakur, the officer in charge of the small squad of Royal Guards on board. As Sikander understood things, Zakur commanded Ranya's security detail. As the ranking officer at Socotra, Zakur had decided to personally lead the Royal Guard force headed for the suspicious freighter, leaving the defense of the sultan's island villa in the hands of his subordinates. "Any signs that we're expected, Captain?" Sikander asked him.

The big Gadiran sat in the copilot's seat. A mediocre pilot, he'd been happy to relinquish the flying to Sikander. Instead, he busied himself monitoring the local emergency channels and keeping an eye on the vid feed from *Hector*'s orbital observation. If he knew where Sikander had spent the night—and Sikander had to imagine that he did, or he wouldn't have been much of a security chief—he gave no sign. "None as yet, Mr. North," he answered in Montréalais-accented Anglic.

"I'm beginning to think Ranya was right," Sikander said. He'd felt like a heel for asking the Socotra Island staff to wake her before dawn, and could only imagine what she must have thought. But as soon as he'd explained what *Hector* suspected about *Oristani Caravan,* she'd been quick to grasp the implications. Meknez hosted only a token Royal Guard presence; the city was under Bey Salem's control, and most of the soldiers consisted of his own house troops. If arms were being smuggled through the port at Meknez, someone had already arranged for the local authorities to look the other way, and any attempt to alert the Meknez-based forces to search and seize *Oristani Caravan*'s cargo could tip off the very people they hoped to catch. Speed and secrecy were the order of the day, and that meant using Royal Guard forces available on Socotra—and the contingent of armed sailors from CSS *Hector.*

"In my experience, that is usually the case with the amira," Zakur admitted. "Except, of course, when she thinks she doesn't need to listen to me."

Sikander smiled to himself, replaying the conversation in his mind. Ranya had insisted on coming along, a prospect that had absolutely horrified Captain Zakur. Only a threatened mass resignation by her guard detail had convinced her that her royal person had no business riding along on security raids. Even then Zakur had been careful to check the flyer's storage compartments to make sure she hadn't stowed away before he took off. "I was referring to the idea of keeping the local forces out of this," he told Zakur.

The Gadiran kept his eyes on the vid feed, but nodded. "I am very much looking forward to my next conversation with Bey Salem," he said. "If your intelligence is right, then his men are corrupt, complicit, or just staggeringly incompetent. I would like to know which it is."

Sikander glanced at the countdown clock in the flyer's head-up display. He was running a little ahead of schedule, so he cut his speed a bit and put the flyer into a gentle S-curve to kill a few seconds. It might also help to confuse any observers on the ground about the spot where he intended to land. The port was busy; in addition to the half-dozen spacegoing freighters that were currently loading or unloading in the harbor basin, a similar number of seagoing vessels not much smaller than their spacefaring cousins moored along the concrete piers. In the long centuries of Gadira's isolation from the rest of human space, antiquated rail networks and surface shipping had served as the primary means of transporting goods across the planet. Heavy grav transports with induction drives slowly replaced the old ships and trains, but they could handle only a portion of Gadira's shipping needs, and the planet's infrastructure still featured facilities like the port at Meknez or the rail yards in other cities. For now, a good deal of Gadira's merchant traffic still floated, and that would likely remain true for decades to come.

"Hector-Alpha on final," said Long over the comm channel. "Ten seconds."

"Socotra-Two on final," Sikander confirmed, changing course one last time. He kept up the best speed he could manage safely, now passing by the looming cargo cranes that lined the dock. At the last instant he switched on the landing lights to get one good look at the supposedly empty stretch of parking lot where he intended to set down. Just past the building, he caught the flashing lights of *Hector*'s shuttle, touching down close by the Cygnan freighter. Sub-lieutenant Larkin and her party were responsible for securing *Oristani Caravan*.

The lot looked clear, so he quickly flared out, reduced power, and thumped his landing skids down on the concrete. "Touchdown!" he called out to the others on board.

Darvesh and the guards in the back threw open their sliding doors and bailed out of the flyer; Captain Zakur popped his own door and followed. Sikander paused for a moment to cut the flyer's engine and power it down, then unbuckled and scrambled out of his seat. Darvesh waited for him with the last mag carbine; Sikander checked it quickly as the Gadirans hurried to the warehouse door. While *Hector*'s landing party stormed the freighter, Sikander's small team had the job of seizing the warehouse and detaining anybody they found.

Sikander expected the Gadiran soldiers with him to burst through the door and storm the building, but they surprised him. Gathering by the warehouse door, they quietly tried the handle. It opened easily, and the four Royal Guards slipped inside. Darvesh and Sikander followed after them. Large cargo containers filled the warehouse interior, dimly lit by flickering overhead lights. The big containers formed narrow alleyways in the huge structure, providing the team with plenty of cover as they moved deeper. Open space in the center of the warehouse provided parking for ground transports with flatbed trailers, which could pull in to load or unload containers. At the moment, several transports were parked there with engines idling. A traversing crane mounted on rails suspended from the ceiling positioned a container onto the bed of one of the transports; Sikander heard the echoing calls of men shouting at one another, the high-pitched warning beep of the crane as it moved, and the low rumbling purr of the transports' engines.

A man appeared at the head of the alley between containers. The fellow wore a jumpsuit and a hard hat, and looked like an ordinary port worker . . . except for the automag pistol slung over his shoulder. He wasn't looking in their direction, and seemed to be involved in directing the crane's movement.

Zakur glanced back at his soldiers and signaled with his hands. Two of the guards peeled off to slip down another gap between the cargo units. The captain waited fifteen seconds, then moved forward and broke into the open. "Freeze!" he shouted at the men working in the warehouse. "This is the sultan's guard!" He continued in Jadeed-Arabi that Sikander couldn't follow, but the intent seemed clear. Zakur covered the first man in sight with his carbine, and the fellow slowly raised his hands. The other soldiers pounced, finding targets of their own.

Sikander and Darvesh followed Zakur into the open. Darvesh covered someone to his right, so Sikander swung his carbine to the left, and found two very surprised-looking Gadirans staring back at him. It looked like close to a dozen smugglers in the room, but they'd been caught off-guard. For a long moment, no one moved or said anything. Zakur growled out a set of instructions and nodded at one of the workers; Sikander understood that they had been told to lay down their arms, slowly.

The man Zakur menaced scowled fiercely. He was a heavyset fellow, perhaps fifty years of age, with a thick gray-streaked beard. Glaring at the guard captain, he carefully unslung his weapon and started to lay it down. Then, from outside, a sudden burst of mag-weapon reports and the staccato popping of conventional gunfire broke out. A comm unit on one worker's belt crackled aloud, carrying a rapid stream of Jadeed-Arabi—a warning or a call for help, Sikander guessed.

The insurgents in the warehouse panicked. The man in the blue hard hat suddenly raised his weapon at Zakur, but the Royal Guard captain did not hesitate. His mag carbine whined twice, hurling its lethal darts through the center of the older man's chest. The fellow staggered back and collapsed, but in the blink of an eye, gunshots and screams filled the air. Insurgents lunged for their weapons or dove for cover; the outnumbered Royal Guards opened up on anyone holding a weapon.

Both of Sikander's targets went for their guns at the same time. He hesitated for a critical instant, not sure who to shoot, before he slewed his barrel to one side and drilled a mag-carbine round just under the chin of the one on the left. The back of the man's neck exploded in blood and bone; he crumpled nervelessly to the floor. The other man shot wildly in Sikander's direction, and Sikander ducked back around the corner of the cargo unit. Slugs thudded into the container's metal side, adding the clatter of their impact to the bedlam of the scene.

"Take some alive!" Zakur shouted in Standard Anglic for the benefit of the Aquilans. "We need intelligence!" Then the Gadiran captain cursed and spun to the ground, knocked off his feet by a slug that struck him in the shin.

Sikander crouched low, and quickly popped back around the corner of his cargo unit. The second man he'd been covering continued to spray bullets around the room while sidestepping toward the massive shape of the nearest ground transport, evidently moving toward cover. Sikander quickly sighted on him and pulled the trigger; the mag carbine jumped against his shoulder. He meant to knock the man down with a couple of shots in the legs, but instead he caught the fellow with a short burst right through the front pockets of his trousers, riddling his hip and pelvis. The insurgent collapsed, screaming in pain; Sikander hurried over to kick the man's weapon away from him, then turned to look for another target.

Darvesh calmly shot down an insurgent who paused to switch magazines, then turned and crippled another with shots through knee and shoulder. Sikander fired a burst in the general direction of another fellow targeting Darvesh's back; he missed, but the man ducked out of sight, and a moment later one of the other Royal Guards lobbed a stun grenade almost on top of the insurgent. The blast shook the warehouse and hurled the unfortunate rebel a good three meters in the air.

The fire slackened, replaced by the angry shouts of Zakur's men and the moaning of the wounded. Sikander moved cautiously around the parked transports, looking for anyone who might be trying to keep out of sight. Then, the heavy transport beside him roared to life and surged forward.

"Sir! Look out!" Darvesh shouted from across the warehouse.

Sikander threw himself out of the transport's path. He hit the floor hard and rolled, his mag carbine clattering across the floor, but he caught one good look at the cab as the vehicle passed. To his surprise, the driver was fair-skinned, lean, with sandy-colored hair and light eyes. *I've seen that man before!*

Mag-weapon shots erupted as Darvesh and the Gadiran Royal Guards opened fire, riddling the cab and motor compartment with shot after shot, but they failed to stop the massive transport. The driver plowed through the closed loading doors with a spectacular crash, hurling them into the parking lot beyond, and drove off into the night.

Sikander picked himself up off the floor, and recovered his carbine just as Darvesh hurried up to him. "Sir, are you hurt?" the valet asked.

"Just bruised." Sikander glared after the transport, its taillights disappearing into the port. He keyed his communicator. "Long, are you listening? A transport just smashed its way out of the warehouse. Get airborne and stop it!"

"Sorry, sir, I can't," the shuttle pilot replied. "The shuttle took a rocket when the fighting started. It's damaged, I'm not sure it can fly. I'm restarting the bird now."

Sikander scowled. "Damn. All right, let me know when you can get in the air."

"Did you get a good look at the driver, sir?" Darvesh asked.

"It was the Dremish consul. I don't recall his name, but I met him on board *Panther* last week." Sikander considered the implications of that for a moment, and decided he didn't like them at all. He sighed and returned his attention to the warehouse. "What is our situation here?"

"One of the Gadiran guards is dead. Captain Zakur is wounded and needs attention, but I think he should be fine. There are six enemy fighters dead, and four others wounded."

Sikander smiled. "I saw that one fellow you put on the ground. Nice shooting, Darvesh."

The Kashmiri nodded gravely. "Thank you, sir, but I regret he is unconscious. We may have to bring him around before we can question him."

"It looks like Captain Zakur's men have this place well in hand. Let's go see how Ms. Larkin did." Sikander took a moment to get his bearings, waved at the Gadiran officer to let him know that they were leaving, and then headed out through the destroyed vehicular door. Circling around the outside of the warehouse, he and Darvesh came out onto the working area of the pier. The Cygnan space freighter towered over the pier on his left, and the sprawling warehouse stretched for a couple of hundred meters to his right. A cargo crane mounted on rails stood motionless between the ship and the building, a container hanging from its hoist. *Hector*'s shuttle was parked on the pier not far from the gangway leading to the ship.

They trotted over to the shuttle, where they found Petty Officer Long inspecting a blackened patch by the vertical stabilizer. Two more sailors worked in the open cockpit, running systems checks. "Are we going to need to call for a ride?" Sikander asked as he approached.

"Beats me, sir," Long replied. "The control surface is chewed up and the damage knocked the flight-control systems off-line, but they're rebooting. I think we'll be okay for non-aerodynamic flight, but I want to perform some checks first."

That made sense to Sikander. The shuttle's powerful induction drive could get through a vacuum without any lift from its wing surfaces at all, and it had to be able to maneuver with or without atmosphere to push against. "Where is Ms. Larkin?"

"Cargo deck, sir." The pilot nodded in the direction of the gangway. "She's checking the freighter's manifest."

"Thanks, Long." Sikander headed up the steeply sloping gangway to the freighter's personnel hatch. On the quarterdeck he found four more of *Hector*'s sailors standing guard over two dozen of the freighter's crew. Most sat on the deck, looking dejected or frightened. None of them appeared to be Gadiran, and Sikander wondered if *Oristani Caravan*'s deckhands and engineers had any idea that they'd been involved in arms smuggling; freighters didn't normally open their cargo containers in transit unless something went wrong. He made a mental note to bring up the question of leniency for the freighter's crew later on, and continued to the ship's vast cargo deck.

At first glance, it looked a lot like the inside of the warehouse he'd just been in. The containers were racked and stacked in sets of revolving brackets affixed to the big cargo-handling rails in the curving overhead, rather like cartridges in an ancient revolver. The bigger freight carriers of the Coalition's core worlds simply strapped their containers to the outside of the hull, and never actually entered atmosphere. However, ships servicing backwaters such as Gadira needed to be able to land and unload on the ground if there were no orbital facilities to use, and were designed to carry their cargo internally. Sikander and Darvesh found Larkin, Chief Trent, and half a dozen more armed sailors about halfway down the deck, rotating a container down for inspection.

Larkin glanced up, and saluted. "We've secured the ship, sir," she reported. "Four casualties, one serious—Deckhand Gardner was shot, but the medics think they can stabilize him."

Sikander returned her salute. "What happened?"

"We ran into some insurgents standing guard over the operation on the pier. They opened fire on us, and we took them out. The freighter's crew offered no resistance, although the captain protested our boarding and search."

"There were more insurgents in the warehouse," Sikander told her. "We'd better set up a perimeter and keep our eyes open in case they have friends nearby."

"Already done, sir. Most of our force is cordoning off the area."

"Good work, Ms. Larkin." Sikander turned his attention to the cargo container, which was now rotated down to their level. "What have you got here?"

"I suggested to the freighter's captain that he'd better cooperate if he didn't want his ship impounded here for a few months." Larkin allowed herself a predatory grin. "He took me at my word, and pointed out the containers he thought might be 'questionable.' Most are already in the warehouse, but this one was the next to be off-loaded."

Chief Trent punched an access code into the container's door. It opened with a hiss of air pressure equalizing. The master-at-arms waited a moment, then pulled the door the rest of the way open, and let out a low whistle. "Sir, ma'am, you'll want to take a look at this," she said.

Sikander strolled over to look in the container's open end. Inside, two insect-like shapes filled the cargo unit. A web of wire ropes secured to cleats on the container's floor and ceiling locked them in place and plastic sheeting covered their bulky outlines, but it was clear that he was looking at a pair of heavily armed combat flyers secured for transport. "Well, well. It looks like the Caidists ordered something special this month," he observed.

"But they don't have any mechanized forces," Larkin said.

"I suppose they intended to remedy that oversight, Ms. Larkin." Sikander moved in, looking for identifying marks or registration numbers. "I wonder how many of these cargo units are full of combat vehicles?"

"Enough that someone is going to be really unhappy when they don't show up," Chief Trent said.

"Specifically, the Dremish consul," said Sikander, thinking of his narrow escape from the heavy ground transport in the warehouse. "I saw him in the warehouse." He considered the significance of their discovery here. If the Dremish were involved in shipping arms to the Caidists—and not just small arms or rockets, but weapon systems as large and expensive as combat flyers—then what was the troopship doing in orbit? Dremark certainly wouldn't arm rebels its own soldiers might end up fighting, would it?

"The Dremish were here?" Larkin asked.

The name finally came to Sikander's mind. "Bleindel, that was his name. We met the fellow on board *Panther* over dinner last week. Apparently he's up to no good." If this was all a Dremish operation . . . He needed to bring this to Captain Markham, and fast. "Let's finish up here as quickly as we can, Ms. Larkin. There is a lot more going on here than we thought."

18

There is nothing quite so unlovely as a mining town, Otto Bleindel reflected. The Dremish agent gazed over the dusty boulevards and ugly refineries of Meknez from the fiftieth-floor lobby of the Najmah Tower. Tanjeer was located in the planet's fertile equatorial belt—warm and humid throughout the year, but pleasant enough with its orange and olive groves and well-watered gardens. Meknez, on the other hand, was carved out of the true desert fifteen hundred kilometers to the south. With the Bitter Sea too small to exert much in the way of a moderating influence on its climate, Meknez was brutally hot and dry for most of the year. Even the offworlder-friendly business district and the small cluster of diverse neighborhoods around the university looked dreary and dirty.

The luxurious décor of the sky lobby in which he stood could not make up for the eyesore outside the windows. Najmah Tower—the nerve center of the el-Fasi mercantile empire—did, however, offer an excellent view of the port facilities from which he'd escaped just a few short hours before. From his vantage he could easily make out the boxy hull of *Oristani Caravan* alongside the pier, the white arrowhead shapes of the Aquilan shuttles, and the cordon of local police vehicles surrounding the area. He had no idea how the Aquilans had pinpointed the largest and most important arms shipment the Security Bureau had routed into this backwater planet to date, or how they had managed to keep his allies in the Gadiran security establishment from learning about their discovery and warning him that they were moving in on the Cygnan freighter. Thanks to their unexpected interference, everything he'd done on this remote planet was now in danger of unraveling. Bleindel's mouth tightened as he gazed down at the distant scene, leaning on a cane he'd found in a secondhand store. He'd gotten away, but not without a little reminder of how close it had been.

The answer to unexpected developments, he reminded himself, *is flexible planning.* The fact that so few people seemed to be capable of dealing effectively with the unfolding of events in unanticipated ways had always puzzled him. No one could expect all possible outcomes, of course, but simply building plans that offered lots of redundancy and kept important assets in reserve could go a very long way toward mitigating what would otherwise be disasters. No doubt this loss was painful, but after a few hours of evaluating the impact of the raid and considering alternatives, he'd come to realize that this did not have to be a disaster.

"Bey Salem will see you now," the secretary announced from behind him. Bleindel turned around and limped across the reception area at the young woman's invitation. Her sleeveless dress, a little immodest by Gadiran standards, might have passed without remark in any Coalition-power city if not for the old-fashioned comm headset she wore. Like a number of wealthy Gadiran men, el-Fasi liked to surround himself with beautiful women, and had evolved certain private tastes he did not indulge in public.

"Thank you," he told her, and entered el-Fasi's cavernous private office. The rampart of gold-tinted windows to his left looked out over the mountains, something of an improvement over the refineries and port visible from the waiting room. A tiny artificial brook wandered through the room, and a variety of abstract paintings decorated the walls. Most Gadirans honored the old Quranist aversion to depicting the human form in artwork, and the bey decorated his office accordingly.

Bey Salem stood up and came around his desk to greet him. "Mr. Bleindel!" he said. "I was not expecting you."

"I hope you will forgive the intrusion," said Bleindel. "In light of the morning's events, we need to update our plans."

"I assume you refer to the Aquilan sailors who currently occupy one of the piers in my port," the bey said with a sour expression.

"I do," Bleindel replied. "We need to accelerate our time-table."

Salem el-Fasi looked doubtful. "Let us discuss it over coffee." He pressed a button on his desk, and spoke. "Zineb? Coffee for Mr. Bleindel, please. Bring something to eat, too." He moved to a pair of couches by the window, and motioned for Bleindel to join him.

"Thank you," Bleindel answered. He was in fact hungry, since the morning hadn't allowed him any opportunity for breakfast.

Bey Salem frowned as he took note of Bleindel's cane and his limp. "Are you injured, Mr. Bleindel?"

"I was in your warehouse when the Aquilans landed, and I found myself in the line of fire. Fortunately the cab door of a transport took most of the impact, but I still ended up with a mag dart in my calf." It was a testament to the thoroughness of Bleindel's preparations that weeks ago he'd anticipated that he might need to drop out of sight and set up a bolt-hole in Meknez. He'd prepared similar hiding places in half a dozen spots around the planet, not knowing if he would ever need them. And, naturally, he'd stocked his bolt-holes with basic medical supplies. Of course, he hadn't *planned* on getting shot, but the fact that he'd anticipated the unexpected meant that he could tend to the mag-carbine dart in his left leg, stop the bleeding, disinfect and bandage the wound, then get going again in less than an hour.

"God is merciful! Should I call for my physician?"

Bleindel shook his head. "It's not serious—I was able to bandage it myself. I will have it looked at later, but today I have no time to waste. Bey Salem, are your household troops in place for the Casbah operation?"

"Some of them are. I know that *Tanjeer Nomad* is already in position, and I think *Nador Prosperity* is only a few hours from docking—I would have to consult with Colonel Idhari to determine his exact state of readiness. I have also secured the allegiance of two division commanders in the Royal Guard. Why do you ask?"

"Because I think you'll need to launch Casbah twenty-four hours from now. Possibly sooner."

"Within the day?" Bey Salem's eyes widened in surprise. "I did not expect to move for another week or more. Many of my troops are in the wrong place!"

"That was the original plan, yes. The discovery of *Oristani Caravan*'s cargo means that we need to move immediately." Bleindel nodded in the direction of the piers a few kilometers distant. "Between the Aquilans and the Royal Guard, they'll trace the distribution network for previous arms shipments in a matter of hours. We can't give them the time to figure out the nature of your involvement. I have already contacted Alonzo Khouri in Tanjeer; he is massing his followers even as we speak. By noon, the capital will be in flames."

Zineb, the bey's secretary, entered with a soft knock, carrying a silver tray with a coffee service and a selection of pastries and fruit. The two men waited as she set the tray down on the low table between the two couches. "Please hold my calls until Mr. Bleindel and I are finished," Bey Salem told her.

"Of course, Bey Salem," she replied, and quietly retreated.

The bey returned his attention to Bleindel. "You will excuse me if I am not terribly confident in coffeehouse revolutionaries. I was under the impression that Khouri would remove Sultan Rashid from office ten days ago. The fact that Rashid remains alive after those idiots riddled his transport group with your missiles troubles me. Either your missiles are defective, or you're working with complete incompetents."

"I assure you, there's nothing wrong with the ZG-4s we provided to Khouri. They are twenty years old, true, but each missile was tested for operability when they were uncased. I know, because I oversaw the testing myself." Bleindel shifted in his seat, stretching out his injured leg. He'd allowed himself only the minimal necessary dose of painkillers, and he was paying the price already. "As far as the personnel involved, I had the opportunity to work with the people I wanted to, and they performed well."

"Performed well? They shot down everybody but the sultan!"

Bleindel considered his words as he measured sugar for his coffee and took a bite of an almond danish. He needed to strike the right note of reassuring Salem el-Fasi that things were under control and that he was committing to the right course of action, but he also needed to make the Gadiran understand that the opportunity was fleeting. If he expressed too much confidence or too little, the bey might wait to see how events unfolded. That would not be in Dremark's interest.

"Bey Salem, the goal was not to kill Sultan Rashid," he explained patiently. "The goal was to launch the attack."

"What is the point of launching an attack that fails?" Bey Salem demanded. "Khouri merely warned Rashid that he needed to be more careful. I admit I am not particularly worried that Rashid might suddenly become more competent, but the Royal Guard is a different story!"

"The point, Bey Salem, is that we provoked an escalation. We wanted the Royal Guards to hit back at the Caidists. They provided us with exactly the response we hoped for. Oh, I would have been happy enough to see Sultan Rashid dead. Whoever took the throne after such a spectacular assassination would pretty much have had to launch an immediate set of sweeps and reprisals against the revolutionaries and Caidists. But it didn't matter that much whether Rashid or his successor initiated that crackdown."

"It may not matter to you, Mr. Bleindel, but it certainly matters to me," Bey Salem retorted. "I can hardly assume the throne while Rashid's still sitting upon it."

"In that you are mistaken, Bey Salem. History is full of examples of rulers forced to abdicate by their successors." Bleindel straightened and set down his coffee, ignoring the ache in his wounded leg. "If we manage this properly, the people will beg you to take power and restore order whether Rashid is alive or dead. And I assure you that the moment is at hand. Is it a few days ahead of schedule? Yes. Will that make a difference? No, it will not. Your positioning may not be optimal, but it is good enough—especially if you can arrange for part of the Royal Guard to stand aside or back you. By tomorrow there will be a need for a new sultan. That sultan should be you."

"They will beg *someone* to step in," Bey Salem muttered. He leaned back into the plush offworld leather of his couch. "I can think of three or four of my peers who might regard themselves as likely sultans, too."

"Your likely rivals lack one key advantage you possess: the friendship of the Empire of Dremark. Even if several claimants move on the throne at the same time, we will back *you,* Bey Salem. All you need do is ask us to help restore order. I can confirm that you will have a full regiment of crack Dremish regulars on hand to cement your control of the capital." That, of course, was the crucial fig leaf of legitimacy before the other great powers in the Coalition of Humanity. So long as one plausible governing figure emerged to request Dremish intervention, Bleindel's countrymen would be able to respond with the necessary level of military support. In fact, Bleindel had quietly arranged lines of contact with a couple of Bey Salem's most promising rivals so that Dremark could quickly shift its support to another Gadiran possibility if for some reason Salem el-Fasi suddenly became a liability . . . which el-Fasi did not need to know, of course. "As soon as you commit your forces to Operation Casbah, we'll move to support you. But it must be *today*."

"Your ships have that many troops on board?"

"And the orbital firepower to erase anything that gets in their way." Bleindel studied the bey closely. "If you have any doubts or reservations, now is the time to back out, Bey Salem. From this hour forward we are on a timetable, and we can't change course. Are you committed?"

The Gadiran noble met his gaze. The air of kind joviality he cultivated in public was nowhere to be seen; Bleindel read naked ambition and cold calculation in el-Fasi's face as he weighed the answer. "My only reservation is the price for your assistance," he finally said.

"There will be a treaty spelling out commercial access, military assistance, basing rights, and more," said Bleindel. "We have plans for industrializing Gadira and expanding its offworld commerce threefold above what Montréal has been doing, and the first beneficiary of that flood of wealth and influence will be you. Yes, the Caidists will be outraged. We'll give you the modern troops you need to solve that problem permanently." He paused, taking another sip of coffee and allowing the bey to absorb his words before continuing. "All rulers are indebted to those who support them in power; I won't try to tell you otherwise. But the Empire is good to its partners, Bey Salem."

Bey Salem thought for a long moment. "So be it," he finally said. "I will summon Colonel Idhari and consult with him about timing our actions to take advantage of the unrest in the capital."

"Good," said Bleindel. "Might I suggest that you begin by arranging for your forces to seize control of *Oristani Caravan*'s cargo before sultanate forces arrive? It should only take a few hours to ready the combat flyers for service, if you have trained pilots available."

"I thought you intended those for the caids."

Bleindel smiled. "We have now reached the point where it's no longer useful to sponsor an uprising among the desert tribes. I would much rather put that firepower in your hands."

The bey gave a small snort. "Of course. Yes, I will see to that. We'll tell the Aquilans that we need to impound the cargo for evidence."

"Good thinking," said Bleindel. "Now, if you will excuse me, I must be on my way. Time is running short, and I have things to see to in Tanjeer today."

"Make sure that you are not seen with your revolutionary friends. It's bad enough that I am connected to off-worlders. If my fellow beys tie me to the support of the rebels, not even the friendship of Dremark will be enough to carry me into power."

"I am the very soul of discretion," Bleindel promised. "I'll see you tomorrow or the day after in the gardens of El-Badi, and we will talk more about your alliance with Dremark. Until then, farewell."

"Go with God," Bey Salem replied. He stood and showed the Dremish agent to the lobby; they shook hands and parted.

Bleindel made his way to an elevator, leaning on his cane. In fact, it might someday be very useful to remind el-Fasi that the Dremish Security Bureau could provide the bey's enemies with proof that he had armed the rebels for the purpose of providing himself a reason to assume power; he made a mental note to record that suggestion in his final report for Gadira. That was one of the reasons he favored el-Fasi as the most useful tool for establishing Dremish control of the sultanate. The bey was compromised, and he had too much to lose by turning on Dremark now.

The elevator whisked the agent up to the rooftop garage, where he'd parked a very fast private flyer. It was more than fifteen hundred kilometers to Tanjeer, and he needed to be there by midday. Moving awkwardly, he climbed into the driver's seat, tossed his cane onto the seat beside him, and started up the engine. Then he roared out of the exit doorway, and began to put on speed. Even as he climbed away from Meknez, he switched the comm unit to its secure setting and keyed it. "SMS *Panther,* this is Consul Bleindel," he said. "Put me through to Fregattenkapitan Harper, please. It's going to be a busy day."

19

Meknez, Gadira II

In all, *Hector*'s landing party captured twenty-four combat flyers in twelve containers, plus five containers filled with bombs, missiles, and heavy mag darts for the flyers' onboard weapons systems, and three additional containers full of contraband small arms and ammunitions. It was enough to start a good-sized war, Sikander decided—which, when he thought about it, was exactly what someone was trying to do. It took hours to inventory the arms, but by noon Sikander decided that they'd done everything they could in Meknez. *Time to turn it over to the locals—and perhaps get something to eat and a bit of sleep.*

The chirping of his personal comm unit interrupted those pleasant thoughts. "This is Lieutenant North," he answered, stifling a yawn.

"Mr. North, this is the XO," said Peter Chatburn over the link. "Are you finished there?"

"Yes, sir. The local police forces say they can handle matters from here. What do you need?"

"We're recalling the shore party. There's something unusual going on up in Tanjeer, and major riots have broken out all over the city. We may need Ms. Larkin's force to evacuate more private citizens from the city's offworld district. Is the shuttle flyable?"

"Petty Officer Long says so, sir. He pulled a couple of damaged boards and it checks out for nontactical maneuvering."

"Very well, then. Get back up here quick, Mr. North. There's a lot going on."

Sikander glanced around. Angela Larkin stood with her hand to her ear, evidently receiving the same recall notice from *Hector*'s comm techs. A short distance off, Captain Zakur was busy with his own comm device, speaking rapidly in Jadeed-Arabi. If he'd received the news about riots in the capital, he would be heading back to rejoin Ranya's protective detail . . . and that suggested a different course of action than returning to *Hector*. Whatever was going on, Ranya el-Nasir was likely to be in the middle of it.

Sikander believed in listening to his intuition. The moment the thought crossed his mind, he made his decision. "With respect, Mr. Chatburn, I would like to remain planetside and rejoin the amira. You may need a pair of eyes close to the situation."

"That is not an option," the XO replied. "Everything we're looking at up here suggests heavy fighting in a matter of hours. We don't need the added responsibility of worrying about your safety while Gadira burns."

"I think it may be important to stay close to events and keep you posted on the Gadirans' concerns," Sikander replied. "In my estimation, it's worth a small risk. Oh, and Chief Reza will be with me. I won't be alone."

There was a long silence on the other end. Sikander formed the impression that Chatburn took a moment to talk it over with the captain, which was confirmed when Elise Markham's voice came onto the comm unit. "Very well, Mr. North," she said. "Watch yourself down there. And if I order you to return to *Hector*, I expect you to do so at once. Am I understood?"

"Yes, ma'am. North out." Sikander ended the call. Of course, he assumed that his invitation was still good, but given the fact that Aquila had just provided the Royal Guard with actionable intelligence and intercepted a major arms shipment, it seemed like the sultan's officers wouldn't object to his continued presence.

He quickly conferred with Larkin and Chief Trent, confirming that they'd received their orders to return to *Hector*. Then he hurried over to Captain Zakur, who was stowing his own gear in the flyer they had taken from Socotra. A temporary walking cast encased his lower right leg, but the big Gadiran paid little attention to his injury. "Do you have room for two more, Captain Zakur?" Sikander asked him.

Zakur straightened and gave him a measured look. "You are not returning to your ship, Mr. North?"

"It seems events on the ground are more interesting today. I'd like to stay somewhere close to the amira and observe developments."

"It may be dangerous," said Zakur. "The amira flew back to El-Badi two hours ago. I am going straight to the palace, and you must know there are very serious riots in the capital."

The palace? What in the world possessed her to head for such an obvious target? Sikander wondered. But as he thought about it, he decided that he could guess at her reasoning—symbolic actions had value. Sultans who fled to safe and distant refuges in the face of danger were not likely to keep their thrones for long, but a show of personal courage might reinforce wavering loyalties. He wished she had told him her plans, but it wasn't as if she needed his permission to be Amira Ranya Meriem el-Nasir. She did what she thought was right.

On the other hand, Captain Markham had very probably *not* anticipated that he would immediately head for the middle of the rioting when she granted him leave to remain on the planet. It might be for the best if he neglected to bring that to her attention now. "I understand," Sikander told Zakur. "Perhaps we can find a way to help."

The Gadiran thought it over for only a moment. "Very well, then. I cannot promise that you will have access to the amira when we arrive, but I have no objection if you wish to come along."

Sikander and Darvesh tossed their bags into the flyer's cabin and racked their weapons inside. Sikander took the pilot's seat, and began to warm up the engines. As soon as Zakur and his remaining Royal Guards took their seats, Sikander lifted off, and pointed the flyer's nose toward the distant capital. Figuring that speed was of the essence, he configured the vehicle for high-altitude flight and climbed to twenty thousand meters, taking it supersonic.

Even at the flyer's best speed, the flight from Meknez to Tanjeer was not short. He ate a small snack and caught a twenty-minute nap over the southern arm of the Silver Sea in the middle of the flight, compensating at least a little for the late night and early morning he'd just had. Sikander made sure he was back at the controls a good five hundred kilometers from Tanjeer. Beside him, Tarek Zakur's face grew sterner as the minutes ticked by. He seemed to be working with at least three different comm channels, trading rapid-fire orders in Jadeed-Arabi that exceeded Sikander's limited vocabulary in the language.

Sikander waited until Zakur seemed to be between calls. "Should we continue toward the palace?" he asked the Gadiran officer.

"Yes, as quickly as possible," Zakur told him. "There is heavy fighting near El-Badi. You should assume you may be landing under fire."

"The insurgents are that close to the palace grounds?"

"They are, but the street fighting is not what concerns me," Zakur replied. "There is an unidentified column moving on the palace from the west. Apparently a large force of regular troops debarked from seaborne freight carriers docked in the cargo port. They deployed light armor and air cover while the Royal Guard dealt with widespread riots in other districts."

"A coordinated attack with the urban insurgents?" Darvesh asked from the backseat.

"Or opportunism," Zakur answered. "The commander of the palace garrison has tried to summon reinforcements from the Royal Guard bases on the outskirts of the capital, but there seems to be some trouble in getting them out of their barracks."

"That is beginning to sound like a coup," Sikander said. "Who is behind it?"

"One or more of the beys. They maintain private armies, and they can afford mechanized formations. The Caidists don't have any heavy forces." Zakur allowed himself a grim smile. "The traitors might not be as clever as they think, though. The sultan left last night for the Khalifa Palace to visit his daughters. He is in Toutay, not Tanjeer."

Ahead of him, Sikander caught the first distant glimpse of the brown smudge of Tanjeer. Even at this distance, he could make out thin black plumes of smoke drifting into the sky. He glanced over his shoulder. "Darvesh, contact *Hector* and tell them what's going on. I'd better pay attention to the flying."

He heard Darvesh relaying the report to *Hector,* and took a moment to acquaint himself with the defensive systems of the Gadiran flyer. He also did his best to dredge up any recollection of tips for avoiding enemy fire. When Petty Officer Long had flown into Tanjeer's spaceport for the sultan's garden gathering, he'd descended to just a few meters above the ocean and slalomed back and forth on his approach. *Good enough for him, good enough for me,* Sikander decided. He put the flyer into a steep dive, bleeding off altitude.

The maneuver brought him to sea level about twenty

kilometers from the palace; he could clearly see its golden domes and spires above the low cliffs. Doing his best to keep up his speed while zigzagging sharply, Sikander streaked over the long, rolling swells. Navigation markers and small working boats flashed by under his wings; distantly he noted more plumes of smoke rising from Tanjeer's business district, and streets barricaded with abandoned ground cars or heavy transports. *It looks like a war zone out there.*

"Where should I land?" he asked Zakur.

The Gadiran monitored various vid feeds on his dataslate. "Head for the south terrace and land on the lawn between the palace and the ocean. The palace landing pads may be under observation."

"Understood." Sikander replied. He kept his speed up and altitude down until the last possible moment, coming in below the level of the twenty-meter cliffs that marked the seaward edge of the palace compound. Then he killed the flyer's speed, flaring and powering its braking thrusters as he popped up over the edge. He eased forward over the gardens and verandas, and didn't immediately see any patch of ground that seemed especially good for a landing. Sikander settled on a narrow strip of green between two arbors and rotated the flyer sideways as he dropped down.

He managed to knock down one of the arbors with the rear fuselage of the flyer, but the vehicle settled on its struts more or less evenly. "Er, sorry," he said to Zakur.

"Think nothing of it," the Gadiran replied over his shoulder as he opened his hatch and scrambled out. Sikander, Darvesh, and the remaining Royal Guards followed suit.

The instant Sikander got out of the flyer, he realized the seriousness of the situation in the capital. The smell of smoke was heavy, and the sound of gunfire—the distant popping of firearms, the shrill whine of mag weapons, and the occasional muted *whump!* of an explosion—rolled over the palace grounds like an approaching thunderstorm. He could hear crowd noise, too, the angry roar of many people gathered together not too far away. As bad as the situation in Sidi Marouf had been a week ago, the current troubles seemed to be an order of magnitude worse. Darvesh shot him a look of warning, but said nothing. This was the sort of situation he was supposed to keep Sikander out of, after all.

Sikander and Darvesh followed the limping Captain Zakur into the palace. Inside, the marble-floored hallways echoed with the shrill crackle of voice comms and people shouting urgently. Pairs of Royal Guard sentries manned post after post within the building, looking angry and tense. Sikander glimpsed palace staff hurrying to hide various treasures, removing pictures from the walls and small statuary from display stands. *Are they expecting El-Badi to be looted?* he wondered. That certainly did not seem to be a good sign.

They took several quick turns, and then entered a very modern-looking command center hidden in the middle of the palace. Large vidscreens loomed on every wall; Sikander saw images of riots breaking out in Tanjeer's downtown areas, angry crowds surging along the boulevard just outside the palace grounds, armored scout-cars advancing slowly down a deserted street. A dozen Royal Guard officers and orderlies manned the room, all of them talking at once.

This looks familiar, Sikander decided. The Aquilan consulate was fresh in his mind, but he remembered observing other protests from the security center in his father's palace at Sangrur . . . *when Devindar came home, after the attack. That's what this reminds me of.* The night was hot—

—*and humid. Sikander sleeps little. Near dawn he grows restless, and goes down to the palace's command center to see if there is any news of the investigation. Nawab Dayan is there, watching the vid feeds from several different cities at the same time. Dozens of dragoons and civilian police crowd the room, filling the room with a tense buzz of activity.*

Somehow Nawab Dayan notes Sikander's approach without glancing away from the displays. "How are they?" he asks.

"Mother and Gamand are both sleeping," Sikander tells him. The danger is over—he knows they will both survive, although Vadiya North will require extensive reconstructive surgery for her ruined face, and Gamand is in for months of difficult physical rehab to regain the full use of his arm. In fact, his mother will never look quite the same again, although Sikander doesn't know that at the time.

"The nationalists could have killed us all," the nawab says.

Sikander's gaze falls on a news feed showing the site of the attack. The crawl at the bottom of the screen puts the death toll at seventy-three. The sheer shock of the attack is wearing off; now that he is no longer in the middle of the carnage, he is beginning to piece together exactly what he'd seen. "Good God. Who would do such a thing?"

Sergeant Reza of the nawab's dragoons answers Sikander. "The Sons of Palar are claiming responsibility for the attack, Nawabzada." That is the terrorist branch of the Kashmiri Liberation Party. Most KLP members stop just short of advocating open revolution or acts of terrorism, but the radicals call for more direct action against Kashmir's aristocratic classes and their Aquilan patrons. Sikander can guess which faction is dominant this morning.

He shifts his attention to the vid displays his father is watching. They show the nawab's soldiers descending on nationalist agitators all across Jaipur, and the KLP taking to the streets in protest. He recognizes one scene in particular: the administration building of the university in Ganderbal. A number of soldiers surround the building; he wonders what's going on.

"*Father, you must stop this madness!*" Devindar hurries into the command center, angrily gesturing at the vid feed from Ganderbal. Sikander turns in surprise: He hadn't realized that Devindar has returned already. His brother is bandaged on the side of his face and across his left arm. Sikander starts to welcome Devindar, but Devindar ignores him and confronts their father. "*No one at Ganderbal is a terrorist!*"

"If no one at the university is a terrorist, how is it that three of your fellow students set upon you with knives?" Nawab Dayan replies. "And why is Professor Howell barricaded in the chancellor's office with a bomb? The matter seems clear enough to me, Devindar."

"Dr. Howell had nothing to do with it," Devindar says. "You are making a mistake."

"Parmad Howell spent six years in prison before you were born because he was convicted of terrorist acts. He's spent the last twenty years radicalizing any students stupid enough to listen to him." Nawab Dayan folds his thick arms like a battlement across his chest. "After today, no more. Professor Howell can explain his incitements in court."

"You can't criminalize dissent!" Devindar snaps. "You are acting exactly like the tyrant the KLP says you are!"

Dayan North turns away from the vid displays, his eyes flashing dangerously. "The Ganderbal police inform me that there are eight or ten students holed up in there with Howell. I wonder whether some of them are friends of yours, Devindar."

Sikander glances over at Devindar, and their eyes meet. The dark look in Devindar's face tells Sikander that his brother is wondering the same thing. Devindar has made no secret of his attraction to the supposedly less radical elements of the KLP for four or five years now . . . but for the first time Sikander wonders where his loyalties lie.

Devindar does not answer Nawab Dayan. He straightens

his shoulders, holds their father's gaze for a moment, then turns and strides out the door without looking back.

Six hours after the argument in the command center, Sikander boards the warp liner for High Albion. . . .

That was the moment the breach between Devindar and Father became irreparable, Sikander reflected. His father hadn't allowed Sikander to return to Kashmir until he'd graduated from the Academy. It was four and a half years before he saw either of them again. *By then, everything was different.*

Darvesh tapped him on the shoulder. "The amira," he murmured. The Kashmiri sergeant nodded at the far corner of the room. Ranya stood there, arms folded as she watched the chaos unfolding on the screens. Her olive Montréalais-style skirt suit was probably the closest she could come to being in uniform.

"Of course," said Sikander. "Thank you, Darvesh." He dismissed the old memories, focusing on what was going on around him this very moment, and followed Tarek Zakur across the room. The two of them joined Ranya by the displays.

Ranya glanced around as they approached. "Captain Zakur, you're back! And I see you brought Lieutenant North, too."

"He insisted, Amira," Zakur answered. He bowed, then took a sudden interest in one of the vid feeds nearby.

"Concerned for me?" Ranya asked Sikander with a small smile.

"Well, yes," Sikander replied. He nodded at the chaos on the vidscreens. "I wouldn't have left you on Socotra if I had realized that all this was about to break loose."

"I wouldn't have headed off to Socotra in the first place," Ranya replied. "Then again, I succeeded in confusing Bey Salem's forces. A squadron of flyers carrying his soldiers landed at the villa an hour ago, looking for me."

"Salem el-Fasi?" Sikander asked. "Is he the one behind the troop column moving in from the port?"

"His troops are hanging back for the moment, probably hoping the mob outside our gates will break in and over-run the palace. But yes, el-Fasi just issued a global broad-cast to the effect that he has been forced to step in and restore order." Ranya pointed at a screen showing a slow-moving aerial view from rooftop height, following the progress of troops riding light armor. Her face tightened, and for an instant Sikander caught a glimpse of the anger and anxiety she kept carefully hidden. "He spent years insisting he wanted nothing more than to protect me and telling me what a great man my father was. I knew there was a whiff of rottenness to all that attention he showered on me."

"I am sorry, Ranya," he said. He studied the image of el-Fasi's column, working through the pieces of the puzzle. He'd assumed that local involvement in the *Oristani Cara-van*'s arms smuggling was more or less incidental. After all, it seemed likely that the Dremish agent Bleindel would have selected the spaceport and freight-handling services that best suited his needs for moving contraband into Gadira without attracting too much attention. But if this Bey Sa-lem was in position to move on the palace *today,* he must have known what the Caidist sympathizers in Tanjeer planned to do days in advance. That suggested coordina-tion between the bey and the rebels.

The dark look on Sikander's face caught Ranya's atten-tion. "What is it?" she asked him.

"Is there any chance that Salem el-Fasi is secretly allied to the insurgents and Caidists?"

"It's almost unthinkable. He made a vast fortune partner-ing with offworld business and modernizing our indus-tries, which put many of the urban extremists out of work." Ranya nodded at the images of the el-Fasi forces. "Look, you can see there that insurgents are harassing his soldiers.

They are angry with the sultanate, but they *hate* the beys and what they stand for."

"Then this isn't about the Caidists, and it isn't about an el-Fasi coup," said Sikander. "It's about Dremark taking control of Gadira. They've been supplying arms shipments to insurgents through el-Fasi's ports with one hand, and preparing el-Fasi to overthrow you with the other."

"Dremark?" Ranya looked at him. "All the arms our soldiers have recovered from rebel caches have been of Cygnan manufacture. Why do you think Dremark is involved?"

"I ran into the Dremish consul in the warehouse at Meknez. Well, to be honest, he did his best to run into me. He almost flattened me with a heavy ground transport." Sikander smiled grimly. "I'm afraid he escaped, but I got a good look at him as he drove off. It was definitely Bleindel."

"Otto Bleindel?"

Sikander glanced at her. "You've met him?"

"He has been working with Salem el-Fasi, passing himself off as a trade representative." She thought furiously for a moment. "God is merciful! That explains everything. The Dremish manufactured the crisis so that Bey Salem could launch a coup. And once he takes power . . ."

". . . they'll negotiate with their puppet for whatever they want in Gadira," Sikander finished her thought. The Republic of Montréal might not be willing to commit thousands of soldiers to an effort to pacify the insurgents and prop up the el-Nasirs, but the Empire of Dremark had no such reservations. They only needed a plausible reason to intervene. The real question was what part the Dremish cruiser and troop carrier in orbit were intended to play, and whether or not anything could be done about it. "Damn. I need to tell the captain."

"Protesters are massing by the east gate," one of the guards announced, listening to a headset. "Lieutenant Imamovic reports that his platoon is taking mag-rifle fire from snipers hidden in the crowd. He requests instructions."

Ranya hurried to peer over the man's shoulder at the console he was watching. Sikander followed her; the screen showed one of the gates leading into the palace grounds. A thin line of Royal Guards—these men wore dappled sand-olive camouflage, not the black-and-scarlet dress uniforms worn inside the palace—sheltered behind a barricade near the fence, rifles at the ready. Outside, a mob of hundreds, perhaps thousands, shouted and shook their fists. A constant shower of rocks and debris sailed over the fence, pelting the palace grounds.

"Do not fire on the crowd," Ranya ordered. "Nonlethal defenses only. I won't have this turn into a massacre."

"Amira, that may not be up to you," Captain Zakur said, standing close behind her. "If the crowd breaches the gate and you are still here, we will have no choice but to employ all means necessary to defend your person. You should think about moving to a safer location."

"If we surrender the palace, then Bey Salem will be happy to liberate it for us," said Ranya. "El-Badi is a crucial symbol of the sultan's power. We cannot allow it to fall into his hands."

"If we allow you to fall into the hands of the Caidists or el-Fasi's forces, the status of the palace becomes irrelevant," Zakur said. "Please, consider—"

"Intruders on the grounds!" One of the guards monitoring another set of security feeds slapped an alarm button and pointed. "Sunrise Park, sector three! They drove a ground car through the fence!"

Zakur spun around to study the camera the guard pointed at. Sikander couldn't make out much more than a stalled-out ground car—more of a truck, really—with smoke spewing from its engine compartment, and a rush of protesters. Some waved pistols or combat rifles, but many were armed with nothing more than sickle-shaped swords or curved daggers. The Gadiran captain keyed his comms. "Reserve platoon to Sunrise Park at once!" he ordered. "Seal that breach!"

Some of the attackers staggered and dropped as Sikander and Ranya watched, struck by fire from the palace defenders, but more streamed in to replace them. One small group found a spot by a barricade and set up a heavy autorifle, opening up on the Royal Guard's positions. Sikander could distantly hear the shrill stuttering sound of the weapon echoing down the hall. It stood as a chilling reminder that he watched events taking place just outside the palace, not a feed showing some far-off disorders.

A flash of light flickered across another screen. A moment later, Sikander heard a loud rumble, and the floor beneath his feet trembled slightly. He looked back, and realized that the east gate—the one so many people had been crowded near—no longer existed, blown into a tangled mess of twisted metal. Scores of bodies littered the street. *A bomb,* he realized. There was a moment of stunned silence, and then bystanders slowly began to pick themselves up off the ground. Some remained too dazed or injured to move, but others seized whatever weapons were close to hand and surged toward the gap. "Dear God," he murmured.

Zakur turned to Ranya. "Amira, I beg you: We must go. We do not have enough men to defend the palace grounds against the mob. All we can do is buy a little time."

Ranya nodded slowly, still shaken by what she saw on the screen. "Very well."

The Gadiran officer took her by the arm and steered her out of the center, as more Royal Guards joined the entourage. Sikander and Darvesh followed in their wake. They hurried through more parts of the palace he hadn't yet seen, and emerged in a spacious garage filled with a dozen or more ground cars and flyers of varying degrees of luxury. A large landing pad stood just outside the garage doors, occupied by three military flyers; beyond those, the parklike palace grounds looked down on olive groves and outbuildings. Once again the roar of the angry mob rose in Sikander's ears, along with the constant popping of gunfire.

The Royal Guards ringed Ranya and moved toward the nearest of the flyers—but a sudden burst of small-arms fire erupted in front of them. Sikander caught sight of armed men in mismatched working clothes scuttling under the branches of the olive grove before he threw himself to the ground. Captain Zakur pushed Ranya down and covered her with his own body, while the other guards returned fire. Mag-rifle rounds chirped and whined as more men opened up. "Get some covering units into the air!" Zakur shouted at his troops.

Sikander rolled behind a large planter, and drew his pistol. He'd left the mag carbine he'd carried in the raid at Meknez racked behind the pilot's seat in the flyer on the south terrace. A pair of Royal Guards ran into the rebel fire, heading for the parked flyers. Bullets struck around them, but the two reached the combat flyer and scrambled into the cockpit. A moment later, the engine hummed to life, and the autorifle turret below the flyer's nose kicked into motion, swiveling to find a target. Two blurred silver streaks shot out from the shadows of the grove and slammed into the side of the flyer—antiarmor rockets, screaming across the landing pad with deafening roars. The flyer exploded, hurling pieces of fuselage and landing gear across the field and knocking everyone to the ground, Royal Guard and insurgent alike.

Sikander picked himself up, his ears ringing. *Now what?* Maybe there were no more rockets ready to fire on the remaining flyers at the palace landing pad—and maybe there were. He didn't know if he would be willing to risk his life on that gamble, but they clearly couldn't stay where they were.

Darvesh shook his shoulder. "The flyer we came in might be a better option, sir," he said.

"I agree." Sikander raised his voice and shouted at Zakur. "Captain! The south terrace!"

Zakur glanced over his shoulder, and nodded. He tapped the soldiers near him on their backs, and called out hurried instructions to the rest of his group. Half the group laid down a furious barrage of fire, lashing every conceivable bit of cover in sight with bursts of mag-rifle darts. The rest of the men got to their feet, doing their best to keep their bodies between Ranya and the insurgent riflemen, and then ran back into the garage. Sikander and Darvesh sprinted after them.

They raced back through the palace. Sikander caught the distinct chatter of gunfire echoing through the marble halls, and realized that somewhere in the sprawling building insurgents were already on the loose. The thought was not remotely reassuring, and he breathed a sigh of relief when Zakur burst out of a door onto the terrace with its pools and sweeping view of the sea. The flyer they'd arrived in remained parked on top of the unlucky arbor.

This time, one of the Royal Guards headed for the pilot's seat. Sikander happily presumed the fellow was rated as a combat pilot, and settled for piling into the back with Ranya, Darvesh, and four more guards. The pilot lifted off before he'd finished strapping in, and raced away from the palace by dropping over the cliff's edge and heading west across the bay.

Ranya gazed back at the palace through the rear window. To Sikander's surprise, she did not have a scratch on her, although she'd managed to lose her shoes in the race through the palace. She took several deep breaths, then looked at Zakur, in the copilot's seat. "Where are we going, Captain?" she asked.

"We are still considering options, Amira," Zakur replied. He had a bad cut on his scalp that was bleeding freely, but he ignored it as he scanned through the flyer's comms again. "At the moment I simply want to get you out of the area."

"Head for Toutay," she said. "The sultan will need our help."

"I don't think that is a good idea," said Sikander. Ranya gave him a startled look, so he continued. "Bey Salem needs the el-Nasirs either captured or dead for his coup to succeed. For that matter, the Dremish would prefer Bey Salem to be the only thing resembling a planetary authority for them to deal with. It won't take them long to figure out no one is left at El-Badi, so it seems to me that going anywhere near your uncle might be the most dangerous thing you could do right now."

Captain Zakur nodded in agreement, his face set in a hard scowl. "Lieutenant North is correct, Amira," he said. "We should keep the royal family dispersed if possible."

"Then where should I go?"

"Some place where you'll have the ability to communicate with loyal forces and maintain command, but your enemies won't be able to find you," Sikander said. *Hector*, perhaps? Would Captain Markham be willing to extend an offer of refuge, or not? He couldn't even begin to imagine what sort of diplomatic headaches that might lead to . . . but perhaps a different ship might be a better choice. "You told me that *Shihab* is equipped with a modern comm suite and defensive systems. Where is she now?"

"She departed Socotra early this morning, right after the amira left," Zakur replied. He pulled out his dataslate, and studied his reports. "Yes, she's about halfway between Socotra and Tanjeer. It's as secure as any other option at the moment, and we can meet her at sea."

Ranya thought it over for a moment, then nodded. "The *Shihab* will do. Take me there, please."

"Yes, Amira." Zakur nodded to the pilot, who banked sharply and turned the flyer away from the coast, heading out over the Silver Sea.

Sikander glanced out the window at the gleaming white walls of El-Badi, quickly falling behind them. He wondered whether the palace would still be standing the next time he saw it, and whether Ranya would be safe anywhere on Gadira today. Salem el-Fasi's forces or Caidist insurgents probably didn't have the means to locate or attack her if *Shihab* stayed well out to sea, but what about el-Fasi's Dremish friends? If he was right about their intentions, then it was only a matter of time before Dremark moved in force. *And what does Captain Markham do then? Just how far do her orders extend?*

Ranya noticed his silence. "What is it?"

"I hate to leave under these circumstances, but I can't stay on *Shihab*," Sikander told her. "I think I need to get back to my ship."

20

CSS *Hector*, Gadira II Orbit

An hour after seeing Ranya el-Nasir safely to *Shihab*, Sikander and Darvesh returned to *Hector*. The sailing yacht's tiny landing spot couldn't accommodate the cruiser's shuttle, so Petty Officer Long had been obliged to land in the water beside *Shihab* and bring the shuttle alongside so that Sikander could board. Ranya had sent him off with a chaste kiss on the cheek, since a large number of very anxious Royal Guards watched over her like eagles guarding their nest. The last Sikander had seen of her, she was hurrying down to the yacht's command facilities as *Shihab* furled her sails and lifted her hull up out of the water on her induction drive, headed for the crowded shipping lanes in the open ocean south of Tanjeer. If el-Fasi's forces received any kind of orbital feed from their Dremish allies, blending in with other shipping would be the best way for Ranya to conceal her exact location.

The instant Long settled the shuttle into the hangar bay's docking cradle, Sikander headed straight for the captain's cabin. He still wore his battle-dress uniform and carried a noticeable aroma of smoke with him, but he thought that Markham would agree that the circumstances dictated a timely report. He took a moment to doff his cap and run a hand through his hair outside her door, then knocked and entered. "Captain?" he said. "I am back on board."

Markham looked up. She was not alone—Peter Chatburn sat across the desk from her. Evidently they had been in the middle of a conversation. She took in his unusual appearance with one raised eyebrow, and nodded. "So I see. What's the news from the ground, Mr. North? Any word about the sultan?"

"The last I heard, he was in the Khalifa Palace at Toutay," Sikander replied. "I am afraid that a mob in Tanjeer overran El-Badi Palace, but Amira Ranya is safe for the moment. I left her on board the royal yacht, which should keep her well out of reach of urban insurgents."

"Your news is a little out of date, Mr. North," Chatburn observed. "The insurgents no longer hold El-Badi. Apparently Salem el-Fasi's forces moved in and recaptured the palace shortly after the amira fled the scene."

"I hadn't heard that, XO," Sikander admitted. Conditions on the ground changed rapidly today, it seemed. "However, that brings me to the real problem facing us today: Dremark." He quickly recounted his encounter with Bleindel in the warehouse at Meknez, the appearance of el-Fasi's troops in Tanjeer, the defense of the palace, and Ranya's description of Bleindel's dealings with Bey Salem. "I think we are facing a wide-ranging Dremish plot," he concluded. "First they arm the rebel elements, then they choose a new strongman to support when the el-Nasir sultanate crumbles. If they haven't landed Imperial troops to support el-Fasi yet, then they will do so soon."

"I don't know," Chatburn said slowly. "The fact that this Bleindel character was associated with el-Fasi doesn't mean that he coordinated the whole thing. For all we know, he merely rented el-Fasi's facilities to deliver the arms aboard *Oristani Caravan*. Corruption is endemic here."

"I would agree, sir, except for the fact that el-Fasi's forces were waiting in Tanjeer this morning for trouble to break out," said Sikander. "The bey knew ahead of time that the insurgents planned a major uprising today and pre-positioned his forces. Either he is coordinating directly with the Caidists—which seems unlikely, since he claims that he's taking over in order to defeat them—or some other party is arranging events and making use of them both."

Captain Markham leaned back in her chair, a thoughtful frown on her face. "And let's not forget that SMS *Panther* and SMS *General von Grolmann* have also conveniently arranged to be on hand for this moment. They weren't sent here by accident—the Dremish thought that their warships might be needed in Gadira. One wonders how they knew."

"Damn," Chatburn muttered. "What do we do if they put troops on the ground?"

"Let's hope that we can persuade them to avoid further escalations," Markham replied. She looked at Sikander. "Thank you for your report, Mr. North. Get something to eat and take the opportunity to rest if you can; I've a feeling this is merely the beginning, and I will need you at your best later."

"Yes, ma'am." Sikander stood, saluted, and left.

As per the captain's orders, he stopped by the wardroom for a hot sandwich before returning to his cabin to shower and change. His anxiety about events on the ground didn't allow him to sleep for long, but he catnapped, and dozed off daydreaming about swimming with Ranya amid the sea flowers of Socotra. He awoke feeling much better—a hot meal, a shower, and some rest had dispelled most of his fatigue.

When he returned to his station on the bridge, Sikander found the compartment already three-quarters full. Most of Hiram Randall's Operations Department specialists stood at their posts, carefully monitoring *Hector*'s orbital reconnaissance drones and doing their best to keep up with events on the ground. Captain Markham and Commander Chatburn were on hand as well; the ship's senior officers congregated around the center of the action. For his own part, Sikander suspected that he had plenty of routine work to catch up on after being absent for a couple of days, but it could wait for now. He'd spent more time on the ground than anyone else on *Hector,* and the captain might need his insights and observations.

Lieutenant Commander Randall glanced up as he paused to study the displays. "Welcome back, Sikander," he said. "Nice work at the palace. El-Fasi's troops are turning Tanjeer upside down looking for the amira."

"Thanks, Hiram," Sikander replied. If nothing else, it seemed he'd finally earned the operations officer's respect. He studied the tactical displays for a moment, focusing on *Panther* and *General von Grolmann.* "What have the Dremish been up to in all of this?"

"Early this morning, the transport began launching reconnaissance flyovers around the major cities. They've also landed observation and contact teams, especially around the capital." Randall motioned at the main bridge display, which showed an overhead image of the city of Tanjeer with the positions of different forces marked.

Sikander nodded. Aggressive reconnaissance was the least he expected from the Dremish warships. "Are there any new developments with el-Fasi's forces?"

"Well, they re-seized the arms shipment Ms. Larkin's landing party impounded in Meknez. Around the planet, they're securing government buildings and transit hubs. There's fighting in some places between Royal Guard units and el-Fasi's troops, but in other places they're cooperating to quell the insurgents. It looks pretty confused to me."

Sikander nodded to Randall. "It appears that I have some catching up to do."

He sat down at the weapons console and examined several different feeds, looking for the latest information on the fighting near the capital. First he checked on *Shihab,* and found the royal yacht a good eighty kilometers south of

Tanjeer, motoring along slowly as it did its best to blend in with the waterborne shipping on the Silver Sea. It seemed that Ranya was safe for the moment, at least. Then Sikander turned his attention to the Dremish ships in orbit, looking for any clues as to their intentions. *Panther* simply maintained her station, not maneuvering or conducting any shuttle operations. The transport *General von Grolmann* was significantly more active, though. Several assault shuttles kept station on her, and she continually adjusted her orbit to linger over the capital. *Grolmann* was easily twice the size of *Panther,* although of course she was not anywhere near as heavily armed. She carried plenty of bomb cells and low-velocity K-cannons for ground-fire missions, but only a handful of point-defense lasers for protecting herself. Assault transports didn't fight other ships; they carried large numbers of troops instead. "What are you up to?" Sikander muttered to himself.

Because he happened to be looking at *Grolmann,* he was the first to notice the change in operational tempo. A group of shuttles—first four, then eight, then a full dozen—detached from her troop bays and began to descend toward the planet. Sikander wasn't terribly familiar with Dremish small craft, but similar vehicles in Commonwealth service carried as many as thirty troops. That would be a couple of companies, at least, or possibly a full battalion if they launched a second wave.

"Captain!" he called. "The Dremish are launching assault shuttles from *General von Grolmann.* It looks like a large landing force."

Markham glanced at the display showing the Dremish ships. "It seems so. Mr. Randall, I need your best guess about their combat power and their intentions. XO, let's go to Condition Two. We're almost there anyway."

"Yes, ma'am," Randall replied. He conferred with his intelligence specialists.

Chatburn stepped over to a nearby comm station and

thumbed the all-call selector. "Now set Condition Two. Repeat, now set Condition Two throughout the ship." That would bring *Hector* to one step short of general quarters; at Condition Two, half of the ship's crew reported to their battle stations, and the ship's engineers readied the ship's power and damage-control systems for potential action. A ship could stay at Condition Two for hours by rotating personnel on and off watch, but wouldn't be caught completely unprepared if action threatened.

Captain Markham moved over to her battle couch and took her seat. "Communications, transmit to SMS *Panther*," she said in a cool voice. "*Panther*, this is *Hector*. What is the destination of the landing force currently deploying from *General von Grolmann*, over?"

There was a short delay before the Dremish cruiser's reply came over the bridge speakers near the captain's seat. Sikander recognized Captain Harper's voice. "*Hector*, this is *Panther*. The Gadiran government has requested our assistance in dealing with the ongoing unrest in Tanjeer. We are complying with their request, over."

Markham looked over to Randall. "Mr. Randall, check with our contacts in the Royal Guard and find out whether they asked the Dremish for help."

Randall nodded. "Yes, ma'am. We're on it."

"*Panther*, this is *Hector*," Markham said, renewing her transmission. "Where do you intend to land your troops, over?"

"*Hector*, we are deploying to establish a safe perimeter around the Tanjeer spaceport," Harper replied. "No Aquilan citizens or property will be threatened by our forces. Restoring order is frankly to the benefit of any power with interests in Gadira, over."

"This isn't your problem, in other words," Markham said without transmitting. Her frown deepened.

"Captain, we have a quick assessment on the landing force," Randall said. "Twelve of their Falke-type assault shuttles can land a combat team consisting of an infantry battalion with a dozen light combat flyers and a heavy-weapons section. If *Grolmann* is fully loaded, she'll have two more infantry battalions backed up by a heavy-armor company on board. They might not have the numbers to garrison the capital, but they can smash up any number of insurgent formations."

"Or Royal Guards," Sikander pointed out. Gadiran soldiers in obsolete Montréalais vehicles wouldn't stand much chance against the soldiers of a first-rate Coalition power such as Dremark; numbers might not matter much in that kind of confrontation. The flight of assault shuttles accelerated down and away from the big Dremish transport, weaving and jolting as they entered atmosphere.

Markham nodded, but did not reply to Sikander. "Did the sultanate request their help?" she asked Randall.

"No, ma'am. They have no idea what the Dremish are talking about and want to know where they're going."

"I feared as much," the captain said. She glanced up at Chatburn. "We can't allow an outright occupation of the planet. How do I convince Harper to stand down?"

"Stall for time?" Chatburn suggested. "Give them a chance to think it over and decide whether they're ready to risk a major incident."

Markham keyed her comm panel again. "*Panther,* this is *Hector* actual. Captain Harper, we are aware of no request for intervention from the Sultanate of Gadira. Given that, your landing force appears to be substantially in excess of the limits imposed by the Tanjeer Agreement of 3062. We request that you suspend your landing operations until the situation can be clarified, over."

This time there was a long pause. "*Hector,* this is *Panther* actual. Captain Markham, we have learned that Sultan Rashid el-Nasir is no longer the head of the planetary government," Captain Harper said over the comm link. "We are engaged in discussions with the provisional government of

Bey Salem el-Fasi, the new planetary authority. They have asked for our help in restoring order, and we feel compelled to safeguard our interests by providing whatever assistance we can. Our ground operations will continue. *Panther,* out."

"That arrogant bastard hung up on us!" Markham snarled under her breath. Sikander tried to think of another time he'd heard Markham swear, and couldn't come up with one; her patience was fraying rapidly, not that he could blame her. The captain took a moment to compose herself, then spoke to Chatburn. "I think we may need to express our disapproval more forcefully. XO, please set Condition One."

Chatburn nodded, and pressed the general-quarters signal. "General quarters, general quarters! All hands man your battle stations," he announced. "Set Condition One throughout the ship. All stations report readiness."

Sikander did not have far to go; his battle station was the master weapons console. He stood up and pulled his battle armor from the storage bin behind his seat. The standard Navy working uniform could be sealed to create a serviceable vacuum suit for a short time, but for full combat readiness all hands pulled on torso armor, heavy gauntlets, magnetized boots, and armored helmets. He left open the faceplate for ease of communication; if the compartment was suddenly holed, his helmet was designed to close instantly. While Sikander shrugged on his gear, the bridge crew quickly changed over. Some hands currently on watch left to go to battle stations elsewhere in the ship, while others who hadn't been on the bridge hurried into the compartment; Peter Chatburn left to go take up his position in the auxiliary bridge, while Angela Larkin and Karsen Reno joined the rush of incoming personnel and quickly pulled on their own battle armor before taking their stations at the torpedo console and the secondary-battery console. A well-drilled crew aimed to set battle stations within three minutes; Captain Markham usually insisted on two and a half.

The captain donned her armor, and returned to her couch. She waited a few moments, studying the display that showed the ship's various action stations—weapons mounts, damage-control parties, sick bay, redundant engineering stations, and the auxiliary bridge—reporting their readiness. The noise and chatter that had filled the bridge compartment beforehand dissipated. "All stations manned and ready, Captain," Randall reported from his position at the tactical console.

"Very well," Markham replied. "I'm going to speak a little more sternly to Captain Harper. Mr. Randall, Mr. North, be ready, but do not engage any active targeting without my express command. If necessary we'll fire a warning shot one hundred kilometers in front of *Panther*'s bow."

Sikander looked down at Ensign Girard and nodded. "Set it up, Mr. Girard," he said quietly. "No active targeting. We don't want to paint their hull or they might mistake our intent."

"Yes, sir," Girard replied. He busied himself with calculating trajectories on the main-battery console.

Markham opened her comm channel again. "Captain Harper, we do not recognize the authority of the el-Fasi government. In the absence of such authority, your operations are in violation of Article Six of the Tanjeer Agreement. Suspend your landing operations immediately, over."

The bridge fell silent as officers and ratings alike listened for the Dremish reply, whether it was their job to do so or not. There was none.

"The Dremish assault shuttles are engaging Gadiran Royal Guard defenses at the Tanjeer spaceport, ma'am," Randall reported. "Four shuttles are splitting off and appear to be headed toward the northwest. We're not certain where they are headed."

Sikander adjusted his console display, bringing up the imagery that the operations team was observing. He had a suspicion about that secondary flight . . . a suspicion he was able to confirm with a cursory glance at the map. "I believe they're headed for the Khalifa Palace in Toutay, Mr. Randall," he said. "That's where Sultan Rashid is."

Markham shifted in her seat. Only the flat monotone of her voice betrayed her anger. "Captain Harper, I must inform you that if your ground forces continue their attacks on the legally constituted government of this planet, I will be obliged to fire upon them. The Commonwealth will not stand by and ignore your efforts to overthrow the government of this system. I repeat, cease your offensive operations at once, or I will open fire on your troops, over."

Larkin and Girard exchanged glances in front of Sikander. He imagined they were thinking what he was: *Dear God, I hope she is bluffing. And I hope the Dremish believe her.*

Harper responded swiftly to Markham's threat. "Any attack upon Imperial forces operating in this system is an attack upon the Empire of Dremark, Captain Markham. We will reply with all necessary force, over."

"Captain Harper, your violation of the diplomatic accords both our nations have agreed to leaves the Commonwealth of Aquila with no alternative," said Markham over the comm channel. "If you mean to start a war here, you're making excellent progress. Recall your landing force immediately, or face the consequences. *Hector,* out."

Sikander realized he was holding his breath, and forced himself to exhale. He'd thought of Elise Markham as an excellent commanding officer before this day, but he was in awe of the unyielding iron she now revealed. Did her orders extend to firing the first shot if necessary? Perhaps more important, did Captain Harper believe that they might?

"Mr. North, are you prepared to fire a shot across *Panther*'s bow?" the captain asked Sikander.

Sikander glanced at Girard's fire mission, repeated on his display. "Yes, ma'am."

"Then, on my command, one and only one main-battery

round, one hundred kilometers ahead of *Panther*'s bow. Activate no targeting system, and mind the planet, we don't want to hit something on the ground. Train battery . . . and fire."

"Train battery and fire, aye!" Sikander repeated. He released Girard's fire order, and watched the icons on his console flash green. A mechanical whine and thump came from the hull ahead of the bridge, followed by the heavy thrumming sound of the Mark V kinetic cannon spitting out its round. The ten-kilo projectile left little in the way of visual evidence of its passage through vacuum—a K-cannon shot needed to hit something to produce any spectacular explosions. But the standard sensors of any warship within a couple of million kilometers couldn't miss the short-lived pulse of EM energy from the rail cannon, and radar systems watching for micrometeorites and orbital debris likewise tripped automatically when the fist-sized rod of tungsten moving at one percent of the speed of light hurtled through the area before disappearing into deep space beyond. In all likelihood the shot set off half a dozen blaring alarms on *Panther*'s bridge, and Sikander supposed that would be spectacular in its own way.

"*Panther*'s painting us with fire-control systems," Hiram Randall reported. Warning lights flashed on the tactical console.

"Return the favor, Mr. Randall," Markham ordered.

"Designate Dremish cruiser *Panther* as Target Alpha," Randall ordered. "Designate the transport *General von Grolmann* as Target Bravo. Illuminate Target Alpha and commence tracking."

"Illuminate Target Alpha, aye," Sikander replied. He marked the Dremish ships as hostile on his console; Ensign Girard quickly brought up *Hector*'s targeting systems and activated them. Sophisticated radars, lidars, and passive gravitic systems instantly measured the distance, course, and speed of the Dremish ship. At the moment, she was only about three thousand kilometers distant, lower in her orbit than *Hector* and moving at a correspondingly higher speed—knife-fighting range by the standards of modern fire control.

For several minutes, nothing more happened. The two cruisers locked each other with their fire control, the naval equivalent of two duelists pointing their pistols at each other but holding their fire. Sikander switched his attention from the weapons console to the main bridge display, now adjusted to focus on the orbital situation. *Panther* slowly rotated to keep her broadside on *Hector; Hector*'s helmsman likewise adjusted the ship's attitude to keep the maximum firepower focused on the Dremish cruiser. "Steady, everyone," Sikander said softly to his weapon officers. "Keep your hands well away from the firing keys."

Then *General von Grolmann* opened fire.

The troop carrier's K-cannons were not pointed at *Hector,* and *Hector*'s automated defenses did not register the barrage as an attack. But half a dozen K-rounds went streaking down into the dusty skies below. "*Grolmann* is firing on Gadira, Captain!" Randall said.

"What's she shooting at?" Markham demanded.

"The rounds appear to be targeted in the Toutay area, ma'am, probably the Khalifa Palace," said Randall. "Impacts are visible now."

It's not Ranya, Sikander told himself. He risked a quick glance at the vid feed that Randall's team monitored. Giant dust plumes obscured the area, but the display retained a faint outline of the original structure underneath. El-Fasi forces ringed the palace at a safe distance; he guessed that Bey Salem had called upon his Dremish friends to soften up the fortresslike palace for his troops to mount an assault. Until the dust cleared, it would be hard to assess just how much damage the Dremish bombardment was inflicting, and whether Gadira still had a sultan or not.

Commander Chatburn's voice came over the ship's internal command channel; the XO stood watch in the auxiliary bridge, ready to take over if an enemy hit took out the main bridge. "They aren't firing on us, Captain," he said. "They're only hitting the ground targets. The Commonwealth has no vital interest here worth starting a war over."

"The Empire of Dremark has taken that decision out of our hands, Mr. Chatburn." Markham stared at the Dremish ships, her face grim, then turned to Randall. "Break orbit and engage *Panther,* Mr. Randall. If we disable her fast, we might put a stop to this before it gets any worse."

"Aye, Captain," Randall replied. "Helm, ahead full! New course zero-seven-zero, up sixty. Bring us to ten thousand kilometers from Target Alpha and commence evasive maneuvering. Main battery, engage Target Alpha!"

"Engage Target Alpha!" Sikander echoed. He released the weapon hold icons on his console; an instant later Michael Girard opened fire from his station.

"Commencing fire!" Girard reported. *Hector* shivered with the immense power of the K-cannons blasting their deadly projectiles at the Dremish cruiser. At the same time, the deck tilted and the main view showed the planet drawing away as *Hector* moved to open the range and gain maneuvering room.

"*Panther* is returning fire!" Sublieutenant Keane called out from the sensor station.

"Understood," Captain Markham replied. "Mr. Randall, Mr. North, give me continuous fire on that cruiser until she's disabled. Now that we're in a fight, I have no intention of losing it."

"Continuous fire, aye, Captain," Sikander replied. *And God help us all.*

21

This day cannot end soon enough, Ranya el-Nasir told herself. There was simply too much to take in: uncertain alliances, unexpected betrayals, revolutions and coups and invasions . . . the whole planet was mad today, and she couldn't even begin to imagine what it all signified in the end. She steadied herself with one hand on the seatback of the specialist manning *Shihab*'s main communications console, rocking with the gentle motion as the yacht lolled in the heavy swells, and tried to understand what the orbital vid feed showed her. She could make out small slivers of light against the blackness of space and tiny bursts of light erupting around them, but its meaning was beyond her.

"Can someone explain what we are seeing here?" she asked the soldiers around her. "I can't make heads or tails of it."

"I beg your pardon, Amira," the technician said. "Let me see if I can improve the image." He adjusted the controls, and the view suddenly shifted, zooming in on one of the blurry slivers. It was a warship painted in white and buff, maneuvering frantically as its turrets swiveled to remain trained on target.

"It's the Aquilan cruiser," Tarek Zakur said, studying the

image alongside her. "They are fighting the Dremish warships."

Sikander! Ranya drew in a deep breath, doing her best to master her sudden surge of worry. Regardless of what she felt for the Kashmiri officer, she had many more important things to concern herself with than the fate of one man, no matter how much she cared for him. She whispered a swift prayer for his safety, and focused on what she was seeing. "Who is winning?" she asked Tarek Zakur.

"I couldn't say, Amira. I haven't seen many space battles." Zakur looked to the technician. "Where are we getting this feed from?"

"The Montréalais orbital traffic-control station," the man said. "They are watching the battle with great interest."

"I'll bet they are," Ranya said. She made herself straighten up and look away from the console; she could not afford to spend time watching a battle whose outcome she could not influence in the least. In fact, she didn't entirely understand why *Hector* and *Panther* were firing on one another. Dremark certainly indicated its hostility to the sultanate by attacking Royal Guard strongpoints in Tanjeer and providing fire support for the el-Fasi forces attacking the Khalifa Palace, but as far as she knew Aquila had no obligation to intervene on behalf of the el-Nasirs. *They must see a compelling interest of their own in foiling the Dremish schemes,* she decided. For the moment, she would have to content herself with the simple fact that the Commonwealth's interests appeared to align with her own; she'd piece together the consequences once she knew whether the Commonwealth of Aquila or the Empire of Dremark controlled the approaches to the planet. "Update me if it becomes clear that one side or the other is winning the battle in orbit," she told the technician.

She turned away from the space battle and moved over to study a holo-table map depicting the fighting going on around the planet. *Shihab*'s command center was a cramped space at the aft end of the main cabin, partitioned off from the luxurious living areas. Four or five people in the room would have filled it, but almost twice that many tried to cram into the room at once: sensor operators manning the yacht's defensive systems, comm experts trying to maintain secure channels to key Royal Guard commands throughout the world, and high-ranking officers coordinating the response of the sultan's army as they tried to simultaneously manage the street fighting against extremists in the major cities, Salem el-Fasi's developing coup, and now the overwhelming firepower of Dremish forces landing at key spots around the planet. So far, it seemed that three major crises held equal importance: the multisided battle for control of the capital, the attack on the Khalifa Palace, and a bold assault against the Royal Guard base in the city of Nador by Caidist forces out of the Harthawi Basin.

Nador does not matter, she decided. Tomorrow she could worry about whether or not Gadira's second-largest city was under the control of Caidists or not. Nor could she do much about the standoff around the Khalifa Palace. That left Tanjeer. The Royal Guard regiments stationed at the Abdelkadar Barracks seemed to be paralyzed by conflicting orders; perhaps that was something she could sort out—

"Amira, Sultan Rashid wishes to speak with you," Captain Zakur said, interrupting her train of thought. "The situation at Toutay is becoming more serious."

More serious? she wondered. There didn't seem to be much room left for things to get any worse. She steeled herself to maintain a calm demeanor, and simply nodded. "Of course. Which channel?"

"Here, Amira," Zakur replied. He guided her over to a seat by one of the comm consoles and handed her a headset so that the din of alarms, signals, and people talking loudly all around her wouldn't drown out her conversation.

Ranya adjusted the headset, and looked into the screen. Her uncle gazed back at her from what seemed to be the passenger seat in a transport; the image shook and bounced, most likely from the hand of whoever held the mobile comm unit. A small trickle of blood from a cut at his hairline streaked the dust on the side of his face. "Ah, there you are," he said over the channel, and gave her a small smile. "Are you safe, Ranya?"

"For the moment," she told him. "Where are you? What is happening?"

"General Mirza has informed me he can no longer defend what is left of the Khalifa Palace. We are attempting to withdraw through the mountains above Toutay. The decision has been made to shift command to Ben-Daleh. I am told that it remains in loyal hands." Someone spoke to Rashid from off the comm unit's camera; he nodded before looking back into the screen. "We may be out of communication for a while; *Shihab* will be our primary command center until we reestablish ourselves at Ben-Daleh."

"I understand, Uncle," Ranya said. "Go with God."

Rashid nodded. He looked weary, more exhausted than Ranya had ever seen him. He had made a life of avoiding difficult things, and now that they had found him anyway, he was not ready to meet them. "There is something more," he said, and his face seemed to crumple as she watched. "Your aunt Yasmin is dead, Ranya. She was in the Blue Tower when one of the orbital strikes made a direct hit. No one . . . no one survived."

Ranya felt a dagger of grief in the center of her chest. "Lina and Sabrina?" she whispered. Her cousins were only children!

"Sabrina was with Yasmin," Rashid said. "Lina is alive, but she was trapped in a different part of the palace and the guards couldn't get her to my transport. They're going to try to get her out on foot."

"Uncle—" she began, but then her voice caught in her throat. She couldn't think of anything to say.

A sudden jarring movement made Rashid grasp his seat

restraints as he shook from side to side. Ranya heard voices shouting in panic and warning. When the image steadied again, he had to raise his voice to make himself heard. "It seems that there are Dremish combat flyers in our vicinity," he told Ranya. "We may not be able to continue this conversation for long."

Ranya finally found her voice. "Get to safety," she urged the sultan. "We will find a way to fight back. This will not be the end for us, I promise you."

"Fighting back is the only thing Gadirans know how to do," Rashid said sadly. "We are a contentious race. Our great tragedy is that all our power of defiance is spent on the wrong targets. The caids are not wrong to—"

The screen went black. Static burst in her ears, and then images flickered across the screen—fire, smoke, a startling blue glimpse of tumbling sky and mountainside— accompanied by a terrible roar. Ranya snatched the headset away, and stared at the screen. "Uncle Rashid!" she cried. "Uncle Rashid!"

Around her, the command center erupted into chaos. Shouts and cries of panic filled the room. Desperately, Ranya tried to restore the connection. "Captain Zakur!" she called. "I've lost the sultan!"

Zakur didn't answer. In fact, the whole room fell silent a moment later. Ranya looked up, and found every man in the command center staring at one small screen. It showed the wreckage of a transport scattered over the barren shoulder of a mountain; a heavy flyer of a design unfamiliar to her orbited the crash site lazily, and then drifted away. "What is it?" Ranya demanded. "What happened?"

"The sultan's transport," Zakur said. "It's been shot down."

Ranya stared at the screen, hoping for some hint of a miracle. Perhaps he'd somehow been thrown clear of the wreckage, or perhaps there was a mistake and he wasn't actually on board that transport, but in her heart she knew that she gazed on a scene of grim finality. There would be no miraculous escape this time. "He is dead," she said slowly—a statement, not a question.

"Yes, Amira," the guard captain said. He covered his eyes and looked away, the first time in her life that Ranya had ever seen Tarek Zakur flinch from anything. "He is."

Slowly, Ranya got to her feet. She felt the eyes of the soldiers in the crowded command center shifting to her, and suddenly she felt the overwhelming need to get out of the room. Somehow she retained the presence of mind to walk deliberately instead of running, brushing tears from her eyes as she fled out to the yacht's aft deck.

The daylight dazzled her eyes after the dim illumination of the vid displays and comm screens. *Shihab* was far enough out to sea that even the tallest buildings in Tanjeer were not visible over the horizon, but she could easily make out the jagged brown rampart of the coastal mountains east of the capital. *God, lend me strength,* she prayed as she gazed out over the bright sea. Her own fate didn't concern her, but there seemed no end to the grief and sorrow that had been laid in store for the people around her. She thought of the gardens her uncle Rashid had tended so diligently on the grounds of El-Badi, and suddenly found herself filled with an overwhelming grief for her homeworld. The cycle of death and rage had to be ended, but how? If she somehow survived the day and defeated Salem el-Fasi, the caids would still be her enemies. And if she did not survive the day, then the caids would fight on against el-Fasi and the Dremish until they forced the offworlders to burn half the world in order to pacify them.

The caids . . . She thought about what Rashid had said just before the missiles hit. Was that what he was suggesting? She took a deep breath, examining the idea taking shape in her mind. It couldn't possibly work, but what other choice did she have? Her own fate meant nothing when weighed against the fate of the whole planet.

Tarek Zakur approached slowly, hesitant to intrude on her. "Sultana, I am sorry," he said in a ragged voice. "Your uncle was a better man than most people knew."

Sultana? Ranya wondered. The title sounded ridiculous to her, almost disrespectful; she couldn't make any claim to the throne. Someone would have to be chosen, there would have to be a logical decision about the succession . . . but she realized that she held the throne, whether she was ready for it or not. Ranya took a deep breath, and turned to face Zakur. "Thank you, Tarek. You served him well. What happened was not your fault."

The captain bowed deeply, acknowledging her words. He straightened, his face once again impassive. "There are new reports of heavy fighting in Nador between Caid Ahmed el-Manjour's people and our garrison there. And the Dremish have secured the Tanjeer spaceport. We are too close here; we need to set a course and get farther away from the capital before our enemies figure out where you are, Sultana."

"If the Dremish cruiser remains in orbit, then nowhere on the planet is safe," Ranya told Zakur. She glanced up at the sky; there was no hint of the furious battle raging overhead. "Pick the course that seems best to you."

"Yes, Sultana." Zakur hesitated. "What do you mean to do?"

"Am I that transparent?" Ranya asked.

"Only because I know you well, Sultana. You have decided on something, and you think I will not like it."

"I think *I* will not like it," she replied, and allowed herself a small ironic smile. "Contact all Royal Guard formations under our command. Order them to cease operations against Caidist forces and disengage to the best of their ability. We will turn our full force against Salem el-Fasi and his Dremish allies—they are the only enemy that matters. In fact, broadcast the command openly, and authenticate it as needed with our field commanders. I want everyone to know who we are fighting and why."

Zakur nodded. "At once, Sultana. Our forces may need to defend themselves if the Caidists and insurgents continue their attacks, though."

"Only to the minimum degree necessary," Ranya said. "As for the Caidists, let me see what I can do about that. Put a call through to Hadji Tumar ibn Sakak."

"The scholar?" Zakur frowned, a puzzled look on his face.

"Yes. It is my hope that he can help us."

"As you wish, Sultana. I will have your orders relayed and I will have our communications specialists find Hadji Tumar for you." Zakur bowed and went back belowdecks, heading for the command center.

Shihab turned toward the southeast and accelerated; the distant brown haze that marked the location of Tanjeer swung around slowly until it was directly astern. Evidently Tarek Zakur had some destination in mind, although Ranya doubted whether the yacht could get far enough away from the enemy forces in the capital to gain any measurable degree of safety. Even at her best speed, *Shihab* could not outrun Dremish assault shuttles—or kinetic strikes from orbit. Their best defense was looking innocuous. She moved to the lee rail and stared out over the waves, deliberately pushing her grief for her uncle and his family out of her mind, and thinking carefully about her next move.

A few minutes later, Captain Zakur summoned her back to the command room. "We have Hadji Tumar, Sultana," he told her.

Ranya followed him below. One of the communications consoles had been cleared for her use; she sat down and activated the screen. She found the lean, spectacled visage of Hadji Tumar regarding her from what appeared to be a cluttered and disorganized private office. "Good afternoon, Amira," he said to her.

"Thank you for taking my call, Allameh," she replied. "I hope you are safe from the fighting."

"As safe as anyone can be today," the old scholar said. "But I have a feeling you did not call me to inquire after my safety. How may I be of service?"

"I have a favor to ask of you. I need you to speak to the Caidist leaders on my behalf, and ask them to hear me out." Ranya gestured helplessly at the air. "We all face a very dangerous new enemy, and I do not believe they understand the threat. I have to try to convince them."

Tumar studied her through the screen. "Are you speaking on behalf of the sultan, Amira Ranya?"

Ranya steeled herself. "Sultan Rashid is dead. His transport was shot down near the Khalifa Palace."

The old scholar flinched. "God is merciful," he whispered. "I see. This has been a terrible day—I am sorry for your loss. What do you wish me to convey to the caids?"

Ranya told Tumar what she meant to do. When she finished, the allameh looked dubious, but he nodded. "I will ask, Amira," he said. "I cannot promise that they will agree, but I believe they will at least listen. Give me half an hour."

It ended up taking almost an hour to make the arrangements for the next call. Ranya spent the time rehearsing what she meant to say, while doing what she could to keep up on the military developments. She lost track of the battle between *Hector* and *Panther;* the orbit of the Montréalais traffic-control station carried it out of sight of the fighting, leaving her to wonder if the battle had concluded, which ship had won, and whether Sikander had survived the day or not. The Dremish troops finished securing the spaceport in Tanjeer and turned their attention on the Abdelkadar Barracks on the outskirts of the capital, heavily damaging the base with airstrikes. Whether they knew it or not, the Dremish might have aided her there, since many of the troops at Abdelkadar were under the control of commanders who had refused the sultanate's orders, declaring for Salem el-Fasi. *But not all of them,* Ranya reminded herself. Many of the men would be confused or torn by their conflicting orders, and every Gadiran who died today, loyal or disloyal, was one of her people.

Finally Captain Zakur appeared and led her to one of the yacht's conference rooms, hastily refitted with comm gear to provide her with more privacy than the crowded command center. She sat down, composed herself for a moment, then activated the vidscreen.

In one panel of the divided conference display she saw Tumar ibn Sakak, still working out of his old-fashioned office. In three additional panels she faced two sun-darkened, gray-bearded men in the traditional garb of the desert tribes, and a younger man with olive skin and black, curly hair, who wore a keffiyeh over the dirty jumpsuit of an urban laborer. She recognized the first of the gray-bearded men as Harsaf el-Tayib, but she didn't know the other two. All three started in surprise as they realized who she was.

"Hadji Tumar, you have deceived us!" the desert chieftain she didn't know protested. He was a short, round-bodied man, and it appeared that he was taking the call from a mining pit or quarry somewhere in the deep desert. "This is the amira!"

"Forgive me, Caid Ahmed," the old scholar said. "She asked to speak with you, and I did not think you would agree if I told you first. I would regard it as a great personal favor if you would consent to hear her out."

"It is not fitting for a man of God to employ falsehoods," the chieftain said with a scowl.

"It is not fitting for servants of God to kill one another, and there has been far too much of that of late, especially when their strife profits the godless," Tumar answered. The protesting chieftain's scowl deepened, but he fell silent. "Amira Ranya, this is Caid Ahmed el-Manjour. The other men you can see are Caid Harsaf el-Tayib and Alonzo

Khouri. Several others are listening in but do not wish to reveal themselves at this time."

"I remember Caid Harsaf from the time when my father was sultan," Ranya said. She looked at the lean, bearded chieftain. "I thank you for hearing me out."

"It is only because of my respect for the allameh that I am listening," Harsaf el-Tayib replied. "Where is the sultan? The allameh said he wanted to warn us of a danger threatening us all."

"Sultan Rashid el-Nasir is dead," Ranya said, keeping her voice even. "His transport was shot down a little more than an hour ago as he left the Khalifa Palace."

"Rashid is dead?" Caid Harsaf said, surprised. He glanced at the others in his display. "Who is sultan now?"

"I am now the eldest surviving heir of Sultan Kamal, and the head of House Nasir," said Ranya.

"A woman cannot be sultan!" Caid Ahmed blustered.

"No, but she can be sultana," Ranya replied. "I do not claim that title yet, however. It is my hope to serve as regent only until the proper succession can be determined, and today is not the day to do that."

Caid Harsaf gave el-Manjour a humorless smile. "You see, Ahmed? Hadji Tumar did not lie. He promised the head of state, not Sultan Rashid by name." His eyes shifted to the allameh. "But I must wonder if the amira can be regent."

"There is precedent," Tumar answered. As a scholar and jurist, his view on that question carried a good deal of weight. "Speak your mind, Amira."

"We share a common enemy," she told the rebel leaders. "I told you that Sultan Rashid is dead, but I did not tell you who killed him. He was shot down by a Dremish assault shuttle, after the Dremish warship in orbit over our planet launched a kinetic bombardment that destroyed much of the Khalifa Palace. I understand that Sultana Yasmin and at least one of her daughters were killed in this bombardment, too. One of my cousins may still survive—I simply do not know." A surge of anger and grief welled up in the core of her being at that thought, but she fought it down and continued. "You all know by now that Salem el-Fasi is attempting to claim the throne. What you might not yet realize is that Dremark is backing him with troops and warships so that they can seize control of Gadira and install el-Fasi as their puppet."

"Montréal, Dremark, what is the difference?" Alonzo Khouri asked, speaking for the first time. "Any of the Coalition powers would be happy to be our master. They will still get rich from our labor while we remain buried in poverty."

"The difference is that it's been twenty years since a Montréalais garrison occupied Gadira," Ranya answered. "Yes, they provided my uncle with military aid and investments, but they gave up on stationing troops here a long time ago. Today Dremark's soldiers saw fit to obliterate a six-hundred-year-old planetary treasure with bombs from orbit and assassinate my uncle. How do you think they will deal with riots and protests in the poor neighborhoods of our cities?" She shifted her gaze to the desert chieftains. "Or open rebellion by the free desert tribes?"

"If they think they can crush us under their heels, they are fools," Caid Ahmed snarled. But Caid Harsaf said nothing, shifting in his seat and reaching up to stroke his beard.

"There is something else I need to show you," Ranya said. She linked her dataslate to the vidscreen and brought up an image to show the others—a slender, sandy-haired offworlder, captured in midstride by a security cam near the parade ground of El-Badi Palace. "This is a man who calls himself Otto Bleindel. He is the Dremish consul in Gadira."

To her surprise, all three rebels showed signs of recognition. Caid Ahmed leaned closer, and muttered something under his breath. Caid Harsaf paused in stroking his beard. And Alonzo Khouri frowned. "I know him. He told us his name was Hardesty, and he said he was a mercenary."

"He has been supplying you with your modern Cygnan weapons, correct?" said Ranya. "He was spotted in Meknez with the latest arms shipment, which the Royal Guard intercepted. It turns out he has also been arming Bey Salem." She adjusted the footage, expanding it to show Salem el-Fasi walking beside Bleindel on the palace grounds. "I think he has been playing us all for fools. While he was giving you the firepower you needed to attack my uncle, he was also arming Bey Salem's forces."

"To what purpose?" Khouri asked.

"So that Bey Salem could overthrow the sultanate," Hadji Tumar answered for Ranya. "This offworlder armed you so that you would weaken or defeat Sultan Rashid, and make it possible for Bey Salem to seize power and sign a treaty of cooperation with Dremark. I know little about such things, but it appears to me that his plan is well on its way to succeeding."

"Can you prove this?" Caid Harsaf asked Ranya.

"You know where your weapons came from. As for Bey Salem's exact bargain with Dremark, I admit that I am guessing. But Salem el-Fasi's troops are now sitting in El-Badi Palace, and Dremish troops are firing on the Royal Guard. What other explanation is there?" Ranya allowed the question to hang in the air.

There was a long silence as the three men considered her words. Finally Caid Harsaf spoke again. "Assuming everything you say is true, Amira, what exactly do you propose?"

"I am ordering the Royal Guard to disengage from all actions against your forces," said Ranya. "We are turning our full strength to putting down el-Fasi's coup attempt and fighting back against Dremark. I beg you for your help in fighting our common enemy, but if you cannot bring yourself to fight alongside the Royal Guard, I hope you will at least stand aside and let us fight for you."

"For us? You fight to keep yourself in power," Alonzo Khouri observed.

"That may be true today," Ranya replied. "Tomorrow, it will be up to you. I will not reign without the consent of the people. Assuming I am not killed by Salem el-Fasi or his Dremish allies, I promise before God that I will convene an assembly to decide whether Gadira should have a sultan, what place our Quranist beliefs should have in our society, and whether we will welcome or shun offworld contact. But if you do not help me now, you'll have to ask the Emperor of Dremark what kind of world he will allow you to live in." Ranya looked at each of the men in turn, and then back to Khouri. "Gadira for Gadirans, isn't that your slogan?"

The rebel leaders looked away, perhaps trying to gauge each other's reactions or listening to people who were not on Ranya's screen. The silence stretched on for long seconds, and then Caid Harsaf spoke. "Very well, Amira," he said. "Speaking for the el-Tayibs, we will hold our positions if your Royal Guard does not attack us, and we will not move against you as long as you are fighting Dremark or Bey Salem. As for allying with you . . . I must think on it more."

"The el-Manjouri will do the same," Caid Ahmed growled.

"I can only speak for my own people in Tanjeer," said Khouri, "but we have been fighting el-Fasi and his imperialist allies all day, and we will continue to do so. We will avoid engaging the Royal Guard if they do not attack us."

Ranya let out a breath she didn't realize she had been holding. "I can expect no more. Go make whatever arrangements you have to; we will speak again later." She looked at each man in turn, and gave them one small nod. "Now, if you'll excuse me . . . I have an invasion to repel."

22

CSS *Hector*, Gadira II Orbit

Panther was ready for trouble. The moment *Hector* opened fire, the Dremish ship accelerated and replied with her own K-cannons. At their current range, the flight time of the K-rounds was less than a second, not enough for any kind of deliberate evasion by either ship. Despite that, most of the cruiser's salvos missed each other, simply because both ships were accelerating at full military power. A half second was enough time for *Hector* to change her vector by several hundred meters, and thus not be quite where she'd been when *Panther* returned fire. *Panther* had less of an opportunity to move, since *Hector* fired first, but even so Mark V rounds streaked past her, missing by a dozen meters or less in most cases—and for a kinetic round, missing by a meter was the same as missing by a thousand kilometers. Without direct impact none of the frightful kinetic energy of the tungsten-alloy projectiles could be turned into damage on the target, and a phenomenal amount of energy was thus wasted on missed shots.

But not all missed.

One of *Hector*'s shots grazed *Panther*'s stern, wrecking a main drive plate. Another gouged her belly, failing to penetrate her armor but creating a brilliant spray of molten metal that blossomed behind the Dremish ship. And one solid hit impacted just below *Panther*'s second main-battery turret, drilling a hole through the barbette armor. The Aquilan shot transformed instantly into a ragged spray of dense, incandescent plasma, driven to unimaginable temperatures by the transformation of sheer kinetic energy into heat. It vaporized the capacitor room below the turret, and compartments all around buckled or melted in turn. The Dremish cruiser shuddered under the secondary explosions, an expanding ball of white-hot plasma streaming from her wound.

"Hit!" Girard yelled, raising a fist in triumph.

Sikander grinned fiercely, and started to congratulate the ensign—but at that moment *Panther*'s return fire struck *Hector*.

Like *Hector*'s initial volley, most of *Panther*'s shots missed. But Oberleutnant Helena Aldrich's gunnery team was every bit as well trained as Sikander's, and *Panther*'s K-cannons were actually a little larger and more powerful than *Hector*'s. A grazing hit just aft of *Hector*'s superstructure sliced through the power conduit feeding the number-three main-battery turret, and a second round found *Hector*'s main hangar bay and incinerated a docked shuttle in its cradle. The ensuing fireball blew the hangar hatch completely free of the ship, but also ejected a good deal of the molten debris; two of *Hector*'s shuttles spun away from the ship as blazing meteors that would streak across the sky above the Bitter Sea ten minutes later. The hangar explosion jolted every compartment like a giant pounding the side of the ship with a sledgehammer. Sikander was wrenched sideways and bit his tongue hard enough to draw blood before the inertial compensators kicked in and suppressed the movement.

"Number-three turret out!" Sikander called, reporting the damage blinking on his console. He had no idea what had happened; the turret icon flashed red, and that was all he could tell. Other damage reports echoed around the bridge. He heard Magdalena Juarez on the command channel, reciting a list of damaged or off-line systems. Her battle station was down in the engineering control station, where she monitored the power plant and induction drives.

"Hit them again!" Randall shouted.

"Recharging main battery, sir!" Girard called back. The Mark V couldn't throw ten-kilo slugs over and over again; each K-cannon had a firing cycle of about fifteen seconds. The deck lurched again under Sikander, and he realized that Chief Quartermaster Holtz was doing his best to throw the ship into every jink, roll, and sharp turn he could manage while climbing up out of Gadira's gravity well.

"Box your fire, Mr. Girard!" Sikander told the ensign. "They'll be evading now." K-rounds moved so fast relative to targets that anticipating enemy evasion essentially became a two-dimensional problem—it was important to spread a salvo a little ahead, a little behind, a little above, and a little under the apparent target so that no matter which way it dodged, it stood a good chance of running into a K-round's path. He didn't want Girard to get locked in on aiming his full salvo at the spot where *Panther* happened to be the instant he fired.

"Yes, sir!" Girard replied. "Firing!" Another volley of Mark V K-rounds hummed and crackled as they blasted toward the enemy cruiser. The range opened as both ships clawed up away from the planet, seeking room to dodge and weave. It seemed Captain Harper had no more taste for knife fights than did Captain Markham. *Hector* scored again with a hit that wrecked an auxiliary engineering room; *Panther* hit back and damaged part of *Hector*'s folded warp ring.

On his own initiative, Sikander keyed a fire mission to the secondary battery. Sublieutenant Reno had control of the ship's UV lasers, and while unlikely to cause serious damage to an armored warship, they could vaporize antennas and sensor arrays, slagging or jamming weapon mounts with lucky hits. "Knock out their sensors and secondaries, Mr. Reno," he said. "Anything you see that looks delicate and important. Mind our heat budget, only fire when you see something worth burning."

"Aye, sir!" Reno replied. He opened up with the laser battery, using high-magnification targeting to hunt for vulnerable spots and burn them. Lasers didn't carry the hitting power of rail-gun rounds, but nothing material could completely ignore a few million joules of energy arriving in a concentrated area. Puffs of vaporized hull metal began to appear beneath *Hector*'s searching lasers—and naturally *Panther*'s own lasers burned *Hector*'s hull structures, too.

The two cruisers hammered away at each other, continuing to salvo their K-cannons and maneuvering wildly in an attempt to dodge fire. Neither ship carried enough heavy armor to shrug off a kinetic round from the other, but obtaining a square hit was harder than Sikander would have guessed. Most hits struck on the curve of the hull, deflecting a good deal of energy out and away from the interior systems while leaving spectacular gouges and furrows of shattered hull and incandescent metal. *Hector*'s K-cannons had a more rapid firing cycle; *Panther*'s hit harder. Again and again impacts hammered the ship, and Sikander found himself so busy with managing the battle damage to *Hector*'s batteries and fire-control systems that he forgot to be frightened for his own life. He noticed the Dremish transport breaking orbit, and fleeing from the dueling cruisers at her best speed. *At least we've succeeded in interrupting the landings for the time being.*

"Weapons, I need a torpedo spread on Target Alpha!" Randall ordered.

"We're still inside minimum distance, sir!" Sublieutenant Larkin replied. "We need another thousand kilometers of range for a clean run!"

"Damn it," Randall snarled. "Stand by and be ready with

a spread as soon as we open the distance! Helm, come right and get us more separation!"

"Aye, sir," the chief helmsman replied. *Hector* leaned into the turn, still surging and twisting in its evasive maneuvers.

"New target, Target Charlie!" called Sublieutenant Keane from the sensor console. "Range thirty-five thousand, bearing one-three-five! Waffe-class destroyer, accelerating to intercept us."

"Damn the luck," said Captain Markham. "It's *Streitaxt*. I suppose she didn't leave the system after all."

Hiram Randall grimaced. "She probably hid behind the moon," he said. "They must have slipped back to park in a dark-side crater when we were on the wrong side of Gadira II. Sorry, Captain. We should have confirmed that she left the system after she bubbled up."

Markham nodded, and leaned back in her seat. "Very well," she said, maintaining her calm demeanor. "It looks like we've got a harder day ahead of us than we thought."

For the first time in the encounter, Sikander felt the icy touch of fear at the nape of his neck. Dealing with the *Panther* was a fifty-fifty proposition, but they seemed to be holding their own for the moment. *Streitaxt* was a powerful new destroyer, and even if she was not the match of a cruiser, she didn't need to be in order to shift the odds decisively in *Panther*'s favor.

"Captain, we may need to consider a withdrawal," Commander Chatburn said from his post in the auxiliary bridge. "We're outgunned, and we've made our point. There may not be much more we can do here."

"As matters stand, we can't avoid *Streitaxt*'s engagement envelope," said Markham. She studied the displays for a moment, then made her decision. "Mr. Randall, plot a course for disengagement once we get past the destroyer. Mr. North, split your batteries. Keep up the fire on *Panther* but engage *Streitaxt* as she bears. We might as well run through with guns blazing, because they'll certainly be shooting at us."

"Aye, Captain," Sikander replied. He didn't like the idea of admitting defeat, but it wasn't his call. The tactical situation was clearly unfavorable: *Hector* would pass between the two Dremish warships no matter how she maneuvered. "Mr. Girard, I'll take the starboard-side battery and engage the destroyer. You keep the port-side battery and continue firing on *Panther*."

"Releasing the starboard-side battery," Girard replied. "Hit 'em hard, sir!"

Sikander nodded but did not reply, already setting up his console to take control of the Mark V mounts that faced the right-hand side of the ship. It wasn't strictly by the book, but this orbital battle had proved to Sikander that trying to outguess the defensive maneuvers of one target at a time was enough for any gunnery officer. He deliberately pushed the Dremish cruiser out of his mind, leaving *Panther* to the ensign while waiting for the range to *Streitaxt* to close; destroyers were agile targets, and a thirty-five-thousand-kilometer shot would give her almost twelve seconds to dodge. He'd only be wasting power and K-shot, so he held his fire for the moment.

Hector shuddered again with more impacts from *Panther*'s K-cannons and pounded back at the enemy cruiser as the range to the destroyer steadily narrowed. Sikander studied the engagement with a momentary detachment, reviewing all his training and countless hours of discussion and speculation with other officers. He began to suspect that he didn't know as much about ship-to-ship combat as he'd thought he did—a realization probably shared by most of *Hector*'s crew and the Dremish, too. There simply hadn't been many serious engagements between modern warships in the last twenty years or so, and the Aquilan navy based most of its tactics and expectations on theory, not practice.

Hitting a live target that shot back proved a good deal more difficult than simulations or range exercises suggested, and the predicted one-hit kills he'd been told to expect hadn't happened, at least not yet. This was a battle of attrition, not a quick-draw contest, and if they happened to survive until the end of it, *Hector*'s experience would necessitate the rewriting of quite a few training manuals.

"Damn it!" Angela Larkin snarled, and punched at her console in frustration. "We just lost tubes one and two, sir!"

"Destroyed or off-line?" Sikander asked.

"Off-line, looks like we lost the capacitor for the upper launch tubes." She twisted in her couch to look up at him. "Sir, those were the two good Phantoms."

All that work to figure out what was wrong with the torpedoes, and the only two good ones we have on board are dead in their tubes! Sikander grimaced. Torpedoes in dead launch tubes were not going to be very useful, and right now *Hector* needed all the firepower she could get. "Tell Chief Maroth to rig a jumper cable from the other tubes," he told Larkin. The crewmen manning the torpedo room were probably already working on it, but maybe they'd be able to get tubes one and two operational by cross-connecting the power feeds from tubes three and four.

"Aye, sir," Larkin replied. She turned back to her console.

"Weapons, I need that torpedo spread," Randall called back to Sikander. "The range looks good to me!"

"Torpedoes off-line, Mr. Randall," Sikander said. "We lost power to the launch tubes. No ETA on repairs."

Randall swore under his breath. "Very well," he replied. "Keep it up with the main battery, then."

"Aye, sir!" Sikander returned his attention to *Streitaxt*, now well within his engagement envelope. At twenty thousand kilometers, he opened up on her. "Salvo starboard!" he called, and hit the firing keys. It was perhaps a little long for shooting at a destroyer, but it wouldn't hurt to force *Streitaxt*'s crew to start thinking about taking evasive action. He quickly tuned out the chatter of reports and commands not directed at him, concentrating on directing his share of *Hector*'s main battery. Minutes crawled by as *Hector* began taking fire from both sides, and the pace of the battle threatened to overwhelm the bridge crew altogether. More hits rocked the cruiser, setting off a chorus of alarms.

"Damage report!" Magdalena Juarez barked over *Hector*'s command circuit. "We've lost generator three, effective power ouput now at sixty-five percent capacity! Drive plate two is off-line, estimated time to repair ten minutes! Hull breaches in the mess deck, personnel office, Auxiliary Engine Room One!"

Sikander winced at the growing list of things that no longer worked on board *Hector*. He could smell burning insulation nearby, although it was not yet so toxic that he needed to close his visor. Red lights blinked on a dozen consoles around the bridge, and not a few of them flashed on his own weapons display. Two of *Hector*'s main-battery turrets had been knocked out, and a third was power-starved until the gunner's mates stationed there could rig a jumper cable big enough to take the energy load needed to fire one of the Mark V K-cannons. The ship's inertial compensation no longer worked at full effect, either; every jink and swerve from the helm threw Sikander from side to side in his battle couch, and the hull shuddered and groaned under each new impact. Like tired boxers, the two cruisers continued to wear each other down, but neither had yet scored a knockout punch.

"Acknowledged!" Captain Markham replied. "Can you get generator three back on-line, Ms. Juarez? We need the power."

"It's destroyed, Captain," the chief engineer replied. "Half the casing is gone, looks like primary impact from a heavy K-cannon. I can redline the remaining units and give you a little more, but it's dangerous."

"Do so," Markham ordered. "We no longer have the luxury

of safety margins." Her voice remained admirably calm, but her fingers clenched the arms of her couch with fierce strength. Sikander swallowed the words of warning that came to his lips. It wasn't his job to second-guess the captain on damage management, and for all he knew, she might be exactly correct in her decision.

"Salvo port!" called Michael Girard. So far it seemed like the ensign was doing well with his half of *Hector*'s main guns: Half a dozen major hits scored and pocked *Panther*'s hull, and she appeared to be sluggish at the helm. Sikander hadn't yet landed a good hit on *Streitaxt,* but he'd grazed her twice, and the destroyer danced wildly at the edge of its own effective range to dodge his fire.

"Tactical, tubes three and four are ready to launch," Angela Larkin called out. "We have good solutions on Target Alpha!"

Sikander looked up in alarm. "Those are bad torpedoes, Ms. Larkin!"

"They'll work, sir! I set up a new attack program that won't trigger the reset."

"Weapons, do we have torpedoes or not?" Randall demanded from the tactical console.

Sikander realized that while he'd been absorbed in the task of trying to hit *Streitaxt,* Larkin had stayed focused on her job. The older torpedoes faulted out in the standard attack program, so she'd punched in custom settings for the weapons that were in functional tubes rather than wait for power to be restored to the off-line weapons—and she'd managed it in ten minutes. *A month ago I asked her what would happen if we had to fire torpedoes in anger,* he remembered. *Now we find out.*

"Tactical, the torps are good. We can take the shot," he told Randall. Maybe the effort to isolate the torpedo failure hadn't been wasted, after all. Trusting Larkin to execute the attack, he focused on *Streitaxt* again and resumed fire.

"Helm, torpedo attack," Hiram Randall ordered. "Target Alpha, two torps! As weapons bear . . . fire!"

"Firing!" Larkin's console briefly assumed control of *Hector*'s maneuvers. Expertly she spun the ship on its vertical axis, bringing *Hector*'s bow-mounted torpedo tubes to face *Panther,* and punched the keys to fire two Phantoms. These were not practice torpedoes—these were war shots, fitted with deadly fusion warheads. The ship shuddered as the tubes ejected the heavy missiles; they streaked away from their launch tubes, and vanished into warp bubbles.

"*Streitaxt* firing torpedoes!" Sublieutenant Keane shouted from the sensor station. On Sikander's display, the Dremish destroyer suddenly wheeled to point her bow at *Hector* and release her own spread. For an instant, she couldn't dodge—and his K-cannons were ready.

"Evade torpedoes!" Randall shouted.

Sikander hit his firing keys just before Chief Holtz at the helm wrenched *Hector* into an emergency torpedo-evasion maneuver. "Salvo starboard!" Sikander called out. *Hector* rocked and hummed with the magnetic recoil of the big Mark V K-cannons hurling their lethal shot at the oncoming Dremish destroyer. And then several things happened almost at once.

Hector's torpedo spread arrived at *Panther,* the weapons dropping their warp bubbles and twisting through terminal maneuvers in the fraction of a second between returning to normal space and detonation. Each Phantom carried a rugged fusion bomb of almost half a megaton. In direct contact they would vaporize a battleship, but warp torpedoes weren't fused for impact—they were proximity weapons, designed to detonate as soon as they were sufficiently close to the target to cause crippling damage. Larkin set up her attack as a one-two punch; the first Phantom dove in and burst a few hundred meters from *Panther*'s waist, boiling off the outer skin with the fusion blast just before the second torpedo appeared out of nowhere and detonated even closer, wrecking the cruiser's main power rooms and sending a wave of impulsive shock racing through her structure. *Panther*'s armored hull protected the crew from lethal radiation, but shock and spalling fragments wrecked vulnerable control stations and vital systems throughout the Dremish ship.

Because *Hector* had turned to hit *Panther* with her torpedoes, her stern faced *Streitaxt* when the destroyer's own torpedo spread exploded just behind the hull. The sternmost section of the ship contained few vital control stations or engineering spaces; those were protected in the center of mass, guarded by the heaviest armor *Hector* carried. But the drive plates for the ship's induction engines and the retracted warp ring were located at the aft end of the hull, and *Streitaxt*'s salvo vaporized large portions of *Hector*'s drive system. Hull plates exploded into vapor, kicking *Hector* forward so suddenly that Sikander suffered more than a little bit of whiplash—as did something like two-thirds of the cruiser's crew—before the inertial compensators could react. Sensors, power generators, and control systems were knocked off-line by the jarring hits. Most came back on almost at once, but not the drive plates shattered by the torpedo bursts. In one savage moment, *Hector*'s legs were slashed out from under her, leaving her in a tumbling, out-of-control spin.

Alarms flashed and wailed throughout the bridge, and half the screens went dark. But weapons controls were especially well hardened against shock, and Sikander could observe the effect of his previous salvo on *Streitaxt*. As before, five-sixths of his K-cannon shots sailed past the destroyer with little effect, although one rod grazed the hull and left a fifty-meter scoring of molten metal only a few centimeters deep. But the sixth round hit dead center in the destroyer's bow, still facing directly at *Hector*. While it was the most heavily armored part of the hull, no destroyer in any fleet could stand up to a direct hit from a cruiser's

K-cannon. The blast incinerated *Streitaxt*'s forward torpedo room, and touched off a wave of secondary explosions as the bursting charges in the weapons stored in the torpedo tubes detonated. The first fifty meters of *Streitaxt* simply ceased to exist as a recognizable hull, blasted into streamers of incandescent metal and shattered armor plates spinning off in all directions.

Larkin let out a whoop of exhilaration. "Hits on *Panther*!" she called out.

"Hit on *Streitaxt*!" said Sikander. He risked a quick glance away from his display to look at Larkin's console. "Good work, Ms. Larkin."

"Well done!" Captain Markham answered, raising her voice to be heard over the din of screeching alarms and confused reports. "Engineering, what's our status?"

"Acceleration effectively zero, Captain!" Magda answered. Sikander could hear the strain in her voice and a din of shouts and alarms from the engineering control room, carrying over her link to the command circuit. "We can't maneuver!"

"Helm doesn't answer, Captain," Chief Holtz announced from the pilot station. "Attitude control only, and not too much of that."

"Get me a working drive plate, Ms. Juarez," Markham ordered. "Mr. North, what's our main battery—"

"Oh, fuck me," Hiram Randall said laconically, interrupting the captain. He stared at the tactical console. "*Panther* is firing, Captain. We can't evade."

23

Sikander had time to briefly lock eyes with Elise Markham as they both absorbed the import of Randall's announcement. Then *Panther*'s ragged salvo arrived. Though badly damaged, the Dremish cruiser still had power for some of her main battery, and *Hector* could no longer actively dodge. She was merely a target moving in a ballistic arc, although her three-axis tumbling motion made her a somewhat complicated one, and the Dremish fire-control systems assumed that *Hector* could still perform evasive maneuvers and therefore did not aim exactly at where she was. Several rounds missed, fooled by the unexpected motion. Others did not.

One of *Panther*'s K-rounds punched into *Hector*'s port side, a brilliant lance of tungsten alloy. In the space of an instant, a spray of molten metal and jets of gas erupted from the bulkhead on the left side of the bridge. The wall crumpled inward and the deck buckled; a deafening roar blasted the room. Sikander's visor slammed shut; he felt himself picked up and thrown down again, although his seat restraints held and he was not flung from his battle couch. Everything went dark; he heard and saw nothing.

When he could see again, he blinked and looked around.

There was a large, jagged hole in the port side of the bridge compartment; a fiery orange glow gleamed through. Vapor streamed out of the bridge through the hole, the unmistakable sign of a hull breach. He wondered what compartment was between the bridge and the port-side outer hull and what was left of it, but at the moment his ability to picture the details of *Hector*'s internal arrangement wasn't quite up to the task. Shattered control consoles and vidscreens dangled and sparked fitfully on that side of the room. There had been a couple of manned consoles on that side of the bridge, but they were simply gone. Only twisted, hot metal and torn scraps of armored suit remained.

Bridge hit, he realized. A bad one, although he'd been lucky. The weapon-control stations were at the aft end of the compartment, so he and the other Gunnery Department officers seemed to still be in one piece. His ears buzzed and crackled, and he was sore all over, but his arms and legs moved when he wanted them to and his suit remained intact. Already he could see Girard shaking himself and punching at his console, while Larkin—how had she been knocked out of her seat?—picked herself up off the deck and returned to her station. He looked over to Captain Markham to see if she was all right.

She was not.

Molten shrapnel from the hit that had breached the hull had cut through her battle station like a white-hot scythe. She'd been thrown against the far bulkhead in the wreckage of her restraints. A thick, charred line as deep as Sikander's fist snaked across her back, her shoulders, her head. Her suit was torn open . . . but he doubted very much that Elise Markham had lived long enough to die of decompression.

Hiram Randall was luckier. He hadn't been hit directly by the shrapnel, but he'd been struck by what was left of the port-side bridge displays, dislodged by the explosion. He slumped in his battle station, motionless. Whether alive or dead, Sikander could not say.

"Bridge! Bridge! Is anybody up there? Respond!"

Sikander shook his head, and realized that the buzzing he heard in his ears was what remained of the command circuit. Commander Chatburn shouted at him over and over again from his position in the auxiliary bridge. "Bridge, report!"

"This is Lieutenant North," Sikander said. His tongue felt thick and clumsy, but as he spoke he began to rally; the ringing in his ears faded a bit and he felt his wits coming back into focus. "We took a bad hit on the bridge. Captain Markham is dead, and Mr. Randall appears unconscious. I'm the senior officer remaining here."

"Good God," Chatburn replied. There was a long silence. "What's going on? Do you still have sensors and weapons? We've got a power outage here, we can't see anything."

"Heavy damage on both *Panther* and *Streitaxt*. Us, too, I guess. I don't know what we have left, XO."

"You're certain about the captain?"

"Yes, sir." Sikander couldn't even bring himself to look in her direction. He turned his attention to the bridge crew, and keyed the all-bridge circuit. "Dolan, Reese!" he said to two of the hands manning the tactical displays. "Get a patch on the port bulkhead, we'll need atmosphere in here as soon as we can get it!" Armored suits could stave off the effects of exposure to vacuum as long as the suit wasn't breached in the wrong spot, but treating the injured would be next to impossible in a compartment open to space.

"Record in ship's log, effective immediately," Chatburn said over the circuit. "Peter Chatburn, Commander, Commonwealth Navy, assumes command. All stations report condition."

Sikander ignored him. Chatburn already knew what he needed to know about the bridge, and he had other things to do. He unbuckled himself from his couch and stood up. "Mr. Reno, take the weapons console," he ordered. "Attention on the bridge: I am taking tactical control."

His legs were not as steady as he would have liked, but he made it over to Randall's station and unbuckled the operations officer's restraints. Randall's suit indicators suggested that he lived, but his helmet was noticeably dented and Sikander could see a trickle of blood from his nose beneath the faceplate. He could do nothing for Randall at the moment, but he needed the tactical console; as gently as he could, Sikander lifted him out of the battle couch and lowered him to the deck. Then he strapped himself in, and took stock of the situation displayed on Randall's station.

Gadira II gleamed half a million kilometers behind them, a golden crescent against the stars; in their weaving and maneuvering, the two cruisers had traced a ragged helical path around each other, climbing up out of orbit. *Panther* paralleled *Hector* about fifteen thousand kilometers distant, while *Streitaxt* drew back, turning her shattered bow section away from *Hector*'s guns. *Where is the transport?* Sikander wondered. The whole point of this affair was to interrupt Dremark's attempt to land an occupying force. He scrolled and panned his display until he found *General von Grolmann* lurking out near the moon, Hala. Troop carriers had no business being anywhere near a ship-to-ship engagement, although *Hector* was far enough off now that *Grolmann* might be able to return to planetary orbit and resume her ground operations.

"Helm, get our spin under control, and bring us to new course one-nine-zero, down twenty," Sikander ordered Chief Holtz. "We're getting too far away from the planet."

"Aye, sir," the chief pilot replied. "I'm working on the spin, sir, but changing course is going to take a while. We have a lot of velocity in the wrong direction and not much acceleration ability."

"Would it be faster to slingshot around the moon?"

"Yes, sir, by quite a bit. That would require . . . course one-three-five, as soon as I can stabilize our spin."

"New course one-three-five, as soon as you can get us stabilized," Sikander said. "Best speed you can put on, Chief." He looked back to his gunnery officers. "Mr. Girard, damage assessment on *Panther*! Mr. Reno, same on *Streit-axt*! What do they have left?"

"One moment, sir!" Girard replied.

While Reno and Girard studied the sensor imagery of the Dremish warships, Sikander took a long look at his own damage displays. The Old Worthy had taken a serious beating. They'd lost a third of their K-cannons to direct hits or internal damage that disrupted power or fire-control systems. Casualties numbered fifty or more, the warp ring was inoperative, and they limped along at barely three-quarters their normal power generation. The engines suffered the worst damage, of course . . . but hull and armor integrity was good, and other than a distinct lack of maneuverability, the ship was still combat effective. *Hector* still had a little more to give, if he had to ask it of her. However, they could no longer dodge enemy fire worth a damn, with so much damage to the drive plates.

Sikander returned his attention to the damaged K-cannons. The number-one turret flashed red—that was Darvesh Reza's battle station. *Cascading system failure from the bridge hit, or direct hit on the mount?* He knew he shouldn't pay attention to a single indicator, not with the whole ship to worry about, but he quickly selected the local comm circuit anyway and called. "Number-One Mount, Bridge. Are you still there?"

To his surprise, Darvesh answered. "Bridge, this is Mount Number One, Chief Reza speaking."

"Darvesh? My board shows your mount inoperable. Where's Chief Valenzuela?"

"The last hit damaged the train mechanism, sir. Chief Valenzuela is directing repairs. We should be able to resume fire momentarily." Darvesh paused. "Have we stopped maneuvering?"

"We've lost a lot of our drive capacity, but we're still in the fight. Keep me posted on repairs. Bridge, out." Sikander allowed himself a small sigh of relief. Darvesh had been with him for most of the last ten years; it was good to know that they hadn't parted ways just yet.

"Report on *Streitaxt*," Sublieutenant Reno announced. "She's got most of her power and engines, sir, but her torpedo battery is gone, and she lost most of her forward armament. All she has left are aft-mounted K-cannons and lasers." Sikander allowed himself a grim smile at the results of his handiwork.

"Report on *Panther*," Girard said a moment later. "Power fluctuation and visible damage in the middle of the hull suggests that she might have lost most of her fusion plants. Her main battery is mostly intact, but I don't think she has the power to use it."

"She knocked the hell out of us just a minute ago," Sikander said in a sharp tone.

"The capacitors for each mount must have been charged up before our torpedoes hit her. If they're discharged now, it's going to take her a long time to build up a sufficient charge for another salvo."

"Good point, Mr. Girard. New firing orders: Focus all main-battery fire on *Panther*'s bow. Her torpedo battery is the last thing the Dremish have got that can kill us quickly. Wreck it, if you please."

"Aye, sir! Shifting all main-battery fire to *Panther*, targeting her torpedo battery."

The command circuit crackled in Sikander's ear. "Mr. North, you are maneuvering. What are you doing?" Commander Chatburn asked.

"The battle has carried us a long way from Gadira II, sir. We are correcting our spin and setting course to slingshot around Hala and reestablish control over the planet's orbital approaches. It's going to take a while."

"Belay that command, Mr. North. Set your course to

disengage from the Dremish warships by the most expeditious route."

Sikander shook his head, uncertain whether he'd understood Chatburn's order. "Sir?"

"We're crippled, and we are in no position to continue the engagement," said Chatburn. "There's nothing more we can accomplish in Gadira; the Dremish brought more ships to this godforsaken system than we did. Given that, we are responsible now for preserving the ship and its crew."

"XO, *Panther* and *Streitaxt* are hurt worse than we are!" Sikander protested. "We're in position to secure the planetary approaches and put their ground forces under our guns. The one thing we can't do effectively is run away, given the damage to our drives!"

"Salvo!" called Girard. The ship shook with the power of the heavy K-cannons unleashing a fresh barrage of destruction at the Dremish cruiser. Sikander checked quickly to make sure *Streitaxt* was keeping her distance; the destroyer came to a parallel course so she could bring her aft batteries into play. *Hector* was theoretically protected against destroyer-weight battery fire, but given her limited maneuverability, *Streitaxt* could stand off at a much longer range and fire with impunity. Somebody on her bridge knew what he was doing, which was unfortunate.

"That is *Captain,* not XO, Mr. North," said Chatburn. "I am now in command. Cease fire and disengage, is that clear?"

"Sir, just look at the Dremish ships. We have them!"

"Destroying *Panther* is not our mission, damn it! Our rules of engagement from Fleet Command specify that we are only to use force to prevent a Dremish occupation of the system. The system is now under occupation. The situation's now in the hands of the diplomats or the battle fleets. We have done exactly what we were ordered to do."

"Mr. Chatburn, the Dremish position can be reversed. If we hold the planet's orbital—"

"Mr. North, this is not a democracy," said the commander. Sikander could hear the icy anger in his tone even through the audio circuit. "I don't know what traditions you may be accustomed to in the navy of Kashmir, but in the Commonwealth Navy, orders are meant to be followed. I will charge you with insubordination if you do not immediately cease fire and disengage."

"Salvo!" Girard called. The hull boomed and shook with the fire of the K-cannons.

Sikander winced at the poor timing of the shot, but before he could reply, Magda Juarez spoke; the chief engineer's station was part of the command circuit, too. "Commander Chatburn, the bridge still has power, but most of the sensor feeds in aux control are out. Mr. North has the best view of the situation. I recommend you leave him in tactical command until you can acquaint yourself with developments. May I suggest that you relocate to the bridge?"

"Hit!" Girard shouted. "I think I got *Panther*'s torpedo room, sir. No secondary explosions, but it's the right part of the hull and a solid impact, not a graze."

"Good work, Mr. Girard!" Sikander replied. He noticed that the vertigo-inducing motion shown in the bridge's horseshoe-shaped viewscreen had slowed and leveled out. Chief Holtz was slowly gaining control over the ship's attitude. "Split the battery again and engage both targets. Fire for effect!"

"All right, Ms. Juarez. You make a good point," Chatburn said. "Is there a clear route from my station to the bridge?"

There was a brief pause as Magda considered the question; she had the best information on the damage *Hector* had suffered. "Yes, sir. Take the starboard-side passage on the third deck forward to the ladderway by Engine Room Two. Go up to the first deck and detour around the mess deck, it's been hit bad. You should be able to take the ladder on the port side to Deck Two and reach the bridge. It's depressurized but clear."

"Very well," Chatburn replied. "I'm on my way. And, Mr. North, this is a direct order: Cease fire immediately! I will decide whether to continue the engagement when I reach the bridge."

Sikander punched at the arm of the tactical station in frustration, then punched it again. "Yes, *sir*," he snarled, acknowledging the order. He looked back at his weapons team. "All stations cease fire!"

"Cease fire, aye," Reno replied.

"Cease fire, aye," said Girard. He leaned over his console. "Sir, *Streitaxt* is still firing on us. I don't know if we should let up on her yet."

"Mr. Chatburn's orders," Sikander explained. He leaned back at the tactical console, thinking furiously. The auxiliary bridge was at the aft end of the hull, just behind the main power plant. He wasn't surprised that it had been knocked out by the torpedo hits in the stern; it was Peter Chatburn's good fortune that he hadn't been wounded or killed. In normal conditions it might take five minutes for someone to move from the auxiliary bridge to the main bridge. Given battle damage, destroyed or depressurized compartments, the circuitous route described by Magda . . . it might take Chatburn ten minutes or more to get to the bridge and assume tactical control as well as actual command. *He has the right and the duty to do that,* Sikander reminded himself. Junior officers simply didn't have the option of ignoring their commanders just because they thought mistakes were being made.

Assuming that Chatburn saw no reason to change his mind and broke off the action, it certainly would save lives. It might also minimize the diplomatic fallout of an exchange of fire; damaged ships would be less provocative than destroyed ones. On the other hand, leaving Dremish troops on the ground and Dremish warships in control of the system would certainly lead to the establishment of a planetary government that Dremark could claim to be protecting.

Maybe that was a question for the diplomats as well, but it seemed to Sikander that the arguments to follow (assuming a general war didn't break out) would be a lot more effective if the Empire of Dremark failed to put Salem el-Fasi on the throne.

"Sir, what are we doing?" Angela Larkin asked him. None of the junior officers had access to the command circuit; they hadn't heard anyone other than Sikander. "Are we going to finish this, or not?"

"It's not a war yet," Sikander said, somewhat grudgingly. He averted his eyes from the remains of Captain Markham. He noticed that the technicians working on an emergency patch for the hole in the port-side bulkhead had almost finished; they'd be able to restore atmosphere in just a moment. "Mr. Chatburn hopes that we can still avoid one. Breaking off the action is the best chance for that."

"Begging your pardon, sir, but why are *we* breaking off? As things stand now, we've got twice the combat power of both the Dremish ships put together." Larkin pointed at the pitted and blackened main screen, which showed the shattered shape of *Streitaxt*. "They're the ones who ought to be running!"

"Tell the Dremish," Sikander muttered—and then sat bolt upright. Why not do exactly that? He wouldn't fire against Chatburn's direct order, but the Dremish didn't know that. By custom, nothing other than routine navigational communication went out from a Navy ship without the commanding officer's direct approval, but he knew that Chatburn was going to be unreachable for the next ten minutes as he picked his way through the ship to get to the bridge. He just might be able to make a case for acting on his own initiative later. More important, it was the right thing to do; if it came at the cost of his career, then so be it.

"Communications!" Sikander said sharply. "Signal SMS *Panther: Panther,* this is *Hector.* I am holding my fire because I believe you no longer have the ability to threaten me, and I have no wish to inflict any more loss of life. You have three choices: First, retrieve your ground forces from Gadira II and withdraw your vessels to a distance of at least one light-minute from the planet. Second, instruct your landing force to lay down their arms, and power down and surrender your vessels for unlawful action against the recognized government of this system. Third, you can force us to continue this action, which will end in your destruction. Which will it be? Over."

Sikander felt the eyes of the bridge crew on him. Behind him, Michael Girard let out a low whistle. Whether he was struck by the sternness of the demands or Sikander's sheer audacity in issuing them at all was hard to say. No one else said a word. *Panther* did not reply, and Sikander began to wonder whether the damage inflicted on the Dremish cruiser had perhaps knocked out her communications, or whether the senior officer remaining might actually be on *Streitaxt* or *General von Grolmann*.

"Sir, signal from *Panther*," the comm tech said. "It's on your display."

Sikander looked down, and found the lean, bearded visage of Fregattenkapitan Georg Harper gazing at him. He wore an armored suit with a closed visor; his helmet showed sooty black streaks on one side, although Harper appeared uninjured. "*Hector*, this is *Panther* actual," Harper said wearily. "Under my orders, the forces of His Imperial Majesty operating in this system will withdraw to the distance you specify. Be advised that retrieving our landing force cannot be done in less than two hours, and SMS *General von Grolmann* will need to return to low orbit to recover her troops, over."

Sikander thought over the request. He was inclined to tell Harper no, since he didn't trust them to bring their ground operations to a timely halt . . . but the Dremish would have to be completely mad to risk the troop transport if she was under *Hector*'s guns. "Granted," he told Harper. "We expect troops on the ground to hold their positions until retrieval. Any other movements will be construed as hostile."

The Dremish captain's face was stone. "This is a complete outrage. You understand that your reckless attack upon our forces is an act of war. Captain Markham will be called to account for her actions, I promise you."

"Not by any human power, Captain Harper. I regret to inform you that Captain Markham is dead. Commander Peter Chatburn is now in command of CSS *Hector*." Sikander met the Dremish captain's eyes with an expression as hard as steel. "As for the question of war, that will be for our governments to decide. But I remind you, sir: *You were warned. Hector,* out." He cut the channel.

Three minutes later, Commander Chatburn reached the bridge.

24

Tanjeer, Gadira II

Otto Bleindel crouched behind an overturned writing desk in the shattered lobby of the First Bank of High Albion building, studying the dispositions of half a dozen insurgent fighting units in the Sidi Marouf. Tanjeer's revolutionaries more or less controlled the city's offworlder district, and Bleindel was satisfied that he'd arranged Khouri's followers in a defense that should present the Royal Guard with a long and bloody challenge if they wanted to restore order. The Royal Guard, however, was not cooperating. Instead of pushing in to clear the district, they seemed happy to let the misguided revolutionaries keep the Sidi Marouf for the moment.

What can I do to provoke a more satisfying reaction? Bleindel wondered. It would have to be something the Royal Guard could not tolerate, but he didn't want his coffeehouse revolutionaries to guess that he had lured the surviving sultanate forces into pouncing on them. He looked around, seeking inspiration, and spied disorganized gangs of young men—and a few boys who really shouldn't have been allowed to roam the streets at such a dangerous time—gathered in the street outside the lobby. They threw bricks through windows and set ground cars on fire, to no particular purpose that he could see. Perhaps he could trick the Royal Guard into bombing the crowd outside, or even call in the airstrike himself. Arranging for a crowd massacre might be just the right way to get a last little bit of use out of Khouri's followers.

A clatter at the bank's back entrance drew his attention. Alonzo Khouri and half a dozen of his revolutionaries trotted into the lobby, taking up positions alongside Bleindel and the handful of insurgents who made up his little command team. "I've been looking all over for you, Mr. Hardesty," Khouri remarked. "You're a difficult man to catch up to."

"Events are moving quickly today, but not here. I'm afraid the Royal Guard doesn't seem interested in storming our defenses." Bleindel nodded at the crowd outside. "If those are your people, perhaps you could convince them to locate a nearby detachment for us? Since the sultan's men won't come visit, we should restate our invitation."

Khouri glanced at the crowd outside and watched them for a long time. "They are all my people, Mr. Hardesty," he said. "And I don't like the idea of encouraging boys to go throw stones at grav tanks."

Bleindel lowered his voice. "Revolutions sometimes demand sacrifice. They would be proud to take the risk, if you asked it of them."

"You seem to have a talent for convincing others to take your risks, Mr. Hardesty—or Mr. Bleindel, if you prefer," Khouri said. He looked back, and his eyes grew cold. He deliberately swung the muzzle of his mag rifle to cover Bleindel. "I think we don't need much more of your help. Surrender your weapons, please. Slowly!"

"What is the meaning of this?" Bleindel demanded.

Khouri regarded him with contempt. "The meaning of this is simple—I've learned who you are really working for, Bleindel. You're a Dremish operative, and you mean to put Bey Salem on the throne as a puppet. I have no interest in trading a Montréalais master for a Dremish one."

"I see," Bleindel replied. He studied Khouri for a long moment, considering his answer and calculating his chances. He'd hoped to be long gone from Sidi Marouf before his role in things came to light, but it seemed that was not to be. Carefully he relinquished his pistol, and made a show of reaching into his jacket to hand over another one tucked into a shoulder holster. Instead, he armed and dropped a grenade on the floor between them.

The Gadirans goggled at the small black sphere for a moment, stunned. Bleindel took advantage of the momentary surprise to hurl himself up and over the heavy table he crouched beside, hoping its thick marble slab would be sufficient protection. The revolutionaries around him shrieked or cursed in sudden panic. The quicker among them leaped for cover, while others fumbled for their weapons or tried to scramble to their feet. Alonzo Khouri snapped off three quick shots at Bleindel, and hit the Dremish agent in his arm and buttock as he dove for cover. Then the grenade went off with a shattering blast.

Dust, debris, and pieces of human bodies flew past Bleindel in his improvised shelter, as every surviving window in the bank lobby blew out into the street. Ears ringing from the blast, he dragged himself to his feet and limped away into the smoke and dust as quickly as he could. Screams and mag-pistol shots sounded behind him, although he could hardly hear them. He didn't think Khouri was dead—he'd seen the revolutionary throw himself flat just before the grenade exploded—but the odds were good that he was injured or unconscious, and that would be enough.

He made it to the street, and ducked around the corner to the alleyway before anyone managed to pursue him from the lobby. He reached for his comm device with blood-dripping fingers, and punched in a special code he'd hoped he wouldn't have to use.

"Major Kalb," the voice on the other end answered.

"This is Bleindel," he said. He could barely hear his own

voice. "Execute Parachute protocol. I am in the Sidi Marouf, just behind the First Bank of High Albion. There are armed insurgents in the area, so approach with care."

Kalb hesitated for a moment, perhaps verifying the code phrase. "Acknowledged," he finally replied. "Can you get to the Sultan Hassan Mosque? We can have transport there in fifteen minutes."

Bleindel leaned against the wall, and noticed that his right cheek ached abominably. When he gingerly set his hand on the wound, it came away dripping with blood. "Doubtful," he replied. "I'm wounded and I'm not sure how fast I can go. Give me half an hour."

"That's not an option, Mr. Bleindel," Kalb replied. "Every flyer we have on the surface needs to be off the planet in twenty-three minutes."

"What?" Bleindel glanced over his shoulder; there was a commotion in the crowd just outside the alley mouth. Grimacing in pain, he limped farther down the alley, and ducked into a doorway to make sure he was out of sight. "What are you talking about?"

"We have been recalled to *General von Grolmann*," Kalb answered. "All ground operations are to be suspended immediately."

"*What?*" Bleindel asked again, shocked. He prided himself on careful preparations and flexibility in his plans, but this was something he had not anticipated. "We hold the airport and the barracks, el-Fasi's forces hold the palace. We can mop up the Royal Guard and suppress the Gadiran insurgents in the capital any time we like! What idiot is ordering you to withdraw?"

"Fregattenkapitan Harper of SMS *Panther,* who happens to be the senior officer in His Imperial Majesty's service present in this system," said Kalb. His voice took on a tone of disgust. "The Aquilans objected to our landing. There was a battle in orbit, and the Aquilans won. They require us to withdraw from the planet."

"They can't do that!" Bleindel checked to make sure the alley was clear, then headed off in what he thought was the right direction, making the best speed he could. "As long as we're in control of the capital, the question of which government is legitimate remains open. This situation is retrievable."

"Not while the Aquilans are in orbit and we are not," Kalb said. "They can scrub us off the planet any time they please with targeted kinetic strikes, and I have no ground-based batteries that can take on an enemy cruiser. Now, you must excuse me—I have twenty-two minutes to get the rest of my troops off this miserable hellhole. And that means you have twelve minutes to get to the mosque, or we'll leave without you. Kalb, out." The screen went dark.

Bleindel swore and came within a hair of throwing his comm unit against the alley wall. He looked around once more, then broke into a ragged, painful lope.

He made his pickup with thirty seconds to spare.

25

Tanjeer, Gadira II

Five weeks later, the gardens of El-Badi Palace still showed the scars of the fighting. Sikander could see ugly bare patches where mortar bombs had scythed down flowering shrubs or blasted away century-old trees, and one of the more handsome fountains was now missing its centerpiece sculpture; as he understood it, the leaping dolphins had been deliberately riddled with mag-rifle fire by insurgents who could find no other way to express their anger at the sultan after occupying the palace grounds. He wondered if the sculpture would be repaired, replaced, or perhaps redesigned entirely.

"I am glad they allowed you to come down and say goodbye, Sikay," Sultana Ranya Meriem el-Nasir said to him, and drew herself closer to his side. They strolled slowly through the least-damaged part of the gardens, surrounded by vigilant guards who kept a respectful bubble of space around the two of them as they walked. "I was worried that I would not get a chance to see you before you left."

"A request from a planetary sovereign requires attention. Commodore Thompson really had no choice but to comply." A small Aquilan squadron now orbited overhead: *Pandarus* and *Paris* had arrived shortly after the Dremish withdrawal, along with a commodore and his staff to establish a temporary Commonwealth station in what had clearly become a sensitive system. *Hector* herself had departed ten days ago with the aid of a fleet tug, returning to Caledonia for repairs . . . and leaving Sikander behind, since Acting Captain Chatburn had thrown him off the ship at the first opportunity. Now a courier ship prepared to depart for Caledonia in a few hours, and Sikander had been ordered to be on board.

"Are they really going to charge you?" Ranya asked. "From what I have heard, you are the hero of the day."

"The board of inquiry has not even begun its deliberations," said Sikander. That, of course, was why he was no longer serving aboard *Hector*. Officers facing accusations of the sort hanging over his head couldn't remain in their billets, especially not when their commanding officers had drawn up the charges. Consequently, Sikander and Darvesh had been temporarily assigned to the Fourth Cruiser Squadron staff while the Commonwealth Navy tried to decide what to do with him. "Commander Chatburn filed serious charges against me, but I've heard that Commodore Thompson is something of a poker player. Apparently he was quite impressed by my so-called bluff against the Dremish, and it helps that I was right."

"I once read that back on ancient Terra, there was an empire that had a military decoration for officers who won battles by disobeying orders," Ranya said.

"The Military Order of Maria Theresa, from ancient Austria. I ran across that story just a few days ago when examining my own situation. It turns out that it's a little bit of a myth that it was only awarded for disobeying orders." Sikander looked back at Ranya and smiled. "But it was awarded for officers who exercised their own initiative, especially for acts 'that might have been omitted by an honorable officer without reproach.' If this were ancient Austria, I'd like my chances."

Ranya laughed. "I will see to it that you leave with a Gadiran decoration, by the way. Your superiors may have a hard time censuring you after the Sultanate of Gadira publicly thanks you for your intrepid actions."

"For that reason only I would be honored to accept. There are others who deserve recognition more than I. Captain Markham, for example." Sikander paused to study a flower bed full of spectacular yellow-orange blooms—Gadiran sunroses, perhaps? He was not entirely sure, but he thought that it might have been the very spot where Sultan Rashid had captured Elise Markham during his garden party on the day he'd met Ranya. The memory of Captain Markham brought both a smile and a shadow to his face; far too many of his shipmates had joined her in death. Chief Torpedo Mate Maroth had been killed by a grazing hit near the torpedo room. Pilot Second Class Long had died in the hangar conflagration, Lieutenant Isaako Simms when sick bay was smashed by a direct hit from a K-cannon. Many more had been injured, some severely: Magdalena Juarez had lost most of her hand to a bad electrical burn, but remained on her station without even acknowledging her injury for twenty-four hours straight as she fought to keep the Old Worthy under power and patch the worst of its damage. Hiram Randall had survived a fractured skull and severe concussion, but it would be months before he could return to active duty. The engineering experts on Commodore Thompson's staff doubted whether *Hector* herself was worth repairing; at the very least, she'd be in the yards for the better part of a year.

Ranya recognized that his thoughts had turned to more serious matters. She merely stood and waited by his side for a long moment while he gazed over the tropical flowers and thought about the men and women he knew who would not be going home. Finally, Sikander gave himself a small shake and smiled for her sake. "I saw the intel reports this morning," he said. "Congratulations on the capture of Salem el-Fasi. That must come as a great relief to you."

"It does," Ranya replied. "He didn't really pose a threat, not after the insurgents stood down and allowed the Royal Guard to retake Tanjeer, but there is much he must answer for. Weeks of pointless fighting around Meknez, for example."

"Any sign of his friend Bleindel?"

She shook her head. "As far as we can tell, he disappeared in the Sidi Marouf after the Dremish withdrawal. I suppose he saw no reason to prop up a puppet if that puppet wasn't actually on the throne. Which reminds me: Please let the Commonwealth authorities know that Gadira would be greatly interested in extraditing him if he turns up again."

"I will," Sikander promised. He doubted that Otto Bleindel would present himself for apprehension any time soon; as far as he could tell, it was still an even chance whether the Empire of Dremark would go to war with the Commonwealth of Aquila over "the Gadira incident," as it was being referred to in general newscasts. The diplomatic furor almost defied description, but the fact that both sides seemed unwilling to push the issue to general hostilities struck him as a hopeful sign. The Dremish had gambled on bold action to improve their position, and lost: The whole business of being caught backing coups and launching small invasions had left them with little support from the other great powers in the Coalition of Humanity. Sikander had heard that Dremark might disavow the whole thing as a case of local commanders exceeding their orders, in exchange for which the Commonwealth government would pretend to believe them.

They walked on, moving around the palace toward the seaward side. Sikander noted that the arbor he'd managed to crush under the combat flyer's tail had been rebuilt. "So what happens next?" he asked her. "Will the caids accept you as sultana? Will the peace hold?"

"It's not the caids I'm worried about," Ranya replied. "It's the beys. They have the most to lose when change comes to Gadira. Yes, the caids are socially conservative, but there is nothing in the Quranist tradition that prohibits a female ruler."

"Really? I didn't know that."

"There is a surprisingly large gap between what people think is in the Tharsisi Quran and what it really says. The Martian scholars who examined the old suras were quite moderate in their outlook. Attitudes on Gadira are founded in our culture, not our faith. And culture can change." Ranya reached out to take his hand. "The caids and the urban classes want a sultan who looks out for their interests, not the beys' fortunes. I mean to give them one, and then build a constitution to make sure it stays that way when I am no longer on the throne."

"The beys will fight you," Sikander observed.

"Not for a few years." Ranya smiled a little. "Salem el-Fasi's defeat should serve as a warning to the others, at least for a time—perhaps even long enough for my reforms to take hold."

Sikander's comm unit chimed softly. "Sir, I apologize for the interruption," said Darvesh over the link. "The captain of CSS *Merope* wishes you to be informed that departure is drawing near."

"Thank you, Darvesh," he answered. "I promise I will not keep him waiting."

"It seems you must be on your way," Ranya said.

"I am afraid so," said Sikander. He looked into her eyes, and raised his hand to brush her lustrous black hair from the side of her face. "Will you be all right?"

"Have no fear for me," she said. "There are many long days ahead, but I'm the daughter of Sultan Kamal. I am equal to the test. And, as you said about your own challenges a moment ago, it helps that I am right." She glanced over at Captain Zakur, who stood a few meters off watching over the two of them. The big officer inclined his head, and turned his back to studiously examine a potted plant that suddenly caught his attention. Other guards in sight followed his lead.

Sikander smiled, and bent down—only a little, since Ranya was almost as tall as he was—and kissed her for a long, perfect moment. Then he straightened again. "Good-bye, Ranya Meriem el-Nasir," he said in a soft voice. "I wish you knew how sorry I am that we did not meet under other circumstances."

"I wish you knew how glad I am that we met at all," she replied. "Good-bye, Sikander Singh North. You will always be welcome here; may the stars steer your path back to me someday."

He embraced her one final time. Then he let her go, and strode away without looking back.

Read on for a preview of

RESTLESS LIGHTNING

·

RICHARD BAKER

Available in October 2018 from
Tom Doherty Associates

TOR   A TOR BOOK

1

Bagal-Dindir, Tamabuqq Prime

T his is a damned peculiar way to travel," remarked Commodore William Abernathy in a sour tone. He waved one hand to indicate the open-sided carriage in which they rode, the elaborately dressed Tzoru driver with his—or her?—painted dermal patterns, and the *alliksisu* yoked to the boatlike prow. The Aquilan flag officer fidgeted in a vain effort to find a comfortable posture for his seat. Short and slight of frame, with iron-gray hair and a stiff terrier's mustache, Abernathy disliked sitting still, especially on a cold and damp day. "It'll take us half an hour to reach the embassy at this pace, and I'll be damned if it isn't snowing by the time we get there."

Lieutenant Commander Sikander Singh North, Commonwealth Navy, noted that his new commanding officer's favorite word appeared to be "damned" and carefully hid a smile. He found the cold, clammy weather uncomfortable too, but he had about thirty kilos on Abernathy, all of it muscle. Most people from his homeworld—Jaipur, in the Kashmir system—possessed the stocky, broad-shouldered frames common among natives of planets a little over standard gravity. If *he* felt the chill through his Navy overcoat, the commodore probably felt like he was sitting in a freezer.

"It's tradition, sir," he told the commodore. "At least the ride is smooth." Maglev rails buried under the avenue powered every street in the Tzoru capital, providing a wheelless suspension for the carriage. The transportation network had been installed around the same time ancient humans had first figured out agriculture. Time and again during Sikander's tour of duty in the squadron posted on the Navy's Helix Station he'd started to believe he might actually understand something about the culture or psychology of the alien Tzoru—and time and again he'd been confronted by some new piece of evidence that humans didn't really understand the Tzoru at all. *For example, powering the roads but not the vehicles. Leave it to the Tzoru to come up with that one!*

"Tradition? A damned stupid one, I suppose," Abernathy muttered, confirming Sikander's suspicion about his favorite word.

"Powered ground cars would challenge the place held by the carriage-driver *sebetu,* sir," Captain Francine Reyes explained to Abernathy. Tall and poised in comparison to her wiry, energetic superior, she wore a more or less permanent frown of disapproval at the various idiosyncrasies of the Tzoru. Abernathy had taken command of the squadron patrolling Helix Station only a week ago, but she'd served as deputy commodore under his predecessor for more than a year. Like Sikander, she'd had plenty of time to experience the peculiarities of Tzoru customs.

"*Sebetu*—those are the Tzoru clans, right?"

"Something about halfway between a clan, a guild, and a caste, yes." Reyes had anticipated that the weather might be cold; she at least had dressed warmly for the carriage ride. She continued her explanation: "Taking away the role of the carriage-driver *sebetu* would upset the harmony of things. The Tzoru simply don't do that unless they must."

"Are you serious, D-Com?" said Abernathy. "In ten thousand years no one's convinced the taxi drivers to retire their ridiculous draft beasts? So why couldn't we just land at the embassy grounds and skip the whole thing?"

Sikander took that as his cue. "Sir, no one flies over Bagal-Dindir except for members of the aristocratic *sebetu* or their soldiers. If it's any consolation, the privilege of an official carriage is a sign of Tzoru deference to your rank. Otherwise we'd have to take the trolley or walk." He'd learned more than a few hard lessons about Tzoru inflexibility during nineteen months as Helix Squadron's intelligence officer, especially when it came to Tzoru military protocols. Sikander was a line officer by trade, but not even a career intelligence specialist could be expected to make sense of the contradictions and challenges every Commonwealth officer who rotated through Helix Squadron encountered. In fact, the Admiralty staggered relief assignments specifically to ensure that the squadron staff always included at least a few officers who'd been on Helix Station for some time.

"Walking might be warmer," Abernathy said with a snort. He shivered inside his overcoat, and leaned forward to address the driver. "You, there. Can we go a little faster? I want to beat the snowstorm." The translation device clipped to his collar emitted a string of guttural Tzoqabu a moment after he finished.

The driver turned to regard the small party reclining in the open carriage, twisting easily in a motion that would have tested a human contortionist. He (or so Sikander guessed, since humans could have a difficult time telling Tzoru of different sexes apart) replied to Abernathy in Tzoqabu; Sikander's own translation device fed the interpretation into his ears: "The *alliksisu* has no interest in hurrying, honored friends, but if you are cold I can activate the heating plates."

"There is a heater?" Abernathy asked in a flat tone.

"Yes, honored friend. I shall activate it." The Tzoru adjusted controls on a small panel near his left hand, then returned to the task of directing the *alliksisu*—a creature that looked like a blue, scaly rhinoceros with long legs and three wide toes on each foot. A moment later, a pleasant warmth enveloped Sikander's legs and began to well upward from the floor.

"Could've used that ten minutes ago," said Lieutenant Mason Barnes, leaving his translator off. The fourth in Abernathy's small party, Barnes—Sikander's roommate in their Academy days, and one of the closest friends he had in the Navy—served as Helix Squadron's communications officer. He had the pale complexion, red hair, and rural accent of a Hibernian. People who evinced characteristics of the old Terran races were somewhat unusual in the metropolitan worlds of the Aquilan Commonwealth, or any of the other great powers in the Coalition of Humanity. Noticeably distinct traits like the fair skin of the Hibernians, or the coppery complexion and wavy black hair common in Kashmir, indicated descent from populations that had been isolated at some point or other during humanity's expansion to the stars. Mason caught Sikander's eye and nodded at the driver's back as if to say, *A Tzoru being Tzoru, what can you do?*

Sikander answered with a small shrug. Humans had encountered only four other starfaring species and the long-dead ruins of a few others in nine centuries of interstellar travel. Of the living four species, Tzoru were perhaps the most humanlike, but despite bipedal morphology and technology comparable to human technology, Tzoru were indeed *alien*. They had evolved from semiaquatic pack hunters millions of years ago; a sort of stiff cartilage made up their skeletons, and they had tough rubbery crests with breathing apertures instead of noses. In place of skin, Tzoru had a gray, leathery dermis with patterns of scales—broad and thick on the back and shoulders, finer and more colorful around the face. Their eyes were large and dark and set almost on the sides of their bullet-shaped heads, and their wide, lipless mouths were filled with serrated teeth. Tzoru dressed themselves in kilts and sleeveless tunics for everyday wear, layered robes in cold weather, or elaborately ornate robes when they wished to demonstrate their social status . . . which was at every opportunity, in Sikander's experience.

Tzoru thought processes and emotions likewise ranged from near-human to coldly pragmatic and uncompassionate. They had nothing like the human drives of romantic love, ambition, restlessness, or a craving for thrills, but they showed great affection for friends and relatives. And they had exactly zero empathy for strangers, which meant that a carriage driver bundled up against the chill of a cold day would never even begin to imagine that his passengers might be cold if they didn't bring it to his attention.

"I knew it. Now it's snowing," Abernathy observed. Sikander glanced up; sure enough, wet, heavy flakes drifted down from the gray clouds overhead. The commodore drew his overcoat more snugly over his chest and settled back in his seat with a sigh of resignation.

"If you'll look over thataway, sir, you can see the Anshar's Palace," Mason said, perhaps hoping to distract Abernathy's attention from the cold, wet ride. "Just through that gap in the treeferns, there. Those're the monuments of the Royal Ward." Slender spires, mighty domes, and steepsided ziggurats loomed a kilometer or two from the boulevard down which they rode. Bagal-Dindir had the population of any large human city, but Tzoru built few high-rise buildings; as a result the capital sprawled over a vast area. In some neighborhoods one could hardly tell that one was in a city at all, but the Thousand Worlds ward—the city's "Embassy Row"—stood in an old temple district not far from the seat of the Dominion's government. The drive from the spaceport to the Aquilan embassy offered some of the better views to be found in the city.

"That big ziggurat with all the gold on it?" Abernathy asked, craning for a better look.

"Yes, sir. They say that one building covers almost three square kilometers."

"Impressive," Abernathy admitted. "Have any of you been there?"

"No, sir," said Sikander. "Only a handful of humans have ever set foot in the palace."

Reyes gave a small snort of disgust. "The Anshar's attendants almost never permit non-Tzoru to sully the grounds with our presence. It's rather insulting, if you ask me."

"Hmmph." Abernathy grunted and looked away, turning his attention to their immediate surroundings. Private homes, workshops, and small businesses dotted both sides of the boulevard, interspersed with open spaces that allowed longer views. Tzoru dressed in the colors of many different *sebetu* hurried from one establishment to another or rode along in carriages and carts that cluttered the street. Quite terran in many ways, Tamabuqq Prime had breathable air, oceans filled with water, natural flora dominated by green plants, and more or less Earthlike seasons and weather. But even after a year and a half stationed in the heart of the Tzoru Dominion, Sikander still found it disconcertingly alien. The sounds and smells were all wrong: the avians hissed and clicked instead of singing, overpowering spice-like scents filled the air, and the sky on a sunny day was a pale green hue.

Five more months, Sikander told himself. His tour in Helix Squadron would soon be over. The Tzoru frontier lay more than a month from Aquila's core systems; it was the sort of place where ambitious officers went to make names for themselves without the oversight of their superiors, and superiors who didn't want to deal with troublesome subordinates could send them out of sight and out of mind. Sikander belonged to the latter group: Very few Kashmiris served in the Aquilan navy, fewer still came from families as pedigreed or powerful as the Norths of Jaipur, and exactly one had taken command of an Aquilan warship in the middle of a battle, fighting through to victory in the face of orders to withdraw. After the prominent role Sikander had played in the Gadira incident, half the Admiralty had wanted to commend him, and the other half had wanted to court-martial him. The compromise that had eventually won out was evidently to hide him in the most remote post they could think of. *But which side of the debate does Abernathy favor?* The new commodore hadn't bothered to tell Sikander whether he approved or disapproved of his actions at Gadira.

A snowflake slipped past the visor of his cap, narrowly missing his eye. Sikander brushed at his face, noting that the flurry seemed to be growing heavier. He hadn't seen snow in years, a simple accident of assignments to bases in temperate climes and periods of leave that never seemed to align with the cold season at home. Now that he thought of it, it had been snowing the first time he met William Abernathy. Fourteen years ago, back at the Academy, a day filled with heavy flurries—

—*dancing outside the high windows of Powell Hall's formal hearing room. The afternoon is cold and gray; the furnishings are dark, old wood, massive as battlements. Sikander, a freshman, faces the Disciplinary Committee: five senior midshipmen with faces that might have been carved from stone. A dozen of Sikander's classmates and upperclassmen from his company sit behind him; he can't see them, but their silence is a tangible weight at his back. At the side of the room, Commander Abernathy, staff advisor to the committee, sits with his head leaning on his hand, watching the scene. His posture suggests he is falling asleep.*

The committee chairperson, a senior named Adelaide Wallace, reads from a document: "Midshipman Fourth

Class North, you have been placed on report for the infraction of striking a superior officer. Your company commander states that on the evening of February tenth, he found you engaged in a fistfight with Midshipman Second Class Gray. During this altercation he saw you throw several punches at Mr. Gray, and that you continued to do so even after you were ordered to stop. The purpose of this proceeding is to examine the facts of the report, provide you an opportunity to make answer, and then determine the appropriate punishment. This is an administrative proceeding and is not a hearing under the military justice code, but any statements you make here are considered to be in the public record and you are expected to be truthful under the Academy honor code. Do you understand?"

"I do, ma'am," Sikander answers.

"Midshipman Second Class Gray and your company commander have already stated that they agree with the facts as stated in the report. Do you dispute any part of the report?"

Sikander hesitates before he speaks. "No, ma'am. The report is correct."

Midshipman Wallace looks up at that. "You are admitting that you are guilty of striking Mr. Gray? The customary punishment is expulsion, Mr. North."

"Ma'am, Midshipman-Commander Farrell accurately reported what he observed when he arrived on the scene and what Mr. Gray said to him at that time. But the report says nothing about what happened before Mr. Farrell got there, or whether Mr. Gray was telling the truth."

"You dare to call me a liar, Snottie?" an angry voice snarls behind Sikander. A clatter of scraping chairs follows.

Sikander can't help it; he turns around. Midshipman Victor Gray, a junior in Sikander's own company, knocks his chair over as he springs to his feet. He is a tall, sandy-haired young man, stocky and strong for an Aquilan, and his face is twisted in fury.

Sikander looks him right in the eye. "Yes, sir. I do."

Gray takes a half step toward him and balls his fists. The midshipmen that make up the Disciplinary Committee look at each other in confusion. Several people start to speak at once. But Commander Abernathy sits up straight and slaps his open hand on the tabletop in front of him so loudly everybody in the room jumps. "Strike that from the record!" *he snaps.* "And Gray's remark too. We will have no such insinuations on the transcript, is that clear?"

Adelaide Wallace stares at Abernathy in surprise before nodding to the underclassman who serves as the committee clerk. "As Mr. Abernathy requests," *she says to him.* "Strike the last two remarks, please."

"Ms. Wallace, I suggest a brief recess," *Abernathy continues. Without waiting for her reply, he stands and marches over to where Sikander stands. He's easily ten centimeters shorter than Sikander or any of the other midshipmen, but in that moment the only commissioned officer in the room seems to tower over everyone. It's all Sikander can do to stand his ground without flinching.* "North, come with me. I need a word with you."

He spins on his heel and strides away as the midshipmen watch. Sikander stares after him for a moment, then hurries after him—

"What's going on here?" Abernathy asked suddenly, rousing Sikander from the old memories. The commodore had a little more gray in his hair and gold braid on his uniform than the officer Sikander remembered from his Academy days, but seemed otherwise unmarked by the passage of fourteen years.

Sikander turned to see what had caught the commodore's attention. Scores of agitated Tzoru crowded together in front of an open-sided shelter or hall a short distance up the street. Many wore green, double-pointed caps of a design he hadn't seen before, and one individual standing on a parked cart led a responsive chant. At each pause, the Tzoru in the crowd raised their hands in the air and shouted wildly in response: *"Ebneghirz! Ebneghirz!"*

"Some kind of religious procession," said Deputy Commodore Reyes with a scowl of disapproval. Like many Aquilans, Reyes had no use for religious beliefs of any sort, human or alien. "There's some such nonsense every day in Bagal-Dindir. That building behind the crowd is a shrine—they're all over the capital."

"They seem worked up about something," said Abernathy. The crowd slowly drifted into motion, streaming down the street toward the carriage. "Is this typical?"

"It's the first time I've seen something like it, sir," Sikander said. It didn't seem to be any kind of religious event; Tzoru shrine processions were celebrations, not protests or rallies. Perhaps that distinction was lost on most Aquilans—secularists and rather smug about it—but as a Kashmiri he'd been raised in New Sikhism and surrounded by Hindu friends and acquaintances. That didn't make him an expert on Tzoru public displays, but it did mean that he was not as quick as his Aquilan comrades to assume that religious beliefs were at the root of any inexplicable or belligerent behavior. He looked up at the carriage driver, activating his translator. "Excuse me, driver—who are those Tzoru over there?"

"They are *warumzi agu*," the driver replied. "I did not know that there would be a gathering at this hour."

"What are they going on about?" Mason Barnes asked.

"They are praising Ebneghirz," the driver repeated. The name seemed familiar to Sikander. He thought he might have seen something about it in recent intel summaries—a passing mention, perhaps. The Tzoru Dominion simply didn't have any kind of media culture, and finding out what any large number of Tzoru thought about something was surprisingly difficult. The driver seemed annoyed rather than concerned, but of course that might mean anything. On the other hand, it only took Sikander a few moments of watching to decide that he didn't like the look of the crowd at all. He'd never seen a Tzoru mob in person, but he'd seen more than a few human ones, and something about this group shouted *danger!* at him.

"Driver, are they angry at us?" he asked directly. Sometimes that was necessary to get a Tzoru to consider a situation outside of his or her own narrow interests.

It worked—the driver glanced down at Sikander, back to the *warumzi agu* procession, and back to Sikander again before nodding. "They may be," he conceded. "Honored friends, it would be better if we went a different way." He made a clicking sound at the *alliksisu* and touched its flank with a long, reedlike goad, turning the creature toward a cross street before the crowd reached them. Driving an *alliksisu* carriage seemed to involve a good deal of suggestion and persuasion, and few actual controls.

The Tzoru leading the crowd caught sight of Sikander and his companions in the carriage, and suddenly raised their voices in excitement. "I think that's a good idea," Abernathy said. He and Reyes occupied the rear seat of the carriage, so they now had their backs to the crowd; the wiry commodore twisted in his seat, scowling at the approaching Tzoru. "Driver, get us out of here."

Francine Reyes glanced back as well, then keyed her comm device. "*Exeter* shuttle, this is Captain Reyes. Stand by for immediate retrieval of our party. We have a situation developing."

"Ma'am, the Tzoru authorities will never permit an overflight," Sikander said.

"I don't intend to ask them," said Reyes. "Better to—oh, *damn*."

Behind the carriage, the leading ranks of the *warumzi agu* broke into a run, bounding after the carriage in short, springy strides that swallowed up the distance with alarming speed. "Look out!" Sikander shouted. He rose from his seat and crouched upright in the carriage, ready to fend off anyone trying to climb aboard. He had no idea if unarmed combat against a Tzoru was a good idea or not, but he'd rather go down swinging if it came to it. Mason Barnes followed his lead, and got up to guard the other side of the carriage.

"*Exeter* shuttle, come get us!" Reyes shouted into her comm unit.

The carriage driver flicked his goad again, and the *alliksisu* fell into a clumsy trot . . . but the mob continued to close the distance. Some of the *warumzi agu* drew close enough to pelt the humans with small stones, bottles, and even round, hard fruit of some sort, an angry hail that clattered against the metal sides of the carriage or bounced back into the street. Sikander ducked and raised a hand over his head to protect himself—and then a fist-sized bottle sailed out of the crowd, striking the driver in the back.

The driver gave a sort of whistling hiss and suddenly abandoned his post, leaping down to the street and scuttling away. "Do not hurt me!" he shouted before the translator lost his voice. Sikander caught a glimpse of the fellow scissoring his hands in front of him and bowing as he hurried off, a Tzoru gesture more or less equivalent to a human raising his hands over his head. The pursuing Tzoru swarmed around him; several began to tear at his robes and pummel him savagely.

Confused, the *alliksisu* began to slow again—and then something else was thrown into the carriage, a clawed creature about the size of a large rat. It had a spiky carapace and a barbed tail equipped with a jabbing sting, and it scrabbled about the floor of the carriage, clacking its mandibles. All four humans flinched away from the repulsive little monster.

"What is *that*?" Abernathy snarled.

Sikander had no idea, but when the creature darted after Reyes, he saw his opportunity. He stepped forward and swung his right foot through the creature in a magnificent soccer-style kick that punted the thing a good six meters through the air. It disappeared into the crowd. At the same time, Mason scrambled up over the passenger bench to the driver's position, seized the slender goad, and whacked the *alliksisu* across the rump with a blow so forceful that Sikander heard the *crack!* above the shouting and screams all around them. The draft beast let out a roar of pain and bolted away, throwing the passengers back into their seats and scattering the crowd surrounding the carriage. Sikander lost his balance completely and fell heavily onto Abernathy and Reyes.

By the time he extricated himself from his superiors, the mob of green-capped Tzoru had fallen far behind. Barnes stood in the driver's position, guiding the galloping beast with the goad. He managed to coax the *alliksisu* into turning down a cross street, and let it gallop on for a few hundred meters. Astonished Tzoru stopped in their tracks to goggle at the carriage and its human occupants racing past. Sikander ignored them and kept watch on the street behind the carriage, making sure the mob couldn't catch up to them.

"Mr. North, any sign of pursuit?" Abernathy said, raising his voice to be heard over the draft beast's bellows of protest and galloping footfalls. Sikander noticed that at some point in the encounter the commodore had lost his gold-braided cap.

"They gave up two or three hundred meters back. I think we're clear for now, sir."

"Very good. Mr. Barnes, see if you can slow this thing down before we flip the carriage or run over somebody. D-Com, cancel the shuttle, if you please."

"*Exeter* shuttle, belay your orders," Reyes said into her comm unit. "We are no longer in immediate danger."

"Yes, sir." Mason glanced around the driver's post, and carefully adjusted a lever. The carriage magnets changed their orientation, applying a smooth braking resistance to the *alliksisu*. The beast immediately responded to the signal, slowing to a walk.

"Well done," Abernathy said. "When in the world did you learn to drive one of these ridiculous things, anyway?"

"I'm Hibernian, sir. Not the first time I drove a horse-drawn carriage. Or whatever the Tzoru call their horses."

The commodore snorted. Hibernia had a reputation for being rural and backward, at least by Aquilan standards. "It would seem so. Now, where is our embassy again?"

"I know the way, sir," Mason replied. "We're not that far off. But shouldn't we go back for the driver?"

"Of course not," Abernathy said. "If he didn't want us to leave without him he shouldn't have abandoned his post in the face of danger. Mr. Barnes, the embassy, if you please."

"Yes, sir." Mason applied the goad again, gently this time. The draft beast picked up its pace; the lieutenant guided it onto another crossing avenue, and settled into the driver's position. He looked ridiculously out of place, but he seemed to have the draft animal under control.

"Very good. Now someone explain to me what just happened there. Who are these Warzi Gooey fellows? Why did they chase us? Mr. North?"

"I'm not sure, sir. I think it's some kind of popular movement—the Tzoru have a lot of them, but nothing that makes it onto our threat assessments." Sikander shrugged helplessly. "I'm afraid the only intelligence the squadron staff collects on local civilian matters is what the Tzoru report on their own broadcasts."

"That's not good enough," Deputy Commodore Reyes said to Sikander. "You should review local conditions with the embassy before we even set foot on the ground, Mr. North. An intelligence officer is supposed to anticipate trouble, especially when a flag officer's personal safety may be at risk."

Sikander bristled, and barely succeeded in fighting down a sharp retort. In the first place, it was not a fair criticism—

local developments weren't really part of his job as squadron S-2. His team focused on the formations and capabilities of the Tzoru military *sebetu,* as well as the squadrons of half a dozen other human powers that maintained a presence in Tzoru space. Tzoru politics were *complicated,* and even the expert diplomats of Aquila's embassy had trouble interpreting events here. Secondly, he didn't care at all for Reyes making a point of criticizing him to their new commanding officer. She'd done enough of that with Commodore Morse; the last thing he needed was for her to continue that sort of harassment now that Commodore Abernathy had assumed command.

Unfortunately, arguing against a superior officer's criticism rarely improved matters. So instead he said the only thing he could in reply: "Yes, ma'am. I will touch base with our embassy staff."

Commodore Abernathy let the exchange pass without comment. Instead he made a show of studying the ancient walls surrounding the Thousand Worlds ward, now coming into view, and gave his stiff mustache a small tug. *A note of approval, or disapproval?* Sikander wondered. For a man who carried himself with such energy and wasn't shy about sharing his opinions, William Abernathy could be surprisingly hard to read at times.

Mason tapped the *alliksisu* on its flank and turned the creature and the carriage to the right, passing beneath the ceremonial gateway leading into the Thousand Worlds ward. The ancient fortifications rose up around them, then gave way to a crowded district of homes and workshops and mercantile establishments huddled together within the old walls. More floating *alliksisu*-drawn carriages crowded the narrow streets, but here human diplomats and businesspeople mingled with Tzoru servants, shopkeepers, and retainers in the service of one or another of the noble clans. No less than nine different human powers maintained embassies in the Thousand Worlds ward, not to mention a sprawling Nyeiran mission and a Velar consulate hidden in one of the back alleyways. In eight square kilometers of the old walled district, humans and nonhumans from almost all of civilized space met and interacted with each other in a disorderly, chaotic cauldron of activity.

"Here we are, Commodore," Mason announced. He guided their draft beast into a circular driveway in front of a sprawling building—recent human construction, not ancient Tzoru—that reminded Sikander of the governor's mansion on New Perth. Aquilan marines in dress uniforms stood watch by the main entrance; their crisply pressed uniforms were much the same as the ones their predecessors had worn for centuries, but the mag rifles at their sides were brand new and very, very functional.

"Very good," Abernathy grunted. He stood and hopped down from the seat without waiting; Sikander and Reyes followed, while Mason handed the goad to a Tzoru attendant who hurried up to relieve him. Sikander took a moment to check his uniform for any unsuspected tears or marks, and discovered a section of ripped seam along his side and a purple stain—probably from some foodstuff or other thrown at the carriage—on his left shin. The others in the party likewise took note of smudges or damaged uniforms with various scowls.

A short, broad-shouldered woman in the uniform of a marine major emerged from the embassy and marched out to meet them. She glanced once at the disheveled carriage, but said nothing before snapping a salute to Abernathy. "Commodore Abernathy, welcome to Bagal-Dindir. I'm Major Constanza Dalton, officer in charge of the protective detail. Ambassador Hart is waiting to see you; there have been some unusual developments today."

"The *warumzi agu*, we know," said Abernathy. He returned her salute. "Excitable fellows—they let us know that they didn't appreciate humans riding about in the capital."

"*Warumzi agu*?" Major Dalton frowned. "We've been

getting reports about them in other cities, but this is the first I've heard about any in the capital. However, that's not what I referred to. I was speaking of the trouble in the Dominion High Council."

"Trouble? What trouble?" asked Sikander. After five visits to Bagal-Dindir in nineteen months, he'd come to know Constanza Dalton fairly well. She prided herself on maintaining a certain decorum as the commander of the embassy's marine detachment, and that meant a mild term such as "trouble" likely carried a great deal of understatement with it.

"The first councillor just announced that he's stepping down," Dalton replied. "The news broke an hour ago. It's all the buzz in the streets of the Thousand Worlds today."

Reyes shot another look at Sikander, but he ignored her. "Sapwu Zrinan is no longer in power? Who's in charge at the Anshar's court?"

"That's the question, isn't it?" Major Dalton returned her attention to Abernathy, and gestured toward the embassy's front door. "Right this way, Commodore. Ambassador Hart said that you were to go on up as soon as you arrived."

TOR